CW01560337

Satan's Church
Cam Lavac

Satan's Church

Cam Lavac

NEW
HOLLAND

First published in Australia in 2005 by
New Holland Publishers (Australia) Pty Ltd
Sydney • Auckland • London • Cape Town

14 Aquatic Drive Frenchs Forest NSW 2086 Australia
218 Lake Road Northcote Auckland New Zealand
86 Edgware Road London W2 2EA United Kingdom
80 McKenzie Street Cape Town 8001 South Africa

This edition published in 2006

Lavac, Cam.
Satan's church.

2nd ed.
ISBN 1 74110 476 9.

I. Title.

A823.4

Publisher: Fiona Schultz
Managing Editor: Martin Ford
Production: Grace Gutwein
Design: Greg Lamont
Printer: Kyodo Printing Co. (S'pore) Pte Ltd

10 9 8 7 6 5 4 3 2 1

Cover Pic: Greg Lamont

This one's for Jill

ACKNOWLEDGMENTS

I would like to thank my friend, David Hickie, for his initial encouragement and enthusiasm when he first read the synopsis of this book. Without his encouragement and 'getting the ball rolling' I may have long ago, simply given up.

My special thanks to my friends and literary agents, Clare Calvet and Xavier Waterkeyn of Flying Pigs. Thank you Clare for your steadfast faith in this book, which proved an ongoing source of inspiration, and thank you for seeing merit where others did not. Xavier, thank you for your mentorship and for always being available when I needed you, irrespective of the time. Your incredibly analytical mind was an enormous help in pulling a plot to pieces and then reconstructing it so that it made sense.

Your steadfast faith in me and this book, as well as your refusal to accept rejection made this book happen.

Through your dedication, optimism and sheer hard work, you have truly proven that, 'Pigs will indeed fly.'

Chapter 1

Cardinal Luca Morova stared intently at the dying Pope, wishing he would just hurry up and get on with it. The sound of the Pope's laboured breathing competed with the hushed murmuring of the gathered cardinals mouthing the rosary, while their fingers moved from one bead to the next, silently counting out the Hail Marys.

Morova felt increasingly uncomfortable in his black cassock, a rivulet of prickly sweat trickling from under his arms. The room was like a sauna, with the sickly, sweet pungent odour of impending death permeating the breathless air. He glanced around the room at the black robes and red sashes of his fellow cardinals standing vigil over the dying Pope. He caught the eye of one of the cardinals who smiled sadly, bowing his head respectfully.

Sycophant! Morova thought with contempt, returning the sad smile, seemingly sharing the man's grief. Morova noted the man's own discomfiture as he tugged at his collar and mopped the sweat from his brow with a handkerchief. At least I'm not the only one roasting in this stinking room, he thought, with some small sense of satisfaction. The air-conditioner was out of the question, the doctor had explained, as the dry air would further impede the Pope's breathing.

Morova knew the cardinals hated him, but he did not care. What mattered was that they respected him and many even feared him, which was a good thing. The College of Cardinals was jealous of his meteoric rise to the red-hat brigade. As the youngest cardinal in modern times, he had been accused behind his back of being overly ambitious, of climbing his way to the top on the backs of others, using the knives he'd planted there as handholds.

But idle gossip did not concern him. Morova was secure in the knowledge it was his talent for matters financial which had brought him success. As a monsignor in the Vatican Bank he had trebled the bank's cash reserves through cunning and astute investments. He was aware of the rumours of mafia connections, and of deals that were dubious if not criminal. Let them think what they like! The fact remained that by the time he had been made cardinal, the Church's financial health had never been better.

Any jealousy the College may have felt at the time of his elevation to cardinal was overshadowed by outrage when Alexander IX named him Cardinal Camerlengo of the Holy Roman Catholic Church. The humble title 'Camerlengo', literally 'chamberlain' in Italian, hid the reality that it was the highest rank bestowed on a cardinal. The Camerlengo administers the property and revenue of the Holy See, as well as verifying the death of a Pope. He directs the funeral arrangements and then the preparation and management of the conclave. He is also responsible for the continuing government of the Church during a *Sede Vacante*, the vacant seat of St Peter.

Morova pictured in his mind the thousands of grieving Catholics holding vigil in St Peter's Square, awaiting the inevitable death of their Pope. The only sounds to be heard would be the fluttering of pigeons and the hushed prayers of the faithful as they gazed expectantly towards the Pope's balcony where a black flag would finally announce the end.

Fools! What did they know? Morova thought. They didn't realise that towards the end of his reign, Alexander had all but brought the Church to its financial knees. Morova had warned the Pope that aligning the Church with social reform for workers could alienate the corporations. When the Pope failed to heed Morova's warnings, big business accused the Papacy of Marxism and, as he had predicted, donations and favours quickly dried up.

The grinding wheels of the Vatican required enormous amounts of money to keep them greased and now all of Morova's good work had been undone and the Church was hurting where it mattered most, the hip pocket.

Morova snapped out of his reverie, sensing that something was wrong. He looked around. The room was quiet. The cardinals were no longer praying. They were watching him expectantly. He looked at the Pope. The sound of tortured breathing had stopped and the Pope looked at peace.

'Quickly,' Morova ordered, 'get the doctor.'

The man closest to the door hurried out, calling for the doctor who was waiting to be summoned.

The doctor entered the room, walking quickly and with authority towards the Pope's bed. The cardinals watched anxiously as the doctor pressed a stethoscope to his patient's chest. He listened intently, moving the stethoscope from one spot to another. After a while, he removed the stethoscope from around his neck and shook his head.

As the doctor moved back away from the bed, Cardinal Morova stepped forward to take charge. As tradition commanded, he picked up the golden hammer that had already been placed in anticipation by the Pope's bed. Then, in a loud voice he called the Pope's birth name, 'Orazio,' and gently tapped the dead Pontiff's forehead with the hammer. He repeated this ritual again, then once more. Replacing the hammer, Morova reverently picked up the Pope's hand and gently removed the Ring of the Fisherman. The cardinals watched solemnly as Morova placed the ring on a small metal plate. He picked up the hammer and raising it above his head, smashed the ring. Turning to the assembled cardinals, he announced in a pious voice, *'Papa mortus est.'* The Pope is dead, and then added, 'The Pope has gone to his reward.'

As one, the assembled cardinals blessed themselves with the sign of the cross. 'Now I would ask your Eminences,' Morova continued, 'to leave us, so that I can personally bid farewell to His Holiness.'

The cardinals nodded their understanding, and as they filed out of the room each of them made the sign of the cross over the deceased Pope. As the last of them passed through the door, Morova overheard, 'The Camerlengo was very close to His Holiness. His grief will be heavy.'

Morova smiled at the observation, closing the door and sliding the bolt, assuring that his privacy with the dead Pontiff would not be disturbed. He then strode past the bed without even a cursory glance at the corpse whose arms were crossed on the chest, a rosary clutched in the lifeless hands. Morova headed straight for the papal bathroom and didn't bother to close the door. He lifted his cassock and lowered himself onto the bowl, noting with satisfaction that from his position on the toilet he had a clear view of the dead Pope. With a contented grunt he vented an explosive bowel motion.

After meticulously washing his hands he dried them with the soft white towel bearing the Papal insignia. Replacing the towel, Morova looked into the mirror over the wash basin. He rested his hands on the basin and leaned towards his reflection. The dark eyes stared back at him and he licked a finger to preen his bushy brows. He turned his head from side to side, examining his reflection, and decided that at fifty two he still looked good. He noticed a few strands of white at the temples, in stark contrast to the blue-black hair, but decided they added dignity to his appearance. Frowning, he spotted a blackhead. He leaned closer to the mirror to squeeze the offending blemish, then stepped back to gain a better perspective of his image and was satisfied with what he saw. Morova knew that as Camerlengo he was automatically disqualified from being a Papal candidate, but this did not concern him. He had his own plans, which did not include being elected Pope. Such an eventuality would prove disastrous to his long-term ambitions. As Pope he would be terribly stifled by the office of Pontiff, constantly under the glaring scrutiny of the world. The Pope couldn't fart without making world headlines, he thought irreverently. No, the Papal office would not suit him at all. He could wield far more power as the grand puppeteer, pulling the Papal strings. The recently deceased Pope, although weak and indecisive, had become a great disappointment. The old fool had developed an alarming degree of independence, Morova thought, and look where that had got him. The Church was almost in a state of anarchy with many clergy leaving and international funding all but drying up. The Vatican coffers had never been so low, and Morova was determined to change that.

As he left the bathroom he looked forward with eager anticipation to the canvassing of votes, the power brokering and secret deals that would lead up to the coming conclave and he had no doubt as to the outcome. He paused at the body of the Pope and reflected aloud, 'What great profit we have made from the myth of this man called Christ.' He gestured with his head towards the bathroom and said, 'One does not have to be a Pope to sit on the most exalted throne in Christendom, Alexander.'

Chapter 2

Traffic was chaotic along Viale Vaticano as limousines lined up depositing their ecclesiastical passengers who were arriving in record numbers for the conclave of cardinals to elect a new Pope. One vehicle stood out from the rest. Sandwiched patiently between limousines was the driver of a battered Fiat Bambino. In its glory days the tiny car would have been a shiny blue, but now most of the paintwork had either rusted away or worn to the dull red undercoat. Thick clouds of smoke spewed from the car's exhaust, intermittently letting off a loud backfire. The harassed portiere greeting the cardinals watched bemused as the Fiat finally pulled up in front of him. Impatiently he stepped up to the car and with undisguised distaste leant down to address the driver. He was careful not to lean too closely for fear of catching something nasty from the dishevelled occupant. He removed a silk handkerchief from his pocket to shield his face. 'You can't stop here. You must drive on immediately.' He pointed with his finger. 'The tourist car park is on the other side of the plaza.'

'But I am not a tourist,' the driver protested, 'I have business here.'

The portiere took a closer look at the man behind the wheel. He was thin and unkempt, of unspectacular appearance dressed in a black, stained smock. He had greasy, thin receding hair, his 'beard' a grey stubble. Behind the steel-rimmed spectacles a pair of bright blue, bloodshot eyes smiled up at him. The portiere thought he looked like a drunk badly in need of a bath. Then, for the first time, he noticed the yellowing Roman collar in contrast to the black smock. 'Scuse, Father,' he apologised, bowing his head, 'I did not notice you were a priest. What business do you have here at the Vatican?'

'I have come for the conclave of cardinals,' the driver explained.

'I am sorry, Father, but only cardinals and their staff are permitted to alight here.'

'But I am a cardinal,' the man replied, lacking conviction.

'Of course you are,' the portiere responded mockingly, 'and I'm the Pope. I'm sorry, but you're holding up the traffic. You must drive on,' he said, dropping the title Father, by now not at all sure if the man was even a priest. Rome was full of fanatics masquerading as clergy, especially now.

With a resigned sigh the man decided not to pursue the matter further. With a loud crunching of metal, he put the car into gear, and with a final noisy backfire drove off.

⁎⁂⁎

After parking the Fiat in the giant tourist car park, the man retrieved a battered, cardboard suitcase from the back seat and shut the door without bothering to lock it, figuring that if someone stole the car they needed it more than he did. With suitcase in hand, he walked back to the main door of the Secretariat of the Vatican where the portiere was still busily greeting cardinals and their entourage. He confronted the portiere again, who at first did not recognise him.

'Can I help you, Father?' the portiere asked, with thinly disguised contempt as he eyed the priest's shabby dress and suitcase. Then came recognition and he scowled. 'I thought I told you to be on your way.'

The man smiled. 'Yes, I did as you told me. I parked in the tourist car park.'

Frustrated, the portiere seemed about to give him a piece of his mind when he was interrupted by a voice calling from a limousine. 'Cardinal Salvatore, could it truly be you?'

13

The man and the portiere looked towards the voice. The door of the limousine swung open and out stepped an imposing man resplendently dressed in the full regalia of a cardinal. He was already striding purposefully towards the two men, arms flung wide in greeting. The dishevelled priest recognised him immediately as none other than Cardinal Alphonso Bacherelli, Prelate of Venice. To the portiere's amazement the two men embraced in a warm hug. Cardinal Bacherelli noticed the portiere gaping and asked, 'Why are you just standing there? Why don't you help Cardinal Salvatore with his luggage?' Then turning back to his friend he said, 'My dear, Giuseppe! It is so good to see you after all these years. But where is your motorcar and driver?'

'My motorcar is in the car park,' Giuseppe answered, 'and as for my driver,' he grinned, 'well, you are looking at him.'

Cardinal Bacherelli draped an arm around Giuseppe's shoulder, steering him towards the door of the Secretariat where a Swiss Guard saluted them. 'Come, my friend,' he said, 'we will see to having you outfitted in the attire befitting your rank.'

'But I have brought clothes with me,' Giuseppe protested, indicating his suitcase. 'What I have is quite comfortable and adequate for a humble priest.'

Bacherelli chuckled. 'You are a Prince of the Church,' he chided gently.

Giuseppe smiled, shrugging his shoulders and resigned himself to the care of his friend.

⁂

When Cardinal Salvatore retired to the privacy of his allocated apartment within the Apostolic Palace, he surveyed his surroundings, finding the apartment to his liking. It was simple with none of the expensive trappings of art and antiquity adorning the walls of the public areas of the palace. There was a single bed, an armchair, and a small kitchenette where he could cook breakfast or make coffee. The only decorations were a crucifix and a framed photograph of the deceased Pope.

Giuseppe knelt on the floor in front of the photograph and reflected on his friend. His mood was a mixture of sadness and exaltation. The fact that he would never see his friend again was tempered with the firm belief that Alexander was sitting at the right hand of Christ.

He remembered when he had first answered the calling from God, aspiring to serve humanity as a simple priest with no higher ambitions than that. His best friend at school had also received the calling and they entered the seminary together. His friend was ambitious and knew how to play the political game. His rise through the ecclesiastic ranks was nothing short of spectacular and, understanding the need for a confidant and ally, he dragged Giuseppe along with him.

Giuseppe's mentor became Pope Alexander IX and after his coronation he elected his reluctant friend to the rank of bishop, later bestowing him with the red hat of a cardinal.

Giuseppe accepted this without protest, firmly believing it to be the mysterious will of God.

He was given the archdiocese of Venice, but before too long he unhappily begged to be allowed to return to his beloved village in the foothills of the Dolomite Mountains in the north of Italy. He pleaded that he was not an administrator and could serve God more effectively by ministering to his flock of poverty-stricken parishioners in the village and surrounding districts. Reluctantly, the Pope acquiesced to his friend's pleas making him the highest-ranking parish priest in the history of the Church.

When Cardinal Salvatore stepped down as Prelate of Venice, Bishop Bacherelli was promoted to cardinal to fill the void.

Chapter 3

'Papa, please! Don't let him take me!' the child pleaded.

'It's for your own good, Luca. You are weak of body, and of mind – like your mother was. The fathers will make you strong.'

The monk stood like a terrifying apparition, his features hidden deep within the hood of his black habit. He approached the boy menacingly, hand outstretched. The boy shrieked, crying now, begging his father to let him stay. Behind the father, arms folded, expressions grim, stood the boy's two half-siblings.

'Don't be such a baby, Luca,' the girl mocked.

'Try to be a man, for once,' the boy chided.

'But I don't want him to take me. I want my mother.'

'Your mother's dead, Luca,' the father reminded him.

This caused the boy to cry even harder. The monk grabbed his hand and started dragging him towards the door. Luca dug his heels into the ground, shrieking, but he was no match for the monk's superior strength.

Cardinal Luca Morova woke with a start from his nightmare, lathered in sweat, and for a moment he wasn't sure where he was. The phone was ringing incessantly and he remembered he was in his office. He had been sleeping on the makeshift bed he'd had set up. He looked at the luminous dial of his watch. It was four in the morning. He'd been asleep for two hours.

He rubbed his eyes, trying to wipe away the grogginess as he picked up the phone. 'Pronto!'

'Did I wake you?' the American accent drawled.

16

'It doesn't matter. I was due to wake up anyway,' Morova replied, hearing the telltale echo of the trans-Atlantic cable. He was alert now. 'Did you secure the funds?' he demanded.

'No problem,' the American assured him. 'Just make sure our man gets the nod.'

'You worry about your end, and I'll worry about mine,' Morova snapped testily.

'Two hundred million US is a shit load of money,' the man said dryly.

'A small enough investment, I would suggest, all things considered.'

'Yeah, well, provided you get our man in the chair. Otherwise …' the American's voiced trailed off.

Morova ignored the veiled threat. 'When will the money be transferred?'

'It's taken care of.' The line went dead.

Morova replaced the handset and headed for the bathroom to freshen up for another long day of phone calls. Two hundred million dollars would go a long way.

Chapter 4

Conclave. From the Latin Con and Clavis, meaning 'with key', liberally translated as, 'under lock and key'. Or: a gathering of a group.

The bronze doors of the Sistine Chapel shut with a reverberating clang, locking the cardinals from the world, isolating them to commune with the Holy Spirit to reach an enlightenment of conscience from God. The first session of the conclave had begun and Cardinal Salvatore was relieved to find he had been seated next to his friend Cardinal Bacherelli. He leaned back into the high, throne-like chair, gripping the rich, red velvet armrests as he surveyed his surroundings. A heavy mist of incense hung in the air, lending an ethereal quality to the legacy of Michelangelo, whose genius adorned the walls and ceiling. Glancing around at the other cardinals, Giuseppe realised there were few faces he knew. As he watched, they were in the process of sitting down in similar chairs, spaced evenly around the rectangular perimeter of the walls of the chapel, which measured 40.93 metres long by 13.41 metres wide, the exact dimensions of the Temple of Solomon, as given in the Old Testament. He recognised Cardinal Morova who was patiently waiting at the altar, flanked by assistants.

With his back to the altar wall, the Cardinal Camerlengo seemed dwarfed against Michelangelo's depiction of the Last Judgement, which rose an impressive 20 metres to the ceiling. Giuseppe stared in fascinated amazement at the composition of Christ gesturing in judgement over the damned, whirling down to Charon of the underworld.

Cardinal Bacherelli leaned across, capping a hand to his mouth. 'Once everyone has settled in, the Camerlengo will lead us in prayer.'

Salvatore nodded. He had read up on the protocol he'd received on arrival, but he was nevertheless grateful to have his friend keep him abreast of procedure. Church politics had never been an important consideration in Giuseppe's life.

'After prayer,' Bacherelli continued, 'we take the oath to maintain absolute secrecy on proceedings, under pain of excommunication. Then, Cardinal Morova will extol the Holy Spirit to guide us in our deliberation.'

Giuseppe nodded again, but he was perplexed. There was one very important detail about the procedure that worried him.

Bacherelli must have noticed the concern on his friend's face. 'Is something troubling you Giuseppe?'

'Well, yes. I have been out of touch with Church hierarchy for a long time, and you are one of the few cardinals I know.'

'Yes,' Bacherelli prompted.

'Well, how do I know who to vote for? I mean, I do have utmost faith in the powers of the Holy Spirit, but ...' his voice trailed off.

Bacherelli gave him a quizzical look. 'You mean, no one has spoken to you about a favoured candidate?'

'What do you mean?'

'Leading up to this day, most of the cardinals have been busy debating the merits of the candidates among them. Did not Cardinal Morova speak to you?'

'No. Not since he wrote to me, asking me to be sure I attended the conclave.'

'I see.'

'I did think it strange at the time, and I admit that originally I had no intention of attending. You see, I don't think of myself as a cardinal. I feel I am here under false pretences.'

Bacherelli smiled at this. 'My dear Giuseppe, I believe you have more claim to the title than all of us.'

Giuseppe felt himself blushing at his friend's compliment and was about to launch into a denial when they were interrupted. Cardinal Morova asked the cardinals to take the oath of secrecy. He then led the final prayer before the first vote began.

'In the name of the Father and of the Son and of the Holy Spirit.' Cardinal Morova began. 'We beseech Thee O Lord to send down the Holy Spirit to enlighten us, Your servants, in the election of Your new representative on earth, to lead and to guide us and to steer Your Holy Church through the troubled waters of modern times.'

As one, the assemblage responded. 'Amen.'

They were ready to cast their first vote.

Giuseppe picked up the ballot paper, rubbing it between his thumb and forefinger, noting it was of high quality, parchment-like material. He read the neat, handwritten, copperplate script. *Eligo in suumum pontificem* ... – I elect as supreme pontiff ...

He looked across at Alphonso and whispered, 'I still don't know who to vote for.'

'You could always vote for me,' Bacherelli chortled. 'But seriously, there is no need for concern. This is only the first of many ballots. If you have no candidate in mind, simply leave your ballot blank. You will have ample time over the next few days, or weeks, to get to know the cardinals. This is just a warm up.'

Giuseppe was relieved. He could not cast a vote without a clear understanding of the candidates and what they stood for. He still found it hard to grasp that he was participating in the voting process to elect the next Vicar of Christ. He looked up and noticed the cardinals were writing on their ballot paper or in the process of folding it, so he picked up his own peacock feather quill as if to examine it. He replaced the quill in the inkpot without marking the paper, which he then neatly folded.

One by one, in order of seniority, the cardinals approached the altar where the Cardinal Camerlengo stood waiting, three assistants standing behind him. As each cardinal reached the altar he turned back towards the assemblage and holding the ballot high above his head for everyone to see, announced in a loud voice, 'I call to witness the Lord Christ, who will be my judge, that I am electing the one whom, under God, I believe ought to be elected.' The cardinal then placed the ballot on a paten on top of a large, golden chalice on the altar. The Camerlengo then slid the vote into the chalice.

After the last cardinal deposited his vote Cardinal Morova took the chalice and removed a ballot paper. He unfolded it and read the name before handing it to the first assistant who read it and passed it on to the second assistant who wrote the name on a tally sheet. He then passed it to the third assistant who stuck a needle and thread through it. Once this had been done Cardinal Morova called out in a loud, clear voice, 'Giuseppe Salvatore.'

Giuseppe looked up, surprised to hear his name being called. 'Why has he called out my name?' he asked Cardinal Bacherelli.

'Because it is your name on the ballot paper.'

Momentarily confused, Giuseppe frowned, and then, figuring what had happened, he smiled knowingly. 'Alphonso, you wrote down my name. That was a kind thing to do. But why? It will only cause me embarrassment with the cardinals.'

Before Bacherelli could answer, the second ballot had been threaded and Morova announced, 'Giuseppe Salvatore.'

Now Giuseppe was really confused. 'But, but, Alphonso. You are only allowed one vote! How could you have voted for me twice?'

21

Morova read the third ballot. 'Giuseppe Salvatore.'

But this is impossible, he thought. No one here knows me, except for Alphonso. It is a practical joke.

'Giuseppe Salvatore.'

Giuseppe looked frantically around the room searching for confirmation that this was some sort of initiation prank on a cardinal they knew did not belong. All eyes were solemnly riveted on the Camerlengo.

'Giuseppe Salvatore.'

Giuseppe looked to his friend, eyes pleading. 'Alphonso. What is going on? Tell me this is some kind of a joke.'

Alphonso smiled at Giuseppe, but there was no mirth in his eyes.

'Giuseppe Salvatore.'

The string of ballot papers was growing thick and every one that was opened was declared a vote for Giuseppe. After the next paper was threaded, the Camerlengo broke the monotony by declaring, 'No vote.'

Oh my God, Giuseppe thought, surely mine was not the only no vote.

⋆⋆⋆

When the first ballot finally reached its conclusion, Morova solemnly addressed the cardinals. Triumphantly he surveyed the expectant faces before him. I have my puppet pope, he gloated to himself. Everything had gone according to his plan.

'Holy Eminences,' he began, 'having completed the count you are witness to the wisdom and the will of the Holy Spirit. We, as the Sacred College of Cardinals have, almost unanimously, agreed on a successor to the throne of St Peter.'

An excited murmur began to spread among the cardinals.

Morova held up a hand for silence and then continued, 'Would Your Eminence, Cardinal Giuseppe Salvatore please approach the altar.'

For a moment there was no movement, as though Giuseppe had either not heard or had not comprehended. The assembled cardinals began to rise from their seats, converging towards Cardinal Salvatore. Morova watched as the moving mass of black and scarlet blocked Salvatore from his view. Then slowly, a path began to open between Cardinal Salvatore and the altar. The Cardinal Camerlengo waited patiently. As if in a daze, Salvatore rose to his feet and tentatively began to move forward. Hands reached out to touch him, heads nodding approval, and as he passed, the path closed behind him. Softly at first, the cardinals began to chant, 'Papa, Papa …' and by the time he reached the altar the sound had swelled until it was like a wave carrying him forward on its crest to his destiny.

When he reached the altar Morova bade him kneel and then said, 'Cardinal Giuseppe Salvatore, it is the will of the assembled cardinals, princes of the Roman Catholic Church and through the Divine intervention of the Holy Spirit that you be elected the two hundred and sixty-fourth Pontiff, successor to the throne of St Peter, Bishop of Rome and Keeper of the keys to Heaven. I now ask you, do you accept this cross?'

Giuseppe Salvatore remained silent, his lips mouthing a prayer. He raised his eyes to Michelangelo's ceiling, as though he might find an answer there. Prostrating on the floor, he lay still for another full minute while the cardinals waited patiently in silence. He rose to his feet and looking directly into the eyes of Cardinal Morova he spoke in a trembling voice, 'If this is God's will, I humbly accept His cross.'

Bowing his head Morova said, 'As God wills. And what name shall Your Holiness assume?'

To Morova the man looked a little in shock, and the new Pope pondered a while before answering. 'There are two predecessors I admired,' he said, 'Pope Leo for his abounding humility, and my own friend and mentor, the recently departed Pope Alexander. I will take their names.'

Morova struck his crosier three times on the tiled floor and then proclaimed in a loud voice, *'Annuntio vobis guadium magnum. Habemus Papam. Qui sibi accipit nomen Leo Alexander I.'* I announce to you great joy. We have a Pope. Who takes for himself the name, Leo Alexander I.

⚜

Outside in St Peter's Square thousands of pilgrims waited patiently for the telltale smoke from the Sistine Chapel, which would inform the world of a decision. Journalists and news crews from almost every nation had set up residence in Rome, but it was too early for them to join the gathered faithful. They knew from historical experience not to expect a result within the first few days, maybe not even the first few weeks.

The one exception was Rodger Carroll, a junior reporter for BBC television. When the news director in London had decided to include him in the crew to cover the conclave, Rodger saw this as his great opportunity. Before departing, he spent every spare moment in newspaper libraries, swatting up on the history of papal elections and Church protocol. By the time the crew arrived in Rome, Rodger was almost an authority on the subject. While the crew headed for a local bar, Carroll chose instead to mingle with the crowd in the Square.

'You never know, sir,' he argued to his boss, 'something newsworthy just might happen. But if not, at least I'll get a feel of the mood.'

His boss laughed, while the rest of the crew ribbed him good-naturedly for his enthusiasm. The crew boss jotted down the phone number of the bar and stuffed it into Carroll's pocket. 'Just in case,' he winked.

⋆ ✧ ⋆

Carroll did not immediately notice the thin wisp of smoke that began to curl in a lazy spiral from the narrow chimney of the Sistine Chapel. Piazza San Pietro, St Peter's Square, was filled to overcrowding by those determined to stand vigil until a new Pope was elected, and like Rodger, no one was watching the chimney with interest or expectation, because everyone knew this was only the first ballot.

Carroll could not help overhearing a young American priest absently comment to his companion, 'Shows how much I know, I could have sworn black smoke meant they haven't elected a Pope.'

'It does,' his companion assured him. He went on to explain. 'At the end of each session they burn the ballot papers, adding wet straw which makes the smoke black.'

'Then why is white smoke coming out?'

Rodger turned his attention to the chapel, as others began to notice the plume of smoke, nudging those next to them and gesturing in the direction of the chimney. At first, most shared the American's initial confusion, until slowly the unthinkable became a reality and a few voices began to call, 'We have a Pope, we have a Pope … Papa, Papa …' Slowly the call was taken up, spreading through the masses in a rising chant, in a multiplicity of languages.

With a reporter's eye for history in the making, Rodger saw eyes turning expectantly to the central balcony within the façade of the Vatican and from where they knew the announcement of a newly elected Pope would be declared.

Having left nothing to chance, Rodger had made arrangements with the owner of a nearby café to be allowed the use of his phone at a moment's notice. It had cost him a few thousand lire, but now, as he raced out of the Square to phone his boss, he figured it had been a worthwhile investment.

'What do you mean they've elected a Pope?' his boss asked. How could they? I mean, that's impossible. They only just went into their first meeting.'

'All I know is that there's white smoke coming up from the chapel,' the young reporter insisted, 'and the crowd's going berserk. Listen to this.' Rodger held the phone towards the door of the café, relaying the din of thousands of voices chanting in unison, 'Papa, Papa …'

Replacing the phone to his ear, Rodger could hear his boss screaming at his crew across the bar. 'Get into St Peter's now!' he yelled. 'We've been caught flat-footed. The shortest Papal election in history and we don't even have a camera in there.' He spoke back into the phone. 'Rodger, you still there? Good! Stay exactly where you are. Understand? Don't move! I'll get the crew in there as fast as I can. And, Rodger, listen up. You're it. Get it? As soon as the cameras get there, you're on.'

Rodger smiled, but said nothing.

'Rodger, did you hear me? I said you're it. Casey can't do it. He's pissed. You're all I've got. Now get ready.'

'I'll be ready, boss,' Rodger assured him. He'd been ready for this all of his life.

As Rodger shouldered his way through the mass of people, the crowd erupted, and he looked up just in time to see a smiling Cardinal Camerlengo appear on the balcony, flanked by other cardinals. Morova stepped in front of a microphone and in a grandiose manner, spread his arms towards Heaven and waited for silence. Without lowering his arms, he waited, standing like a statue caught in time, till the chanting died, replaced by an expectant hush, broken only by the flapping wings of the pigeons. Still he waited, allowing the expectation of the crowd to build like the charge of electricity preceding a lightning strike.

'*Habemus Papam* ...' We have a Pope ...

St Peter's Square exploded into a riot of noise as strangers kissed and embraced, while others danced and jumped up and down in a frenzy of unbridled joy. Morova continued to stand, arms still raised, waiting to continue. For a long time it seemed it would be impossible to quieten the crowd, but slowly the tumultuous noise began to fade. Again he waited for absolute silence.

'Through the divine intervention of the Holy Spirit, the Sacred College of Cardinals has unanimously voted for His Eminence, Cardinal Giuseppe Salvatore, formerly the Patriarch of Venice.'

This time the silence continued in an anti-climax as confused people looked at each other, trying to digest what they'd just heard.

'Who's he?' the American priest asked his companion, reflecting the question on thousands of lips.

'Beats me,' his companion shrugged, 'never heard of him.'

✦

The flustered news crew found Rodger Carroll and as they were setting up the camera, the crew's boss shouted to no one in particular, 'Find out what you can about a Cardinal Giuseppe something or other, and do anything to get a photo. Find out who his relatives are. Someone must know who this guy is. We've got to interview someone.'

'His name is Cardinal Giuseppe Salvatore,' Carroll said, 'and he used to be the Prelate of Venice.'

'What? How do you know that? Never mind.' The boss shook his head, with an unfamiliar look of respect in his eyes that was new to Rodger.

Cardinal Morova continued, 'I present to the world the new Vicar of Christ, Pope Leo Alexander the First.' The curtain

27

behind Morova parted and he stepped aside to make room for the new Pope to take his place before the microphone. The white soutane and skullcap stood out in stark contrast to the scarlet and black of the flanking cardinals.

Rodger Carroll turned his back on the new Pope and straightened his tie as he watched the cameraman count down with his fingers. His hand clenched into a fist and then pointed at Carroll indicating he was live to air. The red light on top of the camera began to glow, and Rodger brought the microphone to his mouth and smiled.

'This is Rodger Carroll reporting live in St Peter's Square for the BBC.'

Around the world, millions watched the unknown Rodger Carroll, as the crowd sank to its knees, heads bowed in anticipation of the first apostolic blessing.

'Behind me, Pope Leo Alexander I, elected in the shortest conclave in history, is about to deliver his first blessing to the world ...'

Chapter 5

Cardinal Morova was in his office when he was summoned, but he was in no hurry to respond. After all, he was busy, and he was annoyed at being disturbed. Besides that, it was important he set an early precedent. He was not a junior cleric at the beck and call of the recently elected Pope. Let him wait, he thought. He continued to pore over the documents on his desk for another half an hour before he was satisfied they were in order. Then, with a resigned sigh he pushed his chair away from his desk. He would soon see what was so urgent. Nevertheless, he would have to be careful. It may be prudent to humour the Pope, let him think he is the boss for a while. Morova had learned from past experience that the best way to manipulate a Pope was to let him think his ideas and decisions were his own.

As he walked the short distance along the corridor separating his office from the Pope's, within the confines of the Apostolic Palace, he was oblivious to the priceless artworks he passed on the way. When he reached the Papal office, the Swiss Guard stood respectfully to attention and knocked loudly on the huge door.

'Avanti,' the familiar voice called from within.

The guard opened the door and with the confidence of familiarity, Morova strode with determination to where the Pope was seated. His shoes beat a hollow staccato on the marble floor, causing the Pope to look up.

'Ah, Eminence,' he acknowledged from behind the great, carved desk.

'Holiness,' Morova greeted, 'I heard news you wished to see me.'

'Yes indeed, Eminence,' the Pope replied, glancing at his wristwatch.

Morova ignored the gesture. 'And how can I be of assistance, Holiness?' he asked.

Without preamble, the Pope came straight to the point, gesturing to a letter on his desk. 'I received this letter this morning. It is a request for an audience.'

'Holiness, please,' Morova interrupted. 'It is most important that Your Holiness accustoms himself with the usage of the royal plural when referring to himself.'

'Tush,' the Pope waved a hand dismissing the correction. 'I could never get used to that.'

'But Your Holiness, there is protocol to observe.'

'I would much rather be myself.' He waved the letter at Morova, bringing him back to the point of his summons. 'Now, about this request.'

'Holiness, I am afraid that is out of the question,' Morova said without bothering to ask who the letter was from.

'The request comes from a person for whom I have great admiration.'

'Holiness, with respect, you have only recently been appointed Pope. Your schedule for personal audiences is full for at least six months.' Counting off on his fingers he continued. 'World leaders, heads of state, royalty, heads of multi-national conglomerates ...' He waved a hand in the air, emphasising the enormity of the Pope's commitments. 'Holiness, really, the list goes on and on. And that does not include the other day-to-day duties of your Papacy.'

Leo Alexander brushed aside Morova's objections with an impatient wave of his own hand. 'I will see her, Cardinal, and I would thank you to arrange it.'

Morova was taken aback by this unexpected display of defiance. It was out of character. Perhaps it would be best to indulge him, he thought. Sometimes it is better to acquiesce on the small things in order to win on the things that count.

'Why, of course, Holiness. I was only concerned at your very full schedule, not wishing to burden you unnecessarily. I am sure we can squeeze this special person in briefly between scheduled audiences.'

'You do not understand, Eminence. It is my intention to go to her.'

Morova blinked. 'I'm sorry, Holiness, I don't understand.'

'She is in Portugal. And I am told she is not well. Travelling to the Vatican is out of the question. So you see, I intend to go to Portugal. And without delay,' he added for emphasis.

Morova could scarcely believe what he was hearing. 'But, but Holiness,' he stammered, 'this is entirely without precedent.'

'Perhaps,' the Pope responded with determination, 'but be that as it may, precedent or no precedent, I intend to go.'

Morova decided to take a different tack. He smiled indulgently. 'Holiness, I apologise. How insensitive of me. This is obviously of importance to Your Holiness. But does Your Holiness have any idea of the logistics and protocol involved in organising a Papal visit to a foreign country?' Without waiting for an answer he continued. 'Firstly, we would need to move through the correct diplomatic channels. The Vatican ambassador to Portugal would need to broach the subject with the foreign secretary of that country. This would be followed by an official letter of intent to the government of that country. We would then need to wait for an official response as to when would be the most convenient time of year for your visit, taking into consideration that country's previous political engagements. This would then be followed by an official invitation, followed by our official acceptance. And only then would arrangements begin for your security, which would consist of liaising between the Swiss Guard

31

and the heads of security of the foreign country.' Morova smiled condescendingly. 'So you see, Holiness, it is out of the question.'

The Pope waited patiently for Morova to finish before replying. 'Then my visit will be unofficial. Incognito, if you like.'

Morova stared at the Pope as if he had gone mad. 'Incognito?' he blurted. 'Holiness, you have obviously not come to terms with the gravity of your position. You are the Pope. The Head of the Holy Roman Catholic Church. The Vicar of Christ on Earth. You are the Chosen Successor of St Peter. You wear the Fisherman's Ring. You are the infallible and undisputed leader of one billion Catholics worldwide! Holiness, you simply do not travel incognito.'

Morova paused to draw breath, fearing he had overstepped himself.

The Pope smiled. 'It is no use, Eminence. I am determined to go. Sorry. *We* are determined to go.'

It would seem that nothing Morova could say would sway the Pope. His mind was racing with the political implications of cancelling even one of his scheduled audiences. This was turning into a potentially serious situation and short of placing the Pope under house arrest, Morova was running out of options.

He changed tack once again, cursing his own stupidity. He decided to ask the obvious question he should have asked right up front. Know thine enemy.

'Very well, Holiness, it would seem you are unwavering on this quest of yours. Might I be so bold as to ask the name of this person who is deemed so important by Your Holiness?'

'Yes, you may, Cardinal Morova, but I have one condition.'

'And that would be, Holiness?'

'That you drop the formality of your address, at least when we are in private discussion. Can you not address me by my given name? My friends call me Giuseppe?'

Morova stared at the Pope as if he'd been asked to blaspheme. 'Very well, Holiness. Whatever Your Holiness wishes.'

The Pope gave a resigned sigh. He picked up the letter from his desk and pressed it to his cheek. 'The letter is from dear Sister Lucia.'

Morova's heart missed a beat. His thin lips compressed into a grimace and he cursed himself for not anticipating this most obvious eventuality. He had been so distracted by the conclave that he had forgotten that sooner or later that witch would get her claws into this Pope, just as she had with his predecessor and his predecessor before him. This was far more serious than Morova had suspected. Regaining his composure, he struggled to smile. 'Then I will travel with you, Holiness.'

'No, Cardinal Morova. Your place is here at the Vatican.'

Chapter 6

During the short flight to Lisbon, Leo Alexander had time to reflect on what he knew about the amazing woman he was about to meet.

Lucia de Jesus was born in 1907 in a hamlet called Aljustrel of the township of Fatima in Portugal. At ages ten, nine and seven, Lucia and her cousins, Francisco and Jacinta were unremarkable children, with nothing distinctive to set them apart from other, healthy young children of similar age. But that was before 13 May, 1917. The events of that day were unparallelled in Church history and are considered the most momentous and important since the resurrection of Christ.

At about midday, while playing in a field owned by Sister Lucia's parents, the children saw what appeared to be a bright flash of lightning. Looking up they saw an apparition, swathed in light, hovering about a metre above a holm oak.

The children later described the apparition as a lady dressed in white, with a face that was indescribably beautiful, neither sad nor happy, but with an air of mild reproach. They said they were close enough to be enveloped by the light radiating from her.

The apparition spoke to the children, assuring them they had nothing to fear, explaining She was from heaven. She asked them to meet Her at the same spot on the thirteenth day for the next five consecutive months. She promised to reveal who She was and what She wanted from them. Before departing She told the children to pray the rosary every day for peace and an end to the war. The apparition then rose serenely, and surrounded by intense light, disappeared into the east.

Word that the children had experienced some sort of mystical vision spread, so that the following month, some fifty or so spectators had gathered in anticipation of the next, promised visitation. True to Her word, the apparition appeared on the thirteenth day of the following month, and as the small crowd watched, the sun grew dimmer and they heard a whispering sound like the humming of bees. It was on this visit that the apparition revealed Herself to be Our Lady, the mother of Jesus. Lucia asked if She would take the three of them to heaven. Our Lady told the children that She would be taking Jacinta and Francisco soon, but that Lucia would stay a long time as trustee of the secrets to be revealed and to deliver Her message to the world.

On the third apparition on 13 July, 1917, Our Lady told the children that She would perform a miracle in October for everyone to see, so that the world would believe. She then spread Her hands and a great radiant light streamed forth, seemingly penetrating the earth. It was then that the children saw the first vision, or secret of Fatima. They saw a great sea of fire, within which were submerged tortured souls shrieking in anguish and despair, surrounded by hideously grotesque shapes of devils and demons. This vision only lasted a few moments, but it was long enough to strike terror into the hearts of the children. Our Lady explained that they had witnessed a vision of hell, a warning to the world to heed Her words.

Our lady then went on to reveal the second secret, telling the children that the Great War would end, but if the world did not mend its ways, this would be followed by another war, far worse, and that it would begin in the reign of Pius XI and that nations would be annihilated. She demanded the consecration of Russia by the Pope and in the event of that happening, prophesied that Russia would convert to Christ. She warned that failure to consecrate Russia would result in that country spreading its terrors throughout the world, promoting wars and persecution. By the fifth apparition a crowd of twenty thousand people gathered to witness what was about to take place. As the crowd waited expectantly they observed unexplainable phenomena. The air cooled suddenly and the sun dimmed so that stars could be seen, and a rain fell that was like snowflakes, but disappeared before touching the ground. Then the crowd witnessed a luminous ball moving slowly through the sky in a westerly direction and then back again.

The following month, the crowd had swelled to seventy thousand, because word had spread of Our Lady's promise to perform a miracle on this, Her sixth and last appearance.

As the multitude waited expectantly, it soon became apparent that something was happening. Like the previous visitations, the temperature suddenly dropped and a fine drizzle of rain began to fall.

All of a sudden, Lucia cried out, 'Look at the sun.'

The crowd looked up and the clouds parted, revealing the sun as a giant silver disk shining more intensely than ever before, yet people were able to stare at it without being blinded. Then, witnessed by the crowd of more than seventy thousand, the great disk began to dance, spinning like a colossal ball of fire, spraying bright flames across the sky. Then abruptly it stopped. The multitude held its breath. The sun started again, this time travelling in the opposite direction. This was repeated three times. It stopped again. The great sphere of light began to quiver and reverberate. Suddenly it plunged, twisting and turning, plummeting on a collision course with the terrified crowd. The miracle lasted a full ten minutes and then the fiery orb returned to its place in the sky, and was normal again.

As well as the seventy thousand people in attendance, there were witness reports of the phenomenon from as far as 40 kilometres away.

It was after this miracle that the Lady then went on to reveal the third and most terrible secret.

⟶✦⟵

True to Our Lady's word, Francisco and Jacinta became ill at almost the same time at the end of October 1918. Francisco was taken on 4 April, 1919 and buried in the cemetery at Fatima. Our lady took Jacinta on 20 February, 1920, and she was buried in the cemetery of Vila Nova de Ourem. In 1935, Jacinta's remains were transferred to a tomb in Fatima, prepared especially for her and her brother. At the time of her exhumation, fifteen years after her death, her face was found to be perfectly preserved. Later, the remains of the children were moved again, this time to the crypt of the Basilica of Fatima, where they remain to this day.

Giuseppe's reverie was interrupted by the captain's announcement. 'Ladies and gentlemen, please fasten your seat belts as we begin our descent to Lisbon.'

⟶✦⟵

A taxi deposited the Pope in front of the Carmelite Convent of St Theresa, where the driver gratefully thanked the kind father for his generous tip. Leo Alexander's hand was still on the bell cord when a smiling nun who introduced herself as the Mother Prioress opened the gate. She ushered him in, where he was confronted by a line of shy, grinning nuns. The Prioress explained that she had lifted the vow of silence for the day, in honour of the Papal visit and apologised that as Sister Lucia had not been well, she thought it best that she wait inside for His Holiness.

Although anxious to meet Sister Lucia, the Pope took his time, greeting each of the nuns individually with a question and a few words, delighting them with his near-fluent Portuguese, explaining that his mother had been born in their beautiful country.

The Pope was shown into a drawing room, where the nuns fussed over him, offering tea and cakes, which he happily accepted.

My, my, he thought, I'm still the same person I was before, and yet how differently I am treated.

I think I preferred the before.

Leo Alexander surveyed his surroundings as he waited for Sister Lucia.

The room was Spartan – hardwood floors bleached from years of scrubbing, with a simple table surrounded by hardback chairs being the only furniture. Two framed pictures hung on either side of a wooden crucifix hanging in the centre of a whitewashed wall. One was of Our Lady of Fatima, which he thought appropriate, considering who lived here. The other was a portrait of his recently deceased predecessor, with a black ribbon of mourning stretched over one corner of the frame.

'I'm so sorry, Holy Father,' the prioress apologised, 'we have still not received a photograph of your Holiness.'

The Pope dismissed the apology with a wave of his hand, joking, 'How fortunate for you and the sisters.'

A younger nun assisted Sister Lucia into the room, and the Pope stood up to greet her. She tried to genuflect, only managing a half curtsy, bowing her head to kiss the Papal ring. The Pope withdrew his hand, resisting the courtesy.

'It is I who should be prostrating to you, Holy Mother' he said, kneeling to kiss the hem of her gown. He helped her to a chair, ensuring she was comfortable before joining her at the table. The Pope observed a burning intelligence and awareness in her eyes, which twinkled with good humour as she assessed her visitor.

'How very good of you, Holy Father, to go to so much trouble to visit an old nun,' she started.

'It is my privilege,' he said, causing her to smile.

'But you are such a busy man, Holiness, she continued, 'with so many problems and responsibilities. I am sure we could have managed to get these tired old bones to the Vatican.'

'I was thrilled to receive your letter, Sister, and meeting with you supersedes the petty problems of state and meetings with people who bask in their own importance. All of my life I have dreamed of meeting with you, and hearing from your own lips about your most extraordinary and privileged experiences.'

'Then your Holiness should have visited with us earlier.'

'Ah, but I was not the Pope then.'

'I am always happy to receive those who are devoted to the Blessed Virgin.'

'Holy Mother, nothing would please me more than to spend our time together reminiscing about the incredible events of Fatima. But your letter mentioned a matter of grave importance. Imperative that it be brought to my urgent attention.'

'For reasons best known to Her,' Sister Lucia began, 'I have been chosen by Our Lady to be Her emissary to the world, and it is Her business which I wish to discuss with Your Holiness.'

With a tingle of anticipation the Pope encouraged her to continue.

'As a wise man, Holiness, you may have pondered why it is, that Pope after Pope failed to reveal the Third Secret of Fatima.'

'Ponder it I did, Mother,' the Pope agreed, 'but being a simple priest, it was not for me to question the infallible wisdom of a Pope.'

'But now *you* are the Pope, Holiness, and there are things you must know.'

The Pope shivered with a sense of foreboding at what was to come, and he felt almost superstitious awe to be in the presence of a person who had spoken with the mother of God.

'Our Lady was explicit in Her instructions that Her third message was to be revealed to the world by no later than 1960.'

The Pope wasn't sure whether she expected him to respond or just listen. He said, 'As I recall, when the time of revelation came in 1960, the Pope declared the world was not ready.'

Sister Lucia smiled gently, as though addressing a gullible child. 'Are you suggesting, Holiness, that perhaps the Queen of Saints and Angels somehow got it wrong? And that perhaps She got the date mixed up?'

The Pope already felt humbled in the presence of a living saint, and now, following the mild rebuke, he also felt foolish. 'No, Sister, of course not. It is just that, well, it is what we were told at the time.'

Sister Lucia continued. 'As you correctly recall, Holiness, Pope John XXIII announced in 1960 that the world was not ready. And now, eighteen years later, Our Lady's message is still being suppressed.'

'I, I really did not give it much thought,' Leo Alexander admitted. 'I suppose I just blindly accepted what I was told.'

'Yes, Holy Father, that is the problem. You, along with the millions of faithful around the world, accept with blind faith and obedience all that is declared by the Vatican.'

The Pope felt uneasy. 'But Holy Mother, isn't that what we are supposed to do? Obey the Pope and his bishops unquestioningly?'

Sister Lucia smiled sadly. 'Firstly,' she replied, 'it is important for Your Holiness to understand the chain of events leading up to the suppression. You see, it wasn't until 1944 that I wrote down the revelations of the Third Secret, having been ordered to do so by my bishop. I was ill at the time and the bishop feared the secret could die with me. He had no idea of its contents, but accepted that should it die with me then the Church would potentially lose an exceptional grace from God. This was true, but the bishop had no idea of the shocking and devastating revelation the secret contained, nor the potential ramifications.'

'Is it because of the nature of the revelations that the secret has been suppressed?'

'Yes, but allow me to continue.'

The Pope nodded, apologising for the interruption.

'I had to be sure, so I asked the bishop to put his order to me in writing, which he did. But it was not to be that simple.' She frowned. 'For three months I could not put pen to paper. I wrestled with my order from the bishop daily, but I just could not write. There was no logical explanation for it and I was becoming extremely frustrated at being unable to fulfil a simple directive from my superior. It was during this time that Our Lady appeared again, assuring me that it was God's will to reveal the secret.'

Leo Alexander once again thrilled at the thought of Our Lady appearing to this woman and he felt privileged to be in her presence, if not slightly envious.

Sister Lucia took a sip of water before continuing. 'Please excuse me, Holy Father, my throat is dry. I don't often get the opportunity to speak.' She took another sip, replaced the glass on the table and continued. 'Our Lady went on to explain why I had been unable to write down the secret as ordered, and the reason was incredible.'

The Pope leant forward in eager anticipation of what was to come. 'Yes, yes, please continue Sister,' he prompted.

'The Holy Mother told me that Satan had blocked my will to stop me carrying out my order.'

Leo Alexander's brow shot up.

'Yes, I admit it does sound incredible. You see, Holy Father, Our Lady has been in a continuing conflict with the powers of darkness, which are increasingly winning the struggle to enslave humanity. Satan knows that should the Third Secret be revealed, then centuries of his work will be instantly undone.'

The Pope felt confused. Despite his unerring faith, this was beginning to sound a little metaphysical. 'I don't understand, Mother. Are you saying the Third Secret has been suppressed all these years through Satan's intervention?'

'Yes.' Her answer was matter of fact.

'But, but, to what purpose? Is there a hidden message within Our Lady's revelation?'

'No, certainly not. I assure you, Holiness, that Our Lady does not speak in riddles. Her message to the world is abundantly clear.'

The Pope gestured for her to continue.

'Be assured, Holiness, that the forces of evil are strong and they grow stronger daily, as Satan gains more and more disciples in high places within the clergy, politics and business.'

'Satan has disciples within the clergy?' the Pope marvelled.

'Be guarded, Holiness, for they are within the very walls of the Vatican,' she warned.

The Pope was shocked at this revelation, but said nothing.

'I'm sorry, Holy Father, I digress. Once I had written the secret down, I sealed it in an envelope as instructed and gave it to the bishop, who never opened it. Is that not peculiar?' she asked rhetorically. 'It then took thirteen years before the document finally arrived in Rome in 1957, when it was placed in a locked chest by Pope Pius XII, and amazingly he did not read it either.'

'Yes, I know that,' the Pope said, 'but I thought it was because it was not to be read until 1960.'

'No, Holiness, that is not quite correct. The instruction was explicit; it was to be revealed by no later than 1960. There is much hypothesis on why Pius XII chose not to read it. It is thought he may have had an inkling of the contents, fearing them too terrible to contemplate, and what he did not know he did not have to act on. He decided he would wait until the latest date decreed by the Blessed Virgin, but he died without ever having read it.

'The envelope was finally opened by Pope John XXIII in 1959, a year after Pius XII's death. As 1960 approached you would have known there was a growing sense of expectation throughout the Christian world, with a renewed movement of devotion to the Immaculate Heart of Mary.'

'Yes, yes,' the Pope agreed, 'I was one of the many looking forward to the revelation and suffered bitter disappointment.'

'And rightly so, Holiness. When the time arrived in February 1960, the world was simply told that the Third Secret of Fatima would not be revealed.'

'I seem to recall,' the Pope said, 'that at the time the Vatican issued a terse press release, something about not wishing to be responsible for the accuracy or reliability of your interpretation of the Blessed Virgin's message.' He paused, feeling embarrassed. 'I must admit, Sister, that at the time I thought it a plausible explanation.'

Sister Lucia smiled at the Pope's discomfort. 'You were not alone in your acceptance of that nonsense. My cousins and I were chosen by the Blessed Virgin Mary for reasons best known to Her and to God. By suggesting that my interpretation may be anything but accurate is to propose the possibility of the Mother of God making a mistake in Her choice of messengers. Is it conceivable that She would entrust a message to humanity to someone who could not be trusted to pass that message on accurately?'

Once again the Pope felt chastened. 'All that you say, Mother, is undisputedly logical, but I have to admit, I am still perplexed.'

Sister Lucia sighed. In the depths of her calm eyes, Leo Alexander saw peace and tranquillity, yet at the same time, a terrible intensity of sorrow. 'The secret is a key, Holy Father,' she said, her voice troubled. 'It is a key given to people by God through His mother. It is the key to avoiding the Apocalypse.

43

This threat is looming over nations and humankind. To continue to ignore this gift, this opportunity, will result in the world's enslavement to the Antichrist. Nations will be annihilated from the face of the earth.'

The Pope sat stunned, lost for words.

Sister Lucia continued. 'Others have had the opportunity to turn the key, but they refused. Now it is up to you, Holy Father.'

Leo Alexander was finally able to speak. 'And now, tell me, Mother, what is this terrible secret? This secret that is a key.'

'It is not just a key, Holy Father, it is also a cross. A terrible cross that God has chosen you to bear. I will pray you have the strength to carry it to your own Calvary.'

Chapter 7

It was early, but already St Peter's Square was filling with brightly coloured umbrellas held high like beacons by the tour leaders signalling to their flocks of eager-faced tourists. The Pope stood at his office window overlooking the Square. How enthusiastic they looked. Hanging on to every word, gazing from left to right in wonder as the glory of Renaissance architecture is pointed out to them. The Pope could almost hear the words.

'We are standing in front of St Peter's, which is without doubt the finest church ever built in all of Christendom. Built on the site of St Peter's tomb in 315 by Constantine, it was re-built in the sixteenth century by Pope Julius II. The dome is mainly credited to Michelangelo and it soars 119 metres above the high altar. The interior is so vast it can accommodate sixty thousand people.'

The Pope watched one of the guides spread his arms, no doubt gesturing at the piazza, its colonnades reaching out in a symbolic embrace of the Christian world. The guide pointed at the Pope's window, causing Giuseppe to instinctively withdraw.

If they only knew what I now know, he thought, they would not be so carefree. His mind could barely accept the reality of the terrible responsibility he faced. But there was no escaping it. The meeting with Sister Lucia had shaken him, and as a result, changed him forever and he prayed to God that he would have the strength and wisdom to implement what was demanded of him.

He left the window and pressed the intercom on his desk, summoning his secretary. The elderly monsignor, who had served three Popes, entered the Papal office carrying an appointment book. 'Good morning, Holy Father,' he greeted. 'During your, ah, absence we re-scheduled as many appointments as we could, but I'm afraid that these just will not wait.' He opened the book and began to read the day's gruelling schedule of appointments.

The Pope cut him off. 'Thank you Monsignor, but there is a more pressing matter we need to attend to.'

'Holiness?' The monsignor looked up from his book.

The Pope continued. 'Please arrange to bring us the writings of Sister Lucia.'

'But, Holiness, your schedule of appointments …'

'Please cancel my appointments.'

The monsignor looked as though he'd been struck a blow.

The Pope felt sorry for the little priest and for a moment he thought the man might actually cry. 'Monsignor, I am truly sorry. I know you have my best interests at heart and I know it has been difficult for you, but I do not have time to see anyone today. There are more urgent matters I need to attend to. Now please, would you arrange to bring me Sister Lucia's account of the Third Secret of Fatima. I understand it is filed within the Vatican archives.

The monsignor made no attempt to move, he looked unhappy, eyes downcast, his feet shuffled uncomfortably.

'Is there a problem?' the Pope asked.

The old man hesitated. 'Are you sure you really want this document, Holiness?'

'Of course,' the Pontiff replied, 'and without delay. Why, is there something I should know?'

The priest continued to hover nervously, looking increasingly uncomfortable. 'Holiness, I'm afraid it is not that easy.'

'I don't understand, Monsignor,' he said puzzled, 'you do know what it is I'm talking about, don't you?'

'Oh yes, perfectly, Holiness. It's just that …'

'What is it? Why is it a problem to bring me Sister Lucia's document? It is in the Vatican, isn't it?' The man was now positively agitated, and the Pope encouraged him to answer. 'Don't be afraid, Monsignor. What do you know about this?'

'The problem is, Holiness, that the last person to read the document was your predecessor, Pope Alexander, and that was early in his reign. I remember it clearly. He became terribly upset after reading it. He was in mental turmoil for weeks, praying constantly. He became ill as a result of it. So you see, Holy Father, I'm only trying to save you from similar anguish.'

'That's thoughtful of you, Monsignor, but nevertheless, I would still like you to bring me the document. I will see it.'

Still the priest made no move to leave.

'Please, Monsignor, what is it now?' the Pope pleaded, becoming frustrated.

'There is more, Holiness,' the priest continued hesitantly.

'Well?' the Pope pressed.

'Once Pope Alexander recovered from his upset, he ordered Cardinal Morova to take charge of the document with instructions that it was never to be shown or revealed again.'

'What? Are you telling me it has been destroyed?'

'Ah, no. At least I don't believe so, Holiness. But might I make a suggestion?'

'Yes, of course. What is it?'

'Perhaps it would be best for me to summon Cardinal Morova. He may be able to enlighten you.'

'Yes, yes. That's an excellent idea. Please send for him at once.'

⚜

'You sent for me, Holiness?' Morova asked as he entered the Papal office.

'Yes, I did, Eminence. Thank you for your prompt response.'

Morova had made a point of keeping the Pope waiting for more than two hours and now he wasn't sure whether he was being sarcastic. He chose to ignore it.

'Cardinal Morova,' the Pope got straight to the point, 'it is our understanding that you have some knowledge of the Third Secret of Fatima.'

Morova did not blink. His smile was condescending. He had anticipated this.

'Now, why would your Holiness wish to bother himself with such a matter?'

Leo Alexander was visibly taken aback by this unexpected response, replying in a tone alien to his usual good nature. 'Why we would bother with anything is hardly your concern, Cardinal Morova. We would suggest your attitude is bordering on insolence.'

Morova was surprised at the sudden change in the usually meek and humble man, and that he was now referring to himself in the formal plural, was not lost on him. 'Then please forgive me, Holiness,' he said, lacking sincerity, 'it was not my intention to be insolent. I was merely hoping to protect you from a subject that has been closely examined by your predecessors, who agreed it was a matter best left alone.'

Perhaps this Pope was a mistake after all, Morova thought. Could it be this peasant has a mind of his own?

'On the contrary, Cardinal Camerlengo,' the Pope said, addressing him for the first time by his official title, 'it is a matter long overdue for action.'

Morova decided to take a different approach. This man may be sharper than he'd given him credit for.

'Sister Lucia is old, Holiness, and her interpretation of the revelation is, um, perhaps a little clouded, or let's say the accuracy of her understanding is questionable, and has already caused undue grief.'

'She was not so old when she wrote down the revelation,' the Pope countered.

'Ah, yes, that may be correct, Holiness, but nevertheless, she lacks education. Her interpretation is still highly questionable, as is her ability to write it down accurately. After all, she did not even learn to write till she was an adult.'

'Cardinal Morova, are you suggesting the Blessed Virgin Mary, mother of God, Queen of Angels and Saints made an error in judgement in Her choice of messenger?' he demanded, echoing one of Sister Lucia's own compelling arguments.

Morova stumbled for words.

'Enough Cardinal! We command you to retrieve the document at once.' He punched the intercom button on his desk, summoning the Monsignor secretary to step in at once.

Morova was trembling with rage and it took all his will to maintain control. *How dare he? I made him, and I can just as easily undo him.* His rebellious thoughts were interrupted when the Papal secretary entered the room.

'Monsignor, we would like you to order a Swiss Guard, on our direct authority, to personally escort His Eminence to retrieve Sister Lucia's document. The guard is not to leave the cardinal's presence until we have the document in our hand. Is that understood?'

The monsignor said nothing, glancing nervously at Morova for confirmation of the order.

Morova gave a slight nod, but he was fuming as he backed out of the Pope's presence.

A Swiss Guard escorted Cardinal Morova to the deepest recesses of the Vatican archives where he had secreted the document so many years ago. His mind was racing. *This Pope must not be allowed to read that damned document. I should have destroyed it once and for all, and to hell with the consequences.* He had considered it, but then thought better of it. *As long as that damned nun is still alive, she could just as easily re-write the cursed thing. This damned, interfering Pope may just be fool enough to*

49

act on the document. Morova shuddered at the thought. But how can I stop him reading it? He was almost in a panic and then realised the Swiss Guard was watching him closely.

'Are you all right Eminence?' the guard asked respectfully.

'Of course I'm all right,' Morova snapped. He had no choice. There was no way out. He would just have to wait and see. If nothing else, Morova was confident in his skills of persuasion. Surely the man is reasonable, despite his newly acquired stubbornness and overabundance of sickly humility. Morova would convince him of the folly of taking drastic action. No. He simply would not allow it to happen. The consequences were unthinkable. Morova had far too much invested to allow that to happen.

They had reached the depths of the archive room, surrounded by countless shelves of ancient, musty books.

'Wait here,' Morova ordered. In the middle of the room stood a large, steel safe. The cardinal glanced at the guard, gesturing him to turn his back. Satisfied that the guard was not watching, Morova turned the combination of the safe that contained the most valuable and ancient documents owned by the Church, many of which were highly controversial. Only two people at a time knew the combination. In the event of one of them dying, the surviving partner chose a replacement as the keeper of the key, as they were traditionally referred to. Morova was one of the keepers. Not even the Pope knew the combination. He peered into the safe with his torch and quickly spotted the sealed envelope just as he'd left it years before. With trembling fingers he removed it, placing it inside his tunic and locked the safe. When Morova began to leave, the guard coughed. 'Ah, excuse me, Eminence, you have forgotten something.'

Morova scowled. 'What?'

'You have not signed the register for removal of a document, Eminence.'

Morova scrawled his name in the thick, leather-bound register and slammed it shut.

⚜

The Pope looked up in anticipation when Morova returned. 'You have the document, Eminence?'

'Yes, Holiness, as you ordered.' He made no move to hand it over, reluctant to part with it.

The Pope held out a hand. 'Well?'

'Holiness, please, I really would ask you to re-consider. Nothing good can come of this. There are far more important things your Holiness should be concerning himself with.'

'Such as?'

'The audiences, Holiness. There are many important people we had to put off during your absence. I postponed urgent meetings saying you were unwell. But, I can only delay for so long.' He raised his hands in a gesture of exasperation.

The Pope looked at Morova with mock shock. 'You lied, Eminence?'

Morova squirmed.

'You are dismissed, Cardinal Camerlengo. We will see no one until we have studied the document.' He held his hand out again leaving Morova no choice but to hand over the envelope and then back out of the office.

Once he was alone the Pope slit the envelope, gingerly removing two sheets of paper. He studied the paper before reading. One sheet was of high quality, embossed with a raised watermark of a monk. This was the original document written in the neat hand of Sister Lucia. The other was a typed sheet of plain office paper. This was the official translation to Italian. He decided to read Sister Lucia's original transcript first and then judge the accuracy of the translation.

That he was about to read a direct interpretation of a revelation from the Mother of God was not lost on him and he felt overawed by a sensation of other worldliness. As he began to read, his hands shook as the gravity of Our Lady's message began to sink in. Sister Lucia had given him an overview of what to expect, but it did not prepare him for this. He now understood why she had insisted he read the document himself, rather than hear it from her. He re-read it three more times before he was satisfied there could be no mistaking Our Lady's meaning. But it was all too clear. There was no mistake or chance of misinterpretation. He wondered if he had the strength and resolve to handle the enormity of what was expected of him and decided to retire to the solitude of the Papal apartment.

Secure in the privacy of his rooms, he locked the door and dropped to his knees, sobbing.

'Oh, my God, please give me the strength and wisdom to cope with this terrible cross you have chosen for me. I fear I am not worthy. I am just a simple man and I am afraid. Terribly afraid.'

⚜

For three days the Pope remained locked in his apartment, refusing all entreaties to take meals.

On the fourth morning he opened the door declaring in a loud voice that he would eat. The nuns fussed, tut-tutting at his haggard appearance, and they hurried to prepare a huge breakfast of eggs, salamis, cheeses, rolls and a pot of black coffee.

'There is much to do, Sister,' he told the nun who brought him his breakfast, 'but firstly I must eat to build my strength. We have a testing ordeal ahead of us.'

'In that case, Holiness, may I suggest that after you have eaten, you retire to catch up on some sleep? Your Holiness does look very tired.'

'There is no time for sleep,' he protested. 'Please send for my secretary. We will talk while I eat.'

'As you wish, Holy Father,' the nun replied unhappily.

Within minutes, the monsignor appeared at the breakfast table.

The Pope bade him sit, asking if he would join him for breakfast.

'Many thanks, Holiness, but I have already eaten. I have been up for many hours, praying for you. We were concerned.'

'Thank you for your concern, Monsignor, but we need to concern ourselves with bigger issues. Please make notes while I speak.'

He picked at the food absently while dictating a list of directives. The first task was to arrange an appointment with the Cardinal Camerlengo at his earliest convenience.

'And this time, tell him we do not mean in two hours.'

The second task was to prepare for a convening of the Sacred College of Cardinals, also at the earliest possible convenience.

The Monsignor blinked, 'But, Holiness, the cardinals have only recently departed Rome following the conclave. The logistics …' he lamented.

'I don't care about the logistics. Please, just do it.'

They won't be happy, but …, the Pontiff thought as the Monsignor continued to write the long list of instructions.

'And now for the final, and most important task,' the Pope said after he'd been dictating for over an hour. 'We would write a letter to my oldest and dearest friend in the world, Father Bruno Bracciano. We will write this letter personally and will call for you when the task has been completed.'

Father Bracciano and the Pope had been friends since childhood. They had gone to the same school and had simultaneously answered God's calling, entering the seminary together. While Giuseppe Salvatore had risen through the clerical ranks, albeit unwittingly through his friendship with a Pope, Bruno Bracciano remained a humble parish priest. His flock were the poor people of the tiny village of their birth, tucked away in a valley among the majestic Dolomite Mountains. Giuseppe would turn to Bruno whenever he felt in danger of losing his own humility. Giuseppe loved nothing better than to visit his friend whenever time permitted, and the two of them would take up as though they'd never been separated. The two were accomplished mountaineers and had spent many happy hours together, climbing the fabulous, dizzying, vertical cliffs of the Dolomites.

'One is never nearer to God than when one is hanging precariously from a sliver of a finger hold, with a thousand metre vertical drop beneath one,' Bruno once observed.

Giuseppe agreed with his friend's sentiment, adding one of his own, 'And nor are you closer to your friend, than when he is the one holding onto the other end of the rope.'

The climbs were one of the things from his past life that the Pope would miss the most. An outing on the cliffs left him feeling alive and invigorated of spirit, with a clear head, the tensions of life seemingly to have dissolved into the thin mountain air.

The Pope began to write in his precise copperplate hand.

My Dearest Friend Bruno,

We live in troubled times, as never before. Since taking up the cross as Christ's representative I have become privy to a situation within the Church that is so alarming, and so serious, that I cannot even begin to explain the potential ramifications to Mother Church and to humanity. All I can say is, God help us, and have mercy on our souls. I have had the most alarming revelation, and I beg you to pray for me so that God grants me the wisdom to deal with it. Failure on my part could result in nothing short of Armageddon. You will think I am sounding alarmist, but believe me my trusted friend, when I tell you that the forces of evil are more advanced than you and I would hitherto have ever imagined possible.

How I long for the simplicity of my previous life, and like Christ in the Garden of Gethsemane I would give anything for this cross to be taken away from me. But that is not to be. The Holy Spirit chose me to be Pope, and I have no alternative but to do what I must to resolve what is without doubt the most critical challenge in the history of the world.

I long for the simplicity of striding out with you, my friend, to glean your wisdom among the clean air of the mighty Dolomites. But alas, I cannot. I cannot even entrust in you the true nature of this crisis. Believe me when I tell you that it is for your own safety that I keep you in ignorance to protect you from the evil that surrounds us everywhere. I know not who to trust as the evil has permeated the very walls of the Vatican.

I beseech you to hold a most important document in trust for me, and for the world at large. You are the one person on earth to whom I would entrust this document. Suffice to say that it is divinely inspired and holds the truth and future of mankind. It is a copy of the original, and for your own protection and sanity, I implore you to resist opening it but rather keep it within your most sacred and diligent care.

I have called for an extraordinary gathering of the Sacred College of Cardinals, at which I will make a momentous announcement that will forever change the Church as we know it. There will be those who will stringently oppose what I must do and consequently I have no doubt that my life is already in danger. In the event of my untimely death I have no doubt that those who oppose me will strive to destroy the sacred document. That is why it is imperative that a copy is kept in a safe place.

Only in the event of my death do I ask you to open and read the contents and take whatever action you deem fit.

Should it come to that, I seek your forgiveness in advance for the suffering it will bring to your life. May Almighty God have mercy on us all.

Your friend,

The Pope signed his name to the letter and then stepped out of his office where he beckoned to the first nun he saw.

'Ah, Sister, excuse me. Could you please show me how to use the machine that copies letters?'

The nun was startled by the Pope's sudden appearance. She dropped her eyes and curtsied. Recovering her composure, she said. 'Why, Holiness, I would be happy to make a xerox for you.'

'Thank you, Sister, that would be very kind of you,' he smiled.

She led the way to a general office administration area, and when they entered, the clerical staff jumped to attention.

'I am so sorry to disturb your work,' the Pope apologised with a grin. 'I was merely interested to see how the letter copying machine works.'

The staff smiled, stepping up and forming a curious circle around the photocopier.

'Is it difficult to use?' the Pope asked, frowning.

The nun he'd met in the corridor replied. 'No, Holy Father, it is very simple. I will show you.'

The Pope handed her the document he wished to copy and she ran it through the machine. The Pope grinned at the simplicity of it, and after bestowing a grateful Papal blessing on the surprised staff he returned to his office.

'Holiness,' the nun called after him, waving a sheet of paper, 'you have dropped something.' The Pope did not hear her. 'Never mind,' she said to the collected staff, 'I will keep it for him, just in case he needs another copy later.'

Back in his office, the Pope folded the copy of the Fatima document and inserted it into an envelope bearing the Papal crest. He sealed the flap with red wax, pressing it with the Ring of the Fisherman. Satisfied, he placed the sealed envelope together with his letter into a larger, plain envelope, which he addressed by hand. He rummaged around his desk, searching for the xerox copy of the letter to his friend. Never mind, it will be here some-where. He then called for his secretary.

'Monsignor, please instruct the Captain of the Swiss Guards to arrange delivery of this to my friend Father Bruno Bracciano. I cannot emphasise the importance of this task and it is to be carried out without delay. The messenger must deliver the document person-ally into the hands of Father Bracciano and he must ask for a written receipt confirming the delivery. Is that understood?' he asked.

The monsignor assured His Holiness that he would carry out his instructions to the letter.

'Very good. I know I can trust you. Once you have completed that task you may summon Cardinal Morova.'

The priest turned to leave.

'Oh, by the way, Monsignor, just one more thing.' He gestured to the envelope. 'I would prefer you do not mention this to the Cardinal.'

⁂

Cardinal Morova and the Pope remained in closed conference till the early hours of the next morning. When the Cardinal Camerlengo finally left the Papal apartment, he was the last person to see the Pontiff alive.

Chapter 8

Front page headlines screamed the latest Church scandal.

PRIEST REVEALS COVER UP

PAEDOPHILIA IN CATHOLIC SCHOOL

PRIEST BLOWS WHISTLE ON CHURCH

Television, radio and newspaper reporters hounded Peter LeSarus for an interview, all of which he declined.

McGregor also declined to be interviewed, but his barrister assured the press that the charges would be strenuously denied. He insisted that Mr McGregor was a highly respected teacher, and that the allegations were scandalous.

As the trial commenced at Sydney's District Court, at the Downing Centre Courts in Liverpool Street, the heavy media coverage and resultant speculation assured a packed courtroom.

Peter LeSarus stood in the witness box, a Bible in his left hand, his right hand raised. He swore that the testimony he was about to give would be the truth, so help him God. He glanced towards the jury, unable to read anything in the stern, impassive expressions staring at him. The jury saw a man in his forties, dressed in a stylish, well cut black suit. Although not overly handsome, there was something pleasant in his demeanour, and had it not been for the clerical collar, one would have guessed he would have no trouble attracting members of the fairer sex. Dark brown hair streaked with grey at the temples and piercing blue eyes along with a commanding deep voice, gave the impression of a man of self-confidence and authority. As LeSarus sat, the Queens Counsel for the defence stood up, swirling his black gown in a theatrical gesture of authority.

Addressing LeSarus, he said. 'Please give your full name, title and profession, as well as place of employment and domicile.'

LeSarus leaned towards the microphone and replied in a strong, confident voice. 'Father Peter Francis LeSarus. I am a Catholic teaching priest, attached to St Anton's College for boys, where I am also domiciled.'

'Thank you, Father LeSarus,' the barrister began deliberately, stressing the word Father. 'I see you are wearing a Roman collar. I take it then, you still consider yourself a priest?'

'Of course,' LeSarus answered. 'Once ordained, you are a priest for life.'

'Yes, quite. And as a priest, you take vows?'

'Of course.'

'Of course, you say? Can you tell us about the vow of obedience, Father?' the barrister asked, once again emphasising the word Father.

'Priests vow to obey their superiors without question.'

'Would that include obeying the doctrine of the Church?'

'Naturally,' LeSarus replied, sensing what was coming.

'And isn't one of the most sacred doctrines of the Church the sanctity and secrecy of the confessional?'

'Yes, but we must all answer to a higher power than …'

The barrister cut him off. 'Just answer yes or no, if you please, Father.' He paused to study his notes, before returning his probing eyes to the witness. 'Is it true, that the boy, Julius Wheeler came to you, as a priest, in confession?'

'Yes,' Peter responded.

'And is it also not true then, that what the boy Julius Wheeler allegedly told you in trust, within the sacred confines of the confessional, should never have been repeated outside of that portal?'

'Well, technically, but …'

This time the barrister interrupted by addressing the judge. 'Would Your Honour please instruct the witness to confine his answers to the questions in hand?'

'Just a simple yes or no will suffice, Father,' the judge instructed.

'Yes or no, Father? the barrister pressed.

'Yes,' Peter replied.

'Thank you, Father, you seem to be getting the hang of this. If, as you say, you already knew about the alleged molestations against this boy, why is it that you only decided recently to come forward with your allegation against my client, Mr McGregor?'

'He had to be stopped,' Peter answered.

'He had to be stopped,' the barrister mimicked, 'I see. And so you already knew about all this when the Wheelers attended the school with a psychiatrist, alleging that my client had sexually molested the boy?'

'Yes, but at the time …'

'Please, Father, a yes or no will suffice. I suggest to you that at the time, you didn't believe the boy.'

'That's not true,' Peter protested, 'Not only did I believe him, but …'

Again the barrister cut him off. 'I suggest that you saw through him. That you recognised he was mentally ill.'

'I recognised that he was emotionally disturbed.'

'Emotionally disturbed you say? Isn't that just a polite term for mentally deranged?'

'The boy came to me for help.'

'Oh, he did, did he? And pray tell this court the nature of the help you provided.'

'There was nothing I could do,' Peter protested. 'I was bound by the seal of confession.'

'Father LeSarus. We do seem to be going around in circles here. Your Honour, I have no more questions.' He resumed his seat, smiling triumphantly at his client.

LeSarus began to protest angrily but the judge dismissed him from the stand. As he stepped down he passed McGregor who was smirking and winked at Peter as he passed.

The prosecution called the psychiatrist who had attended Julius Wheeler.

'Dr Hart, would you be kind enough to tell this court about your involvement with the boy, Julius Wheeler?'

'Be glad to,' the psychiatrist replied. Before continuing, he paused to pull a handkerchief from his pocket and began to polish his spectacles furiously, all the while glaring in the direction of the accused. He held the rimless spectacles up against the light, and seemingly satisfied, replaced them on his nose, returning the handkerchief to his pocket. 'Julius Wheeler was referred to me by his family physician who was concerned about the boy's state of anxiety and general depression. I suspected post-traumatic depression. As is typical of this condition the patient suppresses the cause of the trauma. In other words, the mind pushes the experience far into the recesses of the subconscious. It's a protective mechanism,' he explained, as though lecturing to students. 'I decided to place the boy under hypnosis to hopefully get to the root of his problem. Following a number of sessions I succeeded in having him reveal, and in some respect come to terms with, what had transpired. I have no doubt whatsoever, sir,' he said, glaring at McGregor, 'that over a period of time, that man,' he pointed accusingly, 'sexually molested the boy.'

'You bastard,' Mr Wheeler hissed from the back of the court amid a general murmuring.

The judge banged his gavel, demanding order, and then addressed Mr Wheeler. 'Any more outbursts from you, sir, and I will have you removed from this court.'

'I have no more questions, Your Honour,' the prosecutor announced.

The defence barrister rose to his feet. Addressing the witness he asked, 'In the light of your outrageous allegations, was my client given the opportunity to face his accuser?'

'I'm afraid that was not possible, sir,' Dr Hart replied. 'To come face to face with the perpetrator of his trauma could have proved extremely dangerous for his fragile state of mind.'

'How convenient,' the barrister responded sardonically. 'Then in light of the seriousness of your accusations why, may I ask, did you not report the matter to the police?'

'Under normal circumstances I would not have hesitated,' the doctor replied. 'In fact, I am duty bound to report any matters of child abuse that may come to my professional attention.' He paused. 'But once again, considering the circumstances, that the boy would undoubtedly have been subjected to a police interview ...' He paused. 'I believed that in the short term it would have proven detrimental to his mental well-being.'

'So what you're telling us, Doctor, is that you went against your professional and legal duty and failed to report the matter to the police?' the barrister challenged belligerently.

Dr Hart looked flustered, barely able to stammer an attempt at a response.

'I am finished with this witness, Your Honour. The defence now calls an independent psychiatrist to give evidence.'

After the independent psychiatrist was sworn in, the lawyer asked, 'How reliable is information attained while the subject is under the influence of hypnosis, Doctor?'

'Well, that depends upon the state of the subject's mind at the time,' the psychiatrist answered.

'Would you please elaborate on that, Doctor?'

'If a person of sound mind is hypnotised, what he relates can generally be deemed to be quite accurate.'

'I see. And what, pray tell, would be an exception to that?'

'You must understand that hypnosis unlocks a person's subconscious. That is why we often use it to help people remember things from the past. Things they may have forgotten. You see, the mind is like a filing system. The conscious mind generally only remembers most recent events that are relevant to the person's life at the time. If the conscious mind remembered everything we would go insane. We are bombarded with millions of pieces of information every day. Most of that information is irrelevant to us and so we think we don't even notice it. But in reality it is all filtered through to the subconscious mind that acts like a huge computer storage bank. It is that very same phenomenon which explains déja vu which most of us have experienced at some time in our lives.'

'Yes, well, I'm sure that is all fascinating, Doctor, but would you please go back to my question. What is the exception to the accuracy of what one reveals under hypnosis?'

'Yes, well, I was getting to that,' the psychiatrist assured him, warming to his subject. 'You see, the subconscious cannot lie. Only the conscious mind can lie. So that what comes out of that part of the mind under hypnosis must be the truth. And as hypnosis only taps into the subconscious then we can be confident it has not been filtered or distorted by the conscious mind.'

'So what are you saying, Doctor? Are you telling us that what Julius Wheeler told under hypnosis was true?' he asked, feigning theatrical alarm.

'It would have been the truth to him.'

'I don't understand, Doctor. Are you telling us that the truth to Julius Wheeler may not have been the truth to others?'

'If Julius Wheeler had been suffering from a disorder referred to as chronic psychotic delusion, what was true to his subconscious may have been pure delusion.'

'Please elaborate, Doctor.'

'In other words, his sick mind would have believed it to be true even though in reality it would have been nothing more than a figment of a sick imagination.'

The prosecutor called out, 'Objection, Your Honour! There has been no evidence to prove the deceased was sick in any way, mentally or otherwise.'

'Objection sustained. Please rephrase the question.'

'Thank you, Your Honour,' the defence said with mock humility. He returned his attention to the psychiatrist. 'Would you please tell the court then, what are the symptoms of such a disorder, Doctor?'

'Confusion, fear and depression are the early telltale signs.'

'And were these not the precise symptoms that prompted Julius Wheeler's general practitioner to refer him to a psychiatrist in the first place?'

'I believe so.'

'Thank you, Doctor, no more questions. You've been most helpful.'

The prosecution called Father Connery, headmaster of St Anton's College. After he had been sworn in, the Crown Prosecutor stood up behind the bar and peered at him over his half-moon spectacles. Seemingly satisfied he removed the spectacles, placing them on the bar table.

'Father Connery,' he began deliberately, 'as headmaster of St Anton's College are you not responsible for the well-being of your students?'

'Yes, of course,' Connery agreed.

'Are you also responsible for the conduct of your staff, both clerical and lay?'

'Yes, that is also correct,' Connery agreed again.

'Then can you please tell this court why it is that you did nothing to protect a young boy under your care against the advances of a paedophile on your staff?'

McGregor's attorney jumped to his feet, screaming his objection.

'Objection sustained,' the judge ruled, casting a stern gaze at the Crown Prosecutor. 'You know better than that, Mr Ritano,' he admonished.

The Crown Prosecutor put on a suitably chastened look, but was no doubt pleased to have made his point. 'My apologies, Your Honour.'

'The question will be struck from the records, and the jury will disregard it,' the judge ordered. 'Please rephrase your question, Mr Ritano, and I warn you against a similar breach.'

'Thank you, Your Honour. Father Connery, as headmaster of the college, was it ever brought to your attention that a member of your staff had ever acted with impropriety towards a student at the school?'

'An allegation to that effect had been brought to my attention by the parents of Julius Wheeler,' Connery agreed.

'I see, and did they specify who the alleged perpetrator was?'

'Yes.'

'Would you please tell us the name of that person?'

'They named the defendant, Mr McGregor.'

'And as a result of that allegation, I take it you took appropriate action, Father.'

'We gave the allegation serious consideration, but decided it was unfounded.'

'So you took no action?'

'The allegation was not founded,' Connery protested.

'I see,' Ritano mused. 'Can you tell this court what investigations were undertaken to lead you to that conclusion?'

Connery was sweating and pulled at his Roman collar. 'There wasn't enough proof to instigate an investigation.'

'Oh! There wasn't enough proof to instigate an investigation?' Ritano mimicked. Then, more seriously, 'You admitted to this court that the parents of the deceased lodged serious allegations against a member of your staff for whom you have accepted responsibility and you now have the temerity to tell this court that the allegation was not founded, because there was not enough proof to instigate an investigation?'

Connery squirmed under Ritano's barrage. 'I, ah, that is …'

Ritano cut him off, continuing the onslaught. 'How can you say that the allegation was unfounded if you did not undertake an investigation?'

Connery looked confused as he tried to recover his composure. 'We did investigate the matter. I mean, we did question Mr McGregor in the presence of the Wheelers.'

'Oh, you did, did you? So I take it you have experience in criminal interrogation.'

'Well, no. Of course not, not as such.'

'No, not as such, you say,' Ritano mocked. 'I take it then that you conferred with the police on the matter, and that it was they, in their professional opinion, who determined that there was insufficient proof?' Ritano pressed.

'No. The police were not brought in.'

'The police were not brought in?' Ritano asked, looking surprised. 'So if the police were not brought in, how did you conclude there was insufficient proof to instigate an investigation? After all, it was a serious matter, was it not?'

'Yes, the matter was considered extremely serious, but as the parents would not allow the boy to give evidence, we chose not to proceed.'

'I put it to you that your decision not to proceed was based on your fear of the potential scandal, and consequently you expelled the boy, allowing Mr McGregor to continue with his teaching duties.'

'Mr McGregor was rather vocal as to his innocence of the allegations,' Connery explained.

'I'm not surprised!' Ritano exclaimed, which brought an outburst of laughter throughout the court.

The judge called for order and Connery continued. 'Without proof, or at least the testimony of the boy, we felt it prudent to pursue the action we did.'

'Did Mr McGregor threaten to take legal action against the school?'

'Yes, he did, and quite rightly,' Connery added. 'The man protested his innocence most vehemently.'

'And you believed he was innocent of the allegations, Father? Remember, you are under oath.'

Connery squirmed. 'I, ah, I wasn't sure.'

'I wasn't sure,' Ritano repeated. 'So there was doubt in your mind?'

'Ah, yes, there was some doubt.'

'There was doubt in your mind, yet you didn't hesitate to expel the boy and protect an alleged pederast on your staff?'

Father Connery began to protest, but Ritano cut him off. 'Why did Mr McGregor suddenly disappear from the staff of St Anton's, almost immediately following the suicide of Julius Wheeler?'

Connery shifted uncomfortably in his chair, glancing furtively at Peter LeSarus. 'Considering the unfortunate circumstances surrounding the boy's death, following so closely upon the allegations against Mr McGregor, we, ah, thought it prudent to dismiss him.'

'How convenient. By we I assume you mean you and your fellow priests.'

'Yes, that is correct. Such a serious course of action is rarely undertaken without consultation.'

'Isn't it true, Father,' Ritano pressed, 'that Father LeSarus argued strongly against the boy's expulsion and Mr McGregor being allowed to stay on?'

'Yes,' Connery answered lamely, 'I seem to recall he objected at the time.'

'Was Father LeSarus privy to your decision to, ah, dismiss Mr McGregor after the boy suicided?'

'No.'

'Why not?' Ritano demanded. 'Wasn't he present during the initial interview with the parents when the accusations were made against your staffer?'

'Father LeSarus was not consulted. He just wasn't. No particular reason.'

'No particular reason,' Ritano mocked. 'You did say that Mr McGregor was dismissed, didn't you?'

'Yes.'

'And did you not testify, only a few moments ago, that such a serious course of action required consultation? And yet, for no particular reason, you chose to alienate from that consultation the one priest who was privy to all the facts.'

Connery began to stammer his response when Ritano interrupted by continuing. 'I suggest to you, sir, that you chose not to confide in Father LeSarus, because he had already told you of his intention to go to the authorities with what he knew.'

'That is not …'

'You were horrified that Father LeSarus would even consider revealing what he'd learned in confession, and you reported the matter to the bishop. Is that not correct?'

'Yes, but …'

'And the bishop ordered Father LeSarus to take an extended trip abroad to examine his conscience, as he put it. And Father LeSarus refused, and so the bishop suggested you get rid of Mr McGregor post-haste, to shut him up before Father LeSarus went public. Is that not so, Father Connery?'

Without pressing for an answer, the barrister paused and rifled through some papers on the bar table, murmuring with satisfaction when he found what he was looking for. 'Father Connery, isn't it most unusual to provide glowing references to a teacher who has been dismissed?' Without waiting for an answer Ritano read the reference to the court before passing it to the bailiff. 'Do you agree that the signature on this most generous and complimentary reference is yours, Father Connery?'

The bailiff handed the document to Father Connery, who gave it a cursory glance and then feebly nodded his agreement.

'I take it then, that you did furnish this reference, Father Connery?'

Connery whispered, 'Yes.'

'I'll ask you again, Father, isn't it highly irregular to furnish a glowing reference to a teacher you have summarily dismissed?'

'The circumstances were out of the ordinary,' Connery explained lamely.

'I'll say they were,' the barrister agreed. 'And they get even more extraordinary. Is it your usual practice to dismiss a teacher for alleged paedophilia, supply him with glowing references and then pay him off as well?' Ritano demanded, his voice raised. 'Paid off to the tune of two hundred thousand dollars, I might add. Please explain that, Father.'

Connery was shaking and looked as though he might weep at any moment. 'The integrity of the school,' he lamented. 'Don't you see? I had to protect the reputation of the school, and the Church. The scandal. The scandal. And the bishop, he ...' His voice trailed off.

Ritano gave Connery a contemptuous look. 'Thank you, Your Honour. I have no further questions for this, this ... person.'

⚘

Finally, the Prosecution and Defence exhausted all their witnesses and the judge directed Mr Ritano, the Crown Prosecutor, to deliver his closing address.

'Ladies and gentlemen of the jury,' he began formally, 'this is a most grievous and tragic case that you have been asked to consider. A young boy has died a most tragic and unnecessary death. A young boy whose parents, of modest means, saw fit to scrimp and sacrifice to provide their son with the advantages of a private school education. They entrusted their son to the care of the priests at St Anton's College, a Catholic college of high repute, academically and spiritually. They entrusted their son to their care with the firm belief that he would emerge as a young man armed with a superior education and sense of spiritual worth. The Fathers of St Anton's betrayed that trust most despicably. They were more interested in protecting the reputation of the school and of the Church, than in protecting a young boy in their care. This is a betrayal of trust so despicable that it is difficult to comprehend. Some of you may be Catholic, and as such, you may be swayed by a misguided sense of loyalty to your faith. But I say to you, it is that very loyalty that is in question. The school and the Church displayed a flagrant disregard of loyalty to Julius Wheeler, a young boy crying out for help. He turned for help the only way he knew how. He was ashamed and hurting. You heard testimony of how he went to Father LeSarus in the confessional seeking help. With full knowledge of what transpired Father LeSarus maintained a staunch silence when the parents of that boy came to St Anton's seeking answers. It may be argued that Father LeSarus had no choice in the matter. He was bound by the Catholic Church's most powerful edict on the sanctity and secrecy of the confessional. Well, that may be so. But it was only after the boy died tragically that Father LeSarus decided that enough was enough. Father LeSarus then decided that it was time to expose,' the prosecutor dramatically pointed an accusing finger at McGregor, 'that monster for what he was. And a monster he is, ladies and gentlemen of the jury, let there be no doubt about that.'

The prosecutor's pointing finger turned into a hand raised above his head. 'Neither St Anton's nor the Church are on trial here, although they might well be for their lack of action and complicity in the events leading up to this tragedy. The man on trial is the accused.' Once again he turned pointing an accusing finger at McGregor. 'That man sitting before you in this court is on trial for his most heinous crimes against a young boy. The crimes of misappropriating the most sacred of trusts, the trust a parent places with a teacher, to teach, to counsel and to protect. That man defiled that trust in the most abominable manner. He used that trust and respect to lure an innocent boy to fulfil his own perverted and lustful cravings. Time and again, using drugs and alcohol he buggerised that boy while pretending to help him with his studies. Yes, ladies and gentlemen of the jury, the man is a monster of the most depraved kind and I ask you to bring in an unreserved verdict of guilty and by doing so remove this menace from our society so that never again will he be in a position of trust over young boys. Thank you.'

The prosecutor's summation left the jury looking visibly disturbed as the barrister for the defence stood to deliver his own concluding arguments.

'Ladies and gentlemen of the jury, my learned colleague has delivered a fine piece of emotional and eloquent oratory, and is to be congratulated on his skill. But that is all it is, ladies and gentlemen, just oratory – oratory lacking a single shred of proof or hard evidence. The prosecution has dismally failed to prove its case, because there was never a case to begin with. My client Mr John McGregor has been seriously maligned. He is a teacher of repute who is dedicated to his noble profession. So much so, that he was prepared to unselfishly invest his own time to help a student falling behind in his work. It is unfortunate that on this occasion, and unbeknown to him, the boy was unwell, mentally and emotionally. You heard a priest give evidence that the boy made a confession, whereby he allegedly learnt of these so-called molestations. That evidence in itself is an astounding betrayal of that priest's faith, vows and all that the Church holds sacred.

'He is a renegade priest, ladies and gentlemen of the jury. A priest who has turned his own back on the Church and will in all probability suffer the consequences of excommunication. Even were you to choose to believe this priest's evidence you must by law consider this. His evidence has not been, nor can it be substantiated with one skerrick of proof. In other words, ladies and gentlemen of the jury, it is hearsay, and as such is inadmissible. That is law. And even if the revelation in the confessional did occur, as he insists, then you must also consider the testimony given by an eminently qualified and respected psychiatrist. The boy may well have believed that what he was telling was the truth, but that truth was the creation of a sick and disturbed mind. Ladies and gentlemen, you can only find this man guilty if you believe him to be so without any reasonable doubt. I put it to you that not only must there be strong doubt, but also that there is no hard evidence whatsoever to support any of the prosecution's testimony. I ask you to deliver the one and only verdict open to you, and that is, not guilty. Thank you.'

Chapter 9

It took the jury less than one hour to deliberate their verdict. Everyone rose as the judge re-entered the courtroom. Peter LeSarus looked across at McGregor who was looking smugly confident, exchanging what appeared to be a joke with his barrister. At that moment, McGregor looked up and caught Peter staring and stuck out the tip of his tongue in a lewd gesture.

Mr and Mrs Wheeler were holding hands. The judge asked the foreman if they had reached a verdict. The foreman responded that they had, and passed the verdict to the bailiff who then presented it to the judge who studied it in silence. After a while he placed the document on the bench and addressed the court.

'This has been a most perplexing case,' he began. 'It is the opinion of the jury that the school, namely St Anton's, did act with a lack of propriety and failed in its fiduciary duty to a student under its care. However, it is not the school that is on trial and therefore we must confine our attention and findings to the accused, namely John Edward McGregor who has been charged with numerous counts of buggery, indecent assault, procurement of drugs and alcohol to a minor. Having said that though, I feel it is appropriate to issue an admonishment to the school for the way it handled – or rather mishandled – what should have been the best interests of a student in its care and charge. I have no doubt whatsoever in my mind, that the unfortunate child did, as a direct result of the school's action of self-protection, take his own life as a gesture of final and utter despair.'

LeSarus glanced at Father Connery who had visibly reddened at the public rebuke.

'As to the accused,' the judge continued sternly, 'would you please rise to hear the verdict of this court.'

McGregor rose to his feet, his height belying his tendency to stoop, due to his corpulent belly hanging ponderously over a low-slung belt. As a younger man he may have cut an impressive figure, but years of physical abuse was evidenced by the tell-tale ruddy complexion of a heavy drinker with hanging jowls framing a pair of moist, fleshy lips, giving him the appearance of a grotesque cherub. LeSarus noted with some small satisfaction that the smugness had gone and he was looking decidedly nervous, dabbing a handkerchief at the shiny film of sweat glistening on his forehead.

'The foreman of the jury will deliver the verdict,' the judge ordered. 'How find ye?'

'It is our unanimous conclusion that based on the evidence presented to this court, and the failure of the prosecution to substantiate the charges made, due in main to the impossibility of collaboration by, or subsequent psychiatric examination of the alleged victim …'

LeSarus' heart seemed to stop beating. The Wheelers looked pale as they hugged each other and waited for the inevitable, 'that we have no option other than to deliver a verdict of not guilty to all charges.'

As the judge banged his gavel to conclude the proceedings he shot a stern and contemptuous look at McGregor who was laughing and pumping his attorney's hand. He turned, grinning victoriously at LeSarus and the Wheelers.

As Peter LeSarus was leaving the court he passed Father Connery who stopped him and said, 'I envy your courage,' and then hurried away, head down, avoiding the Wheelers' eyes who were moving towards Peter. When they reached him, Peter was about to say something, but he never had a chance as Mrs

Wheeler slapped his face. She looked him in the eye unflinchingly and Peter saw unbridled hatred. 'You knew all along,' she accused. 'You could have saved my boy.'

She began to sob as her husband took her by the arm and led her from the courtroom.

Outside the courthouse reporters mobbed Peter, thrusting microphones into his face. He shouldered his way through, refusing to comment, feeling utterly miserable and dejected. McGregor had been exonerated, free to continue teaching and preying on young boys, while all Peter had to look forward to was the Papal Bull of Excommunication. When he reached the bottom of the steps to the footpath in front of the court building a car pulled up directly in front of him. It was a black Rolls Royce with dark, tinted windows making it impossible to see the occupants. The back door opened and a silver-haired, distinguished looking man in his seventies leaned out.

'Father LeSarus,' he called, 'can I offer you a lift?'

Peter leant forward, peering at the stranger. 'Do I know you?' he asked, puzzled.

'No,' the stranger replied, 'but I know you, and you look like you need a lift,' he said, gesturing at the crowd of reporters.

Peter took one more look at the clamouring reporters and thought, what the hell, and slid into the car beside the stranger.

Chapter 10

As the car drove off into the city traffic Peter thanked his rescuer.

'Where to?' the man asked.

Peter gave his brother's address on the North Shore, which the man relayed to the chauffeur through an intercom.

The stranger held out his hand, introducing himself as Brian O'Shaughnessy.

'I'm pleased to meet you, Mr O'Shaughnessy. You said you know me. I can't recall ever having met you.'

'You're right, Father LeSarus,' O'Shaughnessy agreed, 'we've never met, but I do know a good deal about you, and I know precisely what you're going through.'

'I don't understand,' Peter said, puzzled, not sure he was altogether happy with a stranger knowing a good deal about him, much less claiming to understand what he was going through.

'Let me explain,' O'Shaughnessy offered. 'You see, I've been where you are, Father. I was also a Catholic priest once.'

Peter looked at O'Shaughnessy with new interest. 'I'm sorry, I don't understand. What do you mean, you were a priest?' He gestured at the sumptuous interior of the vehicle, and added. 'If you'll pardon me saying so, you don't seem to be doing too badly for a, a priest.'

O'Shaughnessy smiled. 'An inheritance. But once a priest, always a priest, hmmm? I was excommunicated, Father LeSarus, but that in itself is a long story.'

Peter gave O'Shaughnessy a look as though he may be the carrier of some rare and highly contagious disease.

The look was not lost on O'Shaughnessy. 'You do realise you'll be excommunicated yourself for what you did back there?' he remarked as though suggesting Peter was about to join some sort of elitist club.

'I'm well aware of that. I went into this with my eyes open.'

'Whoa,' O'Shaughnessy said, holding up both hands in a conciliatory gesture. 'Believe it or not, I'm with you, Peter. May I call you, Peter?'

Peter nodded and O'Shaughnessy continued. 'You're going to need a great deal of support to help you get through what's coming. I should know. I had no one when it happened to me. Let's just say I'm here to offer you that support.'

'Why?' Peter asked, puzzled.

'When I joined the priesthood, I had the same high ideals as you did when you answered your vocation. But as a result of certain things I learned, I became disillusioned with the Church and what it stood for. I've been following this case with interest, Peter, and now that it's over, I figured it was time to meet you.'

Peter was perplexed. 'Why is it so important for you to meet me, and what is your interest in all this?'

'Peter, I decided to approach you, because like me, you are seriously questioning the ideals you once held dearest and most sacred. You're highly intelligent, you have to be to make it as a Jesuit, and you still have youth on your side. And yet you are willing to throw away your career because you're no longer willing to blindly accept the dogma and teachings of the Church on mere faith. You are questioning and asking yourself, where did the Church go wrong? You've seen evidence of the length the Church is prepared to go to cover up in order to protect its reputation. But most importantly, you decided to speak out. You spoke out with courage, knowing full well what the consequences would be.'

Peter said, 'Fat lot of good that did. But you still haven't told me who you really are, and what you want from me.'

'I do believe, Peter, judging from the action you have taken that you and I share a commonality, as well as certain ideals, concerns, and aspirations …' his voice trailed off.

Intrigued, Peter asked, 'And what is this commonality you and I supposedly share?'

O'Shaughnessy paused before answering, fixing Peter with steely grey, unwavering eyes. 'The commonality we share, Peter, is the pursuit of truth. Or am I mistaken?'

Peter did not answer.

'I thought as much,' O'Shaughnessy continued. 'There are certain revelations to which I have become privy, which in turn, have led me to certain conclusions,' he said, emphasising the word, 'although I have to admit, there are still some pieces missing from the puzzle.'

'Revelations, missing pieces of puzzles, conclusions … What are you talking about?' Peter shook his head, irritated at the stranger's circumspect manner of explanation.

'To understand, it is necessary for me to give you a little background,' O'Shaughnessy said. 'Not so long ago, people were prepared to accept blindly, or on faith if you prefer, all the dogmatic teachings of the Church. For some time now, these same people have been experiencing a growing sense of disillusionment. There is evidence of this in the continuing drop in numbers at Sunday masses and also in religious vocations. Lay staff now run most Catholic schools because there just aren't enough teaching clergy. They're dying out – without replenishment. These trends will ultimately herald the final demise of the Church.'

'And?' Peter pressed.

'Please, bear with me,' O'Shaughnessy replied. 'It's important for you to understand what led to the questions that came before my conclusions. Many gave up on religion out of sheer frustration, but not quite understanding why. Most either lack the intellect or the interest to probe and figure out what went wrong, or why. So they simply turned their collective backs on an institution they no longer believed in. The Church blames this phenomenon on modern times, claiming that people are turning away from spiritualism in favour of materialism, and yet ironically, the Catholic Church is one of the richest and most powerful corporations on earth, if not the richest. The result is spiritual anarchy. Children have turned to drugs as an alternative to spirituality, because they feel lost. God has been barred from many of our schools and to pray before class has been deemed politically incorrect. We have replaced God with government to set our standards of what is morally acceptable. Young girls can have abortions without informing their parents and it is no longer appropriate to discipline children. The government assists children to leave their parents, supporting them with public money. Pornography is rampant and accessible to anyone with access to the Internet. Movies depicting extreme violence and illicit sex have become the norm. Popular music encourages rape, suicide, murder, drugs and devil worship, with alarmed and confused parents wondering where they went wrong. Their children have no conscience of what's right and what's wrong. Children have ready access to the lewd, the violent, the obscene through their personal computers, yet it is politically incorrect to teach about God. It has become fashionable to no longer believe in God. But isn't it interesting that Satan believes in God,' he finished with a bemused smile.

'And your conclusions?' Peter pushed, wondering where this was all leading.

As the car was about to enter the approach to the Sydney Harbour Bridge on Kent Street, O'Shaughnessy ordered the driver to pull over. 'I'll get out here,' he announced, 'I have business to attend to in the city. But before I go, have you ever asked yourself whether, over the centuries, the Church somehow lost its way and has now got it all wrong?'

Peter had an overwhelming sense of déjà vu, as he had been harbouring that precise thought. He was about to answer when O'Shaughnessy cut him off with a firm squeeze on the elbow. 'I promised to tell you about the conclusions I have reached. But before I tell you, I'd ask you to consider all I've said, and to try to keep an open mind.'

The car had pulled over to the kerb, and the driver was waiting patiently as O'Shaughnessy continued. 'I don't expect you to grasp what I'm about to tell you, but here,' he handed Peter a card, 'that's my address and phone number. I would be pleased if you could join me for dinner tonight. I guarantee you won't be bored.'

O'Shaughnessy opened the car door to get out. Then, as if he'd had an afterthought he paused, and turning back to Peter, he said in a conspiratorial whisper, 'The principle conclusion I've reached is that the Roman Catholic Church is in fact Satan's Church.'

He slid out of the car and before slamming the door behind him he added, 'Piggott will take you the rest of the way to your brother's.'

Peter was not sure he'd heard right. 'Just a minute,' he called, hurriedly winding down the window, at the same time gesturing for Piggott to wait. 'What do you mean, Satan's Church? And why should I come to your place for dinner at your say so? I don't even know you. How do I know you're not some kind of lunatic?'

'Please take Father LeSarus on to his destination,' O'Shaughnessy instructed Piggott, before addressing Peter again.

'Pre-dinner drinks will be served at six forty-five for seven. I do hope you will join us.'

Before Peter could utter another word O'Shaughnessy was gone.

Chapter 11

As Peter pulled over to the kerb in fashionable and leafy Queen Street, Woollahra, he glanced at his watch. It was precisely six forty-five. He was right on time. O'Shaughnessy had piqued Peter's curiosity, and although still sceptical of the man's motives, he'd decided this was one dinner invitation he did not wish to miss. A dozen questions went through Peter's mind as he stood on the footpath surveying the street and his surroundings.

Although not large compared to its neighbours, the house Peter stood in front of was nevertheless a generously proportioned, two-storey residence. A wrought-iron fence surrounded the manicured garden and a large, ornate gate opened onto a white gravel footpath leading to the front door. Peter tested the handle on the gate. It was locked. Looking around he noticed an intercom system and a strategically placed video lens. He pressed the button and almost immediately a small, red light illuminated on top of the lens and he realised he was being appraised. 'Good evening, Father LeSarus,' a metallic sounding voice greeted him, 'We have been expecting you. Do come in.'

The gate began to open on silent, well-oiled hinges and as he walked up the path Peter could not help wondering at the extent of the former priest's inheritance, if that was the true explanation of O'Shaughnessy's seemingly splendid lifestyle. He climbed the few steps to the porch, took a deep breath and with some trepidation, raised his hand to knock. Before he could do so the door opened, revealing a tall, thin, sombre-looking gentleman in formal livery, whom Peter recognised as Piggott the driver. The man's appearance reminded Peter of Ichabod Crane from

The Legend of Sleepy Hollow. He supposed that Piggott must double as a butler of sorts.

'Good evening, sir.' The voice was unmistakably the same as on the security intercom. Piggott stepped aside, gesturing for Peter to enter and politely introduced himself, as if they had never met. 'My name is Piggott, may I take your coat, sir?'

'Good evening,' Peter responded, removing his overcoat and handing it to Piggott who hung it on a coat tree just inside the door.

'Please come this way. Father O'Shaughnessy and our other guest are already in the study.'

Peter followed Piggott along a cedar-clad hallway lined with ancient portraits in ornate, gilded frames, which he guessed to be O'Shaughnessy's ancestors. They reached an imposing set of double doors, which the butler swung open, gesturing for Peter to enter. He found himself in a large room illuminated by a soft light. A full-sized billiard table dominated the room. The walls were covered from floor to ceiling with shelves groaning under the weight of an impressive collection of books. Oriental rugs festooned the floor, with heavy, dark furniture and cushioned chairs. The air was pungent with fragrant pipe smoke. Recessed in a far corner stood a large Edwardian desk. A well-equipped bar was placed strategically near the billiard table. This was clearly a man's room, the room of a man who enjoyed fine things and who cherished books. Peter noticed two people seated side by side on one of the deep, leather divans. As Peter entered the room his host O'Shaughnessy, with pipe clenched firmly between his teeth, stood up to greet him.

'Ah, Peter, I'm so pleased you could join us tonight,' he welcomed warmly. Peter shook his hand and tried to peer over the man's shoulder to catch a glimpse of his fellow guest. The figure on the lounge was turned away from him, but judging from the length of the straight, shining chestnut hair, it was obviously a woman.

'Come, Peter, allow me to introduce you.' He took Peter by the elbow, steering him towards the seated figure. 'Christina,' he announced, 'may I introduce you to Father Peter LeSarus. Peter, allow me to introduce my dear niece, Christina Kelly.'

Peter leant over, extending his hand in greeting. The woman looked up, with a warm smile, and took Peter's hand, giving it a firm squeeze. Her hand felt dry and cool and Peter returned the pressure. She was dressed in a grey, shapeless, wool shift. She wore no make-up, not even the hint of lipstick. The outline of one leg was crossed demurely over the other, concealed by the ankle-length shift. He detected no telltale scent of perfume and to Peter it seemed almost as if she were deliberately trying to underplay her natural beauty. Peter guessed her age at mid thirties, and without make-up her skin had a translucent quality. She appraised Peter with steely, grey eyes, much like her uncle's, and her lips curved upwards in an ever so slight, bemused smile. She brushed her hair lightly with the back of her left hand and Peter noticed the plain gold band on her second finger. She wore no other jewellery.

'It's so good to meet you, Father LeSarus. My uncle has told me a great deal about you.'

Peter realised their hands were still clasped, and for reasons he could not fathom, he felt himself blush. Self-consciously, he withdrew his hand and said, 'Please call me, Peter, uh, Mrs Kelly.'

'Thank you, Peter, but only if you call me Christina.'

'Christina,' Peter said, trying it out on his tongue, and deciding he liked the sound of her name.

O'Shaughnessy broke the spell. 'Christina here, is one of the reasons I invited you tonight, Peter.'

'I see,' Peter said. 'Well, it is a pleasure meeting you, Christina.'

She thanked him with a smile.

Peter turned to his host. 'You most certainly succeeded in gaining my attention, Father O'Shaughnessy.'

'Oh please, Peter, let's not stand on ceremony. Please call me Brian.'

'All right then, Brian.' Peter was about to get straight to the point when O'Shaughnessy interrupted him.

'I know that you have questions, Peter, but come, first things first, dinner is about to be served, and one should never discuss important issues on an empty stomach. Piggott's boeuf bourguignon is excellent! I guarantee you won't be disappointed.'

⚜

O'Shaughnessy ushered Peter and Christina into the dining room, in the centre of which stood a long table that Peter estimated could easily seat thirty, although tonight it was set for only three. Piggott was waiting to seat the guests, pulling out a chair for Christina and then moved to the opposite side of the table to seat Peter, while O'Shaughnessy seated himself at the head. Once satisfied his charges were comfortable Piggott disappeared, reappearing almost immediately, wheeling a cart with a silver tureen, which he then placed almost reverently on the table.

'Thank you, Piggott. We'll serve ourselves.'

'Very good, sir,' Piggott replied, retreating from the room and discreetly closing the door behind him.

'Piggott is more than just hired help,' O'Shaughnessy explained. 'He is a dear and trusted friend, with a great many talents, not least of which is cooking. He used to be my father's manservant, and after Father died, Piggott insisted on staying on to help me.

'Let me be mother,' O'Shaughnessy announced, reaching for Christina's plate.

The soup was a consommé, accompanied by an excellent bottle of Alsatian Gewüürztraminer. No sooner had they finished the soup, than Piggott reappeared to clear the plates. Peter could not help wondering whether the butler had some sort of a spy hole.

O'Shaughnessy was true to his word, the boeuf bourguignon was excellent and the accompanying wine, this time a full-bodied Burgundy, also imported, complemented the meal perfectly.

O'Shaughnessy certainly knows how to live well, Peter thought to himself.

'My father also left me a well-stocked cellar,' O'Shaughnessy remarked, as if reading Peter's mind. He gestured to Christina. 'Christina's mother was my sister, also now passed away, God bless her soul. Her father died when she was only a small child, and since her mother died I have been looking after Christina, as though she were my own daughter.' He smiled with undisguised fondness. Christina returned his smile with equal affection. They were obviously close.

Peter asked, 'Ah, but what about, um, Mr Kelly?'

Christina turned her smile on Peter. 'There is no Mr Kelly, Peter.'

'Oh, I'm sorry,' Peter responded, feeling awkward.

'No, it's all right,' she assured, 'there never has been a Mr. Kelly. Except for my father,' she added mischievously.

'I'm sorry. I don't understand.' Peter felt himself blushing again.

Christina held up her left hand. 'You mean this?' she said, referring to the plain gold band on her second finger.

'I'm sorry,' Peter stammered, confused and feeling somewhat foolish, 'it's none of my business.'

'That's all right, Peter,' she reassured him. 'It's an understandable conclusion to think that I'm married. The reason I wear a wedding ring is because I was married once – to Christ.'

Peter's eyes went wide. 'You mean …'

'Yes, Peter, I'm a nun. Or at least I was.'

Peter looked from one to the other, searching for an explanation. Of course, he thought, that explains the dour clothes and lack of make-up and jewellery.

'After I took my final vows,' she continued, 'I asked to be sent to India, to join The Ministry of Benevolence, a congregation of nuns ministering to the most wretched and poverty-stricken souls in Calcutta. Oh, I was so full of zeal then.' Her eyes seemed to mist over at the memory. She quickly composed herself and continued. 'I was determined to make a difference to the lives of these incredibly underprivileged people. What I didn't realise, was that the Ministry was run by a fanatic, who believed that suffering was a gift from God.' Her eyes blazed and there was anger in her voice. 'Her criterion of doing God's work was based on blind obedience to her by the nuns in her charge. She had us believe that we gained leverage over God through suffering which makes God happy so that He can then dispense grace on humanity.'

'You're no doubt referring to Mother Bernadette,' Peter observed.

'Oh yes, Mother Bernadette.' She made the name sound like it was an obscenity.

LeSarus looked puzzled. 'Aren't you being a little harsh, Christina? Many considered Mother Bernadette to be a living saint. She only died recently but her beatification procedure is already in place.'

Christina laughed without humour as she retorted. 'Let me assure you, Peter, Mother Bernadette was no saint. She was a fundamentalist fraud of the worst kind. I was one of the very few lucky enough to have the courage to walk away. But let me explain. Not long after I arrived at the mission, it became apparent that I had a good head for figures, and so I was assigned the task of recording donations and sending thank you notes with receipts. Let me tell you, this became very much a full-time job, leaving me no time to do those things to which I had originally aspired. Mother Bernadette was a fantastic fundraiser. She never actually asked for money, but when she spoke publicly, she would encourage people to sacrifice until it hurt. She appealed to the rich, many of whom suffer pangs of conscience, which they alleviated by giving money to the world's best-known activist for the poor. And after all, the donations were tax deductible.'

'I don't see anything wrong with that,' Peter said, 'fundraising is an integral part of caring for the poor, and if she pricked the conscience of the wealthy, so much the better.'

'I couldn't agree more, Peter,' Christina said, 'provided the funds are used to help the poor.'

Peter looked perplexed. 'I'm sorry, I don't understand. Are you suggesting that Mother Bernadette misappropriated the donations?'

'No, no, not at all. All donations were deposited diligently into the bank account and every last cent could be accounted for.'

'So where was the problem?'

'The problem was, Peter, that that was where the money remained. Amassed in the bank. Millions and millions of dollars of donations, sent by people, many of whom could ill afford the sacrifice, but all of whom believed that Mother Bernadette was channelling their donations to where they did the most good. Very little money found its way to the starving masses for whom it was intended.'

'But why?' Peter wondered. 'What was the point?'

'The point was, that Mother Bernadette saw the flood of donations as proof that God was pleased with her work. Remember, I said that Mother Bernadette believed that suffering was a gift from God. Why then, would she ease that suffering, which she considered a virtue, not only for the poor, but also for the nuns? She was adamant that we preserve the spirit of poverty within the order. We were issued with the barest necessity in clothing, which we had to keep mending till they were threadbare. She was using those poor wretches and their suffering to advance her own public image of sanctity. The hospital we took charge of was run-down and primitive, and the nursing nuns reused needles till they were blunt. The pain this caused was considered a good thing. Yet, when Mother Bernadette became ill, she flew to a clinic in America. We were made to beg for what we needed, but never allowed to take more than the barest essentials. And we did this while millions of dollars were accumulating in the bank. You see, Peter, Mother Bernadette was not a friend to the poor. She was a friend to poverty.'

Peter shook his head in disbelief. 'I'm amazed. The picture you paint is a far cry from how the world saw Mother Bernadette. When did you finally make the decision to leave?'

'It's a long story. Are you sure you want to hear it?' she said, a sardonic smile gracing her lips.

'Please!' Peter said, already intrigued.

Chapter 12

Mother Bernadette forbade her nuns to form friendships with the people to whom they administered. She argued that this would distract them from their devotion to God. But despite this edict, Sister Christina formed a strong bond with the Pivaris family who had converted to Catholicism. Their decision to convert from Hindu was not so much based on religious convictions but more as a matter of expediency. They realised their six children would have greater opportunities in life by receiving a Christian education and hopefully rise above the vicious poverty cycle.

By the time Christina met Vidya and Raj they had developed into a devout, practising Catholic family, having gradually over the years embraced the Church's teachings with growing enthusiasm. Their six children ranged from ages of one to eight years old. Christina visited the family regularly, often helping out with chores and then staying on to share their meagre evening meal, but she never came empty-handed. She always brought something with her, a chicken or some eggs and a loaf of bread. She became increasingly fond of the Pivaris family; touched by their simple faith and their eagerness to have their children make something worthwhile of themselves. They shared their problems with her, seeking her counsel on religious matters.

After Vidya's seventh child had been delivered, again by Caesarean section, the doctor warned that her body could not stand another assault and that another child would probably kill her. He advised sterilisation, or at the very least, contraception. Vidya and Raj sought Christina's counsel on this.

'Raj and Vidya, children are God's gift,' Christina counselled, 'and you know that to interfere with His natural plan to procreate is a mortal sin. It is not for us to understand His mysterious ways. Had you heeded the doctor's original advice you would now have only one child,' she reasoned. 'Yet you now have seven healthy children and by God's grace, Vidya is healthy.'

'But, Sister, we can ill-afford to be blessed with more children. We barely support the ones we have,' Raj argued.

'God will always provide,' Christina answered lamely, not really believing her own advice. Judging from the look on Raj's face, Christina could tell that his own faith in God providing food on the table was wearing thin as well, so she added, 'Then you must exercise self-control and only come together when the menstrual cycle is appropriate.'

This was not what Raj and Vidya wanted to hear, but such was their faith in Catholicism and in Christina that they heeded her advice without further question.

Christina agonised over the plight of these people with too many mouths to feed, and fervently wished she could have advised them differently, but the Church was emphatic on the subject of birth control.

Raj and Vidya were careful, but despite this Vidya fell pregnant again. Raj was beside himself with worry – not only for his wife's health, but also the extra burden another child would impose on his family. Vidya's mother supported the doctor's insistence that an abortion was not only sensible, but also paramount to save Vidya's life.

Raj was deeply disturbed by his mother-in-law's pleading. He loved Vidya dearly, and the prospect of life without her was too terrible to comprehend. He approached Christina again, to ask what they should do.

'I'm sorry, Vidya,' Christina said, 'I cannot give you the answer you want, the Church can never, under any circumstances, condone the taking of a life.'

When the time came for Vidya's confinement, Raj brought her to the hospital where Christina met them.

A midwifery nun told Christina to stay in the waiting room while Raj accompanied his wife into the delivery room. Christina was beside herself with worry, pacing endlessly, until finally, overcome by exhaustion, she slumped into a chair and fell asleep. She wasn't sure what woke her, but suddenly her eyes opened wide and there was Raj, standing over her. His face was a picture of dejection, with tears forming rivulets down his dark-brown cheeks.

'Raj, how is she?' she demanded, leaping to her feet, fearing the worst. 'How is the baby?'

Raj looked at Christina with vacant eyes as though not recognising her, and without a word, turned away. Eyes downcast, he slowly shuffled towards the exit.

Christina ran after him, and catching him by the elbow she spun him around to face her. She looked up into his eyes and saw such depth of pain and suffering, it frightened her.

'Raj, Raj. Oh, my God, I am so sorry.' She could think of nothing else to say, tears now welling up in her own eyes.

Raj seemed deep in thought, as though measuring a suitable response to a difficult question. He looked up, focusing on Christina, as though noticing her for the first time and his shoulders began to shake, ever so slightly at first, and then he let out an anguished, primeval cry.

Christina shuddered.

'My Vidya is dead, Sister. Do you hear? She is dead.' He tore away from Christina's grip on his elbow, heading towards the exit and suddenly stopping, he turned back slowly and added quietly, as though he'd suddenly had an afterthought. 'She's dead, Sister.

And you know what? The child was stillborn. It was another boy, but he was dead. They said he was dead before the birth process even started. Don't you find that ironic, Sister?' he emphasised the last word. 'And now my beautiful Vidya is also dead. For what? For the teachings of your damned Church.'

Christina winced at the profanity. 'Raj, I'm so sorry,' Christina began.

'You're sorry? Damn your sorry! And damn you, and your stinking Church!'

Christina winced again, but ignored the blasphemy, wrapping both arms around her friend, hugging him to her, sharing his incredible grief. Raj stood stiffly, arms hanging by his sides, not returning the hug. 'Raj, I know how difficult this is my friend but there is one thing I must do. We'll have time for mourning later, but now I must send for a priest to administer to Vidya's immortal soul. She must be blessed with the sacrament of extreme unction.'

Raj tore himself from Christina's embrace. 'You leave her alone,' he screamed, and then in a whisper, 'Leave my Vidya alone. Do you hear me?'

≈❖≈

Christina retreated into a depressed mood of deep brooding, questioning her own faith and wondering about this God she served. That God moves in mysterious ways was no longer a satisfactory answer. Slowly she began to think long and hard about what had happened to Vidya. Her death, Christina began to reason, was not the result of a vengeful God, but rather the teachings of mortal men, entrusted with the running of Christ's Church. She became convinced that many of the interpretations, doctrines, dogmas and rites of the Church had evolved over the centuries through human greed and opportunism, and had little in common with the original teachings of Jesus and His Apostles.

My God, they've got it all wrong she thought. Within two millennia the Church has gone so horribly off the tracks from the teachings of Jesus that today it is completely at odds with His original message.

Despite these dark thoughts she continued her ministry to the poor, her faith in God remaining unshakeable and she began to preach a more tolerant creed. When anguished wives sought her counsel on concerns about family planning she advised them to follow their own conscience.

'If you truly believe what you are doing is not wrong, it is not a sin,' she reasoned, arguing that it was more sinful to bring children into the world without the ability to care for them. If bringing another child into the world jeopardised the health or security of the family, surely that must be wrong.

Word soon passed that Sister Christina was preaching tolerance and offering solutions to the perplexing dilemma of contraception. Her reputation as a mystic began to grow. In the case of abortion she staunchly supported the views of the Church that killing a human being was a mortal sin, except in extreme circumstances where a pregnancy would be of risk to the life of the mother. After speaking to Sister Christina, women were going home to their grateful husbands to confidently share the joy of a loving marriage without the spectre of more unwanted births.

Inevitably, word of Christina's unorthodox teachings reached the alarmed ear of Mother Bernadette who promptly summoned her to a meeting.

When Christina admitted she was preaching action by conscience, the Mother Superior flew into a rage.

'Don't you realise that what you are preaching is heresy?' she thundered.

Christina began to respond, but was cut off in mid-sentence as the Mother Superior continued her tirade, 'don't interrupt me,' she shouted, with the veins bulging in her neck, her face a dark purple of fury. 'In a very short time, you've succeeded in undoing everything the Church has achieved in more than a century of toil, overcoming the most insurmountable hurdles, enduring unthinkable hardships. For God's sake, woman, what possessed you?' Without waiting for a reply she jumped to her feet and with spittle flecking at the corners of her mouth she charged down at Christina, hand raised. Turning away at the last second, she smashed her fist on the desk. 'My God, you've been condoning contraception, and although I still can't quite believe it … abortion!'

Christina continued to sit calmly, genuinely concerned for the woman, fearing she might suffer a seizure, such was her agitated state.

'Mother, please calm down. Can't we discuss this rationally?' she pleaded.

'Rationally? Rationally you say? Where is the rationale in what you have done? You cannot even begin to comprehend the damage you have done to these people, to the Church, to our order? Don't you dare to presume to tell me to calm down and be rational. There can be no forgiveness for what you've done.'

'I've advised people to follow their own consciences.'

'And who are you to give advice? Don't you see? They still have no clear understanding of what's right and what's wrong. Like children, they rely on Mother Church to guide them. And you come along, confusing them by telling them that as long as their conscience is clear they can do anything they please.'

Christina began to try explaining her experience with the death of Vidya, and how this had become the catalyst for her questioning the validity of the Church's teachings.

Mother Bernadette listened patiently for a while until finally she sank back into her chair beckoning Christina to take the one opposite. She let out a deep sigh, shaking her head.

'My dear, dear misguided fool,' she began, 'you've been a nun for a few years and yet you have the arrogance to sit there espousing that you know better than all the wise and sainted men and women who have shaped Catholicism for two thousand years. How dare you presume?'

'I presume to be a thinking woman and none of it makes sense anymore,' Christina answered. She paused, expecting her superior to interrupt, but when no interruption came, she mistook it for permission to continue, so she carried on enthusiastically. 'Mother Bernadette, haven't you ever, in all your years as a nun, questioned, at least in your own heart, the dogma of the Church? Have you never suspected that perhaps they have got it wrong?' Without waiting for an answer, Christina continued. 'Well, I have. And when I compare the beautiful teachings of Jesus, so full of love and compassion and tolerance to that of the Church today …' her voice trailed off, and she shook her head, raising her hands questioningly.

Mother Bernadette stared at Christina in disbelief. 'You're insane!' It was more a statement of fact than an accusation. 'That's it. It's not your fault. You're insane,' she repeated matter-of-factly as if she were telling her she had the flu. 'You're not the first who couldn't cope with the rigours of our life and you won't be the last. Some just aren't capable of dealing with it. It's nothing to be ashamed of. I'll send you home where you'll be able to get the best of care and somehow we'll get through this. Once people learn that you are ill and irrational they'll understand. Maybe the damage isn't irreparable after all.'

'Mother Bernadette,' Christina interrupted, 'I'm not insane, nor am I going home. My work is here, with these people.'

'Your work is where the Church tells you. You'll be sent home. Do you hear? And the sooner the better for all concerned. In the meantime, you are confined to the grounds of the mission. You are to have no communication with anyone but your fellow nuns.'

Peter had listened with rapt attention to Christina's account of her life in Calcutta without interrupting once, and now, as she paused to sip her wine, he asked, 'So what happened, Christina, did Mother Bernadette send you home?'

'No, Peter, I didn't give her the chance. I left of my own accord. I realised then, that the Church and I no longer had anything in common.'

'I can understand your thinking that,' Peter sympathised, 'but surely you would have realised that the views of Mother Bernadette were those of only one person.'

'How can you say that, Peter, after your own recent experiences? The views of the Mother Bernadettes and the Father Connerys of this world are, I'm afraid, endemic of the Church and what it stands for. But forgive me. I did not mean to bore you.'

'You most certainly didn't do that,' Peter assured her. 'In fact, I must admit, I'm fascinated by your story. Please don't stop now. What happened after you left the convent?'

Chapter 13

After Christina left the convent she wandered aimlessly, disillusioned with her faith and not at all sure what to do with her life. She worked wherever she could, just to help out, exacting no pay but accepting whatever food was offered as reward for her labours. One evening, while sharing a meal with a devout Hindu family they began to talk of the pending *Kumbha Mela*. They explained that this festival of the water occurred only every twelve years at Hardwar where the Ganges River enters the plains of northern India after flowing down from the Himalayan Ranges. The family told Christina that this was one of the most important religious events on the Hindu calendar, as those who came to bathe in the river during the festival had their sins expunged. While this information was not exactly portentous in its own right, what did strike Christina as truly amazing was that the festival was expected to attract over fifteen million pilgrims. This was an event not to be missed, Christina thought, and she vowed to go. The family readily agreed to allow their new friend to join them on their pilgrimage. That Christina was a Christian nun elevated her in their eyes to the rank of holy woman.

So in November, Sister Christina joined the family on the fifteen hundred kilometre trek to the small town of Allahabad. The festival was due to begin in January and the family had allowed a little over a month for their journey, as they were too poor to afford the train. They would have to make their journey on foot carting their scant belongings in a kind of wheelbarrow, taking turns to push it. The barrow held a tent and some small items of furniture, including a camp table with stools as well as their sleeping mats and some small changes of clothing and, most importantly rice, cooking pots and implements.

At times the going was tough, but the morale of the journeyers was good, with spirits high. Often as they passed through villages they were offered food and lodging for the night, out of respect for being pilgrims. Other nights they simply pitched their tent on the side of the road and slept wherever they ended up at the setting of the sun. As they drew closer to Hardwar they were joined by other pilgrims, converging from all points of the compass, until their numbers were so swelled they all but choked the road. There was a vibrant force of expectation among the pilgrims, resolutely marching north towards their final destination at the holy Ganges River.

Peter was so entranced by Christina's story that he hung on every word, hardly ever interrupting.

'You could barely see the waters of the river,' Christina said, 'and the banks were hidden from view by the great press of humanity. I'd never seen anything like it in all my life. Can you imagine what it's like to see countless millions of people congregated together in one tiny area? Along both sides of the river a tent city had formed. Those not fortunate enough to own a tent simply slept in the open wherever they could find a space large enough to place their sleeping roll. There were traders and peddlers everywhere, giving a huge bazaar atmosphere. It was a maddening cacophony of sound and colour and of bustle and hustle of crowds and people enjoying the atmosphere, buying and selling, haggling and generally having fun. There were so many people along the riverbanks that the permanent bridge was totally inadequate to handle the traffic, so they'd put in place a number of floating pontoon bridges.

'Then there were the enlightened masters and saints, some of whom had made their way down from the Himalayas. It was strange but somehow you recognised them. They stood out from others even though they did not consciously do anything to stand out. They just seemed to possess some form of charisma or radiance. I was told by the family I travelled with that some of these were considered living saints.'

Christina and her Hindu family managed to lay claim to a small section of ground near the river, where they pitched their tent and settled in for the month ahead. During the evenings there was much visiting with other families and a constant sharing and interchange of ideas. During the month there would be six auspicious bathing days, when the waters of the river were supposedly transformed into healing nectar, washing away the sins of all those who bathed in it.

One evening, following the first bathing day, the head of Christina's family approached her. He told her that a great spiritual master had heard of the Christian holy woman, and he would like to meet her.

'This is a great honour, Sister Christina,' she was assured, 'it is rare that a master of the stature of Chwong Woo would invite you to an audience. Normally people line up with gifts, hoping to catch a snippet of wisdom or perhaps even to have a question answered.'

When Christina was escorted to Chwong Woo she was shown into a large tent, which had a considerable amount of clear space around it. Inside, the tent was adorned with rich cushions of every conceivable colour and material. There were all kinds of goods strewn around the tent from jewellery to spices and food as well as live chickens and ducks in an assortment of cages. The light within the tent was dim compared to the harsh brightness outside and it took Christina several seconds to adjust her eyes to the gloom, when she became aware of a seated figure. As she tentatively approached she noted that the figure was that of a man who sat ramrod straight with legs crossed and hands placed palm up on each bony knee. The man seemed unaware of Christina's presence for he made no move of recognition, continuing to sit as still as a statue. Christina wasn't sure whether she was supposed to come closer, or just wait respectfully. After a while she coughed but still there was no response, so she decided to introduce herself.

'Ah, good afternoon, sir. My name is Christina. I'm sorry to disturb you but they told me Chwong Woo asked to see me. I do hope they directed me to the right place.'

'Welcome, Sister Christina,' the man replied in English, 'it is most kind of you to come. Please come closer and sit with me. Your Hindi is excellent, I must say.'

Christina did as she was bidden, moving closer before tentatively sitting down on a cluster of cushions. She was surprised that the man spoke English with a hint of an accent she couldn't place. The man was dark, wizened and of slight build, with long, dread-lock-style hair hanging below his shoulders, and an equally long and matted beard. He wore an array of beads around his neck and apart from a tattered loincloth he was naked. His eyes were closed and Christina decided it would be impossible to guess the man's age. His skin was weathered from constant exposure to the sun and the elements, and reminded Christina of a well-worn, dark leather couch. When the man's eyes opened Christina realised that he was blind. Lines of mirth appeared around his eyes, adding to the array of deep etchings. The man radiated such an aura that Christina was convinced she could detect a faint halo around him. When he spoke, the voice was kind and gentle, with an added mixture of bemusement. The accent did not seem to belong to the body from which it emanated.

As if reading Christina's mind he said, 'Oxford. As a young man I had the privilege of studying at that fine university.' He paused for a moment. 'A few days ago when I made my way down from the mountains, I was alone,' he said, abruptly changing the subject about the source of his accent. 'If I were a woman wandering alone and unprotected down the mountain people would have thrown rocks at me, but instead they threw gifts and offerings at me. They put me up in this great big tent,' he gestured around at his surroundings, 'large enough to accommodate many families and surrounded me with things for which I have no need. And yet I make no attempt to look different to anyone. I don't do clever tricks of magic. So why do you think I attract this attention wherever I go, Sister Christina?' He was smiling mischievously.

Christina stammered for an explanation. 'You are no doubt a holy man and this is evident to all who see you. I have also been told you are a great spiritual master. It is clear from your presence.'

'And what of you, Sister Christina? They tell me you are a great holy woman of the Christians. You bear the name of your Christ. Do seekers of the truth follow you?'

Christina smiled as she answered, 'No. No one follows me, Swami,' she said, using the term she'd been advised to address this spiritual master who many called saint. 'Nor am I holy. Far from it, I'm afraid,' she added with mirth in her voice. 'I am just a simple nun, seeking answers.'

'And I think modest, for those who tell me of you, tell me you are indeed a holy woman. But tell me, to what is it that you seek answers?' the Swami asked.

'I seek answers to questions that have come to mind since death touched a person very dear to me.'

'But death is merely an extension of life. Why would such a natural event cause you to seek answers?'

Christina thought about this, and then said, 'This person could have been saved. The death was not necessary. It has caused me to question the validity of my religion, of my God, to whom I vowed to devote my life.'

'To question religion is one thing, but to question God is to question oneself. God is within you and you are within Him, and as such you are one and the same.'

Christina could only shake her head at this explanation. It was beyond her understanding or ability to reason. Though the Swami could not see Christina he seemed to sense her unease and asked, 'When you refer to the I or the me and the my, about who or what is it that you are referring?'

Christina thought for a while before replying, suspecting this was a trick question. 'Why, I guess I am talking about myself.'

'And who or what is this self of whom you speak,' the Swami pressed. 'Where is it? Can you show me the self, the I who is you?'

Christina was becoming increasingly confused as she blurted, this time without much thought, 'You seem to be playing with words Swami. I am right here, sitting in front of you. I know you cannot see me but you are nevertheless aware of my presence.'

'I can see all there is to see,' the Swami corrected. 'I destroyed my physical eyes by staring at the sun. They were too much of a distraction to me. Now I see much more clearly. What I see before me is the body that belongs to the I. When you refer to it, you refer to it as my body, my brain, my mind; and yes, even my soul. So what you must ask yourself is, who or what is it that refers to these physical properties and even spiritualities as my?' You must delve into this mystery, for only when you discover who the I is, the you at the deepest level, will you know God.'

Christina sat silently trying to digest this before asking, 'Is what you speak of then, the basis of your own Hindu faith?'

The Swami smiled at this, then quoted: 'Jesus said to Thomas, "I am not your master. Because you have drunk, you have become drunk from the stream that I have measured out. He who will drink from my mouth will become as I am; I myself shall become he and the things that are hidden will be revealed to him."

'What is Hindu?' he continued. 'Did not your own Jesus Christ say much the same as what I just said? And yet you would not suggest he is Hindu.'

Christina said, 'But Swami, with respect, I do not recall having seen such a quote attributed to Jesus.'

'I have quoted from the Gospel of Thomas,' the Swami replied.

Christina was beginning to think that perhaps the Swami was getting mixed up himself. As far as the Gospels were concerned she felt she was on fairly strong ground. After all she'd had them beaten into the marrow of her bones. She could confidently quote all of them, chapter and verse. This time Christina smiled indulgently at the Swami and said, 'There is no Gospel according to Thomas, only the Gospels of Mathew, Mark, Luke and John.'

The Swami returned Christina's smile saying, 'Not only Thomas, but also the Gospel of Philip, and the Gospel of Truth, not to mention the writings of Judas, brother of Jesus.'

Christina felt her head begin to swim. She could only sit and stare. Finally recovering she said, 'Judas? You mean Judas Iscariot? What do you mean, the brother of Jesus? He had no brother.'

The Swami chuckled as he asked, 'Have you never heard of the discoveries at Nag Hammadi in Egypt?'

Christina barely managed to shake her head.

'No, I thought not,' the Swami responded, even though Christina knew his sightless eyes could not have detected the movement of her head. 'The Catholic Church has gone to great pains to suppress the findings, as have most of the branches of Christendom. There are many more Gospels than the ones you cite.'

'Please tell me about these finds you mentioned,' Christina pressed, fascinated. 'Where is Nag Hammadi?'

'It is in Upper Egypt. The story goes that a young peasant accidentally came across an earthenware jar while digging for clay. When he broke open the jar it contained many papyrus documents, bound in leather. He took them home to his mother who had no idea of the value of her son's find. It is thought that many of the documents were used to start the kitchen fire. It was only much later, when a visiting uncle spied the bound documents, and thinking they could be valuable took some of them with him to Cairo to see if he might not be able to sell them. One way or another they came to the attention of a young archaeologist, who recognised them for what they were – documents written in Coptic. Carbon dating puts their age at the year 360, or thereabouts. As I mentioned, they contained numerous other Gospels that place an altogether different slant on the life of Jesus Christ. It would seem that after Christ died on the cross there were many differing factions wandering around who placed different interpretations on His life and what He stood for. As is humanly typical, these interpretations were subject to a liberal dose of exaggeration, and oftentimes were subject to gaining an advantage to the interpreter. When one studies the Gospels of Nag Hammadi, the most interesting observation scholars make is that there was far less differentiation two thousand years ago between what we now call the religions of the East and West. This is not surprising if you understand that in the Gospel of Thomas where he speaks of spending time in India — and many of the things he relates to — could easily be the words of the Lord Buddha.

'As it turned out there grew to be great suppression. Ideals and truths that did not fit in with some extremists of the time were branded as heresy, a term that really means an outlook which someone else dislikes or denounces. Consequently, heretics became as persecuted by so-called Christians as the early Christians were by the Romans. So it is thought that the Gospels discovered at Nag Hammadi were buried for fear of reprisal for heresy.'

As the Swami paused, Christina reflected on what she'd heard, then asked, 'Why did you ask me here? Why are you telling me all this?'

'Word that you are a good woman had reached me. I had also heard that you were deeply troubled, searching for answers. I am trying to answer some of your questions, but ultimately only you can answer your own questions by searching within.'

Christina asked, 'And the documents from Nag Hammadi, they will provide me with answers? I feel more confused than ever.'

'Of course you are, because you stoically hold on to all your past beliefs. Beliefs you have learned from other people, not from your own inward searching. Search inward and you will find the answer.'

'Are you telling me that Nag Hammadi disputes the divinity of Jesus?'

'We are all divine.'

Christina shook her head, confused. 'I am sorry, I just don't understand.'

'There have been many messengers. Some call them prophets. But all of them, including Jesus, came to us to show us the way. Most chose not to listen.'

'Are you one of those messengers?' Christina asked.

'Am I not showing you the way?' he answered, neither agreeing nor refuting the question. 'There is one more thing I will tell you. In nature there is light and dark, and the two are in constant battle and this is true for the entire cosmos. There are messengers of light and there are messengers of darkness. Some choose to follow the messengers of darkness, and their resolve is to put out all light. I tell you this, that for now, darkness has the upper hand.'

'Do you speak of the Antichrist?'

'The one who would put out the light is legion and goes by many names.'

The Swami paused again, as if listening to music that only he could hear.

'Think about what I have said, my child,' he said and, feeling as if she'd received a gift beyond her immediate comprehension, Christina left the tent and returned to her fellow travellers.

⚜

O'Shaughnessy picked up the tale:

'When Christina finally arrived home she felt she had to know more about Nag Hammadi and the suppressed Gospels. While surfing the net she stumbled on the site of an Austrian archaeologist by the name of Herman Muntz. Muntz was convinced that there were many more documents to be still unearthed at Nag Hammadi, and was appealing for sponsorship to fund his dig. When Christina told me about Muntz I shared her fascination for the potential of more documents being discovered. I found myself wondering what other revelations may still be just waiting to be found.

'So I contacted Professor Muntz, and following our conversation and subsequent correspondence, I agreed to fund an expedition to Nag Hammadi.

'The result of this expedition was almost bizarre in its circumstances. While Muntz failed to unearth anything of further interest, he was approached by a goat-herder who had also ostensibly found a papyrus buried in an earthen jar. Muntz's initial reaction was one of extreme scepticism at the unlikely coincidence of a repeat of the initial circumstances of discovery. However, following a closer scrutiny of the document, scepticism was replaced by wonder. Muntz concluded that this papyrus was very different from those previously discovered. He subjected it to

108

carbon 14 dating and was astounded to find it dating back to 1,700BC.

'You can imagine my excitement when Muntz reported his discovery to me. I could hardly wait for the translation which, unfortunately, Muntz said would take considerable time.

'The weeks stretched into months and just when I was unable to contain my impatience, and was about to contact the Professor, I received a call late one night. I immediately recognised the familiar Austrian accent. It was Muntz, and he sounded extremely agitated.

"I have no doubt that what we have found is the genuine writings of King Mentonidus, he told me."

'I was puzzled, having never heard the name before.'

'Muntz continued without waiting for my response. "King Mentonidus was a Mesopotamian King, or so the legend goes. Much like the fabled, King Arthur, no one has ever been able to prove he really existed. You have no idea of the importance of this find," he assured me in a fever of enthusiasm that vibrated down the line, and which I found quite contagious.

'Muntz explained that countless ancient papyruses and clay tablets unearthed by archaeologists over the years related to stories of this mythical king. The stories traced his adventures through the underworld where he was supposed to have discovered the secret of delving into the future.

'The legends claimed that before his death, King Mentonidus wrote down his prophecies for the world and that this document had been hidden away. Scholars agreed that references to King Mentonidus were legends and mythology and as such the supposed prophecies never existed.'

Peter interrupted. 'Why was Muntz convinced that his find related to King, sorry, what did you say his name was?'

'King Mentonidus.'

'Yes, thank you. How could he be so sure?'

'At first, Muntz was convinced it had to be some kind of incredible hoax, but by the time he had translated the document, he was convinced that what he had found was the lost prophecy of the legendary king.'

'That's quite a story,' Peter said, 'but you still haven't explained why he was so sure.'

Christina handed Peter a folder, which O'Shaughnessy told him contained a partial extract of Muntz's translation.

'Read that, Peter, and while you are reading it, remember it was written nearly three thousand years ago.'

As Peter began to read the document his first reaction was that it must be a hoax as he found it impossible to believe that it had been written nearly two thousand years before Christ. When he finished he started again, and then re-read it several times.

In one thousand seven hundred years from this day, a new messenger will be sent from the heavens, preaching lessons of love and peace, which will threaten those that are the leaders of the day, and for this they will nail him to a cross, upon which he shall die, only to rise from the dead three days after and he will herald a new age. Many will follow his teachings, but beware the dark one who will send his own messenger to put out the light, leading the world back into the darkness that was before.

The messenger of the dark one will make his presence in the halls of power, even within the holiest of holies.

He will divide the nations, delivering the greatest of wars unto them.

The heavens shall weep as the teachings of the messenger are maligned.

In two thousand years less eighty-three after the coming of the messenger a divine vision will appear to three innocents who are the keepers of sheep.

Unto these will be delivered three revelations, which, only if heeded, will deliver the nations from the chains of the dark one.

Peter returned the passage to the folder, contemplating what he'd just read. O'Shaughnessy and Christina sat silently without interrupting his thoughts, waiting for his reaction. Peter finally looked up and said, 'I take it this is some kind of a joke?'

'I assure you, Peter,' O'Shaughnessy answered, 'that it is no joke. That is a true translation from a papyrus that was carbon dated to 1,700BC.'

'But why?' Peter wondered.

'Why what, Peter?' O'Shaughnessy asked, perplexed by the question.

'Why are you telling me all this?'

'I understand you have questions, Peter,' O'Shaughnessy said, 'and I promise you won't be disappointed. As I told you in the car, I've been following the paedophile case closely and Christina and I, of all people, understand your predicament. Would it be true to say that you are experiencing a crisis of faith?'

'That would be an understatement.'

'Truly, Peter, we understand your disenchantment with the Church.'

Christina added, 'What you did was a very brave thing' Peter.'

'Yes, it was,' O'Shaughnessy agreed, 'and we all need friends in times of crisis. It may seem that we have gone a little off the track, but I do think it was important for you to understand Christina's background and her motivation for leaving the convent. Christina's story gives you a perspective of where she fits in to all of this and most importantly, how her experiences led me to become involved with Muntz and the discovery of the Prophecy.'

Peter glanced at his watch. It was after nine and he seemed to be no closer to finding out what this was all about.

The gesture was not lost on O'Shaughnessy. 'You've been very patient Peter. Please bear with me a little longer, and you will learn all there is to know. You see, this is not just about any personal crisis. It is about a crisis in our Church.' After a moment he added, 'Are you familiar with the name, Cardinal Lucca Morova?'

Chapter 14

'Of course,' Peter replied. 'Cardinal Morova is the most powerful cardinal in the Church. He has served as the Cardinal Camerlengo since before I can remember. And it's common knowledge that he's the one who is really running the Church."

'And would it surprise you if I were to tell you that he and I were once close friends?'

Peter sat up, his interest piqued.

'As a child,' O'Shaughnessy continued, 'I was brought up by a family of powerful bankers. My great-grandfather immigrated to Australia from Ireland and founded the first private bank in this country. His son, and then my father, followed in the family tradition. As I was the only son, I was groomed to take my place as head of the family bank. You can imagine then, my father's great disappointment when I announced my intention to study for the priesthood. My father pleaded with me to reconsider, and when this failed, he threatened to disinherit me. It was only when he understood that his inheritance meant nothing to me, that he realised I was sincere and determined to pursue my vocation. He decided to try another ploy. He asked me to place my priestly vocation on hold. After all, he reasoned at the time, if I was truly determined to be a priest, then a few years shouldn't make that much difference. He asked me to put in five years at the bank, and then, if I still wished to be a priest, he would not only give his blessing, but he would donate a substantial amount to the Church.

'Anyway, to cut a long story short, I acquiesced to his wishes and spent the next five years working at the bank. At the end of the agreed time, my enthusiasm for the priesthood had not waned, and to my father's great disappointment, I went off to the seminary. I'm only telling you all this, in order for you to understand that after I was ordained, the Church decided to put my banking experience to work by seconding me to the Vatican Bank. It was there that I met a young Monsignor Morova, who was head of the bank and a rising star. He seemed to take an immediate liking to me and took me under his wing, and before long, I was working as his assistant. What I didn't realise at the time, was that Lucca Morova is incapable of liking anyone. He recognised in me someone who could prove useful.'

'I have heard many conflicting stories about Cardinal Morova,' Peter said. 'What is he really like?'

O'Shaughnessy paused reflectively to fill his pipe.

'You really shouldn't smoke, Uncle Brian,' Christina admonished gently.

'Thank you for your concern,' O'Shaughnessy smiled. 'She's right though,' he agreed. 'Damned filthy habit. But I'm afraid it's one of the few joys I have left in my life, in spite of my emphysema. What's Cardinal Morova really like, you asked.' O'Shaughnessy puffed on his pipe thoughtfully, considering Peter's question. 'He's an enigma. I really don't think that anyone truly understands the man. But let me tell you about the time I spent at the Vatican Bank, and then perhaps you can draw your own conclusions.'

❦

When the young Australian priest began work at the Vatican Bank, Monsignor Morova was quick to recognise that Father O'Shaughnessy had a flair for banking procedures, particularly in the areas of investment and loans. His father had taught him well.

When Morova was offered the role as head of the bank, he accepted the position on the proviso that Pope Alexander IX allow him to begin lending money at competitive interest rates.

This was an unprecedented move for the Vatican, as historically the Catholic Church considered lending money as prohibitive due to the biblical ban on usury. Not only did the Pope acquiesce to Morova's demand, he went one step further, giving his blessing for Morova to invest Vatican money wherever he deemed fit. Although it was virtually impossible to accurately assess the true worth of the Vatican, cash reserves held by the bank at the time of Morova being put in charge were estimated at being in the vicinity of eighty five million American dollars.

Morova began to establish links with leading world financial institutions and began buying up interests in corporations. It was not long before the Vatican was enjoying the fruits of a piece of the action from major hotels like the Watergate in Washington, luxury resorts in Mexico and the Bahamas and major apartment complexes. Morova also began heavily investing Vatican money in stocks of major corporations, including a weapons-manufacturing company and a pharmaceutical firm that ironically manufactured birth control pills. Before long, through Morova's astute investing, the original sum had escalated to a staggering one billion dollars.

This newly acquired wealth began to interest the Italian government, which proposed to lift the Church's tax exemptions. Morova thwarted this plan by threatening to sell off all the Church's Italian financial holdings, which would have plunged the Italian financial markets into chaos. Despite the government's back down, Morova nevertheless began to fear that holding so much wealth within Italy left the Church dangerously exposed – all the eggs in one basket, so to speak. So he set up a trust of Catholic financial advisers, calling it *uomini di fiducia*, or men of confidence. It was with the help of these men of confidence that Morova began to move massive amounts of Vatican money offshore.

It was at about this time, that Morova's father introduced his son to Don Amiglio, head of a powerful Mafia crime family in Rome and cousin to the infamous Gambino family in America. As a result of this meeting, the Vatican Bank began to launder Italian and American mob money earned from heroin trafficking and other crime-related activities. Even the US government began to channel huge amounts through the Vatican to bankroll the fledgling Solidarity Union in Poland. In return for this, and other favours, the US gave diplomatic recognition to the Holy See, making it the only religious organisation in the world that the United States recognised as a sovereign nation state. Morova also funnelled huge sums of money to Latin American regimes friendly to the Vatican and the US, where the money was used to finance the international drug trade.

The Pope, of course, had no inkling or understanding of the extremely complicated web of investments that Morova had put in place around the world. He was only interested in the results, of which he was delighted.

⚜

O'Shaughnessy paused his recount to re-light his pipe. Peter, who had listened without interruption now said, 'I knew the Vatican Bank had involved itself in some rather dubious offshore investments, but I must admit I had no inkling that it had become involved with drug money and criminals. It's well known that shaky investments very nearly resulted in the collapse of the Vatican Bank.'

O'Shaughnessy finished re-lighting his pipe and continued. 'Yes, quite right. You're referring to what has been called the Vatican Bank scandal. When world stocks and exchange rates tumbled, the Bank was caught off guard, as were many other worldwide banks. The result was that many speculative and illegal offshore capital venture partnerships went under, with the Vatican

Bank's exposure estimated at something like US$240 million. Although,' he added, 'many have since claimed that this figure was conservative.'

'I was only sixteen at the time,' Peter said, 'but I do recall the scandal. There was a government investigation, but nothing major seemed to come of it. I recall that most of the blame was laid on to a comparatively lowly bank official, who ended up in prison.'

O'Shaughnessy laughed without humour. 'Ha! That lowly bank official you refer to was me.'

Peter blinked. 'You? You mean you were involved?'

'Yes, and no,' O'Shaughnessy replied. 'Yes, it was I who became Morova's scapegoat for the whole sordid affair. And no, I was not involved. Suffice to say, that Morova saved his own neck from official scrutiny by literally stopping investigating agents at the gates of St Peter's. He cited the Vatican's political autonomy and diplomatic immunity to frustrate an in-depth investigation. But he still had to answer to the Pope, who as I said earlier, had remained in blissful ignorance. Morova claimed that his assistant, being me, had deceived him, and without his knowledge, and behind his back, had illegally funnelled enormous amounts out of the country. The Pope believed him, because he wanted to, and subsequently handed me over to the authorities like a sacrificial lamb. I was charged and sentenced to three and a half years in prison on twenty-three counts of misappropriation. As well as that, I was excommunicated. The Church was rescued by Opus Dei, that semi-clandestine organisation of powerful Catholics, who raised the money to get Vatican Incorporated off the hook with investors.'

Peter looked from O'Shaughnessy to Christina, not at all sure how to react to what he'd heard. He sat quietly for a while gathering his thoughts.

'What's the matter, Peter?' O'Shaughnessy asked. 'You look perplexed.' Peter weighed his words before responding. 'Look, Brian, and Christina, everything I've heard tonight has, I must admit, been highly entertaining, but frankly, I'm sorry, it just doesn't gel.'

Christina was startled by Peter's abrupt dismissal, but O'Shaughnessy sat impassive, betraying no emotion. 'I see,' he said. 'Go on.'

'For starters,' Peter began, 'before today I'd never laid eyes on either of you. You waylaid me outside the court and gave me some line about Satan's Church, which was obviously intended to raise my curiosity. Which you knew it would. Then, Christina here,' he gestured at the woman sitting opposite him, 'tells me a story discrediting a nun, who is practically already a saint, and then there's this conversation with a mystic and all this stuff about a prophecy which foretells the coming of Christ and the apparitions at Fatima. And then you proceed to tell me that the most senior person in Christendom, second only to the Pope, is a crook who consorts with mobsters. I'm sorry,' he shook his head, 'it's a bit much to swallow.'

O'Shaughnessy chuckled. 'Coming from a man of your intelligence, Peter, I can't say I'm surprised by your reaction. I would have been disappointed if you had accepted all I've told you on face value and on my word only. You're right. You don't even know me. But wait. There is more. And I guarantee that before you leave here, you will not only understand, but you will believe.'

Chapter 15

꒷꒦꒷

Before continuing, O'Shaughnessy suggested they retire to his den, where they would be more comfortable. Once seated, Piggott reappeared with a tray of drinks. He handed Christina a Tia Maria with milk and offered Peter a balloon snifter of Cognac, which Peter gratefully accepted. O'Shaughnessy accepted the other balloon, passing it under his nose and inhaling the fumes appreciatively.

'Would you like a cigar with your Cognac?' O'Shaughnessy offered. Peter declined, and Christina shot her uncle another disapproving look. He ignored it, making a ceremony of cutting the end off the expensive looking cigar, and then holding a lit match and passing the length of the cigar up and down along the flame. When he'd finally lit it, he blew out a great cloud of blue smoke and continued.

'I don't mean to sound circumspect,' he said 'but there are some things I want you to think about. How do you feel about my saying this: that Jesus Christ, Mohammed, Buddha, Krishna, Emmanuel, to name just a few well-known prophets, were one and the same?' He paused theatrically for effect. Peter looked at Christina with increasing unease.

'I'd say you're echoing the philosophy of Chwong Woo, and that what you are alluding to smacks of blasphemy.'

O'Shaughnessy chuckled. 'Just the sort of response I expected. But of course we don't mean one and the same, literally.'

Peter looked relieved. 'Okay, so what do you mean?'

'What I meant by the same, was that they were all historical figures with great influence on the world and they all preached love and tolerance. They all spoke of God, and they all claimed to be His messengers. Yet not one of them preached that theirs was the one and only religion, and those with a different set of beliefs were to be considered the enemy.'

'That's a far cry from your initial suggestion,' Peter admonished.

'Sorry, Peter, I was merely trying to press a point. Have you ever stopped to wonder why two of history's greatest atrocities were perpetrated by predominately Catholic nations and the Church did nothing to intervene?'

'You're no doubt referring to the Spanish Inquisition and Nazi Germany,' Peter answered.

Christina interrupted. 'But isn't Germany predominantly Lutheran?' she said, challenging them both.

'Many people are surprised to learn that Germany has over twenty eight million Catholics, almost as many as practising Lutherans,' O'Shaughnessy said.

'Not to mention Austria, which is almost exclusively Catholic and was Hitler's birthplace, which he annexed to Germany during the war,' Peter added.

Christina smiled, 'I stand corrected!'

'The Inquisition was responsible for unimaginable suffering in the name of Christ,' O'Shaughnessy continued, 'and one of the main target groups were the Jews. And yet the founder of Christianity was a Jew. Ironic, isn't it!'

'Yes it is,' Peter agreed, 'and it reminds me of an amusing incident when I was a child. I was with my parents, visiting some friends who were devout Catholics, but as it turned out, anti-Semitic bigots. The man of the household referred to the "bloody Jews" to which my father responded that they had a portrait of a bloody Jew hanging in a position of prominence. Naturally he was referring to the picture of Christ. He then added, "And what's more, I see you also have a portrait of a bloody Dago," he said, pointing to the portrait of the Italian Pope.'

O'Shaughnessy and Christina laughed, after which O'Shaughnessy continued. 'Unfortunately, though, bigotry is no laughing matter and when Germany systematically slaughtered millions of Jews, Pope Pius XII didn't lift a finger in protest.'

'Which is why history has judged him as Hitler's Pope,' Peter observed, 'which I've always considered a trifle harsh. It's well known that the Church aligned itself with Fascism, Mussolini and Hitler, as the lesser evil to Communism. No one could have possibly guessed at the time that Hitler would do what he did,' Peter defended.

'Perhaps not,' O'Shaughnessy agreed, 'but by the end of the war, no one could claim not to know about the atrocities. But yet, after the war, the Vatican established what has been referred to as the Ratline, an organisation that helped former SS officers to escape from Europe.'

'Yes, yes,' Peter said, waving his hand impatiently, 'we all know about those shameful pages of Church history, but that is just what it is – history. Today's Church can't be compared to what happened in those days.'

'Oh, but I think it can,' O'Shaughnessy responded, 'when you consider what the Church does, or rather doesn't do, to protect paedophiles.'

Peter looked chastened. He opened his mouth as if to reply, but thought better of it, and said nothing.

O'Shaughnessy continued. 'The only reason the Church has changed its stance is because it knows that in today's world it would never get away with it. The Catholic Church today, as then, has precious little resemblance to the Church that Christ founded. And let me tell you, those atrocities of the past were all part of a bigger plan.'

'A bigger plan for what?' Peter asked, no longer so sure of himself.

'To understand that, you must first accept that it is no accident the Church has evolved as it has. Now I know you will find this hard to swallow, but we have good reason to believe that unwittingly the Church has succumbed to powerful, evil forces.'

'What are you trying to tell me, Brian, that the devil had a hand in the evolution of the Church?' Peter asked. 'Is that why you made that statement in the car, about Satan's Church?'

'I warned that you would have difficulty with this, but I assure you, as I am sitting here, it is true.'

'Well, you are right about one thing, I am having difficulty with all this. I agree that over the years the Church may have had a lot to answer for, but what you're suggesting is taking it a bit far, don't you think?' He looked across at Christina for support, but none was given.

Unperturbed, O'Shaughnessy continued. 'Is it taking it too far?' he challenged. 'Today, the wealth of the Vatican is beyond belief. The Church has become the richest and most powerful political machine on Earth.'

Peter could not disagree.

O'Shaughnessy continued. 'A number of Popes recognised this when they came to office and tried to change it, but to no avail. Those who tried were naïve to the extreme and in their naiveté they believed that as Pope they ran the show.' He laughed. 'They soon discovered they simply could not buck the system of this powerful machine. Pope Leo Alexander is a good example. He only lasted a month in office before dying under mysterious circumstances.'

'Those rumours of the Pope being poisoned are commonplace,' Peter observed, 'but there's never been proof.'

'No, there hasn't,' O'Shaughnessy conceded, 'but neither has there ever been proof to the contrary. Why do you think there was never an autopsy?'

Peter shook his head quietly, unable to answer.

'There are some who believe his successor has been held a virtual prisoner within the Vatican, constantly subdued by drugs during public appearances.'

'Surely that's a little far-fetched,' Peter challenged.

'Is it? Look at him when he makes a public appearance. Most of the time he looks as though he's asleep. He can't even stand on his own feet unassisted.'

'Because he's ill and fragile.' Peter argued. 'But all right, just supposing there may be some truth in what you say, are you suggesting the entire College of Cardinals is in on this, this conspiracy theory of yours?'

'No, of course not! Few people realise what's going on. What I am saying, is that the Vatican and the Church are being run by a handful of men who for various reasons, be it avarice or lust for power, are manipulating the Church to their own ends, with the Pope as their puppet.'

'And who are these men?' Peter asked.

O'Shaughnessy chuckled. 'That's the problem, we don't know for sure but we know they exist. But the one thing I am sure of is who their leader is.'

'You mean Cardinal Morova?' Peter shook his head. 'I'm sorry, but I'm having a problem accepting this conspiracy theory.'

O'Shaughnessy laughed good-naturedly. 'Of course you are. Who would blame you? But let me tell you this. Conspiracies have been rife within the Church for almost as long as it has existed. Let me give you one famous example. Have you ever heard of the *Titanic* conspiracy?'

Peter shook his head.

'Fascinating,' O'Shaughnessy assured him. There are those who say the sinking of the *Titanic* was the perfect crime.'

Peter thought he must not have heard correctly. 'Crime, you said?'

'Yes, Peter. Murder in fact. The *Titanic* catastrophe was an elaborate plan to kill off some of the world's wealthiest and most influential men.' He smiled at the look on Peter's face. 'Yes, I know it is a little difficult to swallow. It's never been proven, of course, but there is some compelling documentation supporting it.'

'You're telling me the people on the *Titanic* were murdered by a conspiring iceberg?' Peter asked sarcastically, looking increasingly sceptical.

O'Shaughnessy chuckled. 'No,' he answered matter of factly. 'Interestingly, the plot was orchestrated by your own order, the Jesuits.'

Now it was Peter's turn to laugh. 'I'm sorry, but I've never heard of anything so absurd.'

Unruffled by Peter's mirth, O'Shaughnessy rang a small bell on the table next to him.

'Yes, sir?' Piggott asked as he materialised almost immediately.

'Piggott, be a good fellow and go to the library and fetch me the volume on the *Titanic* conspiracy.'

Piggott soon returned with a thick, leather-bound volume the size of a broadsheet newspaper, placing it on the table in front of O'Shaughnessy who opened it and began rifling through the pages. It was a giant scrapbook containing hundreds of clippings and notes. 'There are references here by many eminent and learned people relating to what you so flippantly dismissed with a laugh.' He pushed the book towards Peter who flipped through the pages, stopping occasionally to read a few lines.

'There are a few prominent names I recognise here,' Peter conceded.

'Yes, and it would seem they do not share your scepticism on the subject. All of these extracts that I have compiled treat the subject with deadly seriousness. But as I said, the conspiracy has never been proven.'

Peter apologised. 'Sorry to have been flippant. Please, why don't you tell me about this, this *Titanic* conspiracy theory.'

'Very well,' O'Shaughnessy agreed, 'but I won't bore you with the entire, sordid history of the Jesuits. Suffice to say that for centuries they were referred to as the men in black who concealed daggers, carrying out assassinations on behalf of the Church. Many historians refer to them as the ancient CIA of the Church, having taken over from the ancient order of the Knights Templar. Initially it was the Knights Templar who established the wealth of the Church, but after that order was disbanded, the Jesuits took over as keepers of the Vatican wealth.'

'Yes, yes, I am aware of the history of the Jesuits,' Peter said dryly.

'Well then, you may also know that the Rothschilds were the bankers for the Jesuits.'

Peter raised his eyebrows. He did not know this, so he remained silent, impassively hiding his reaction.

O'Shaughnessy continued. 'The Rothschilds, the Morgans and the Rockefellers were the wealthiest and most powerful families in the USA – and they were in fierce competition with each other. Despite this, they decided to join forces by entering into a joint venture to establish a national banking cartel, the Federal Reserve System.'

'Yes, I know all that too. They established the Fed in 1913.'

'Correct,' O'Shaughnessy agreed, 'which incidentally was almost one year after the *Titanic* sunk. But did you also know that the cartel was controlled by the Jesuit order?'

This was now unfamiliar ground for Peter. 'No,' he answered guardedly, 'I can't say I am aware of that. But if they were in control, to what purpose?'

O'Shaughnessy smiled as he dropped his bombshell. 'The aim was to destroy US constitutional liberty and to bring the Pope to world financial domination.'

Peter stared for a moment, trying to digest what he'd just heard. He quickly recovered his composure. 'But that just doesn't make sense,' he countered. 'Why would such a powerful group of bankers get into bed with the Jesuits?'

'Because they shared a common goal and a common enemy – the Jews. By combining forces and establishing the Fed, as you call it, they would dominate the world financially. At the time, it was dominated by the Jews.'

Peter knew better by now not to refute out of hand what he was hearing, so instead he gestured for O'Shaughnessy to continue. 'As you asked, I am trying to keep an open mind on this.'

'Thank you,' O'Shaughnessy said, 'that's all I ask at this stage. There were those who violently opposed the Fed, among them being such prominent figures as Benjamin Guggenheim, John Jacob Astor and Ian Strauss. All immensely wealthy and powerful Jews.'

Peter glanced up. 'So that on its own would have created friction between the two factions.'

'Yes, it did. But the cartel knew they had no hope of succeeding with such powerful adversaries opposing them. J.P. Morgan had taken control of The White Star Lines and the Jesuits connived with him to build the *Titanic* with a registration number of 3909.'

'Is that of significance?' Peter asked.

O'Shaughnessy wrote the number on a napkin and handed it to Peter, 'Take the napkin and hold it up to the mirror,' he instructed.

Peter walked over to a gilt-framed mirror on the wall and held up the napkin. He smiled. 'Cute coincidence,' he remarked.

O'Shaughnessy smiled at his cynicism. 'Perhaps, perhaps not. They had agreed that the only way they could succeed in their ambitions was to get rid of Guggenheim, Astor and Strauss. Well, you don't just get rid of three of the world's wealthiest and influential men. They had to devise a plan that was so outrageous that no one would suspect foul play. They came up with the notion of building the biggest ship in history and claiming it was unsinkable. The maiden voyage would be heralded as the most prestigious event in travel history and would be irresistible to such wealthy men.'

Peter was startled. 'Are you saying that the cartel built the *Titanic* with the intention of sinking it? To kill three men?'

O'Shaughnessy chuckled. 'You've got to admit, it was an outrageous plan.'

'Outrageous is not the word I would have chosen,' Peter said. 'More like preposterous.'

'Good word,' O'Shaughnessy agreed, 'but you have to remember, Peter, these people were playing for stakes so high it is beyond your imagination.'

Peter was incredulous. 'They would sacrifice a ship of the magnitude of the *Titanic*, as well as all the innocent lives, to destroy three men? I'm sorry, I find that impossible to comprehend.'

'Indeed, Peter. It was because it was so preposterous that they knew they would get away with it. And get away with it they did. Secret Jesuit documentation states that innocents can be sacrificed for the greater good. That the end justifies the means.'

'Proof,' Peter demanded, 'what proof do you have?'

'The only proof we have is circumstantial, but I'll let you be the judge. Captain Smith was the captain of the *Titanic*. Unbeknown to most and probably to you too, he was a Jesuit.'

127

Peter vaguely recalled hearing something along those lines. 'In those days you could be a member of the Society of Jesus, or the Jesuits, without being a priest.'

'That's right, Peter. Apart from being a member of the society, Captain Smith was a religious fanatic and he worked for J.P. Morgan. The Jesuit provincial Father in Ireland had a young clerical assistant, who inadvertently came across a correspondence from his master to the captain of the *Titanic*, ordering him on what to do in the North Atlantic. The young man was flabbergasted by this and was at his wits end as to who to confide in. He finally spoke to a reporter in Belfast who undertook investigations, but naturally got nowhere. His notes are contained in this dossier.'

O'Shaughnessy flipped some pages until he came to the copy of the journalist's notes which he gave to Peter to read. Peter read through the notes in amazement. 'This is incredible,' he finally said. 'Why wasn't the investigation taken further after the tragedy eventuated?'

'I suppose it would have been, but not surprisingly, the journalist and the young priest disappeared.'

'And naturally, you believe the cartel got rid of them too.'

'There is no proof of that. But as you can see, Peter, having read his notes, the ship was doomed before it ever set sail. Captain Smith had been sailing the Atlantic for more than twenty years. When they entered an area that was littered with icebergs he gave the order for full speed ahead and retired for the evening. The rest is history.'

'That truly is a remarkable story,' Peter said, 'and I promise you, I am trying hard to keep an open mind.'

'That's good, Peter. I related that story so that you can gain some appreciation of the lengths to which powerful people will go to achieve their ends. There is a whole lot more I could tell you about the *Titanic* conspiracy, but that's not the reason I asked you here tonight.'

Christina now spoke up. 'Uncle Brian, it's getting late. Perhaps it's time to tell Peter about the Third Secret of Fatima?'

'Ah, yes,' O'Shaughnessy agreed, glancing at his watch. 'Sorry, Peter. I do promise this will all make sense soon. Tell me, what do you know about the Third Secret of Fatima?'

'Probably as much or as little as the next person,' Peter answered. 'The secret was to be revealed to the world in 1960, but the Vatican issued a statement that the Pope decided against it for reasons best known to him.'

'That pretty well sums it up,' O'Shaughnessy agreed, 'but haven't you ever wondered why three Popes have chosen to suppress it since then?'

'I suppose, like everyone else, I just accepted the Vatican's edict on the matter. The world simply wasn't ready.'

'Don't you think that's strange considering Sister Lucia was adamant that it was to be made public no later than 1960?'

'When you put it like that, one might consider it a bit strange,' Peter agreed.

'The reason it has been suppressed all these years is because the Popes, apart from Leo Alexander I, could not come to terms with Our Lady's demands. Despite potentially terrible ramifications if Her demands were not met, the Popes chose for reasons best known to them, to suppress it.'

'Has anyone apart from the Popes read the Third Secret?' Peter asked.

'Oh yes,' O'Shaughnessy assured him, 'there are a number of upper echelon clergy, cardinals and bishops, who have read it, and God knows how many more, various clerical assistants, translators and the like.'

Peter fixed O'Shaughnessy with a piercing stare. 'Have you read it?'

O'Shaughnessy exchanged a knowing look with Christina, who gave an almost imperceptible nod. This was not lost on Peter, and he looked quickly from one to the other. 'Well?' he demanded, 'have you read it?'

'No,' O'Shaughnessy answered quietly, 'I haven't read the text personally, but I do know someone who has. But before I go into details you should know that the contents tie in with and continue on from the revelations and predictions of the first and second secrets.'

'Which,' Peter recalled, 'was a glimpse of hell in the first secret and in the second, "The good will be martyred, the Holy Father will have much to suffer and nations will be annihilated."'

'Exactly,' said O'Shaughnessy, raising his index finger to emphasise his agreement. 'Of course, those prophesies had little meaning back in 1918, but now we find they are unfolding in our lifetime. Part of the Third Secret clearly warns that the Antichrist will come among us, and we know he is already here and we have a pretty good idea who he is, where he is, and what his plans are.'

Peter put two and two together and half-laughed as he looked at the older man even more sceptically. 'Are you saying that this prophecy of King Mentonidus, the Third Secret of Fatima, the *Titanic* conspiracy are all linked? Are you suggesting that Cardinal Morova is the Antichrist?' he asked, now laughing in earnest.

O'Shaughnessy smiled. 'No, Peter, but it is likely that he is a disciple.'

Peter grew serious again. 'But how do you know that?' he asked. 'That's almost too fantastic to believe.'

Unperturbed, O'Shaughnessy continued. 'We are told the Antichrist is the prophet of Satan and is here to unleash Armageddon. We have reason to believe he may be hiding behind the veil of Islam, surrounded by gullible disciples. He has beguiled them into believing they are waging Jihad, a holy war in the name of God against Israel and all those who support her.'

'Are you now saying that Islam is in league with Satan?'

'No, not at all. Islam, like Christianity in its purest, most original form, and like most of the other great religions, shares the universality of love and peace. But, as in the Catholic Church, Satan, through his disciples, has infiltrated some of the highest levels of power.'

'And you believe that this is documented in the Third Secret of Fatima?'

'I don't know what is specifically documented in the Third Secret. But the Second Secret goes on to reveal that over the ages a prophet was sent among the people in the name of God to guide people in His loving ways. The dark one has managed to confuse the races by introducing the idea that theirs is the only true god to the exclusion of all others. This confusion has manifested itself in the belief that it is their holy duty to persecute non-believers. Hence, we have terms such as Infidel and Heathen.'

O'Shaughnessy paused, expecting another retort or question from Peter. When none was forthcoming, he continued. 'When you consider the nature of God's love, it is an absurdity in itself that He would need, or want, for that matter, for us to worship Him. It's an arrogant belief, implanted by the Antichrist with one purpose in mind: divisiveness and hatred. As a consequence, we wage war, kill, maim and torture each other, all in the name of God. The dark one and his followers have done their work well. Now that the Antichrist is here, as foretold, we can expect to see atrocities hitherto never before witnessed.

'These revelations are happening now, all around us, Peter, and just as the evil prophet has launched a Jihad against good, we must launch a united Crusade against his terrible evil.'

131

'And how would you suggest we do that?' Peter asked.

'The place to start is to find and eliminate the Antichrist, and send him back to Hell where he was spawned.'

Peter was on his feet now, pacing slowly around the table, deep in thought. O'Shaughnessy and Christina said nothing, waiting for Peter's reaction. He finally said, 'All right, let's assume that I accept what you are telling me. The Antichrist exists but we're not certain who or where he is. Who will lead this Crusade against evil?'

O'Shaughnessy replied, 'As you know, Peter, there are many references in the Bible to the second coming of Christ. But in reality, there have already been many comings. Call those entities what you will – Prophet, Rabbi, Messenger or Teacher. Usually they were sent as figures with whom people could relate in other words, the entity was one of them, someone of their own culture.'

'Are you telling me,' Peter asked, 'that a messenger from God will be sent to lead the world?'

'As is the Antichrist, he is already among us.'

'You know this for a fact?' Peter challenged.

Without hesitation, O'Shaughnessy exclaimed, 'We know it for a fact!' Brian O'Shaughnessy paused for a moment. 'You see, Peter, when I was wrongfully imprisoned, I had a long time to think. At first I was consumed by an insatiable desire for revenge. But over the years, this was replaced by a desire to flush out the truth. Yes, I do want to destroy Morova, but not for my own gratification, but rather to save the Church.'

'Don't you think that's a little arrogant?' Peter suggested.

'Yes, perhaps it is, but I'm the only one who really knows him for what he is. Ever since I returned to Sydney, I've utilised my inheritance on nothing else but to gather facts and evidence.' O'Shaughnessy stood up. 'It's late,' he said. 'You have much to think about. Once again, I apologise that this has taken so long, but I did want you to know all the facts. I'm afraid I'm not as young as I used to be,' he smiled ruefully. 'Think on what you've learned tonight and then, if you wish, we can discuss this further. Piggott will see you out.'

Accepting that the evening was over Peter took his leave, and thanking his host he bade him and Christina goodnight. At the front door the butler handed Peter his coat and opened the door for him. To Peter's mild surprise, Piggott walked out with him, silently closing the door behind them. He then accompanied Peter all the way down the driveway and into the street where he waited till Peter opened the car door.

'I'll be all right now, Piggott,' Peter assured the butler who was still hovering on the footpath. 'And many thanks for an excellent dinner.'

As Peter slid into his brother's low-slung sports coupé he gave a final farewell wave to Piggott who had still made no move to return to the house. Peter shrugged, turning the key in the ignition, and then Piggott seemed to make a decision. He made his way to the passenger door, opened it and quickly climbed in beside Peter. Taken aback, Peter asked, 'Is anything wrong?'

Piggott was agitated and seemed to be wrestling with some inner turmoil. 'Father LeSarus, I am taking a great risk talking to you, but there is something you need to know.'

Chapter 16

It was well after midnight when Peter LeSarus finally left Father O'Shaughnessy's house. Despite the late hour he was not in the least tired. His mind was racing, and he wanted to be alone with his thoughts. With no specific destination in mind he continued driving absently, till he reached the end of the road at the Gap, a place infamous for suicide. Peter parked the car and then followed in the footsteps of the many unfortunates who had come here to end their lives. He climbed through the fence and walked towards the edge of the precipice. Although it was still dark, there was a full moon to light his way. He stopped, just inches from the edge of the cliff and gingerly peered down into the blackness. He could hear the thunder of the waves crashing on the rocks below, and even this far above the sea he could feel the thin veil of spray on his face. He felt an uncomfortable, almost irresistible, force urging him to launch himself into space, so he sat down carefully, dangling his feet over the edge, and continued to stare down into blackness. The sense of vertigo subsided as he lowered his centre of gravity. As his eyes accustomed to the darkness he could see the phosphorescence in the crashing waves below and they became his private light show, and his mind drifted back to the time Julius Wheeler had approached him.

'Bless me, Father, for I have sinned. It has been several months since my last confession,' Julius Wheeler mumbled, head bowed, forehead pressed into his clasped hands.

This was followed by a long silence as though the boy were gathering his courage.

Peter waited a while and then decided to try to encourage him. 'Is there any reason why you haven't taken the sacrifice of Penance for so long?' He waited a while longer and as there was no response he continued, 'Is it because you felt ashamed to come to confession?' Through the veil, he saw the silhouette of Julius' head nod.

Just as I assumed, Peter thought, I will have to tread very carefully here.

'You know that in the eyes of God, there is nothing to be ashamed of. During His life on Earth Jesus loved sinners. He felt nothing but compassion for them and for their human weaknesses and frailties.'

Peter heard another stifled sob from behind the veil, and decided to continue. 'God made us all in His likeness, and He loves us all, despite our frailties.'

The sobbing grew louder and this time Peter decided to wait.

'I wanted to kill myself,' Julius whispered.

Oh, dear God, no, Peter thought.

'My dear child, life is the most precious gift from God. To throw away that gift is the most grievous sin of all.'

Julius lifted his face out of his hands. 'But Father,' he said, 'I'm so ashamed. What I've done; it's just, so embarrassing. And bad,' he added for good measure.

'That is why we have confession, my son. So that Jesus can wash the sins from our souls with His divine blood.' Peter paused. 'Go ahead. Confess your sins and free yourself from your anguish.' He held his breath.

'I accuse myself of committing impure actions,' Julius began.

'I see,' Peter responded, thinking he finally understood where this was heading. 'And were these actions committed alone, or with another person?' There was another long pause and Peter agonised for the boy, wishing he could do or say more to help him. Puberty is tough enough, he thought bitterly, without Church dogma compounding their guilt.

'The worst kind of impure actions,' Julius finally answered, his face firmly buried back into his hands.

'I see,' Peter said, hoping to sound non-judgemental, 'but sometimes, what may seem terrible to you, may just be part of the natural process of growing up.'

'Oh, no,' Julius shot back, 'there is nothing natural in what I've been doing.'

Peter decided he was getting somewhere, sensing he was finally on familiar ground. He now had no doubt the boy had experienced some form of sexual experimentation with another boy, not an uncommon occurrence among adolescents. Some just carried the guilt and shame more heavily than others. He decided to take a different and bolder approach.

'Julius, these, ah, impure actions. Were they by any chance with another boy?' He held his breath.

There was another long silence. 'With a man,' Julius whispered.

Peter froze, blessing himself with the sign of the cross before continuing, desperate to keep his voice steady. 'And this man, this man with whom you committed impure actions … how, how old is he?'

'I, I don't know. But quite old.'

'Very old, like as in a grandfather?' Peter pressed.

'No, not that old, but he looks nearly as old as you, Father.'

Peter felt the blood pulsing in his temples as Julius inadvertently told him he was talking about a man who was probably in his late thirties to early forties. 'I see. And, who instigated these impure actions?'

'He did, Father,' Julius blurted. 'I would never have started something like that. Before Mr Mc …' He stopped himself, pressing a hand to his mouth. He took a deep breath before continuing. 'I meant, before him. Before him, I didn't even know people did disgusting stuff like that. The first time, he told me it was natural. That it was men's stuff, you know, grown-up men's fun stuff.' He stifled another sob. 'Except it's not fun. It hurts. And the pills he makes me take. I can't say no after I take the pills. I sort of get out of control. You know? Like you know you shouldn't be doing something, but you sort of don't care. Until after.'

Peter was sweating. All of a sudden the closeness of the confessional was pressing in on him. He felt a desperate need for fresh air. He tugged at the hard, clerical collar, which threatened to choke him. He realised he was breathing hard, almost hyper-ventilating. Struggling to compose himself, he was grateful for the veil separating them.

Peter took another deep breath, not trusting his voice. 'This, this man. You say he gave you pills. Do you know what kind of pills?'

'He calls them speed. He told me they'd help me with my homework. Make my mind clearer. But when I take them, I can't sleep. My mind just races.'

'And when this man gave you the pills, what did he make you do?'

Long silence.

'Julius. What did this man make you do?' Peter pressed.

'He made me play with his thing.' A pause. 'You know, his dick.'

Peter struggled to keep his voice even. 'Did he make you do anything else, Julius?'

'Yes.'

'What other things did he make you do, Julius?'

'Do I have to tell you?'

'Yes, Julius. It is very important that you tell me.'

'He, he put it in my mouth.'

Peter wiped at the sweat streaming down his face. His brain raged with conflicting emotions of despair and compassion and contempt and hatred and outrage. He felt the bile rising in his throat as he struggled to contain the malignant growth of anger threatening to overcome him.

'Was, was there anything else he made you do, Julius? You said that some of the things he did hurt you.'

Julius began to sob again, more loudly now, with a note of real panic. 'No! Please, Father. I can't tell you that. I'm too ashamed.'

Peter waited, not daring to push harder.

'He, he put his thing in me. He put it in my, you know ...' He was sobbing now in great, gut-wrenching spasms. 'Oh, God, I'm so ashamed,' he cried.

Peter wanted to reach through the curtain. To reach out and hug this poor, tormented child. 'Oh, dear child, you have done nothing to be ashamed of. Don't you understand? Dear God, you're a victim. The man who did these terrible things to you is the one who should feel shame. He'll burn in Hell for the heinous crimes he's committed against you.'

Julius began to calm down, but Peter waited a while longer before continuing. 'Julius, you nearly mentioned the man's name.'

'No, Father, I can't. I just can't. He'd kill me. He said if I ever said anything, he'd kill me. And my parents.'

'But, Julius, he'll never know you told me. I've already explained that I can never reveal anything I hear in confession.'

Julius hesitated. 'Are you sure?'

'Absolutely,' Peter assured him, 'the seal of the confessional is the most sacred tenet of the Church.'

'You promise you won't ever tell him?' Julius demanded.

'Whatever is said in here will always remain between you and me and God. I promise you on everything that is holy.'

Julius agonised a while longer. 'You're sure?'

'Julius, tell me his name,' Peter urged. He waited for a response. There was none. The tension became a tangible thing. Peter could feel it. He could smell it. 'Julius, – tell – me – his - name,' Peter repeated, emphasising each word in a harsh whisper.

'You're sure …?'

'I'm sure.'

'It's … It's … Mr McGregor.'

Oh, good God, please no. Peter struggled to retain his composure. Please don't let it be the new lay teacher.

'Surely you don't mean our, Mr McGregor of St Anton's? Your geography teacher?'

'Yes, Father.'

'Oh, my God,' Peter whispered, struggling to compose himself. 'So when, I mean, how did all this start, Julius?' he asked, unable to control his quavering voice. There was a slight pause, before Julius began again.

'The first time was about a month ago, when Mr McGregor offered to drive me home. He lives close to me, you know.'

Peter LeSarus listened without interruption as Julius recounted how the teacher had driven him home and then offered to help with his homework. That was how it all started and developed into a regular thing.

After Julius finished, they remained silent for a long time. The boy began to sob again, quietly, in anguish, overcome by pain and humiliation.

Peter cleared his throat, composing himself. 'Julius, you did the right thing sharing this bad experience with God. With His infinite love and mercy you will put this behind you and with His grace you will begin to heal. I will now give you absolution for all your sins, past and present. But first, I'd like you to consider approaching me outside of the confessional, so that I can do something about this man, this Mr McGregor. He must be stopped. He must never be allowed to do to another boy what he has done to you. Do you understand what I'm saying, Julius?'

'Wh …, what do you mean, approach you, Father?'

Peter thought his voice sounded as though he were on the verge of panic.

'What I mean, Julius, is that you must come to me outside of the confessional, and repeat everything you have told me here. That way, I will no longer be bound by the sacred seal of confession and I can notify the authorities. They will put a stop to this evil man. He has no place within the teaching profession. He must be locked away.'

'But, Father, you promised. You promised you'd never tell.'

'Julius, this is bigger than you or me. Don't you understand that if this man is not stopped, he will go on? There will be other boys. Do you want what happened to you to happen to other boys? Evil men like this can't help themselves. The man needs help. Don't you understand? He must be stopped.'

'But he'll have me killed. He said so.'

'The police won't let him near you. They'll protect you.'

'No they won't. They can't. He knows murderers. He'll send them after me. And my parents. They'll find out.'

Suddenly the door of the confessional burst open, and little Julius bolted. Peter LeSarus rushed out after him.

'Julius,' he called after the fleeing boy, who had already disappeared out of the chapel, and kept running without looking back.

There was nothing Peter could do. His hands were tied. He spent hours praying, seeking guidance, but none came to solve his quandary. He prayed that Julius would resist any future advances from McGregor.

⤙✦⤚

Peter's prayers remained unanswered, as one day after school he saw Julius stepping into McGregor's car. He wanted to rush over to pull the boy out and give the teacher a thrashing. But he did nothing. He could do nothing. He could not even treat McGregor any differently. And then, as if to add insult to his confusion, McGregor caught his eye.

'Afternoon, Father,' he greeted. 'Just giving young Wheeler here a lift home.'

⤙✦⤚

Peter snapped out of his reverie and realised he was crying. How many times had he agonised over his actions? Of what he could or could not have done. After the school expelled Julius, siding against him and protecting McGregor, the boy had sunk into the depths of depression and it was not much later that he took his young life.

Peter felt a closeness to the boy at this spot where he had died, and where so many others, disillusioned and desperate, had decided that life no longer held meaning for them. He wondered at the state of a person's mind that they should feel so tormented they could see no other way out than ending their life. Had they no one to turn to? Was there no one to whom they could confide their despair? Then he reminded himself yet again that Julius Wheeler had come to him, and he had let him down, failing to protect the boy. He shuddered as though a cold wind had just swept up from the ocean enveloping him in a clammy, deathlike embrace. He wiped the tears from his face with the back of his hand.

As he continued to stare into the hypnotic light show below he thought about all he'd heard that night. Many of the things O'Shaughnessy had said seemed logical, although his years of clerical indoctrination would still not allow his mind to fully grasp and accept what he'd heard. Perhaps it wasn't just the indoctrination

141

but rather that mystical, indefinable quality shared by so few these days: Faith. Despite his own faith he had to agree that something was not right within the Church. What sort of hierarchy would protect a paedophile, to preserve the Church's reputation? The Church had failed miserably, he concluded, in its obligation of morality and duty to protect an innocent child.

Reflecting on the Third Secret of Fatima, his logical mind could not escape the conclusion that it did indeed smell of a cover-up.

By the time Peter had bidden O'Shaughnessy and Christina goodnight his scepticism had been replaced by an acceptance that the prophecy could possibly be genuine, as fantastic as that possibility seemed and then …

An urgent voice brought him back to the present.

'You, yes, you on the ledge, don't move, stay where you are.'

With a start, Peter realised the voice was directed at him. He turned around and was blinded by powerful torch light. He shielded his eyes from the piercing glare and began to clamber to his feet.

'I said, don't move,' the voice commanded urgently, 'this is the police. Stay where you are. Someone will come over to bring you back. Don't do anything foolish.'

Peter stood up regardless, turning towards the light. At that moment the police must have noticed his Roman collar.

'He's a priest,' the voice said to someone else, who then asked Peter, 'Are you all right, Father?'

'Yes,' Peter replied, 'I'm perfectly all right.' He clambered back through the fence, to find himself confronted by two policemen.

'What were you doing on the ledge, Father?' one of the policemen asked suspiciously.

Peter said, 'I'm sorry to have caused concern. I was sitting there, watching the moon, and saying my prayers,' he threw in for good measure.

'Well, sorry to have bothered you, Father, but if I were you, I'd find a safer place to pray.'

Peter thanked the officers and, feeling foolish, made his way back to the car.

As he unlocked the car door it suddenly occurred to him that in spite of all he had learned, he still did not really know why they had chosen to confide in him.

Why me? He thought. What do they want?

And Piggott's astonishing disclosure was something he was completely unprepared for. He found himself hoping that Christina was not privy to Piggott's disclosure, and decided that for the time being he would keep it to himself.

As Peter turned the key in the ignition he knew precisely what he must do.

Chapter 17

Despite having had little sleep Peter LeSarus felt surprisingly refreshed and alert. It was seven in the morning when he dialled O'Shaughnessy's number. The phone was picked up on the third ring, and the unmistakeable voice of Piggott came on the line. He sounded as though he had already been up for hours. Peter identified himself, then apologised for calling so early, explaining his call was of an urgent nature and would it be possible to speak to Father O'Shaughnessy.

Piggott replied in his customary, polite butler's voice giving no hint of the previous night's conversation. 'As a matter of fact, sir, Father O'Shaughnessy is expecting your call. He asked me to put you straight through when you called. He and Miss Kelly are breakfasting.'

Within seconds the now familiar voice of O'Shaughnessy came on the line. 'Good morning, Peter,' he greeted cheerfully, 'I suspected I'd hear from you early. Didn't get much sleep, I wager.'

'No, as a matter of fact I didn't,' Peter agreed. 'You and Christina left me with a lot to digest. As a matter of fact I stayed up to watch the sunrise.'

'So what conclusions have you reached?' O'Shaughnessy asked, cutting straight to the point.

'I don't know that I've reached any conclusions,' Peter answered guardedly, 'far from it. There are now more unanswered questions than ever before. But I have made a decision. Look, I was wondering if I could drop over again. There are a few things I would like to discuss with you and Christina.'

'By all means. You're most welcome,' O'Shaughnessy assured him, 'why don't you come over right away. You should still be able to beat the peak hour traffic. It should only take you twenty minutes or so, and I'll have Piggott hold you some breakfast.'

Less than half an hour later Peter was once again pressing the intercom buzzer on the gate at Woollahra. As Piggott ushered Peter through the house and out into the back garden the butler shot Peter a questioning look. It was almost imperceptible but it was not lost on Peter who inclined his head ever so slightly to assure the butler his confidence was safe. O'Shaughnessy and Christina were seated at a wrought-iron table sipping coffee and as Peter arrived they greeted him warmly. After he sat down Piggott quietly disappeared, reappearing in minutes with a silver tray, setting it down on the table. He removed the cover, revealing a generous helping of crisp bacon, two fried eggs done to perfection, a grilled tomato topped with melted parmesan nestled in a bed of button mushrooms.

Peter suddenly realised he was famished and, thanking Piggott, tucked into his breakfast with relish. After he had mopped up the last of the bacon grease from his plate with a piece of toast and taken a sip of coffee, he sat back and said, 'That was without doubt the best breakfast I've had in a long time. That man of yours is a gem.'

'Yes, he is,' O'Shaughnessy agreed. 'Now then, you mentioned that you'd made a decision.'

'Well, before I talk about that I need to ask you something. Why did you invite me here last night? Surely it wasn't just to relate some stories to me? I mean, it was all very interesting but ...' Peter raised his hands in a helpless gesture, smiling at O'Shaughnessy and Christina.

'No, of course not,' O'Shaughnessy said. 'Peter, we needed to tell you what we did because we knew all about what you were going through. We could hardly help it. It was in all the papers!' O'Shaughnessy smiled sardonically and continued, 'We sensed in you a kindred spirit, someone who had been betrayed by the Church that you had given your life to.'

'I gave my life to Christ,' Peter corrected.

'As did Christina and I. Our initial motive was to extend our hands in friendship – to let you know that you were not alone, and we needed you to understand that we too had had our dark nights of the soul.'

Peter couldn't help smiling at the allusion.

'Yes, quite right,' he replied. As you know I was already experiencing serious disillusionment with the Church. After I testified at the trial I was aware of the consequences my actions would have on my career as a priest.' He gestured at Christina. 'No doubt you went through similar issues surrounding your own vocation.'

'Peter, I knew that after India, I could never return to working as a nun again. I accepted that I would, in all likelihood, be excommunicated, but frankly I don't care. My conscience is clear and the only accountability concerning me is with God.'

'Yes,' Peter agreed, 'I share your sentiments in that regard. But with me it now goes much deeper. Before speaking to you last night I'd already accepted that I no longer have a career within the Church and, more than likely, will also be excommunicated. But now I have to agree that as bizarre as it first seemed there could well be a conspiracy within the Church. Even before last night I had already resolved myself to building a life outside the Church, as much as that saddened me. I wasn't quite sure what I would do, but it seemed the most obvious course of action was to pursue a position as a lay teacher at a non-denominational school. I don't really have other qualifications, certainly not in the corporate sector.'

'So what's your plan now?' asked Christina.

Peter regarded the question and was guarded in his reply. 'I did a little background research this morning on the Internet, and you're right, there's a plethora of information on Mentonidus. He was revered as a mystic as well as a great king, but scholars agree that he was a mythical hero, which makes the discovery of the prophecy all the more extraordinary. If that document does exist, it could be the key to everything you have been alluding to, and could well contain some, if not all of the answers.' He paused, seemingly lost in thought before continuing. 'The original Nag Hammadi find wasn't that extraordinary in its own right, although it did create quite a stir at the time. There were those who attempted to discredit the discovery, claiming the documents were fakes, albeit very clever ones. Over the years most academics lost interest, reasoning that the documents were written by someone and perhaps others, who for reasons that have not been made clear, were attempting to discredit Jesus.'

O'Shaughnessy now joined the discussion. 'Your research is impressive Peter. You're quite right though. The Church did go into a panic. The Nag Hammadi Gospels challenged the very fibre of Christianity and what it stands for. It was in the Church's interest to play it down as quickly as possible. There are of course a small band of stalwarts, the so-called Gnostics, who believe that the Nag Hammadi Gospels are the Gospels of Truth.'

'Yes' Peter agreed. 'Derived from *gnosis*, meaning knowing oneself, and thus human nature.'

Christina smiled, shaking her head.

Peter became vaguely aware that he was actually trying to impress her. He continued, 'They believe that to know oneself at the deepest level of insight is to simultaneously know God. Some even say that the self is divinity, which is what your Swami was alluding to, Christina. I've never really understood that, but there are many adherents to that or a similar belief, particularly among some of the meditation sects who advocate inward journeying through meditation.'

Once more, O'Shaughnessy took up the conversation. 'The documents themselves are common knowledge as you say, Peter, and in most clerical circles they have been strongly discredited with most claiming the Gnostics are a bunch of dangerous fanatics.'

'Anyway,' Peter said, shrugging his shoulders, 'in answer to your original question, Christina, maybe I need something to occupy my mind while I work out what to do with the rest of my life. During the trial I hadn't really considered what I was going to do but you've given me a lot to think about. I still believe in the Church, even if it is in the hands of the powerful and the corrupt. If you don't mind I'd like to write to Professor Muntz. Maybe you're right about the Church losing its way. I need answers and maybe the Professor can give them to me.'

O'Shaughnessy glanced conspiratorially towards Christina, and then turning to Peter he said,

'Yes, well there is just one small detail I did not tell you last night, Peter.'

'I thought there might be more,' Peter said. 'Last night wasn't just about kindred fellowship was it?'

'Our offer of friendship is sincere, Peter. Although I can understand if you're still suspicious. What I didn't tell you, was that since learning about the Prophecy of King Mentonidus, I have not heard one more word from Professor Muntz.'

'What do you mean?' Peter asked perplexed, 'Have you tried to contact him?'

'Of course,' O'Shaughnessy said. 'Frankly, it's a bit of a mystery. It's as though the man suddenly decided to avoid talking to me. I managed on one occasion to speak to Frau Muntz, his wife, but she sounded very agitated and asked me not to call again.'

'That does seem strange,' Peter mused, 'especially considering that you funded the expedition.'

'Yes, that's what I thought. So, you see, under normal circumstances I would have flown to Vienna to get to the bottom of it, but unfortunately the airlines won't let me fly due to this wretched emphysema of mine, which brings me to my other reason for wanting to meet with you.'

'Go on,' Peter said.

'You see, Peter, I needed to get your measure, as did Christina.' He glanced fondly at his niece, patting her knee affectionately. 'She is very precious to me and I needed to know that I could put her in the hands of someone who I not only trusted, but who she could trust too.'

'And your point is?' Peter pressed. He noticed that Christina was giving him that half smile again.

'Uncle Brian is a little old-fashioned and over-protective of me,' she said. 'He nearly died when he discovered I'd been travelling through India on my own.'

'And I'm concerned,' continued O'Shaughnessy, 'I have a bad feeling about Muntz. Most out of character.'

'And?' Peter prompted again.

'Well you see, I was wondering if you would consider escorting Christina to Vienna, to pay Professor Muntz a visit, and hopefully find out what is going on. That is,' he said smiling, 'if you have nothing more pressing to do at the moment.'

Peter was stunned and realised he was gaping.

'Naturally,' O'Shaughnessy added, 'I will pick up all expenses.'

Chapter 18

Peter and Christina booked the first available flight to Vienna but before they left Peter wanted to make some enquiries about the subject of their trip. He decided to call his brother Michael in this regard, as he was currently posted in London in a senior position on the staff of the Australian High Commissioner. Peter's request for information proved to be no trouble for Michael LeSarus.

When they were airborne on the Lauda flight to Vienna, Peter brought Christina up to speed about what he'd learned about Professor Muntz. Sipping a whisky and soda he opened the brief dossier that Michael had sent him and began to read.

'Hans Muntz is married with no children. He and his wife are domiciled in a middle-class apartment in a street called Neustiftgasse, which is in the third ring from central Vienna. He held an associate professorship at the University of Vienna but had never set the world of archaeology on fire.' Peter closed the manila folder and said, 'So that's it, Christina. That's all we have to go on. There's been no information on him since his resignation from the university. It would seem the Professor has dropped right out of academia, becoming somewhat of a recluse.'

'That's disappointing,' Christina said. 'Not much to go on from that.'

Peter said, 'I guess the most logical starting point would be the flat at Neustiftgasse.'

Christina agreed, adding, 'Let's just hope he and his wife still live there.'

The combination of a late night, along with the monotonous droning of the jet engines soon lulled Christina to sleep, and before long, her head dropped onto Peter's shoulder. He did not mind.

⤙ ✦ ⤚

In Vienna, they checked into a modest but clean hotel located on Mariahilfer Strasse, the most lively shopping street, lined with hip shops and cafes, located in the so-called inner district. Although O'Shaughnessy was well off, Christina and Peter were loath to waste his money on luxuries. Peter requested two single rooms, and when the clerk examined their passports he noted they were Catholic clergy, and gave them a warm welcome in reasonable English.

Their rooms were on the third floor and, although simple, proved to be large and comfortable with high, ornate ceilings. Each room had three beds, one double and two singles, obviously set up for budget-conscious families and both Peter and Christina felt guilty that so much space was wasted for their meagre needs. There was a small dining table with four chairs and an ancient, floral-patterned lounge suite, also capable of seating four, around a vinyl coffee table. The share bathroom was located down the hall, but each room had a washbasin with a water pitcher and towel. Their rooms were adjacent, opening onto a common balcony overlooking the busy street below, but when the double glazed doors were closed, most of the heavy traffic noise was shut out, with the exception of the frequent, rattling trams.

Their flight had arrived in the early hours of the morning and by the time they had checked in the city was only just beginning to stir. They decided it was too early to do anything useful so they agreed to retire to their respective rooms and use the time to refresh from the journey and perhaps get a couple of hours' sleep.

Peter flopped on to the double bed, without bothering to even take off his shoes, he was so tired. He closed his eyes, but sleep eluded him. He tossed and turned restlessly, and found himself acutely aware of Christina's presence on the other side of the thin

151

wall. He wondered what she would look like stretched out asleep on the bed. Despite his fatigue, he jumped off the bed and to banish the unwelcome fantasising he decided to take a cold shower, which had always worked before.

After the shower, he realised he was famished, so he wandered down to the desk, where the friendly clerk directed him to a small coffee shop less than a block away, where he ordered a continental breakfast of croissants and coffee for two to go.

Back at the hotel he knocked softly on Christina's door, not wishing to wake her if she was still asleep. She answered the door almost immediately and it was apparent that during his absence she had also showered and dressed.

They sat on the balcony and over breakfast they planned their next move. Christina suggested it would be polite to try telephoning the Muntz's to announce their pending visit.

Peter said, 'Yes Christina, I agree it would be more polite, but not smart. What if he refused to make an appointment? Where would we go from there? The easiest thing in the world to get rid of is an unwelcome telephone call.'

'And a body the most difficult,' Christina added with a grin.

Peter laughed. 'Precisely,' he agreed. 'If we arrive unannounced it's less likely he will refuse us a hearing, particularly when he sees we're clergy.'

Christina looked at him quizzically.

'Yes,' Peter said, 'I think we should wear our clerical garb, that way there is more chance he will trust us.'

Christina nodded her agreement. 'Do you want to go over what we will say?'

'No, I don't think so. I don't want it to sound as though we've rehearsed a speech. It's important that we sound as natural and unassuming as possible to gain his trust.'

Chapter 19

Peter and Christina followed the directions the hotel concierge had provided and they had no trouble jumping a number 48 bus from Belaria. The conductor politely informed the kind-looking, English-speaking Father and Sister that the next stop was Neustiftgasse. The conductor told them that the number they were looking for was in the third district, which although not that far, could prove to be a tiring walk. Peter and Christina thanked him for his concern, but assured him they were fit, and they welcomed the opportunity to walk out the stiffness from the long plane trip, and besides, it would give them a good opportunity to study their surroundings. When he had been a backpacker in his student days, Peter had always made a habit to initially walk a new city. He figured this was the only way to get a feel for it. People who joined guided bus tours never really got inside a city. By walking it you got to smell the smells, see and hear the people. You couldn't do that from the seat of an air-conditioned bus travelling along at sixty kilometres per hour. Peter also believed that it might pay off to walk the street where the Muntz's lived. It just may give them an edge.

When they finally arrived at the address they were relieved to find the building had still not been converted to security, like many of the others they'd seen on the way. They could knock directly on the Professor's door, rather than having to introduce themselves through an impersonal intercom system. After the long walk they were grateful to find the building had a lift. As they stepped into the ancient cage, Peter smiled at Christina, took a deep breath and said, 'Well, here goes nothing,' and pressed the third floor button.

The lift gave a protesting groan and with a shudder began its slow vertical climb. Christina looked at Peter with mock alarm grabbing him by the elbow. 'I hope this thing is safe,' she said.

Peter felt a tingle not unlike an electric shock where Christina's hand gripped his arm. 'I, ah, I'm sure it's all right,' he reassured her, his voice not as steady as he would have liked. 'After all, it's probably been going up and down without incident since the war.'

'I suppose you're right,' she said, not entirely convinced.

'We'd have to be awfully unlucky,' Peter added, trying to sound more convincing, 'for it to suddenly crash, just because we've travelled twenty thousand kilometres to use it.'

'Sorry, Peter,' Christina said. 'I'm just not a big fan of enclosed spaces.'

'You didn't say anything on the plane.'

'Oh, planes are nothing …'

Before she could say anything more the lift arrived at the third floor, jerking to a sudden stop, causing Christina to reach for Peter's arm again. A series of shuddering adjustments began, as the tired mechanism struggled to align the floor of the lift with the floor of the building. After a series of staccato stops it finally came to a stand still and Peter pulled back the metal grille. The lift had not quite managed to line up correctly and Peter had to step up to the landing, offering his hand to Christina. After he closed the door the lift whined back into motion, heading back down to collect its next customer. Peter looked at the numbers of the apartments, and steered Christina left. When they arrived at the number they'd been given they noticed it had a security spy hole in the middle of the door.

They looked at each other nervously and, taking a deep breath, Peter pressed the buzzer. 'Behind that door,' he whispered a hint of humour in his voice, 'could lie the answer to one of the great mysteries.'

Christina frowned in mock disapproval, 'Stop it,' she mouthed.

They could hear faint chimes from within the apartment. Peter waited for a polite time then pressed the buzzer a second time, hoping they were at the correct address and that the Professor was in. He was about to press the buzzer a third time when he heard the unmistakable sound of shuffling feet from within, and then an old lady's voice calling out in German, 'Yah, yah, I hear you. I'm coming.'

Peter stepped back from the door and stood square on, facing the peephole with Christina standing close to him, so that the occupant had every opportunity to recognise their clerical attire. A shadow passed across the peephole, as an eye pressed to it. There was a moment's silence as they were appraised, then the occupant asked who they were, and what did they want.

Peter replied slowly and distinctly, so that he would be understood, in what he hoped was passable German.

'My name is Father LeSarus, and this is Sister Christina Kelly, I'm a Catholic priest and we have come a long way to speak with Professor Muntz.'

There was a long pause as this information was digested from within. 'What do you wish to speak to him about?' the woman behind the door asked suspiciously.

Peter took another deep breath before answering. If he blew it now, he may lose their only chance to talk to him. He felt Christina gently elbow him in encouragement. 'Frau Muntz, we are great admirers of your husband and his work, and we were hoping to ask him some questions for a research document we are working on.'

'You do not have an appointment,' the voice accused.

'No, I'm sorry,' Peter apologised, 'but we have come a long way.'

There was another pause, longer this time, and Peter held his breath. Suddenly, and to his immense relief, he heard the sound of a key turning in a lock. He glanced at Christina who had shut her eyes tightly and had her fingers crossed behind her back. She resumed a suitably innocuous demeanour as the sound of the turning key was followed by a second and then a third, which in turn was followed by the sound of a latch being pulled back. Peter had forgotten how paranoid elderly people could be about their security. Finally the door opened, but only a crack, the old lady still maintained one final security guard between her and a potential assailant. The security chain tightened as the door opened as far as it could go. Peter couldn't help thinking that if he were an intruder it would only take one well aimed kick to break the flimsy chain and the door would burst open.

'Did I hear you say you were a Catholic priest?' the old lady asked, peering through the narrow opening of the door.

'Yes, I am,' Peter assured her, 'and Sister Christina is a Catholic nun.'

'Then why would you be interested in my husband's work?' she demanded suspiciously.

Peter was at a momentary loss for words, and fearing they may lose the moment, Christina blurted in German that was superior to Peter's, 'Frau Muntz, I am Father O'Shaughnessy's niece.'

Suddenly the door slammed abruptly. Damn, Peter thought, but before he could register his disappointment he heard the unmistakable sound of the chain being removed and the door opened wide, revealing Frau Muntz.

'Well, don't just stand there gaping, come in,' she demanded.

Peter and Christina were ushered into the living room of the apartment, which was furnished with overstuffed lounge chairs surrounding an antique looking coffee table. All the walls were covered from floor to ceiling with books, and in one corner of the room stood an ancient roll-top desk and next to that, in stark contrast, a modern computer desk, complete with computer and printer, which seemed out of place.

'Where did you say you were from?' Frau Muntz asked.

'Australia,' Peter answered.

'Austria? You don't sound Austrian. You sound like a foreigner,' she challenged.

'No, no, not Austria. Australia – Or-stray-lia,' he corrected, slowly and loudly emphasising each syllable.'

'There's no need to shout,' she protested in good, but heavily accented English. 'I may be old, but I'm not deaf.'

'I beg your pardon,' Peter apologised. 'You speak English,' he observed unnecessarily.

'Of course I do,' she snapped. 'Do you think I am not educated?' She turned to Christina. 'You say that O'Shaughnessy is your uncle?'

'Yes,' Christina confirmed with a smile, holding out her hand, which Frau Muntz ignored.

'Tell me, why would a Catholic priest and a nun come all the way from Australia, to speak to my husband?' she demanded.

She's a feisty one, Peter thought, full of admiration for the little old lady. She could not have been an inch over five feet, yet despite her age and tiny stature she stood straight and proud. Her eyes twinkled with intelligence and it was obvious she did not suffer fools lightly.

'Is the Professor in?' Peter asked politely.

'No,' she replied gruffly, 'and you haven't answered my question.'

Christina took over. 'Frau Muntz,' she began gently, 'I understand that my uncle funded your husband's recent expedition to Egypt.'

'And so what of it?' she demanded, eyes glaring. 'If he wants his money back, he can't have it. It's all gone.'

Christina smiled. 'He doesn't want any money,' she assured the old lady.

'Are you expecting your husband soon, Frau Muntz?' Peter pressed, becoming frustrated.

She ignored the question, and now that the matter of money had been settled, she gestured impatiently for them to take a seat. 'You will take coffee.' It was more of a statement than a question.

'Yes, thank you,' Christina replied politely for both of them. 'That would be nice.'

Frau Muntz disappeared into the kitchen without another word. Christina placed a finger to her lips and mouthed, 'Be patient.' A few minutes later Frau Muntz reappeared with a tray, laden with coffee pot, cream, sugar, cups and saucers and a plate with a Gugelhoff, the traditional Viennese coffee cake. Setting the tray on the table she poured the coffee and then cut a generous slice of cake for each of them.

Once they had settled down to their cake and coffee she again asked Peter why they had travelled all this way to see her husband.

Christina answered before Peter had a chance to reply. 'Frau Muntz, your husband confided to my uncle what he had found. He was very excited. And when he didn't hear from him for a long time, he became worried that something may have happened, especially after he last spoke to you and you told him not to call you again.'

Suddenly Frau Muntz's eyes glistened with tears. She searched in her sleeve for a handkerchief. Her hard demeanour softened, and suddenly she seemed transformed into a frightened and fragile, little old lady. In a quavering voice she addressed Christina, 'I wish we had never heard of your uncle.' She held up a hand. 'No, I am sorry. That is not correct. He is a very generous and supportive man. It is not his fault. He was not to know.'

Christina leaned forward. 'Know what, Frau Muntz?' she asked softly, concern in her voice.

'He was not to know the grief my husband's discovery would bring him. The discovery your uncle funded.'

'Frau Muntz,' Peter interjected, 'Father O'Shaughnessy was very excited at the potential enormity of your husband's discovery. And then,' Peter held up his hands in a palms-up gesture, 'he never heard from him again.'

'Did Father O'Shaughnessy fear that my husband would cheat him?' Frau Muntz demanded, with renewed hostility in her tone.

'No, of course not,' Christina assured her. 'As I said, he was worried. And when he could not get in contact, he sent me to find out if something was wrong.' She gestured towards Peter. 'Father LeSarus was kind enough to accompany me.'

'So if he was so worried, why did your uncle not come himself?'

'He would have, but unfortunately he is ill, and unfit for such a long journey.'

This seemed to allay Frau Muntz's hostility for the moment. 'So what do you know about my husband's discovery?' she challenged.

'Only what he told Father O'Shaughnessy,' Peter replied. 'That your husband was handed an ancient papyrus by a goat herder who found it when he was digging in clay for water.'

Frau Muntz's eyebrows shot up but she remained silent.

Peter thought he detected a return of suspicion cloud across the old lady's eyes, but continued. 'The coincidence that your husband's find almost exactly replicated the way in which the original Nag Hammadi Gospels were found was not lost on us.'

Frau Muntz gestured with her hand. 'Please do continue, Father LeSarus. What else do you know of my husband's discovery?'

'I understand that the papyrus is alleged to be a prophecy written almost two thousand years before Christ, by a man, a king, who up till now, had been considered a myth.'

'Let me assure you, Father LeSarus, that there is nothing alleged about the discovery. It is genuine,' she added with emphasis.

'Yes, of course,' Peter appeased her, 'that is why Father O'Shaughnessy shared your husband's excitement with equal enthusiasm. As I understand it, the prophecy that your husband discovered predicts among other things the coming of Christ, as well as the apparition of Our Lady at Fatima. I also understand that it contains explicit warnings to humanity to heed the revelations of Fatima.'

Christina spoke up. 'Frau Muntz, my uncle has long held the view that the Church is covering up the facts surrounding the Third Secret of Fatima, and, well, he thinks that the prophecy may shed some light on it, or at least confirm his suspicions, that the Church does have something to hide.'

Peter stood up from his seat and walked around the coffee table. Stopping directly in front of Frau Muntz, he bent down and gently took both her hands in his, and looking intently into her eyes he asked, 'Frau Muntz, does your husband still have this document?'

The old lady shuddered and he saw unmistakable fear in her eyes. She turned her head, averting her eyes from his unrelenting gaze.

'Frau Muntz, please,' Peter pressed, 'it is very important that we know. Where is the document? Does your husband still have it?'

She sat still for a long time, silently weeping, tears rolling down her cheeks, and then finally she shook her head.

'I don't know where it is now, or whether it even still exists. It could have been destroyed for all I know.'

'Did Professor Muntz destroy it?' Christina asked gently.

Frau Muntz shook her head. 'My husband had nothing to do with it. When he received the papyrus for the first time he was very excited with the find. He made the initial translations himself. Then one day he became agitated, telling me that the document was, as you said, a prophecy. Yes, it predicted the coming of Christ, and Fatima, but it foretold many other things, including a cataclysmic event that was to transpire nearly four thousand years into the future.'

'And if the document was dated at about two thousand years before Christ, then that would place that event somewhere in the twentieth century,' Peter interjected.

'Yes, that's what my husband said,' she agreed. 'As you suggested, he said that it coincided with a revelation from the Blessed Virgin Mary, but that was all he said. He was concerned about the risk of the document falling into the wrong hands explaining that this would be catastrophic.'

Peter and Christina exchanged glances.

'Did he explain why?' Christina asked.

'No, I'm sorry. He didn't go into more detail than that.'

'Did he talk to anyone else about his find?'

'After he spoke to your uncle, Sister Christina, he became very agitated as the true ramifications of what he'd found began to sink in. He was astounded at the accuracy of the foretelling of future events, many of which have since been ratified by history. He expressed great concern about what he referred to as warnings of calamitous threats to the world. He felt at a loss as to who to confide in, and your uncle was so far away. He felt the need to talk to someone, to show them what he had. There was only one other person he held in enough esteem, and who he felt he could trust, and one day he decided to confide in this man. You see, he was afraid and could not figure out what to do. He needed to confide in someone who would understand such things.'

161

'Who is that man?' Peter asked.

'Archbishop Voitra, the Prelate of Prague.'

Peter shuddered involuntarily and with trepidation asked, 'Did your husband show the Archbishop the document?'

'Yes, but not at first. He went to Prague to discuss it with him. The Archbishop insisted on coming back to Vienna to see the document for himself. I recall he seemed disturbed when he saw it and became even more so when he read my husband's translation. He wanted to take the document back with him, but my husband refused. They had a terrible row over this, which shocked me. I had never imagined a man of the cloth could talk the way he did. He shouted and screamed and abused my husband who became very upset over this treatment from a man he liked and respected. In the end he asked him to leave. The Archbishop stormed out, yelling that my husband was dabbling in Church business, which he did not understand. He threatened my husband with terrible consequences if he did not hand over the document. My husband was so distraught after the visit that soon after, he suffered a stroke.' Frau Muntz sobbed, dabbing at her eyes with the now soaked handkerchief. After she regained control of her emotions she added, 'He has not been able to communicate since. That is the reason Father O'Shaughnessy could not contact him. And I am sorry. I was too distraught to discuss it. And afraid,' she added.

'We're so sorry to have upset you again, Frau Muntz,' Christina sympathised, reaching out her hand to Frau Muntz, who clung to it as if it were a lifeline.

'We're very sorry, Frau Muntz,' Peter said. 'And I'm sorry to have to keep pressing you but ...'

'The papyrus,' she said, interrupting him, 'has disappeared.'

Peter and Christina were aghast at this news, their hopes slipping away. 'What do you mean, disappeared?' Christina asked.

'My husband kept it in his safe with his other important documents. Some time after his stroke I was sorting through his documents and it simply wasn't there.'

'And you are absolutely positive your husband had left it in the safe?' Peter asked.

'Oh yes,' she replied without hesitation, 'he made a big issue of locking it away in front of the Archbishop.'

'The Archbishop saw your husband lock the parchment in the safe?'

'Yes, I'm positive, my husband made an issue of it. He told the Archbishop he would never get his hands on it and put it directly into the safe.'

'And to the best of your knowledge, no one has had access to the safe since?'

'No, no, I am the only person beside my husband who has the combination.'

'But, is it possible that you may have had a break-in?'

'Anything is possible, Father LeSarus, but I doubt it. Nothing else is missing.'

Christina asked, 'Have you reported it to the police, Frau Muntz?'

'And what would be the point of that? To report a missing papyrus that my husband never acknowledged the existence of? No, Sister, I did not consider it appropriate to involve the police. Ach, I'm glad to be rid of the wretched thing. All it did was bring stress and anxiety to Hans, and ultimately it cost him his health.'

'Frau Muntz, I would like to thank you for your candour and hospitality,' Peter said, standing up, unable to keep the disappointment from his voice. 'You have been very helpful.'

'You are welcome, Father. I sense you are an honest man, but I fear I have not been very helpful.'

'Oh, I assure you that you have. Confirmation that the document exists or existed is very, very important to us. There is just one more question I would like to ask, if you don't mind?'

'And what would that be, Father?' she asked.

'Would it be possible to see your husband?'

'If you like, but I don't see that it would do you any good. As I said, he hasn't communicated since his stroke. It's, it's like talking to a vegetable.' She stifled another sob, dabbing her eyes again.

'Will you be all right?' Christina asked.

'I will have to be, my dear,' she replied.

Peter and Christina thanked her once again, and as they were taking their leave Frau Muntz stopped them, placing a hand on Peter's arm.

'This is important, isn't it?' she asked.

'Yes, Frau Muntz,' Peter answered. 'It could very well be the most important thing any of us will ever have to deal with.'

'If my husband dies, I hope that it will not be for nothing,' she said, quietly closing the door on them.

One by one they heard the locks turning again.

Chapter 20

As they were leaving the Muntz's apartment building Peter remembered something. 'Christina,' he asked. 'Where did you learn to speak German?'

'I studied it in school. Uncle Brian was always a fan of German culture, Goethe in particular, and when I was young Uncle Brian and I were pen friends. One day I wrote to him in German, it started as a joke, but then I realised that not only could I talk to Uncle Brian about anything, I now had my own private language to do it in. I guess that Uncle Brian encouraged me because he used to tell me all of these juicy stories about my mother when she was a child. It was wonderful stuff, especially when you're a teenager, to get the dirt on your mother in letters she'd never be able to read – not that my mother was a snoop, but, you know …' and she trailed off into laughter.

Christina was quiet then, and for a moment her eyes seemed to be staring into the distance. To Peter it seemed as if she was lost in happy memories about her parents. Although he was intensely curious about everything to do with this woman, he suddenly felt uncomfortable about asking her more.

They quickly found themselves on a busy street, and Peter had no trouble signalling a taxi, as he didn't feel up to another long walk back to the bus stop.

'I don't know about you,' he said, abruptly changing the subject as they climbed into the taxi, 'but I'm all for a short trip across the border to Prague. It's a magnificent city and an absolute must on any tourist itinerary.'

'And while we're there,' Christina suggested, with that mischievous grin that Peter thought she must have been practising since she was a child, 'it would be discourteous of us not to pay our respects to the Prelate of Prague.'

'But of course,' Peter said, enjoying the game. 'We wouldn't want the Czechs to think that Australians are rude!'

Back at the hotel they decided to formalise their intention by writing a short letter to the Archbishop, advising him of their impending visit to his city and requesting an audience.

Before they left for Prague they agreed to pay a visit to the institution where Professor Muntz was being cared for. Christina checked with Frau Muntz prior to their visit, and although she still thought it would be futile, she promised to inform the staff at the clinic.

⚜

As they arrived at the clinic, Peter and Christina were relieved that Frau Muntz had been true to her word and they were expected. A nurse escorted them to the garden where the elderly archaeologist was sitting in a wheelchair parked in the shade of a tree.

The nurse told the Professor he had visitors, but she might as well have been speaking to the tree. She smiled apologetically as though blaming herself for the lack of response and then left them alone with Professor Muntz. Peter and Christina sat on a bench opposite the wheelchair, studying the shell of a man. Muntz's head was drooped to one side and a thin stream of saliva dribbled from the corner of his mouth. Christina picked up the towel on the man's chest, and wiped his face. She then introduced herself and although there was no reaction Christina continued to talk as Peter looked on, watching the other man's eyes closely for the slightest sign of awareness. She explained that they had come from Australia to discuss his find and that they had already spoken to his wife. The face remained impassive. She decided to continue.

'Professor Muntz, we have reason to believe that the parchment, the prophecy, may provide evidence which could support there is a serious cover-up within the Catholic Church in relation to the Third Secret of Fatima. If this cover-up is not exposed then we fear the consequences may prove disastrous.'

For a brief second, Peter could have sworn he detected a glimmer of understanding in the man's eyes. Peter stood up and leaned forward, his mouth close to the Professor's ear. 'Professor Muntz, Hans, I think you can understand me.' He took hold of the man's hand. 'If you can hear me, squeeze my finger.' Nothing. 'Hans, I cannot tell you how important it is that we find the parchment. Frau Muntz, your wife, believes that following your stroke, Archbishop Voitra stole it, or had it stolen.'

Peter felt an almost imperceptible pressure on his finger. At first he thought he'd imagined it. But no, there it was again. This time Peter had no doubt whatsoever. He looked up at Christina. 'He can hear me,' he said.

'Are you sure?' Christina asked, doubt mingling with hope.

'Yes. He squeezed my finger,' Peter said, trying to keep his voice calm. Peter stared into the older man's eyes, searching for a sign of something and then Peter's blood froze. What he saw, albeit only for a fleeting second, was unmistakeably, fear.

'Professor Muntz,' Peter urged, leaning close to the man's face. 'You can hear me. I know you can.'

'Is everything all right?'

Peter and Christina turned to see the nurse anxiously hurrying towards them.

'You look as though you've seen a ghost,' she said to Peter.

Peter said, 'He squeezed my finger, and then I'm sure I saw recognition in his eyes.

'That's impossible,' the nurse smiled, 'although it's not unusual to feel some twitching of muscles sometimes. It's only nerves, that's probably what you felt.'

'But his eyes,' Peter persisted, 'I'm sure I saw something in his eyes.' He turned to Christina. 'Christina, you must have seen it too.' Christina reluctantly shook her head.

'It was fear, I tell you,' Peter insisted. 'For a second he looked terrified.'

The nurse smiled dismissively. 'I don't think so, Father.'

Unconvinced, Peter asked, 'Would it be possible to have a word with his physician?'

'I'll check if he's available,' the nurse replied. 'But I assure you, he won't tell you anything different to what I've just told you.'

She came back within minutes and asked Peter and Christina to follow her to the doctor's office, where she ushered them in and introduced them to the man seated behind a desk. The doctor rose from his chair and moved around his desk to greet his visitors. He bade them take a seat and then returned to his own chair. 'How can I help you, Father and Sister?' he asked in English without a trace of an accent. 'I understand you have some interest in my patient, Professor Muntz, and that you have come all the way from the Antipodes to see him.'

Peter thanked the doctor for seeing them. He explained that they had indeed come a long way to talk to Muntz about an important matter pertaining to business between the Professor and Christina's uncle.

'Australians! How wonderful!' the doctor exclaimed. 'This will give me an opportunity to practise my English.'

'I really don't think you need the practice,' Peter flattered the doctor, causing him to smile his appreciation.

'What a pity you have come so far in vain,' the doctor said, referring to the professor's affliction.

'Herr Doctor,' Peter said. 'Professor Muntz was involved in a most important archaeological find. We were devastated to learn of his illness and subsequent inability to communicate.'

'Yes, it is tragic to see a man of his intellect struck down,' the doctor agreed.

Christina asked, 'Tell us, Doctor, is it possible that Professor Muntz will ever regain his senses again?'

'Highly unlikely, I'm afraid. Although his body is reasonably functional, and he appears to be in a conscious state, the mind is just not there.'

Peter continued. 'What would you say then, Doctor, if I were to tell you that I felt a slight pressure on my finger? But not only that, I'm positive I saw something in his eyes.'

'What exactly do you mean by something?'

'What I saw, Doctor, was fear.' Peter insisted.

'And you also saw this?' the doctor asked, turning to Christina.

'No, I'm sorry. I was standing behind Father LeSarus. My view was obstructed.'

The doctor chuckled. 'My dear, Father LeSarus, I hate to disillusion you, but what you saw was in all likelihood an involuntary facial muscle reaction to wind.'

'I beg your pardon?'

The doctor chuckled again. 'In all probability, Father, excuse me Sister, he farted.'

Peter did not believe this for an instant, but chose not to pursue the point. Instead he asked, 'In your opinion, Doctor, what caused Professor Muntz's stroke?'

'One can never be sure of these things, but his wife reported that he'd been in a highly agitated state just prior to it. Severe tension can often trigger something like that, particularly if the patient has a history of high blood pressure.'

Peter paused, head bowed, deep in thought. Then suddenly he lifted his head. He'd just thought of something. 'Forgive me, Doctor, I'm quite ignorant about things medical. Is it possible to bring on a stroke artificially?'

'I'm not sure I understand what you mean, Father.'

'I'm sorry. My question was clumsy. What I meant was, is it possible to bring on a stroke by means of drugs or other form of artificial interference?'

'Now why would someone want to do that?' the doctor asked perplexed.

'Just curious,' Peter said unconvincingly.

'Well to satisfy your curiosity, Father, yes it is possible. The administration of certain drugs can induce a stroke or at least the symptoms of a stroke. But please, why are you pursuing this line of questioning? Is there something you know that I should be made aware of, as his physician?'

'I'm not sure, Doctor. Perhaps I'm just clutching at straws.'

'Bitte?' the doctor asked, looking a little confused.

Christina translated. She had a strange expression on her face and she couldn't keep her eyes off Peter.

'Oh, that's very good. Clutching straws!' The doctor seemed amused. 'Come on, Father,' Christina said turning to Peter and suddenly getting up from the chair, 'I think we have kept the doctor long enough.'

⋆⋆⋆

As they were leaving the clinic Peter said, 'Didn't we take our leave a little abruptly?'

Christina looked at him with her grey eyes and said, 'Peter, I'm no fool. I've read enough mystery novels. You think something's up, don't you? What is it?'

'I think the Professor's being drugged …'

'And you think the doctor's in on it?'

170

'Well, actually no,' Peter said, surprised. 'That hadn't occurred to me, but now that you mention it …' his voice trailed off thoughtfully.

'Well, it occurred to me,' Christina said. 'That's why I wanted to get out of there. I didn't want him to know we suspected anything.'

'Then you agree with me,' Peter said.

'I'm not sure. But I think we should discuss this with Uncle Brian.'

'No. I don't think so.'

'Why not?'

'Because I might just be getting paranoid. I don't want to bother your uncle until we know more. Something about this whole situation is beginning to stink.'

'So what do you suggest we do?'

'We need to think about this some more. We need a strategy.'

They discussed it all the way to Prague.

Chapter 21

Father LeSarus and Sister Kelly presented themselves at Archbishop Voitra's residence formally dressed in their clerical garb. The Archbishop's secretary, a young priest, assured the visitors they were expected and that the Archbishop would not keep them waiting long. Although heavily accented, the secretary's English was passable. He introduced himself to the exotic visitors as Milan Hruska and told Peter and Christina that he'd never met anyone from so far away and that though he personally had never travelled outside of Czechoslovakia, which of course was now the Czech Republic, he still loved to read about foreign places. He spoke to Peter and Christina in a way that was akin to hero worship, as though they were celebrities. He was just asking whether there were many kangaroos in the cities when the buzzer on his desk sounded.

'The Archbishop will see you now, Father and Sister, please to follow me.'

They followed the young priest, who ushered them into a small, shabby office. Against the far wall stood a cheap, laminated desk, behind which sat a slight, elderly man with a stern countenance, dressed in the purple of an archbishop. The framed portrait of a much younger Pope adorned one wall, and on the other was a dusty crucifix. As they were ushered in, Archbishop Voitra stood but remained behind the security of his desk. The young priest backed out of the office, closing the door behind him.

'Welcome to Prague,' he greeted without warmth, also in a heavily accented but fluent English. He presented his ring of office across the expanse of the desk, forcing Peter and Christina to lean and stretch awkwardly to kiss it out of due respect for his rank. With the formalities completed, he gestured his visitors to sit on the uncomfortable, tired-looking chairs in front of his desk. Without so much as offering coffee he came straight to the point.

'You are a long way from home,' he began. 'When I received your letter requesting an audience I was intrigued. It is uncustomary for a nun to travel alone in the company of a priest.' The accusation was subtle but unmistakable.

'Let me assure you, Excellency,' Peter said, with clear resentment in his tone, 'there is nothing untoward about Sister Kelly and I being travelling companions.'

The Archbishop continued, ignoring Peter's self-righteous tone. 'When priests and nuns are sent abroad it is customary for their superiors to write, informing Church hierarchy in the host country, of their pending visit, and yet I received no such notice from Australia.'

Peter replied, 'We are not travelling on official Church business, Excellency, but rather as friends on shall we say, a private sabbatical.'

'That is most unusual,' Voitra observed, 'and what, may I ask, is the purpose of this, ah, sabbatical?'

Peter came straight to the point. 'We are researching the Nag Hammadi Gospels. No doubt you have heard of them.'

The Archbishop nodded slightly, pursing his lips in distaste. 'Heresy!' he spat. 'Those writings were discredited by the Church.'

Peter continued unperturbed. 'An Austrian archaeologist recently returned to the site of the original Gospel discoveries, and we have reason to believe he made another discovery, which may be even more spectacular than the first. The man lives in Vienna, and we travelled there in the hope of interviewing him personally.'

The Archbishop's tone became even frostier, and Peter sensed something else he couldn't quite place.

'Anything your archaeologist may or may not have found will, I daresay, be treated with equal contempt,' said the Archbishop.

'Excellency, we understand that the archaeologist we are referring to is known to you.'

'Is that so? In my position, many people are known to me.'

Peter ignored the sarcasm. 'His name is Hans Muntz. We are led to believe you are friends.'

Voitra's unwavering gaze did not flinch at the mention of Muntz. Without acknowledging or denying a friendship, he said, 'You've wasted your time. If you'd taken the trouble to check your facts before you undertook this fruitless journey, you would have known that Professor Muntz is a vegetable. He can tell you nothing.'

'So we discovered, Excellency,' Peter said dryly.

'And what do your superiors think of you wasting your time researching what has already been decried by the Church,' Voitra demanded, 'and what do you hope to achieve?' The Archbishop's tone was growing more belligerent.

'I guess what we're hoping to achieve, Excellency, is the truth,' Peter LeSarus answered.

'The truth?' the Archbishop exploded. 'Who are you to seek the truth? Is it not good enough for you, that the Church, in Her infinite wisdom, has declared these findings to be not only false but heretic?'

This time Christina, who'd been silent till now, spoke up. 'With the greatest of respect, Excellency, I do believe we have all got off to a bad start. We did not come here to offend you. We are visitors to your beautiful city and we merely came to pay our respects to you as Catholic Prelate.'

With the faintest hint of a smile, the Archbishop seemed to relax a little.

Encouraged, Christina continued. 'Our research is incidental to this visit. As you rightly pointed out, the man we came to see in Vienna is incapable of being interviewed. But as we were so close to Prague, which we heard described as the jewel of Central Europe, we thought we would indulge ourselves with a side trip.'

'Your diplomatic qualities are wasted, Sister,' the Archbishop complimented Christina with a smile. 'You're right. Your companion did get off to a bad start. But then, when I received your letter, I did some research of my own.' All traces of the smile were gone now. 'I emailed my counterpart, the Archbishop of Sydney, who sent me an interesting response.' He picked up a piece of paper from his desk and began to read, moving his lips as he went. He put the paper down and removed his glasses, his face stern. 'It would seem that as clergy you are questionable in your bona fides, if that is the correct expression. Let me see now,' he picked up the glasses again, holding them to his eyes without putting them on and glanced back down at the paper on his desk to refresh his memory.

He levelled his gaze at Christina. 'I understand that Brian O'Shaughnessy is your uncle,' he began deliberately. 'An ex-priest of some considerable notoriety. In fact, it says here,' he gestured with his glasses at the paper on his desk, 'that he has suffered the Bull of Excommunication.' He gave Christina an accusing look before continuing. 'He was expelled from Italy after serving a prison term for embezzling Church money, while working in a position of trust at the Vatican Bank.'

Christina began to protest. 'He was innocent …'

Voitra cut her off in mid-sentence with an impatient wave of his hand. He looked back at the paper. 'Father Peter LeSarus, you were recently involved in a court case where you publicly broke the holy seal of confession, causing irreparable damage to the Church.'

Despite himself, Peter squirmed slightly.

'And finally, our diplomat, Sister Christina Kelly, niece of the infamous Brian O'Shaughnessy.' He peered malevolently over his glasses, this time causing Christina to flinch uncomfortably under his gaze. 'Preaching heresy throughout India and disobeying a clear directive from your superior. Your Bishop leads me to understand that Bulls of Excommunication are being prepared for both of you as well.' He replaced the papers on the desk. 'So, I ask you, what is it that you want from me and what is your real purpose for visiting my country?'

Peter glanced at Christina, catching her eye questioningly. She nodded her head almost imperceptibly. He made his decision and stood up, placing both hands on the desk and leaned towards the Archbishop, looking straight into his eyes.

'Very well, Archbishop Voitra, you want to know why we're here? Then let me be direct. You are right. We did not come here to pay our respects. We are here to retrieve the papyrus you stole from Professor Muntz's safe.'

Peter's blunt approach had the desired effect. Voitra was dumbstruck and could only splutter, his face red with rage, a throbbing vein standing out clearly on his forehead.

'How dare you?' he finally managed, recovering from his initial shock.

At first Peter was seriously afraid the man was going to have a heart attack, but he held his ground, continuing his threatening stance over the Archbishop's desk.

The Archbishop stood up, forcing Peter to straighten up a little. 'How can you dare?' Voitra repeated. 'To speak to me like that. Me, an Archbishop of the Holy Roman Catholic Church.'

'Not long ago, your position might have impressed me, Excellency,' Peter said undaunted, 'perhaps it might even have intimidated me, but not any more. Something is rotten in this state of affairs, and besides, as you've reminded us, I'm due to be excommunicated anyway, so I have nothing to lose.'

Voitra's bright red complexion deepened to purple and the vein on his forehead looked set to burst. His lip trembled as he fought to regain control of his emotions.

'You will burn in Hell for this,' he threatened.

Peter said calmly, ignoring the threat. 'Why not cut the theatrical outrage and admit it? I know that you were with Muntz just before he suffered a stroke. The two of you had a huge row over the document because he wouldn't let you have it. Conveniently, he suffered a stroke soon after you'd left, and after that the document mysteriously disappeared from his safe.'

Voitra had also resumed his seat. 'Precisely what is it that you are trying to say to me?' he demanded in a voice that was a hiss.

'I thought I'd made myself clear, Excellency,' Peter said, placing sarcastic emphasis on the last word. 'Not only am I convinced you stole or arranged to have the document stolen, but I also have reason to believe you arranged for Professor Muntz to have a stroke, or rather what appeared to be a stroke.'

'But that is preposterous,' Voitra spluttered. 'We are friends.'

'Oh, so you're friends now, are you? Well, what would you say if I told you I had a conversation with Professor Muntz?' Peter bluffed. Christina was staring at her feet, not trusting herself to catch the Archbishop's eye.

The bluff paid off, for suddenly, as if by magic, the colour drained from the Archbishop's face, leaving it a deathly pallor of grey-white. The puff was all gone and he looked like a frail old man. 'But, but that is not possible,' he quavered. 'The doctors … They said he would never recover.'

'Well, they were wrong. He told me the stroke-like symptoms were brought on by an injected substance.'

Peter was really pushing his luck now, but he needed to play out his hunch and gauge the Archbishop's reaction. Voitra stared at Peter. The Archbishop's mouth was silently opening and closing, looking for all the world like a goldfish sucking for air.

'So you see, Excellency,' Peter continued, 'we know what happened to Professor Muntz. The only thing we need to find out now, is the whereabouts of the document you stole.'

Voitra looked beaten. All the bravado and brashness had disappeared. 'Father LeSarus, you don't understand what you're dealing with here. That document should be destroyed. It is the work of the devil. You have no idea what powers are involved here. Please, both of you. I beg you to forget all about this. Just let it go.'

'Sorry, Archbishop Voitra,' Christina said, 'even if we wanted to we couldn't.'

'You are fools,' Voitra said, 'you don't know what you are doing, or what you are getting into. Believe me, if you continue to meddle in this you will die.'

Peter and Christina stared at the now visibly shaken Archbishop. Peter no longer felt so sure of his position. Was the Archbishop warning them, or threatening them? The young priest began to wonder if perhaps they had indeed become involved in something they really did not understand, and that they were now way over their heads.

Voitra stood up on shaky legs. He looked older than when they had first come in. 'Now, if you will excuse me,' he said, 'I suddenly feel very tired.' He pressed the intercom on his desk, 'Father Hruska, would you please see my guests out.'

Almost immediately, the affable young man entered the room. His smile froze when he saw the look on his master's face and the tension in the room was like a tangible force. Without a word he held the door open, ushering the visitors out. He closed the door silently behind him and followed them into the anteroom. He only spoke when they had reached the street.

'That was not a happy meeting.' It was a statement of fact, not a question.

'Milan,' Peter said, 'do you know anything about Professor Muntz and the Archbishop's relationship with him?'

'They were friends,' Milan answered. 'The poor man had a massive stroke.'

'Yes, yes, we know all about that. But do you know anything about a document that Professor Muntz had in his possession, an ancient papyrus?'

Milan hesitated for just a fraction of a second and then said, 'I must go, Father, the Archbishop will be needing me.' He turned on his heel, leaving Peter and Christina standing alone.

⸰✦⸰

Milan Hruska hurried inside, concerned for his master. He was like a faithful puppy, having served as the Bishop's secretary ever since leaving the seminary. During that time, over five years now, he'd proven his loyalty time and again and the Archbishop trusted him implicitly. Hruska was privy to all there was to know about the Archbishop, including his dealings with Professor Muntz and the secret document.

He knocked on the Archbishop's office door. When there was no answer he tried again, and after waiting a while he tentatively opened the door. The Archbishop was still seated at his desk, staring into space, a dark, troubled look on his face.

Concerned, Hruska asked, 'Is there anything I can get you, Excellency?'

'They know,' Voitra said without looking up, ignoring Milan's question. He continued, as though speaking to himself. 'The fools may just know. I don't know how, but I'm sure they know, and we're in big trouble.'

Milan didn't have to ask what it was they knew and his face creased with worry.

'But how could they, Excellency?' he asked. 'Professor Muntz will never regain his faculties. We were guaranteed.'

'Nothing is guaranteed, Milan. They claim Muntz has regained his speech, which may or may not be true. It is possible they may be bluffing, but either way that LeSarus is no fool. As for the other one, the diplomat … I just don't know. But one thing you can be sure of Milan, if they don't know all of it yet, they won't let go till they do. They will keep worrying at this till they get to the truth, and then it will be too late. The damage would be irreparable.'

'What do you plan to do, Excellency? What can I do?'

'I don't know, Milan, I just don't know. First poor Hans and now, these two. Where will it end my friend, where will it all end?'

Hruska felt helpless in his impotence to offer a solution. After a few moments of silence he said, 'I assume you will want me to get Cardinal Morova on the phone?'

'Cardinal Morova?' Voitra asked, sounding as though he had never heard the name before. Then after a while, in a very tired and resigned voice, he said, 'Yes, Milan, I suppose you'd better. There's no putting it off.'

Chapter 22

Milan Hruska dialled Cardinal Morova's direct line at the Vatican and in seconds had him on the phone.

'Cardinal Morova? Your Eminence, this is Father Milan Hruska, I have Archbishop Voitra for you.' He handed the phone to Voitra, who took it with trembling hands and began to describe in detail the conversation with his recent visitors. He was not interrupted once. When he'd finished the silence on the other end of the line continued ominously, and after a while, Voitra thought the line must have dropped out. 'Cardinal Morova, are you still there?'

'Yes, yes, I'm still here,' the Cardinal growled irritably, 'I'm trying to think.' There was another long pause before the Cardinal's gravelly voice barked across the line. 'Is it possible that Muntz has regained his faculties?' he demanded.

'I would not have thought so,' Voitra answered with a tremor in his voice, 'but then who can say? Stranger things have happened.' Then as an afterthought, and not meaning to be funny, he added, 'After all Cardinal Morova, are we not in the business of miracles?'

'I hardly think this is the time for jocularity,' the Cardinal snapped.

'Excuse me, Your Eminence,' Voitra mumbled, 'I was not trying to be funny, but there are many cases of seemingly incurable conditions that are suddenly and inexplicably cured. That was all I meant.'

The Cardinal didn't bother to acknowledge Voitra's explanation. 'Well, the first thing you must find out is whether there is any truth to it. Call the clinic immediately and demand a report on Muntz's health. If what you've told me is true, then Muntz will have to be taken care of. He knows too much. We just can't afford for this to go further.'

Voitra was shocked, not quite believing what he'd heard. 'What do you mean, taken care of?' he asked, 'I'm not sure I understand.

'Oh, don't be so naïve, Voitra. You know exactly what I mean. This thing is bigger than both of us, and your sensitivities,' he added with a sneer. 'Now what about these Australians?' he demanded. 'You say it is unlikely they will give up on this and, judging by the way they played you, they already know too much.'

Voitra was now terribly unsure of himself. It was one thing to arrange to have a man mentally crippled. My god, he thought, how many agonising, sleepless nights had he suffered as a result of what they'd done to poor Hans Muntz. It was now clear that it would not stop at that. He had no doubt that what the Cardinal was alluding to was murder. Where would it all end, he asked himself for the millionth time. He now knew that if he conceded that the Australians would pursue this, he would in effect be signing their death warrants. But what could he do? Morova was right, this was bigger than either of them and bigger and more important than the lives of two foreigners. Should they somehow stumble on to the truth and expose what they'd found, well, the repercussions would be nothing short of … unthinkable. But there had to be a way around this without causing the deaths of innocent people.

'Well, what about it, Voitra?' the Cardinal demanded impatiently, 'what of these Australians?'

'I was just thinking, Eminence. Perhaps we could use this to our advantage, use them.'

'And how do you propose we do that?'

'I was thinking of feeding them misinformation.'

182

'Go on,' the Cardinal encouraged.

'I would need time to think it through. Perhaps we could make them think they had discovered the misinformation for themselves. It would need to be important enough to satisfy them, yet not enough for them to pursue it further and maybe even put O'Shaughnessy off the scent.'

The line was silent, as the Cardinal digested the proposal. Voitra uttered a silent prayer, aware that the next few seconds could well seal the fate of the two Australians.

Suddenly, the Cardinal snapped, 'No!'

'I beg your pardon, Eminence,' Voitra asked, 'What, what do you mean, no?'

'Precisely that,' the Cardinal snapped again. 'No. It's too risky. Misinformation may only serve to encourage them to dig deeper. It's clumsy. No. We can't afford the risk. There is far too much at stake. Do what you have to do, and do it quickly.'

'But, Cardinal Morova,' Voitra began to protest.

'Don't argue with me, Voitra. I'm ordering you. Do you understand me? We must protect the status quo. Everyone is dispensable. Use the Russian and call me when it's done.'

The phone went dead.

Chapter 23

꠱ꠥ꠪

Archbishop Voitra sat still for a long time, the silent phone still pressed to his ear. After a while Milan Hruska gently removed the phone from his hand, replacing it in its cradle. He knew better than to interrupt the Archbishop's thoughts, so he just waited patiently in respectful silence. Despite only having heard half the conversation, he had a fair inkling of the result of the call. He'd been party to the assault on Hans Muntz, having helped to arrange it. Voitra had assured him that what they had to do was for the good of the Church, it was a matter of security. As soldiers of Christ they were duty bound to fight the enemies of the Church, and that explanation was good enough for Milan, who blindly obeyed the Archbishop in all things. In war, men sometimes had to do things that were unpalatable, the Archbishop had argued. A soldier's duty was to obey unquestioningly and to do that which had to be done.

When Archbishop Voitra had first learned of the document he'd done the right thing by alerting Cardinal Morova. The Archbishop had suspected the document was important, but he was unprepared for the volatile reaction from the Cardinal, who ordered him to Rome without delay. During a long meeting Cardinal Morova confided just enough information for Voitra to appreciate the gravity of the situation, and the need to get hold of the document employing whatever means necessary.

But now Milan was worried. During their brief meeting he had taken an instant liking to the Australians, and besides, they were fellow clergy. He was certain that Cardinal Morova was intent on having them murdered and most probably Hans Muntz as well. He was deeply troubled by this, but kept it to himself as he waited till his master chose to speak.

Finally, after what seemed like hours, Voitra spoke up. 'My dear, faithful Milan, we live in troubled and complicated times, and it is during extraordinary times like now that we are called upon to do extraordinary work for Mother Church, to protect Her. Do you understand that, Milan?'

Milan hesitated, not at all sure of what was coming, but fearing the worst. 'Yes, I think so, Eminence.' Looking troubled he then asked, 'Does the Cardinal mean to have the Australians …?' His voice trailed off, the question incomplete, as though he could not bring himself to say the word.

'Sometimes we are called upon to do things we do not understand, for reasons that may not be entirely clear to us at the time. Such a time is now, Milan.'

Hruska looked unconvinced, but said nothing.

Voitra continued. 'We must continue to have absolute and unshakeable faith in our Lord and Saviour. And we must extend that faith and trust to his emissaries on earth, our superiors, who in turn are answerable to the Holy Father himself. You do understand what I'm saying, Milan?'

'I think so, Eminence. Do you mean that the order to deal with the Australians is a direct order from the Pope?'

Voitra sighed. 'No, my son, that is not what I mean. But it is as though the order were from him. Cardinal Morova is a prince of the Church whose job is to protect the Church and the Pontiff. It is not our position to question him. He understands the bigger picture, things that we do not understand.'

Milan remained silent. There was no more to be said. To question his master was unthinkable, yet in his heart of hearts he harboured doubt. Murder is murder.

'I appreciate your loyalty more than you will ever know, my son,' Voitra continued, 'but in this instant I cannot ask you to become involved. I will attend to this myself. Please, get me the telephone number of the Russian and then leave me.'

Milan was leaving the office to get the number when Voitra called him back. 'Oh, and by the way Milan, did the Australians mention where they were staying in Prague?'

Milan hesitated before answering. He was about to lie, but could not bring himself to do so. 'Um, yes, Eminence, they mentioned it in their letter.'

'Very good. Get me the name of their hotel as well and then leave me.'

Milan carried out the orders, and then closed the office door. He hurried to his cell, where he put on a coat and quietly slipped out into the streets of Prague.

Chapter 24

⚓

Peter and Christina had taken rooms in a budget hotel in the old city. They were in Peter's room discussing what to do next when there was a hesitant knock on the door. The knock was so light that at first they ignored it, thinking it was someone knocking on the room next door. Then it came again, only this time slightly louder. Christina jumped up. 'There's someone at the door, Peter,' she announced.

Peter pressed his ear to the door, asking who it was. There was no answer, but the knock was repeated, this time more incessantly. 'Who is it?' he asked again. Again there was no response, but the knock was repeated yet again, and this time it was more like a hammering. Peter repeated in a louder and firmer voice, 'Who's there please?'

Following a moments' hesitation they heard a muffled response, 'It is me, Father LeSarus. Father Hruska, Milan. Please, let me in.'

Peter LeSarus opened the door, revealing the friendly priest. No sooner had the door opened a crack than Milan barged in, quickly closing the door behind him, securing it with the chain. There was visible fear in his eyes. 'Please, Father and Sister, you are in great danger. You must leave this hotel at once. Please do not ask me any questions. I am taking a great risk coming here to warn you. You must leave Europe and stop meddling. You do not understand what you are getting into.'

'Milan, Milan, slow down,' Peter said, holding up a hand, 'who exactly are we in danger from, and why?'

'Please! I said no questions. I have warned you. Now I must go. If you stay here you will die.'

They could tell the man was terrified as he headed back for the door. There was nothing more he was going to tell them, he just wanted out. He took the chain off the door. 'I warned you. I have done my duty. I can do no more. Leave! Now! Don't pack. Leave your things. Just get out.' He opened the door and was gone.

Peter and Christina looked at each other, then Christina, looking frightened, said, 'We, we'd be foolish to ignore him.'

Peter had difficulty concealing his own nervousness. 'All right,' he agreed. 'Let's just slip out and keep an eye on the place,' he suggested, 'see what happens. The way Milan was behaving, I'd say that if something was going to happen, it's going to happen soon.'

Heeding Milan's warning to the letter they hurried out of the room leaving all their belongings behind, a decision they would later regret.

They decided against the lift, choosing instead to walk down the three flights of stairs of the fire escape. Upon reaching the street they crossed the road to a café they'd been to earlier and settled down near the front window, where they had a clear view of the hotel across the street.

Neither of them knew what they were looking for and as they sat, sipping their coffees, numerous people came and went from the hotel. After about an hour a black car pulled up in front of the hotel. A large, burly figure stepped out of the car, pausing on the footpath. It was impossible to make out his features as he wore a great coat buttoned up to his chin, with a fedora hat pulled down over his eyes. He paused, looking up and down the street, and then hurried into the building. The driver of the vehicle remained in his seat with the engine running. Five minutes later the figure returned and with one more furtive glance up and down the street he climbed into the waiting car that drove off at a sedate speed. Peter and Christina exchanged nervous glances.

'Are you thinking what I'm thinking?' Christina asked.

At that instant they felt a reverberation, like an earthquake, except it wasn't the ground shaking. It felt more like a concussion of air. The front window of the café imploded, showering Peter and Christina with shattered glass. This was immediately followed by a deafening blast, and then all hell broke loose as a ball of flame erupted from the hotel they had left just over an hour ago.

Chapter 25

Following the explosion, pandemonium broke loose as people screamed and jostled, fighting to escape from the restaurant. Peter and Christina were caught up in the milieu of panicked people sweeping into the street. Once outside, the panic seemed to subside. Curiosity overcame initial terror as realisation dawned that the explosion had gone off in the hotel across the road, and not in the restaurant. Smoke was billowing from the upper floors as dazed people staggered, coughing and spluttering, into the street. The sound of a siren could be heard in the distance, and shortly this was multiplied as more emergency vehicles joined in. Within seconds a police car pulled up in front of the bombed hotel, followed by the first of the fire engines. The firemen jumped out even before their truck had stopped and began unrolling hoses. The scene appeared chaotic, yet organised.

Peter and Christina joined the gaping onlookers, surveying the smoking building from the pavement across the street. Policemen were pushing back the crowd, one warning that the building could come down and that the firemen needed room, while a second policeman, obviously the senior ranking of the two, ordered his colleague to start taking names and details of witnesses.

'I think we're in trouble,' Christina ventured, her voice shaking.

'I do believe it would be politic for us to discreetly leave,' suggested Peter, 'I don't think it's in our interest right now to be interviewed by the police.'

Christina stood transfixed, staring at the now blazing hotel. 'Oh, my God. I can't believe this is happening,'

'Come on, let's get out of here,' Peter said urgently, taking charge.

Christina followed without protest. They walked briskly, but not so fast as to draw attention to themselves. After a few blocks, Christina caught Peter by the arm. 'Where are we going, Peter? Everything we owned was in that hotel. Money, clothes, passports, all gone up in smoke.'

'I know that,' Peter answered a little testily, 'but at least we're alive.'

'That was meant for us, wasn't it?' Christina said, her voice shaking and on the verge of tears.

Peter cursed himself, blaming himself for placing Christina's life in jeopardy. 'We can't be sure of that,' he answered, lacking conviction, but not wanting to panic Christina. 'But either way, at least we've managed to buy ourselves some time.'

'What do you mean?' Christina asked.

'If that *was* meant for us, then whoever did it would think they've succeeded, and so they won't be looking for us.'

'That sounds reasonable,' Christina said nervously, 'but where do we go now? Without money, we don't have too many options.'

'I think we should head for somewhere where there are lots of people, that way we'll be protected by crowds. The central railway station would probably be our best bet.'

'Peter, I really think we should call Uncle Brian now,' Christina said.

Peter nodded, reluctantly agreeing. 'I'll call Brian. He may have connections over here. Our problem is that Australia doesn't have an embassy here, the nearest is in Budapest.'

When they arrived at the station, Peter went straight to a pay phone. 'You keep an eye out for anything unusual while I phone Brian. I suggest you keep an eye on the phone booth from a discreet distance. At least if someone is after us, it'll be harder for them if we're not together.'

Peter placed a collect, station-to-station call to Brian O'Shaughnessy, in Sydney, Australia. He heard a sleepy sounding O'Shaughnessy come on the line and accept the charges.

'Hello, Peter,' O'Shaughnessy greeted. 'All is well, I hope.'

'No, Brian, all is not well, I'm afraid. I think someone is trying to kill us, and we don't have much time, so just listen.'

Peter briefed O'Shaughnessy on what had happened, not going into too much detail, but emphasising they were in trouble and without cash or passports. He then asked O'Shaughnessy if he had contacts in Prague who could help them.

The sleepiness had disappeared from O'Shaughnessy's voice as he asked, 'Christina, is she all right?'

'Yes, she's fine,' Peter assured him, 'she's a little shaken by the experience, but apart from that she's fine. She's waiting for me outside the phone box.'

Peter heard the sigh of relief over the phone. 'Thank god for that. So where exactly are you now?' O'Shaughnessy asked in a clipped no-nonsense voice. 'OK. Stay on the line, don't hang up, I'll be right back to you.'

Peter heard music as he was put on hold.

⚜

O'Shaughnessy dialled a number in Vienna. A female's voice came on the line. In flawless German, O'Shaughnessy asked to be put through to Scott Emery.

'I'm sorry, sir, there is no one here by that name.'

O'Shaughnessy smiled to himself and said, 'This is Brian O'Shaughnessy. The 1967 class reunion is going ahead as planned.'

'May I have your telephone number, sir?'

O'Shaughnessy gave the number and the line went dead. He switched back to Peter. 'Are you still there, Peter?'

'Yes, I'm still here. What's taking so long?'

'Patience, dear fellow, I won't be long.' O'Shaughnessy heard the beep of an incoming call and placed Peter back on hold. 'O'Shaughnessy!' he announced into the phone.

Emery's familiar voice came across the line, 'What's the emergency, Brian?'

'Scott, good of you to get straight back,' O'Shaughnessy said unnecessarily, knowing that having received the code, Emery would contact him immediately irrespective of where he was, what he was doing or what time it was. It was a private code Emery had given him years before, only to be used for a top priority, life-threatening emergency. O'Shaughnessy had never needed to invoke it before, and was impressed it had worked.

'My niece, Christina, is in your part of the world, in Prague as a matter of fact. Seems she and her companion, a priest by the name of Peter LeSarus, have got themselves into a spot of bother. LeSarus said that someone just tried to kill them. Blew up the hotel they were staying in.'

'Were they at the Hotel Medvidku?'

'I've no idea.'

'I'm told it was bombed about twenty minutes ago.'

O'Shaughnessy marvelled at the extent of his friend's intelligence network. Nothing happened in Central Europe without Emery knowing about it.

Emery continued, 'As far as I know, it's a local police matter. No one's figured a motive yet. Where are they?'

O'Shaughnessy repeated Peter's exact whereabouts.

'Tell them to stay put. I'll have a man with them inside of twenty minutes.'

'Thanks Scott, I owe you. How will he know who they are?'

'How are they dressed?'

'Hold on.' In a moment O'Shaughnessy was back on the line. 'They're dressed like a priest and a nun.'

'OK. Tell your niece and her friend that my man will identify himself by asking, 'What platform does the train to Waterloo depart from?' They're to reply, 'You'll need to go to Paddington Station.'

The line went dead.

O'Shaughnessy switched back to Peter and relayed the instructions, warning him to be careful.

'Peter, one more thing,' O'Shaughnessy began. 'Have you been able to find out anything more about the papyrus?'

Peter decided to tell him the bad news. 'It looks like it's been stolen, Brian. It looks like Cardinal Morova's behind it.'

'MOROVA! But how …?'

Peter explained the connection between Muntz, Archbishop Voitra, and Cardinal Morova. The line was silent for a while, and for a moment Peter thought he'd been disconnected.

'This is bad, very bad. I'll need time to think,' O'Shaughnessy finally answered. 'And Peter, please take care of Christina. She's all I have,' he added weakly.

⚜

Exactly eighteen minutes after Peter hung up, a nondescript looking man approached them. He asked Peter a question in Czech, to which Peter gestured that he didn't understand. 'I'm sorry,' he said, 'I only speak English.'

'Ah, but I also speak English,' the man stated proudly in a heavy Czech accent.

Peter wondered if this was their contact, but decided it wasn't. The man looked too pedestrian and Slavic. He continued to look around, his eyes searching through the crowds.

'Have you got a light?' the man asked Peter, holding his unlit cigarette towards him.

'No.' Peter wished the man would go away. 'Look, I'm sorry, but I don't smoke.'

'You are lucky, it is a dirty habit,' the man said, flicking the unlit cigarette away. 'Then perhaps you could tell me what platform the train to Waterloo is departing from?'

Peter was caught completely by surprise, and at first said nothing, staring at the man. Trying to compose himself he said, 'What? I mean, no, it doesn't go from here. Waterloo is in England. No, I'm sorry. That's not what I was supposed to say. What I meant to say was, you'll have to go to Baker Street Station, no, I mean Paddington. That's what I meant to say. You'll have to go to Paddington Station.' Peter was totally flustered by now.

The man smiled. 'You're not used to this sort of thing are you?' His Czech accent had disappeared, replaced by an American drawl. 'Come on, grab your lady friend and follow me. I've got a car waiting outside.'

As they walked towards the car Christina said to Peter, 'Baker Street Station? Smooth, James Bond, smooth.'

Well, at least she still has her sense of humour, Peter thought.

As they left the confines of the station, there was a black Skoda parked at the front entrance in the five-minute passenger pick-up space. The man opened the back door, gesturing to Peter and a wide-eyed Christina to get in. Slamming the door behind them, he climbed into the front beside the waiting driver, who immediately sped off, even before the door had closed.

As they raced through the streets of Prague, the two passengers in the back were thrown wildly from side-to-side.

Peter tried to steady himself as he thanked his rescuer, asking where they were being taken.

'My instructions are to get you off the streets. We'll go to an American safe house. I have no idea what happens after that.'

Neither the man nor the driver volunteered further information. They drove on in silence, twisting through the narrow, cobbled streets of the ancient city. Turning on to the Letna

Bridge, they crossed the Vltava River, leaving the old city behind them. They continued on through the new city and the traffic began to thin as they entered the suburbs and eventually the surrounding countryside. They hurtled on for a couple of hours, the driver never letting up speed, until they reached the small town of Usti, where they finally turned into the driveway of a country cottage. The driver pressed a remote control and the garage silently opened, closing behind them as they drove in.

'Well, here we are,' the American announced. 'You can get out now, you're safe.'

They climbed out of the car, gratefully stretching stiff muscles. The American led them through a door at the back of the garage, which opened directly into the house.

'Where are we?' Peter asked.

'As I said, you're safe for now. Everything you need is here. The fridge is stocked, there's a full larder and a good selection of clean clothing in various sizes in the wardrobes. Male as well as female,' he added for Christina's benefit. 'You'll find toiletries in the bathroom, including unused toothbrushes, and ah, female needs.'

Christina raised an eyebrow.

The American didn't look at Peter or Christina as he scanned the walls, as if checking to see that the building was OK. 'All I ask is that you don't venture out,' he said. 'This is a small town, and strangers attract attention and questions. The telephone is a direct line to our office. If you need anything, or if there's trouble, all you have to do is pick up the phone. It'll be answered immediately. If you need to make a phone call to anywhere in the world, you'll be patched through. It's quite safe and untraceable.'

Peter had guessed that O'Shaughnessy would be well connected, but even so, he was impressed and curious. 'May I ask who you are,' he said, 'and why you are going to so much trouble for us?'

'Who we are isn't important. Why are we helping you? That's simple. Because Scott Emery told us to.'

Peter turned to Christina and mouthed, 'Scott Emery?'

Christina shrugged and mouthed back, 'No idea.'

'Oh, and by the way,' the American continued. 'Scott sends his regards and asked me to tell you he'll be here personally in the morning. Meanwhile, make yourselves comfortable, relax, and remember, don't go out of the house under any circumstances. There's booze in the bar, but I suggest you keep your wits about you.'

Chapter 26

The next morning Christina and Peter were up early. Christina was preparing breakfast when they heard the garage door opening. A car drove in and the door closed behind it. The engine was cut and they heard the car door open and slam shut, followed by footsteps crossing the garage floor. The door opened and in walked the American who had picked them up the previous evening. He was accompanied by a large man with greying hair, which would once have been jet black. He had a swarthy complexion, was of Middle Eastern appearance and was dressed in an expensive looking suit. The man looked to be in his late middle age and even with the generous belly hanging over his belt, he still had the look of someone not to mess with.

The American introduced the newcomer as Scott Emery.

'Mr Emery, it's a pleasure to meet you,' Peter greeted, extending his hand, 'Christina and I are very grateful to you for arranging to bail us out last night.'

'The name's Scott,' Emery grinned, pumping Peter's hand in a vice-like grip.

Peter found himself taking an instant liking to the man. 'OK, thanks, Scott.'

'Good to meet you too, Father Pete.' He turned to Christina, taking her hand, he raised it to his mouth, barely brushing it with his lips, causing Christina to smile at the old fashioned, chivalrous gesture. Emery threw an envelope on to the kitchen table. 'I think you'll be needing these.'

Peter picked up the envelope, and opening it, found two passports. He flicked through them and was amazed they were duplicate passports for himself and Christina, and were even appropriately stamped showing their past itinerary, ensuring there would be no border problems. Once again Peter marvelled at O'Shaughnessy's influence.

'I believe you met Tony last night,' Emery said, gesturing to his companion. 'Tony Gadaleta, meet Father Peter LeSarus and Sister Christina Kelly, Brian's niece.'

Christina handed Gadaleta and Emery a steaming cup of coffee, asking, 'Will you join us for breakfast? I was about to dish up.'

'Best offer I've had all day, considering I've been driving half the night to get here. What about you, Tony?'

Gadaleta declined, explaining he'd already eaten.

After they'd finished eating Christina began to clear the table and Emery got right down to business.

'Brian tells me you're in trouble, something to do with the bombing of the Hotel Medvidku. So tell me, what do you know about it and how are you involved?'

'Ah, sorry,' Peter said, 'I mean we are grateful for all you've done, but, ah, would it be asking too much to tell us who you are? I mean, who you work for?'

Emery laughed. 'Yep, fair question, I guess. CIA,' he said, flicking open a wallet revealing the impressively official CIA ID. He only gave Peter and Christina a cursory glance before flipping the wallet closed again, and returning it to his inside jacket pocket. 'When I was posted to the Italian bureau,' he continued, 'I met Brian when he was seconded to the Vatican Bank. Lucca Morova, who was the boss of the bank at the time, introduced me to him. Brian and I became close buddies. We haven't seen each other since his little problem, but we stayed in touch. Anyway, he called me and told me you were in a jam, and so here I am.'

For the next hour Peter and Christina filled Gadaleta and Emery in on what had brought them to Europe and all that had transpired since they arrived. The two men listened attentively, occasionally interrupting to clear up a point.

When they'd finished, Gadaleta asked Emery, 'Do you think it's possible there may be a connection?'

'I guess anything's possible,' Emery answered.

'Connection to what?' Christina asked.

Gadaleta said, 'The recent escalation in terrorism.'

'What are you saying, Tony?' Peter asked. 'Are you suggesting the Catholic Church may be tied in with terrorism?'

'Not necessarily the Catholic Church,' Emery replied, 'but there's no denying that every religion has its fair share of fanatics. This document the archaeologist, Muntz, uncovered – what do you know about it?'

Christina answered. 'It's a prophecy, purportedly written thousands of years ago by a king called Mentonidus of Mesopotamia. Prior to Muntz finding it, historians agreed Mentonidus was mythical. Well, Muntz's discovery would seem to indicate that the king existed, but how much of the legend is true is debatable. What is extraordinary, however, is the degree of accuracy of his prophecies relative to what we now know to be historical facts. The king foretold the coming of Christ and made reference to the revelations at Fatima. We now know that Archbishop Voitra was prepared to go to any length to get his hands on the papyrus.'

Gadaleta said, 'This Muntz character, you say you thought he may have been coherent when you visited him, but you couldn't be sure?'

'That's right,' Peter replied.

'So when you told the Archbishop that Muntz was lucid, that was a bluff?'

'Yes.'

'That's good, that's very good.' Gadaleta mused, 'It just may push Morova to tip his hand. Any idea if there is a copy of the prophecy?'

'We do know that there was at least one copy of the translation in his safe when the original Papyrus was stolen. It's not there now.'

'I see, and what about this other document you mentioned, the Third Secret of Fatima,' Gadaleta said, referring to his notebook. 'What else can you tell us about that?'

'As far as we know,' Christina answered, 'it has never seen the light of day since arriving at the Vatican. Whether or not it still exists is anybody's guess.'

Emery asked, 'Do you think there is a connection with the Muntz document?'

'Apart from the prophecy referring to it, who's to say. It may only be coincidence,' Christina said. 'That's what we were trying to find out. My uncle suspects a conspiracy.'

'At first, I thought Christina's uncle was being paranoid,' Peter admitted.

'Paranoia doesn't blow up hotels,' Emery said. 'From what you've told me, I wouldn't rule out a conspiracy, and of course if the Church is involved, there may be a crossover of national borders, which naturally would be of interest to the CIA. Whether or not there is a connection with terrorists remains to be seen, although at this point I'd suggest we don't have any hard facts supporting that, one way or another.'

'So where does that leave us?' Peter asked.

'Unfortunately, right now we don't have a mandate to investigate any of this in an official capacity. We have suspicions, but no hard proof. But that doesn't stop us from doing some nosing around out of pure curiosity, just to see where it may all lead. What do you think, Tony?' Emery asked.

'Well, I sure as hell am fascinated. I figure it merits some digging around.'

'What about the people who are trying to kill us?' Christina asked.

'We don't know for sure that the bomb was meant for you,' Emery said.

'Although there is circumstantial evidence which would seem to suggest it was,' Gadaleta continued, 'it could still be a coincidence.'

Emery said, 'And if it is a coincidence, then that Hruska guy's warning may still be valid.'

'What do you mean?' Peter asked, frowning.

'What I mean is, that if the bomb was not meant for you, and if Hruska's warning is to be taken seriously, then someone is still looking for you.'

Peter was sorry he had asked.

'But let's not go jumping to conclusions,' Emery said, noticing the worried looks on Peter's and Christina's faces. 'Meanwhile, the sooner we get Hans Muntz into unofficial protective custody, the better.'

Emery picked up the phone and almost immediately identified himself. 'This is Emery, patch me through to my office please.' There was a slight pause. 'We need to do an urgent snatch. Subject: Hans Muntz. He's in a medical clinic and is oblivious to his surroundings. Yes, it's top priority. I have reason to believe his life is in danger. We'll need to get him to a safe house with medical facilities.' He then gave details of where the clinic was. Peter marvelled at the man's memory. He'd only told him all the details once. 'Call me the minute you have him.'

They all agreed that Peter would accompany Gadaleta and Emery on a visit to see Father Hruska and that for the time being, Christina would remain within the sanctuary of the safe house.

Alone in the safe house Christina felt strange, experiencing a weird combination of shock, fear and boredom. She decided she was suffering from a mild case of post-traumatic stress.

It's hardly surprising, she thought. It isn't every day that someone tries to kill you. I need to get my mind off all this.

She walked toward a bookcase in the living room. There were books in German, Czech, French and even an Asian language she couldn't identify. She found herself wondering about the previous tenants. Who were they and why or how they had come to be here? She finally found some books in English.

The Bellini Blueprint, *The Caravaggio Conundrum*, *The Donatello Dilemma*, she read, but none of the titles held her attention. Finally she settled on another, *The Brownian Motion*. She tried reading a few pages but found the premise ludicrous, the characters two-dimensional and the plot ridiculous. Exhausted, she quickly fell asleep on the couch.

Chapter 27

When Father Hruska opened the door to the Archbishop's residence in Karlova Ulice in Stare Mesto, meaning the old city, he was not surprised to see who was standing there.

'Thank God, you are all right, Father LeSarus. Is Sister Kelly also safe?' Milan asked, concern written all over his face.

Peter nodded. 'Yes, she's fine, Milan.' He gestured to his companions. 'Milan, I'd like you to meet Mr Emery and Mr Gadaleta. They helped us out.' Hruska acknowledged the men with a wan smile. He looked nervous.

'May we come in, please?' Peter asked. 'There are some questions we must ask you.'

'I have been expecting you,' Hruska said. 'The Archbishop said you would not give it up.' He glanced furtively up and down the street. 'But yes, please come in quickly. It is not safe.' They entered the residence and Hruska quickly closed the door behind them. 'Please, come this way.'

He hurried them down a passageway, past the outer office where Peter and Christina had first met him. He gestured with a finger to his mouth, beckoning them to be quiet as they scurried noiselessly along another corridor. Finally he stopped at a door and, opening it, gestured them to enter. They found themselves in a sparsely furnished cell, with a single bed pressed against the far corner of the tiny room. There was a small writing desk, with a straight-backed chair and an uncomfortable looking single seat sofa. The only other furnishing was a wooden kneeler propped against a wall adorned with a crucifix. The knee padding was torn, with stuffing hanging out, and all in all, the room was depressing.

'This is my room,' Hruska announced unnecessarily, 'I am sorry, I cannot make you more comfortable, but here we will not be disturbed.' He smiled sheepishly at Peter. 'I am so glad you are not hurt.'

'We had to speak to you, Milan,' Peter began, 'but firstly, thanks for the warning.'

Hruska gestured towards the bed, 'Please, please to sit down,' as he seated himself on his one chair, facing the bed, with his back leaning against the desk. 'I had no choice. This has gone far enough. I could not, in my conscience, do nothing.'

Peter sat on the bed, while the other men chose to stand.

'So you knew the hotel was going to be bombed?' Emery asked, towering over Hruska's seated form.

'No. I did not know how it was going to be done,' he turned to Peter, 'but I knew your lives were in immediate danger and I had to warn you. I just pray that noone else was hurt or killed.'

'Father Hruska,' Emery continued, 'it's time to be frank with each other.' He spoke slowly, pronouncing each word precisely, so as to be sure the young priest understood him. 'I am a senior officer with the CIA, which means I work for the American government intelligence arm. Mr Gadaleta and I are also accredited officers of Interpol, the International Police.' He paused. 'Do you understand, Father?'

Hruska nodded.

Emery continued. 'We have reason to believe that an attempt has been made on the lives of Father LeSarus and Sister Kelly. My colleague and I,' he said gesturing to Gadaleta, 'have an interest in the case from a wider perspective. You see, we suspect the possibility of international terrorism.'

Emery paused again to give Hruska time to digest this information and allow the enormity of it to sink in. The young priest sat silently impassive, displaying no emotion.

'From what I've been told,' Emery went on, 'I have reason to believe that your boss, the Archbishop, was responsible for the attempt on their lives.' Emery sat on the edge of Hruska's desk, and looking directly down into the young priest's eyes, he asked, 'Now tell me Father, who else is involved?'

Hruska squirmed under the penetrating gaze of the intelligence man, and stood up from the chair. He paced as far as the limiting confines of the room would allow and then turned. He lifted his hands in a helpless, palms-up gesture. 'Mr Emery, it is not as simple as you may think.' He then turned towards Peter as though looking to him for support. Peter gave a slight nod, which seemed to encourage Hruska to continue. 'Archbishop Voitra is good man. I have worked for him since I became a priest. He ordained me. He was a brave and heroic man during the uprising against the Communists. He is now very depressed. He is, ah, how do you say it?' he struggled, looking for the right words, 'He is out of his depth, drowning even.'

'Perhaps you'd better explain, Father,' Emery pressed.

'He is acting under orders from a much higher authority.' Emery glanced knowingly at Gadaleta. Hruska continued. 'But even the Archbishop is now having serious doubts.'

'Doubts about what?' Gadaleta pressed.

'War is war. Even Popes, they rode into war in the early days of the Church, and they killed enemies of the Christ. But that was on battlegrounds. This is assassination he has now been ordered to commit. It cannot be right.'

'Who issued those orders, Father?' Emery asked.

'That I cannot say.'

'Cannot, or will not?'

Hruska ignored Gadaleta's prompting. 'But what I can say is this. When his friend Hans Muntz showed him the papyrus he found, the Archbishop became disturbed over what it contained. I remember him saying that the writings were of a diabolical nature, and could only be the work of Satan. He said to me that the document could finish up the Church. He even used a word, which I think translates to English meaning, Armageddon. You know, the end of the world. He prayed for many days, non-stop. He told me he was not capable to handle such big problems. He then decided to get guidance of what to do from Rome.'

Emery interrupted. 'So Rome gave the order? Who in Rome? Give me a name,' he demanded. 'A city doesn't go around giving orders.'

They were suddenly interrupted as the door opened, and there stood none other than the Archbishop himself. 'Good evening, gentlemen, I heard voices.'

Hruska stared in disbelief, his face red.

'Excellency, I, I did not ask them here, they came …'

'It's all right, Milan,' Voitra reassured him. 'Father LeSarus, you will never know how delighted I am to see you again, safe and sound. I don't believe I have met these other two gentlemen, Milan?'

Hruska hurriedly introduced Gadaleta and Emery.

'I am pleased to make your acquaintance gentlemen, and I am glad you have come. There are things I need to discuss. Won't you come to my office? We will be more comfortable there.'

⸘❦⸘

Once the three visitors, as well as Hruska, had settled themselves in his office the Archbishop addressed Peter without preamble.

'Father LeSarus, again I repeat how pleased I am to see you are alive and well. And your travelling companion, I do hope she is also well.'

207

Peter assured him that Christina was just fine.

'I have been stupid, Father LeSarus, and I fear I have committed a mortal sin. But that is between God and me, and I can only pray for His forgiveness. But meanwhile, I believe I owe you and your friends an explanation. It is true, I arranged for you and your friend to be eliminated. It is also true that I was instrumental in causing my friend, Professor Muntz, to become a virtual prisoner within his own body. What I am now going to tell you is not an excuse for my actions but an explanation as to why, I, an archbishop of the Catholic Church, has stooped to deceit and attempted murder. What I have done is unforgivable, and once I have unburdened myself by relating the facts, then I will be happy to turn myself over to you gentlemen in your official capacity as international policemen.'

Emery said, 'Let's not worry about anyone getting arrested for now, Excellency. Why don't you just go ahead and tell us what it is you know. I can't give any guarantees, but I'm sure my colleague here,' gesturing to Gadaleta, 'would back me when I say that your cooperation would be taken into consideration, should this ever go to trial.'

Gadaleta nodded his agreement.

'Very well then,' Voitra said. 'You know that Hans Muntz and I were close friends, before his, ah, unfortunate, illness. When he discovered the papyrus at Nag Hammadi, Hans was very excited, but his initial excitement turned to deep concern after he had translated it, and so he sought my advice from the viewpoint of a cleric. He told me it was potentially more damaging and controversial to the Church than anything he had ever seen before. I agreed to read his translation, expecting nothing more than an elaboration on the previously discovered and discredited Gospels.

'What I read was disturbing to say the least, and I went into a panic of indecision as to what to do about it. I wished with all my heart that it had not been brought to my attention. I realised it was beyond my scope of experience or authority to deal with. I had to confide in someone, someone who could deal with the potential ramifications it presented.'

Voitra paused. 'What I read, gentlemen, is potential Armageddon for the world as we know it, and believe me, I am not exaggerating. What Muntz had unearthed was a papyrus document that had been carbon dated to nearly two thousand years before Christ. The document had undergone extensive scientific testing. It was genuine. It was amazingly well preserved but, unlike the Nag Hammadi Gospels, it was written in ancient Assyrian, a language in which coincidentally Muntz is a recognised authority. Nevertheless, it still took him a long time to translate. One of the reasons it took so long was his indisposition to believe what he was reading. He kept thinking he had made a mistake in the translation, and so he would laboriously keep going back over his work, checking and re-checking till finally he was convinced the translation he'd completed was as accurate as was humanly possible.'

Gadaleta interrupted. 'You mentioned the document has been carbon dated to two thousand years before Christ?'

'One thousand seven hundred years to be precise,' Voitra replied.

'Is it possible to fake the dating?' Gadaleta asked.

'I asked the same question of Hans, because you must understand I am no expert in these things. He assured me it is not possible to deceive carbon dating devices, but it is possible to forge ancient documents.'

'I don't understand the difference,' Peter said.

'Perhaps I can shed some light on that,' Emery offered. 'I was once involved in an international fraud case involving the forgery of priceless works of art. The forgers got hold of blank canvases that were of the same circa as the originals they wished to forge.

They even managed to get hold of pigment from the same period. They ground this in the same way the old masters used to do. The art forger then used this material to do his work, and when the paintings were presented for sale they passed all carbon dating technology and were deemed original.'

'Yes, I remember you telling me about that case,' Gadaleta said, 'but they came unstuck, as I recall.'

'Yes,' Emery agreed, 'a dealer became suspicious about the authenticity of one piece and had it subjected to a relatively new scientific method, something called prism cryptography. Don't ask me how it works exactly, but it dates to within a year when the medium was placed on to the canvas. In other words, it tells us when the picture was painted. Before that we could only ascertain the age of the canvas and the materials used.'

'That is exactly what Hans told me,' Voitra agreed. 'He told me that he'd had the papyrus subjected to that prism test. Anyway, he was convinced that not only the material was authentic in its age, but it coincided with the year it had been written.

'Hans and I had been friends for many years and as I was an archbishop and his close friend, he figured I would be able to offer advice on what to do about the prophecy. Following my reading of his translation, I became deeply perplexed and afraid. I told him it was beyond me, and that I would like to seek advice and counsel from Rome. Muntz agreed for me to take Cardinal Lucca Morova, the Vatican Secretary of State, into our confidence.'

Gadaleta shot Emery a look, as though to say, 'Aha, at last we have a name.'

'So I wrote to Cardinal Morova,' Voitra continued, 'briefly explaining the matter about which I sought guidance and counsel. As soon as Cardinal Morova received my letter he telephoned me, ordering me to personally bring the papyrus to Rome immediately. Muntz would not hear of it. He simply would not agree to let it out of his sight. He did agree, although reluctantly at first, to allow me to at least take a copy of the translation.

'When I was finally ushered into the Cardinal's office, he bade me sit down and without preliminaries asked, "Have you brought the document?"

'I explained that Professor Muntz would not hear of letting the original out of his sight, but that I had copy of his translation.

"Then please give it to me." Cardinal Morova ordered brusquely. I handed him the translation, and without a word, he began to read eagerly. He said nothing till he had digested the entire document, nor did he display any emotion, so it was difficult for me to gauge a reaction to the reading. When he finally finished, he purposefully unlocked a drawer behind his desk, where he placed the document, re-locking it, and returned the key to his pocket. I remember thinking at the time that this was presumptuous, considering it was neither his, nor my property to dispose of. He removed his spectacles and seemed lost in deep thought. It was almost as though he had forgotten I was in the room. It never occurred to me to disturb his thoughts so I just sat still, awaiting his pleasure.

'Finally he seemed to come to a decision. He rose to his feet and took me by the arm, gesturing for me to accompany him.

"Come, Archbishop Voitra," he said. "It is such a beautiful day, it would be a shame to spoil it by spending it in a stuffy office. Please join me, and I will show you through the beautiful Vatican gardens."

'I followed him onto a veranda overlooking vast, manicured lawns, interspersed with the odd tree. He led me down the stairs and on to the lawn, explaining that this was a side of the Vatican rarely seen by tourists. There were a number of people wandering on the lawn, most of them priests or nuns, with a smattering of the purple and scarlet of bishops and cardinals. Most of these people seemed to be engrossed in deep, animated conversation, but whenever we came close to a group the conversation would abruptly stop, and Cardinal Morova was greeted with a nod of respect, and what I thought was a tinge of fear.

"This is one of my favourite retreats," Morova explained as we began to walk across the lawns. "One can speak candidly without fear of being overheard."

'We continued on in silence, till finally we reached a bench beneath a large, spreading oak tree. Cardinal Morova invited me to sit beside him on the bench. From this vantage spot we had a clear view of the wide expanse of lawn, and it would have been impossible for anyone to approach us without us first observing them from a long way off. "Can't be too careful," the Cardinal said, as he surveyed the grounds. "Now tell me," he said, "who else has read this?"

"To my knowledge, no one, Eminence," I replied.

"Good, and that is the way it must remain," he cautioned.

'The Cardinal then went on to explain that the prophecy document was the work of the devil, who had been undermining the Church for centuries. Only those in the highest echelons of power within the Vatican were privy to the extent of this ongoing battle between good and evil. He continued on to explain that the Church had been uneasily expecting such a document to appear, and that it was meant to undermine faith in the Church and its leaders. What he told me next truly astounded me. I will endeavour to repeat his words as exactly as I can recall them.

"Have you ever wondered, my dear Archbishop, why the Church has suppressed the so called Third Secret of Fatima so steadfastly?"

'I responded that naturally I had given it some thought, especially in 1960. "Well, let me now give you the true facts of the matter," Cardinal Morova said. "A long time ago, following a direct revelation from God himself to the Holy Father, it was made clear that the revelations of Fatima were a hoax, perpetuated by Satan. The Prince of Darkness orchestrated all the miracles evident at the time of the so-called appearance of the Virgin to the shepherd children. The children themselves, it was revealed, were disciples of Satan."

'The appearances at Fatima stand out as the most important occurrences in the modern history of the Church, and their authenticity had been officially ratified by the Vatican. Well gentlemen, you can imagine the turmoil I went through upon hearing this extraordinary revelation from the Cardinal Secretary of State. My first reaction, naturally, was one of utter disbelief. Morova had anticipated this for he went on.

"I hardly expect you to take my word for this, Archbishop, but if you consider, and use logic, then you will conclude that what I have told you makes sense. Why else would the Pope disregard a directive from the Blessed Virgin, if it truly were Her edict? But please, don't take my word for this. It is important you believe what I have told you, particularly in light of this new document you have now brought to our attention. This is a matter of the gravest concern to the Holy See and, as such, requires immediate retaliatory action. To allow this to be revealed to the world would cause such confusion and anxiety among the world's faithful that Satan would undoubtedly achieve his aim of bringing down Christ's Church and all it stands for. The world would enter a period of chaos and darkness hitherto unknown. Evil would finally triumph and the only foreseeable end would be Armageddon. My dear Archbishop, unwittingly you have now become a key player in this ancient drama of good against evil. I must make you understand where you stand and where good stands against evil. His Holiness is not well, as you know, but I feel it is important enough to disturb his rest so that you can hear this from his own mouth. I will request an audience immediately."

'Cardinal Morova had played his hand well for I was aware of the sorry state of His Holiness' health, and the thought of disturbing him was abhorrent. I felt churlish to have doubted the word of the second most senior minister within the Church. I hastily fell into the Cardinal's trap by assuring him it was not necessary to disturb the Pontiff. His bluff had worked. I took him for his word.

"Your faith will be rewarded, my son," he assured me. He then went on to explain that there was absolutely no doubt that my friend Hans Muntz was in league with the devil, for was it not he, who had been chosen to deliver Satan's missive to the world? I argued against this logic by saying, "But Eminence, if Professor Muntz is in league with the devil why would he have brought the papyrus to my attention, and allowed me to deliver it to you?"

'This seemed to stump him for a moment, but not for long. "I grant you," he conceded, "that you may have a point there. I suppose it is not beyond the realms of possibility that your friend, the archaeologist, may be an unwitting party to all of this. Satan's pawn, so to speak. It is not without precedent after all, that men do the work of the devil without knowing it."

'He then gave elaborate instructions on what I was to say to Hans, in order to retrieve the original papyrus and deliver it to the Vatican. Failure on his part to do so would confirm he is working for Satan.

'From Rome I went directly to Vienna where I called on Hans. I explained what Cardinal Morova had told me to tell him. Hans's reaction was anything but cooperative. He flew into a rage, saying his trust in me had been misguided. He accused Cardinal Morova and me of collaborating to steal his precious discovery and ordered me out of his home.

214

'I returned to Prague from where I telephoned the Cardinal, explaining Hans' reactions to his request. I was ordered to retrieve the document immediately and at any cost, and to have Hans killed in the process. He went on to explain that we were Christ's soldiers fighting the battle, which had begun since before time immemorial and when in a justified battle, soldiers must kill.

'This placed me in a quandary of despair. I believed the Cardinal, but what he had ordered me to do was against everything I held sacred. At this point I felt an uncontrollable need to confide in someone else. I just could not make this decision alone, despite my belief in the Cardinal. And so it was, that I decided to bring Father Hruska into my confidence. Even as I made this decision I felt as though I were betraying the Cardinal, to whom I had already sworn my faith and allegiance.'

At this point, Archbishop Voitra paused, casting an affectionate look at the young priest. Milan Hruska took up the story.

'When the Archbishop returned from his trip to Rome I knew that something was wrong, for I had never seen him in such a disturbed state. He heard nothing I said. His mind was elsewhere. The following morning he did not even say mass, which is unheard of. It was not my place however to question or probe what was troubling him. I waited anxiously, hoping I could be of help. Then, a couple of nights after his return, he called for me. He told me everything that had transpired and asked for my counsel. I was overwhelmed that he should trust me so implicitly as to seek my counsel on a matter of such gravity. Although I did not get to read the document he gave me a vague understanding of its contents and the ramifications of it being revealed to the world. He told me it was preferable that I do not get to read it, for the sake of my own state of mind. I was humbled by his trust and the high esteem in which he held me. He needed reassurance that he was doing the right thing, and I gentlemen, gave him that reassurance, and therefore, if there is guilt here, then I must share it.

'I undertook to carry out the instructions on his behalf and ordered the theft of the document. We agreed not to cross the ultimate line by having Professor Muntz put to death, but rather agreed to have him incarcerated as it were, within the confines of his own mind.'

'So, gentlemen,' Voitra said, 'you now know everything.'

'What changed your mind, Archbishop?' Gadaleta asked.

Voitra took his time before he answered, weighing up his words carefully. 'Prayer, prayer, and a lot of it. I examined my conscience and finally came to the conclusion that this was wrong. It was not a course of action that Christ would have taken.'

'And what about you, Milan?' Peter asked. 'You warned us, so you must have changed your mind earlier. Why?'

'It was because of you, Father LeSarus, and your friend, Sister Christina. It was one thing to steal a document and to incapacitate one man, but then to kill a nun and a fellow priest ... well, let us just say I am a good judge of character. I knew within my heart that you are good people. And besides,' he added with a grin, 'you are from Australia.'

'Thank goodness for that,' Peter said.

'So what do you think is the Cardinal's motive in all this?' Emery asked.

'I'm not sure,' Voitra replied, 'but I do know that he will stop at nothing to suppress the prophecy.'

'You read the prophecy, Archbishop,' Emery continued, 'I think it's about time you let us in on what it's all about.'

Voitra answered, 'I'm afraid I can't do that. I can't tell you more than what I've already revealed. You see, strange as it may seem now, Mr Emery, I am still bound by my promise to my friend, Hans Muntz. I gave him my word that I would only discuss the contents with the most senior Church official beside the Pope.'

Emery snorted in disgust. 'So, it's okay to steal the original document and put Professor Muntz into some kind of a coma, just barely short of killing him, but you hold the line at breaking your word to him. Jesus.' He shook his head in amazement.

'I believe I could come up with one or two motives,' Peter ventured. 'Preservation of the status quo of the Church for one. Or, as crazy as this may seem, the Cardinal himself is in league with the devil. Or, he's just insane.'

'I think I could live with the latter,' Gadaleta ventured. 'I'm afraid I don't hold too much store with all this Omen and Exorcist stuff.' He held the index finger of each hand to his head in a mock gesture of devil horns, while at the same time sticking out his tongue. He chuckled, 'Good movies, but really …'

Abruptly Emery spoke up, 'What do you mean by preserving the status quo of the Church, Peter?'

'Well, it's only a theory but the Church has had little tolerance for change throughout its history. Whatever the secret is, it's my guess that it has the potential to shake things up in a big way. Isn't it conceivable that if something or someone were to disturb the Church's status quo, that all hell would break loose in the upper halls of power? Isn't it possible that there are powers within the hierarchy that would do anything to keep control?'

Emery said, 'Whichever way you look at it, we are left with a dilemma. I respect your theory, Peter, but that's all it is at this point. Archbishop, I urge you to report back to Morova as though nothing untoward has happened. He must believe you still have his trust. Assure him that Peter and Christina, as well as Muntz, have been taken care of.'

217

Voitra looked uneasy at the prospect of lying to Morova. Although he had made the decision to go against him, he was still afraid of him. He felt a deep unease, bordering on superstitious dread, at the consequences of misleading him. 'You mean, tell him they've been killed?' he asked.

'That is precisely what I mean.'

'What purpose would that serve?' the Archbishop asked, perplexed and looking uneasy.

'To buy us time, Archbishop, and in the meantime, unless you've forgotten, your dear friend is still in danger. Here's my card. You can get me on that number at any time. If anything untoward happens, please call me immediately.'

* * *

Voitra waited a long time after the three men had gone. He dreaded the thought, but he knew there was no turning back now. He made the call to Morova, his fingers trembling with every turn of the dial.

Chapter 28

Morova replaced the phone in its cradle. The conversation with Archbishop Voitra had left him feeling uneasy, and instinctively he knew he was in trouble. He sat brooding for a long time, his hand still resting on the phone, staring at it, as if it may hold the answer. And then, as if to confirm his apprehension, he felt the fit coming on. It was always the same feeling. He'd lived with it long enough to know it was coming. It started with a strange feeling of becoming disconnected from his body and then, as always, he would become aware of the presence in the room. The hairs on his neck bristled and he shuddered as he felt the familiar cold chill as the temperature in the room seemed to plummet. Then came the musty odour as the air in the room became stale, reminding him of a time he had entered a crypt, which had been opened after being sealed for centuries. A faint whiff of what smelled like sulphur assaulted his nostrils and he marvelled that after all these years he had never become accustomed to the malevolent presence that seemed to invade the depths of his mind. Once again, like all the times before, he felt fear. Morova was grateful the dark one seemed to prefer the shadows of his mind, where he could not quite make out the features. He'd only ever looked into those eyes once in all the years, and the memory still haunted him with vivid nightmares.

Morova quickly reached into the top drawer of his desk, fumbling for the pills that sometimes managed to keep the fit at bay. He unscrewed the lid with shaking hands, and in his haste the pills spilled out onto the floor. Frantically he went down on his hands and knees, groping desperately. His hand closed over one and he thrust it into his mouth, swallowing without water.

He walked over to the divan and stretched out, shutting his eyes, trying to relax, giving the pill every chance to work its magic. As he lay there his mind went back to the first time he'd met the Dark One, as it invariably did whenever he was confronted with the presence.

He had been a young man then, only recently ordained to the priesthood. He recalled his motivation for taking Holy Orders, smiling to himself at the memory.

He had been born into a wealthy, influential Italian family of newspaper barons. His grandfather founded the original newspaper that his father then turned into a conglomerate. His father's political influence was so powerful that on more than one occasion he'd been considered responsible for the toppling of governments. A staunch conservative, he hated communists and, rumour had it, he was connected within mafia circles.

Lucca was born late in the Morovas' marriage, which had already produced a sister and brother twelve and fifteen years his senior. By the time Lucca was born his siblings had already been tempered to the ruthless Morova-style of business where winning and beating your adversary, no matter what the cost, counted for everything. To have expected the older Morova children to dote on their new baby brother would have been a mistake, for they considered little Lucca a nuisance and just one more unwanted potential heir to the dynasty.

Young Lucca was further disadvantaged within his competitive family by being born sickly and weak, in stark contrast to his robust brother and sister. But most of all, with the death of his mother, there was no longer anyone on his side.

By the time Lucca was in high school his brother and sister were already involved in the running of the family business and it soon became apparent there would be no place for Lucca. He was considered too weak, physically and mentally, with his slight build in stark contrast to that of his burly father and brother, and even his sister being considered a big girl. Apart from Lucca, the Morovas were an imposing family with the physical attributes synonymous with the trappings of power and their sheer physical presence alone was enough to intimidate in the hostile world of boardrooms. It was not unheard of for Morova Senior to punch out a disagreeing boardroom executive, rendering him unconscious.

The family were not what one would call religious, being Catholic only by virtue of Italian tradition and outward appearances, and apart from the occasional wedding or funeral, they kept away from churches. Morova Senior was in fact an atheist, as well as Grandmaster of the Masonic Lodge, known as Propaganda Due, or P2. Members of this highly secretive lodge included some of the most influential men in Italy, including members of the military and intelligence services, leading businessmen, bankers, executive staff of various government agencies as well as some high ranking Vatican officials, despite the Church's strict prohibition of freemasonry. During the war, Morova Senior had been a high-ranking officer of the Black Shirt Battalion in Italy, and after the war he became heavily involved with the Vatican Ratline, assisting former SS officers to escape from Europe. A major part of Morova's corporate success was due to his membership of P2 and the ensuing powerful connections. But most importantly, his success was a result of the enormous intelligence files he had collated on anyone of consequence in the Italian corporate world. He never hesitated to use this intelligence if and when it was warranted.

In his final year at high school little Lucca began to plot his future. Being overwhelmed by his dominating family he continually pondered on how to make his own mark in the world, and, at the same time, strike a blow against his family whom he hated. His mother had died when he was only five, and although his memories of her were only vague, they were warm and filled with love. Although Sophia Morova had died of 'natural causes', Lucca felt in a way that he could not quite explain that his father had been responsible for her death. He remembered his brother and sister treating her with contempt and he was certain that they really didn't mind when she'd died.

It was about that time that the idea of joining the priesthood first hatched. It was the perfect solution. The one thing his father would hate more than anything – his son, a priest. At the same time it would present opportunities of power, potentially even surpassing his father's. It was perfect.

And so, to his father's horror and the bemused disgust of both his brother and sister, he joined the priesthood. From his very first day at the seminary he harboured an insatiable ambition for high office and the power that went with it. He held the Church hierarchy in contempt, considering them weak, pious fools with narrow minds and limited imagination, lacking the vision of the giddy heights of glory and power to which the Catholic Church could aspire.

Having a son as a priest became a sore point with the senior Morova, and, although he would never admit it, he was embarrassed. He decided to do something about it. At first he tried to reason with his son, offering him key positions within his empire. When this failed he decided to take a different tack, one that had never failed in the business world. He would bribe the Pope.

The meeting went well and in exchange for an enormous donation the Pope promised that Lucca Morova would move up the ecclesiastical ladder very quickly. He explained to Signore Morova that although it was in his power to make his son a cardinal immediately it would not look good, as he was still far too young for such an exalted role. However he did make him a monsignor, promising that bishop and then cardinal would not be too far off in the future.

～❖～

The young Monsignor Morova made it his business to catch the eye of the Vatican Secretary of State, who recognised a talent in the young priest. Because of Lucca's upbringing – and perhaps also because of the genes he'd inherited – he had a penchant for political manoeuvring, displaying natural diplomatic skills.

The Secretary of State was no fool, recognising an opportunity when it was presented. He knew nothing of Lucca's hatred for his family, identifying only his family's strong political and business influence. He was shrewd enough to realise the political clout a Morova could dispense, so he appointed him to his diplomatic staff, where he dealt with foreign dignitaries and, more importantly, with the highly influential captains of industry from all over the world.

From this position, Monsignor Morova began to build his own important power base within the world of commerce, from whence flowed the all-important funding critical to financing the colossal overheads required to run the Roman Catholic Church.

Having quickly proved his worth to the Secretary of State he moved to a senior position within the Vatican Bank, controlling the flow of billions of dollars of cash and investments including a worldwide, prime real estate portfolio, the value of which could not even be guessed at. This gave Lucca immense satisfaction as he was finally in a position of power controlling wealth against which even his father's billions paled into insignificance.

Although Morova's rise could be considered meteoric for one so young, to him it was still not fast enough. He yearned for even more power, secretly coveting the position of Secretary of State, the real seat of power, but a considerable hurdle stood in the way

223

of this ultimate ambition. He must first achieve the red hat of a cardinal, which was the final stepping-stone to the fulfilment of his plans. Unaware of his father's deal at the time, even under the most optimistic scenario, there was no way he could entertain this for at least another ten years and even then he would have to tread a skilful political path.

It was at about this time that Monsignor Lucca Morova received his first visit from the Dark One.

It was late at night and most of the Vatican household had long ago retired. Morova sat at the desk in his private chambers within the Vatican perusing financial documents by the light of his reading lamp. He removed his glasses, placing them on his desk, and rubbed his tired eyes. He stood up to stretch his aching back, deciding to call it a night. He was too tired to continue and he was afraid of missing something important in the documents he was perusing. He did not like to make mistakes, so it would just have to wait till morning. As he switched off the lamp he shuddered as he felt a coldness embrace him. The cold was as real as if he had opened a window during the depth of winter. His breath seemed to vaporise in front of his face. He looked about him, but could see nothing, yet the feeling of a presence was overwhelming. The drop in temperature was accompanied by a foul smell of stale mustiness. He felt light-headed as though he were going to faint. A strong sulphurous smell assaulted his nostrils and he gagged with nausea, bile rising in his throat. Then his knees buckled and a violent shaking overtook his body. Morova fell to the floor in a spasm of violent convulsions, thrashing about and kicking. The seizure ceased as suddenly as it had began and Morova felt a sense of calm. It was as though his body were floating above the floor, and he felt comfortably warm. Just as he was beginning to enjoy the sensation, the temperature plummeted again, and this time the feeling of another presence in the room was so strong, it caused him to cry out in fear.

'Who's there?' he demanded.

Unexpectedly, and without explanation, the overhead light dimmed, leaving the room immersed in a greenish half-light. Then he heard a soft, almost ethereal voice, which at first seemed to be in his head. The voice was seductive and yet it possessed a nefarious quality, causing him to shudder anew.

'The powers for which you yearn are rightly yours, Lucca.'

'Who are you?' Morova asked, voice quavering. 'Where are you? Is there really someone there?'

The voice answered, 'I am Legion. I have always been, and will always be.'

'I don't understand. Why can't I see you?'

'I am pure spirit, you cannot see me.'

Morova's initial thought was that he was going mad, but this was immediately rejected and replaced by a feeling of foreboding. Although a priest, Morova was essentially an atheist, and like his family, considered the mumbo jumbo teachings of the Church to be just that. And yet Morova harboured deep superstitions, a result of his Catholic schooling. Many an acclaimed atheist has been known to turn to God on his deathbed, begging for a priest, just in case. Now Morova's deeply ingrained subconscious superstition took over. What if there was truth in it all? What if he were experiencing a spiritual visitation? Visitations, appearances, apparitions – the history of the Church was full of them. Could it be possible there was truth in all of it? Mind racing, he reflected on his motivations for priesthood and high office. Could it be he was being paid a visit by a heavenly being, to be punished for his blasphemous motivations?

In a trembling voice he asked, 'Are you an angel?' and immediately felt foolish.

To his immense surprise his question was answered. 'I am an archangel,' the presence replied.

Morova's heart was racing so fast he thought he was having a heart attack. Remembering his catechism he asked, 'Are you Michael, or Gabriel?'

There was a pause, and when the presence spoke again, Morova thought he detected displeasure or testiness. 'I am called by many names, but that is not important for now. Suffice to say I have come to guide you along your path to the greatness in store for you.'

Morova could scarcely believe his ears. A light began to glow in the room and then somehow, magically, he seemed not to be in the room anymore. He felt himself transported to another place and, somehow he knew, into another time, yet it did not feel strange. He seemed to be an observer, and then realised he was in the Sistine Chapel, witnessing a great gathering of cardinals. His vantage point was one of hovering just under the ceiling, witnessing what was going on below. Then he discovered he could somehow control what he saw, or what he listened to. It felt something akin to controlling a camera. He could zoom in or out at will. It was a fantastic feeling, and it all felt quite natural. Then it dawned on him that what he was witnessing was a conclave in the process of electing a Pope. This confused him momentarily for the Pope was alive and well, but then he remembered he was in another time. He did not know why he knew this, he just did. The cardinals were listening to a man at a lectern, and it became apparent he was the Cardinal Camerlengo.

Intrigued, Morova decided to zoom in for a closer look. What he saw was a man of about seventy years of age. Then, to his amazement, he realised the man he was observing was, without a doubt, himself. Slowly, as if viewing a movie, the scene began to fade and he found himself back in his room in the present time, sprawled on the floor.

He must have dozed off, and it had all been a dream, he thought, although he could not believe how realistic it had been. Despite himself, he looked about his room to reassure himself he was alone. He was about to ask if anyone was there, but instead chuckled at his foolishness. Nevertheless he felt disappointed and cheated, as people often do, after waking from a pleasant dream. He sighed and headed for the bathroom to prepare for bed. He took his toothbrush and began brushing his teeth. When he glanced up into the mirror he dropped the toothbrush in shock. The image staring back at him in disbelief was that of a seventy-year-old man, the face he had seen in the dream.

When Morova woke in the morning he was still on the floor. He felt cramped and cold. The nightmare was still all too vivid in his mind. He'd never dreamed anything so realistic. He stretched his aching muscles and shuddered. Then he remembered the image in the mirror and jumped to his feet, hurrying to the bathroom. The reflection staring back at him was of a young man.

⚜

A few years passed and Morova had all but forgotten his fit. Word reached him that the Prelate of Naples had passed away and that the Pope wished to discuss this with him. The Pope saw this as an opportunity to square up with Morova Senior, and, as promised, elevated Lucca to cardinal, posting him to the recently vacated Archdiocese of Naples.

Morova took up residence in that southern Italian city located on the bay across from the ancient volcano of Mt Vesuvius. He revelled in his new role of seniority, proving to be a natural administrator. Months went by and Morova was fitting well into Church politics, concentrating his energies on plotting and scheming on how to return to Rome, where the power was. In

Naples he felt he was marooned in a backwater, deprived of opportunities to shine and excel.

And then late one evening, tossing restlessly in bed, unable to find sleep, scheming about Church politics, he once again felt the presence.

As before, the temperature dropped dramatically, and, without warning, he felt his body spasm into such violent convulsions that he was thrown out of bed, losing consciousness.

When he came to he felt weak and disoriented. As he lay on his back on the floor, waiting for his strength to return, a faint smell of sulphur permeated his nostrils. Oh no, not again, he thought. He made a determined mental note to see a doctor first thing in the morning. Then, without warning, the now familiar voice spoke to him. 'The red hat sits well with you, Lucca.'

Morova sat bolt upright. 'You're not real,' he shouted, 'this is another dream, just like last time.' Suddenly he felt foolish, and muttered to himself, 'I've got to see that doctor first thing.' Then, to his surprise, he heard an audible chuckle, which seemed too vivid to be a dream.

'Of course I'm real. I would have thought your sudden elevation to the exalted company of Princes of the Church would have convinced you of that. Or perhaps you believe it was your own cleverness that convinced the Pope to elevate a forty-year-old, novice monsignor to the red hat?'

Morova was contrite. 'I'm sorry, I'm confused. I don't know what to believe.'

'Well, believe this,' the presence snarled, 'align yourself with me and you will gain all the power you lust for, and more. Your power will be greater than anything your limited imagination can conceive. Align yourself with me and together we will rule the world. Align yourself with me and you will never know what it is to die.'

Morova was at a loss for words and could only stammer, 'Who, who are you? What, what are you? What, what is it you want from me?'

'Questions, questions. Suffice to say, I am Legion,' the presence repeated from their first meeting.

'I don't understand what you mean by Legion.'

'I am as the grains of sand in a dessert. I am as the drops in the ocean. I am at all places, at all times. I am the universe, I am all intelligence and all power.'

Confused, Morova asked, 'Are you God?'

'What is God, who is God?' the presence spat. 'A nice old man with a long white beard who loves everyone? Bah! The stuff of children's stories. Don't be so naïve, Morova. Accept me as your master and I will give you the world as well as immortality. You shall never taste death. Is this not what you desire?'

'Of course,' Morova muttered, 'but I still don't know who you are, or what you are. If only I could see you, then I could be sure that I am not going mad and speaking to myself.'

'And what is it you see when you look in the mirror?' the presence demanded.

'I see myself.'

'Did you not once see an old man?'

'Well, yes. I mean, I thought I did. But it was a mistake. I'm only forty years old.'

'Look in the mirror now,' the presence ordered.

Morova padded barefooted to the bathroom where he switched on the light, stepping in front of the mirror. He reeled at the image, grabbing the towel rail for support. Staring back at him was his reflection, but not as a forty-year-old man, but as a teenager. He continued to stare, and as if by magic, the image began to metamorphose, until Morova realised he was looking at a young, female version of himself. He stared, fascinated. The female he was staring at could have been his twin sister. Then, as he continued to gape in rapt attention, the image began to change again, aging rapidly, like a movie speeded up a thousand times. The female continued to age till Morova was staring at an incredibly ugly, old hag. He tore his eyes away from the mirror, backing out of the bathroom.

'You see,' the presence said, 'you can be anything I choose to make you, as I can be anything I choose to be.'

'But I would just feel more comfortable if I could but have a look at you. To at least see that there truly is someone here. You see, there are times when I think I am going mad. For all I know, I might be mad as a hatter right now, having a conversation with a figment of my imagination.'

'You have little faith, Cardinal Morova. I would have thought my little demonstration would have convinced you there is no need to see me. But very well, if you insist, if it will make you more comfortable.'

Morova waited expectantly, and a soft light began to glow in the centre of the room. It was as if someone was slowly turning up a dimmer switch, only there was no visible source of light. As the light grew in intensity it seemed to gather shape, until it took on the unmistakable shape and outline of a human form. Mesmerised, Morova stared unblinking, his jaw gaping. Slowly the shape began to materialise, and Morova realised he was watching the manifestation of a naked woman.

She was standing with her back to him, and was without doubt the most perfect and beautiful living thing he had ever seen. The shape of the lithe body surpassed in perfection anything he had ever encountered. The skin was smooth and of olive complexion, with long, raven-black, shining hair draping down the shoulders all the way to her waist, finishing just above the perfectly formed buttocks. Morova stared, unable to avert his eyes, realising that for the first time in years he was sexually aroused. Then slowly, she began to turn towards him. Morova took a backward step, not trusting himself, and then the woman was facing him front on. Her beauty was beyond his wildest imaginings. He looked at the face, which was exquisite, but the eyes were downcast and cloaked in shadow. She sidled closer to Morova, who took another backward step. She reached out for his hand, placing it on a perfect breast. Taking his other hand, she placed it on the raised mons Venus, just above the silken hair covering her womanhood. Morova felt an urgent stirring in his loins as she led him to the bed where she laid him down, and slowly and deliberately, began to undress him. She sidled onto the bed beside him and began to make love in a way he would not have believed possible, taking him to dizzying heights of ecstasy. When he felt he would explode and could take no more she expertly slowed her ministrations, only to start again, taking him to renewed heights surpassing the previous ones, until the build-up of sexual tension could be contained no longer, finally exploding in a kaleidoscope of lights and delirious ecstasy.

He must have passed out. He woke in bed alone, drained. Once again, his first conscious thought was that he'd dreamed it all. But when he opened his eyes she was standing over him with just a hint of a bemused smile on her lips. Morova returned the smile, recalling the intensity of his recent pleasure. He reached up to pull her down to him when a light seemed to illuminate her face for the first time, revealing features even more beautiful than Morova had first imagined. As he raised his lips towards her mouth she slowly opened her eyes and Morova was transported through the very gates of Hell. He was staring into an abyss of such putrid evil and malevolence that it was beyond his comprehension. At that instant he became witness to all the evil of time immemorial and understood with absolute certainty that he was damned. He screamed in horror, and lost consciousness.

⚜

Morova was jerked back to the present by the voice. 'Your friend, Archbishop Voitra, didn't sound too convincing,' she growled.

Morova was about to ask how she had heard both sides of the conversation, but checked himself. Tonight the Cardinal felt old and tired. He had been disturbed by the conversation with Voitra, and he knew he would have to give answers. 'I'm sure we can rely on him,' he reassured her unconvincingly.

'Are you? Well I'm not. He's weak. Do I have to remind you what's at stake? Perhaps you're also getting weak, Morova,' the presence challenged.

'No, no,' Morova protested, 'I'm aware of what's at stake, but I don't believe there is anything to worry about.'

'Oh! And why is that?'

'Because I personally destroyed the Third Secret and the Prophecy.'

'And you know for a fact there are no copies of the Third Secret?'

'If there are, they would have come to light by now. We would have known about it.'

'And you're convinced that meddling priest and nun are dead?'

'Archbishop Voitra assured me, just a moment ago. Their bodies were found in the rubble of the blast. They were almost unrecognisable. The Russian did his work well.'

There was a long, drawn-out silence and Morova began to feel uncomfortable. He could feel a tangible build-up of tension in the room, like static electricity preceding a thunderstorm, and then it hit him. He was thrown across the room with such violent force that when he hit the wall on the opposite side he heard, rather than felt, his shoulder blade snap. The picture of the Sacred Heart of Jesus crashed down on his head in a splintering of glass. He shielded his face with his good arm, groaning now with the pain from his shoulder. He was seized by an invisible force and hurled again, back to the opposite side of the room. He crashed again with a sickening thud, his head smashing into the wall, exploding in a burst of white pain, followed by black oblivion.

When he regained consciousness Morova dizzily looked around and his eyes focused on mayhem. It was as though a hurricane had torn through the room that was in shambles. Nothing seemed to have remained unbroken. A sharp pain knifed through his head and he gingerly put a hand to it. It came away covered in blood. He tried to move and groaned as he realised he must have more fractures than just his shoulder. He must have been continually flung around the room even after losing consciousness, with his body causing all the mayhem. It was a miracle he was alive. Then in a calm voice, as if nothing untoward had happened, the voice spoke again.

'Morova, you're a dupe. Voitra lied to you. That fucking priest and nun are still alive. You should know that no one dies without me knowing about it. As we speak they are drawing alarmingly closer to the truth. And don't you kid yourself, you foolish old man. Copies of both documents must still exist, and I want them destroyed. And remember, that what I have given, I can just as easily take back,' she added menacingly.

Morova shuddered and was about to respond when he realised he was once again alone.

Chapter 29

When the three men returned to the safe house Christina greeted them with a message for Emery. Someone had phoned and simply said, 'Tell Emery we have the parcel, but it cost more than we expected,' which Christina correctly assumed meant that Muntz had been safely retrieved, but she was mystified by the meaning of costing more than expected.

'That means we had a casualty,' Emery explained grimly, picking up the phone. He identified himself and listened. Replacing the receiver, he turned to Gadaleta, Peter and Christina. 'Looks like we were just in time. When my people arrived some guy was about to stab a hypo into Muntz. They managed to stop him but one of our boys caught the hypo. They couldn't help him. He died almost instantly.'

'Good God, the poor man,' Christina exclaimed.

'Yes,' Emery agreed, 'a bad break. But at least Muntz is safe.

'What about the killer?' Gadaleta asked.

'Dead. He was shot, so we can't question him.'

The next morning Gadaleta, Emery, Peter and Christina crossed the border and motored into Austria. They continued into and through Vienna without stopping until they arrived at a tiny village called Reckerwinkle, deep within the Vienna Woods, where they finally pulled up in front of a charming alpine cottage, which was like a picture on a box of chocolates. At the front door Emery pulled a key from his pocket and let himself in. Gesturing the others to follow, he closed the door behind them and they found themselves standing in what looked more like the front foyer of an office than the vestibule of what they would have expected of a typical Austrian farmer's cottage. A man wearing a suit greeted them in a distinctive American accent.

'Good to see you made it, Scott,' the man greeted warmly. 'How ya been Tony?' He looked quizzically at Peter and Christina and Gadaleta made the introductions.

'How is the subject?' Emery asked the man.

'Oh, he's as good as can be under the circumstances, I guess. He's asleep right now. The medicos carried out a thorough check on him as soon as we brought him in. Found unmistakable evidence of Nitro Pentasodium in his blood.'

Emery explained for Peter and Christina's benefit. 'That's the drug I told you about. It mimics the symptoms of a stroke, but too big a dose causes death. Once the victim dies all traces of the drug degrade out of the system fairly quickly, or at least more quickly than you can usually organise a post mortem. Careful dosage induces all the symptoms of a stroke, and then subsequent coma, which can be continued almost indefinitely provided you keep administering regular top- up doses.'

'Which would mean,' Peter observed, 'that someone at the clinic must have been topping him up. Maybe, you were right, Christina.'

'Yes,' Emery agreed, 'we'll see if we can get a lead on that from Voitra. He may or may not know who it is.'

'And what happens if you stop topping the victim up with this Nitro whatever you called it?' Christina asked.

'Simple. As the drug leaves the body the victim regains full use of his faculties.'

'You mean Professor Muntz will be all right? We'll be able to talk to him?' Peter asked, excitement in his voice.

'Well, not right at this minute, he's asleep,' the American explained. 'The drug does take its toll though. Over the protracted length of time this guy was having it pumped into him he would have suffered fairly serious atrophy, you know, wasting away of muscles, but with a bit of physiotherapy he should make a full recovery.'

They decided that as Christina had already met Frau Muntz, she would accompany a driver to Vienna to break the good news and bring her back to be with her husband.

⚜

Frau Muntz could barely contain her excitement as she arrived at the cottage, where she found her husband propped up in bed, being fed a thin gruel for breakfast. She burst into tears and ran to him, throwing her arms around his neck. Muntz was delighted to see his wife and although he was still weak, he was plainly lucid and eager to talk.

'It was agony, Anna,' he explained, 'whenever you visited me, I was screaming inside trying to get you to understand that I knew you were there, that I could hear you, understand you. Then this lady and gentleman arrived,' he gestured towards Peter and Christina, 'and I began to have hope because they spoke to me as though they knew I could understand what they were saying to me. And here we all are …' Muntz trailed off, overcome with emotion.

Peter allowed him time to regain his composure before asking if he felt strong enough to talk about the stolen papyrus. 'Yes, yes, of course,' he assured them, 'you've made a long journey to talk to me about it.'

'Professor Muntz,' Emery said, 'Father LeSarus has told us a little about what he knows about this papyrus you found, but perhaps you may care to fill us in on what you know.'

'Certainly,' Muntz agreed. 'The papyrus is a prophecy, but not just any prophecy, it is King Mentonidus' Prophesy of Armageddon.'

'Tell us about this king,' Emery prompted.

236

'King Mentonidus is no stranger to archaeologists. There have been countless references to him in clay tablets and scrolls, although up until the discovery of this papyrus, the earliest references we could find of him were from the Late Assyrian King Assurbanipal, of around 650 B.C.E. This document is incredible in that it dates to almost the dawn of the Assyrian people, over a thousand years earlier. Up until now, it was more or less accepted in academic circles that the king was a legend based on mythology, but this document changes everything. A lot of material has been uncovered recounting heroic tales of the king's exploits and adventures through the underworld. According to the legends he was the protégé of a fearful character referred to as the Necromancer.'

'What does that mean?' Gadaleta asked.

LeSarus volunteered an answer. '"Necro" means dead, and "mancer" means to communicate.'

'Yes, that is correct, Father,' Muntz agreed, 'that is what the word means in its exact form, but, please remember, that although Necromancer is a word Greek in origin, it is itself a translation from the ancient Assyrian language. Even the name, "Mentonidus" is a Greek form. The original word for "necromancer" in Ancient Assyrian is shailu, or mushelu, and some of the precise intended meaning is lost.'

'So what was the intended meaning in your opinion Professor Muntz?' Gadaleta pressed.

'From my readings of the original texts it is my belief that the Necromancer was a kind of mystical being, a magus of sorts, someone who was credited with the power to communicate with those who had gone over to the other side. But perhaps his most important power was the ability to foresee the future.'

'And this Necromancer,' Gadaleta said, 'purportedly passed on his secrets to King Mentonidus.'

'That's right. But as I said, until my discovery, it was all considered mythology.'

'And now?' Gadaleta asked pointedly.

'Ah, good question. You see, there are references aplenty about the legendary prophecy that was supposedly hidden after Mentonidus died and now that I have found it, well it places a whole new perspective on what is legend and what is fact. But there is one other interesting mystery to all this.'

'And what is that?' Gadaleta asked, fascinated.

'The location of where the prophecy was discovered.'

'Wasn't it discovered at Nag Hammadi?' Christina asked. 'The very same place the alternative Gospels were found?'

'Yes, but that adds to the mystery. You see the papyrus is Egyptian, specifically Upper Egyptian, and Upper Egypt is a long way from Mesopotamia. How did the papyrus get there?'

'Any theories, Professor?' Christina asked.

'Yes, I do have a theory but that is all it is, theory. I contend that the alternate Gospels were secreted away by the authors or custodians for fear of persecution. Is it not possible then that the prophecy of King Mentonidus was found and passed on until it found its way into the hands of the disciples of the alternate Gospels?'

'I don't follow,' Gadaleta said.

'I think I understand what you're saying, Professor,' Peter said. 'From what little we do know about the prophecy it would seem there are areas of contention, criticising the way the new Church of Christ would develop.'

'That is why I believe it was hidden away with the alternate Gospels, for fear of destruction by those who would stand to lose, if the prophecy were made public.'

'You also mentioned Armageddon, Professor. Would you care to elaborate on that?' Emery asked.

Muntz paused, looking around at his visitors then said, 'Why, the end of the world. The final battle between good and evil.'

This was followed by an uncomfortable silence, which was finally broken by Peter. 'From your studies of the prophecy, is it your opinion that the end of the world, or Armageddon, is inevitable? I mean, is it a fait accompli, is there nothing that can be done to prevent it?'

'Most certainly there is,' Muntz answered. 'The prophecy is a series of warnings, if you please. But the warnings are about alternative actions. If humanity does not do this, then such and such will eventuate. If it does this, then so and so will happen. Do you understand?'

'Yes, I think so,' Peter replied. 'What you're saying is that it gives various possible scenarios and consequential outcomes.'

'Exactly,' Muntz went on. 'For example, there was an alternate scenario for the Second World War. The prophecy detailed the attempt on Hitler's life by the generals. Had they succeeded, the outcome would have been entirely different. I studied the document laboriously before I fully appreciated its implications. The prophecies are remarkably accurate. Once I had successfully translated the document, I then proceeded to analyse it. If one did not know that it was a document written nearly four thousand years ago, one could be excused for thinking one was reading a documented history of the world to the present and even beyond. Another interesting point is that the prophecy makes detailed reference to the apparition of the Blessed Virgin at Fatima. Mentonidus foretold that event in great detail and warned that if mankind failed to heed Our Lady's message, then cataclysmic events would follow. I believe this refers mainly to the Third Secret, which we all know has been steadfastly repressed by the Vatican. Mentonidus was adamant that this would be a final heavenly warning on what must be done to avert disaster.'

Peter asked, 'And the original papyrus, along with your translation and analysis, were stolen by your friend, Archbishop Voitra?'

'Yes, it would seem so. No doubt, it was the Archbishop who arranged for me to be silenced,' Muntz said, and Peter noted that there was a hint of sadness in the older man's voice.

'And you have no other copies?'

'I'm afraid not.'

'Wait a minute,' Frau Muntz interjected. 'I've thought about this. What about your computer? Wouldn't your translation and analysis still be on the hard drive?'

Muntz sat up in bed, scarcely able to conceal his excitement, while the others stared at Frau Muntz. 'Why, of course,' he said to his wife, 'why didn't I think of that? Unless the computer has been tampered with, the translation and all my other work should still be on it.'

Within a few hours a driver had returned to the cottage with the professor's computer. They set it up on a stand next to his bed and everyone waited anxiously for the computer to boot up. Finally, the screen prompted for a password, which Muntz quickly keyed in. Collectively they held their breaths as he scanned impatiently through the many files. 'Ah, there it is,' he announced triumphantly.

The file opened and finally, there for all to see was Muntz's full translation of the prophecy of King Mentonidus. A collective cheer went up, while Gadaleta raced from the room, returning within minutes with a portable printer, which was impatiently attached to the computer. Muntz hit the print command, and following a series of clicks and electronic beeps, the document began to print. When it had finished, Emery grabbed the pages.

'I'll run out and get someone to make us all a copy.'

Before long, everyone in the room had begun to read their copy of the prophecy.

Chapter 30

Cardinal Lucca Morova had ample time to reflect during his stay in hospital. The doctors said they had never seen a worse case of self-inflicted injury sustained during an epileptic fit.

Of course only Morova knew the true circumstances of his assault and the identity of his assailant. After he'd finally managed to crawl from his chambers to call for help, he claimed amnesia, a claim the doctors readily accepted, considering the extent of his trauma and injuries. He still shuddered whenever his mind returned to that evening, when he'd become the unwitting cause of Satan's displeasure. It was an experience he hoped never to re-live. That Archbishop Voitra's deceit and duplicity were the direct cause of his woes was not lost on him, and in his confinement he'd had little else to occupy his thoughts but revenge. His anger had bubbled and frothed like a living, fermenting thing till it consumed him. He could scarcely contain his impatience to get out of hospital to call Voitra to account for his betrayal.

He reflected on his association with the Dark One, and how over the years more and more had been revealed to him. He now knew, for instance, that he was only one of many disciples chosen from all parts of the world to help fulfil the long-term, worldly ambitions of Satan. Most were people like himself, sharing an insatiable appetite for power or riches, and usually both.

Morova began to understand that many of the world's most powerful politicians, businessmen, media owners, scientists, soldiers and clerics had achieved their positions through Satan's direct intervention. Between them they manipulated an unsuspecting world, steering it slowly but inexorably towards the final confrontation. He recalled the words of St John's Apocalypse.

All alike, small and great, rich and poor, free man and slave, must receive the mark from him on their right hand, and none may buy or sell, unless he carries this mark, which is the beast's name, or the number that stands for his name, and the number will be six hundred and sixty six.

Morova absently fingered the mark on his own right hand. To the casual observer it could have been an ancient burn or even a birthmark yet it had the unmistakable appearance of the number 666, the same sign carried by the prospering Luciferians, who controlled governments and commerce.

Chapter 31

Peter LeSarus was the first to finish reading. He studied the faces around him, trying to gauge their reactions. They were all still engrossed in the document, and occasionally one of them would shake their head, almost imperceptibly, as though refusing to believe what they were reading. Everyone sat stone-faced, oblivious to their surroundings. Christina Kelly was mouthing the words as she read, as though not wanting to risk misinterpreting even one word. Peter glanced at Hans Muntz, sitting impassively patient, and caught his eye. Muntz gave a slight nod, acknowledging the enormity of what had just been read. His wife sat by his side, holding his hand, looking as impassive as her husband, yet no doubt fully understanding the magnitude of the message her husband had unearthed.

As he waited for the others to finish, LeSarus analysed his own reaction to what he'd just read. It had to be a hoax of the most extravagant kind, he reasoned. It was the only explanation that made sense. Nothing else could explain it. Despite the methodology Muntz had used to authenticate the document, there were still a thousand precedents of forgers thwarting the most sophisticated technology known to science. This had to be the case here. What Peter had just read was simply not possible. The odds against someone prophesying to this degree of accuracy were inconceivable. And yet, what if the document was authentic? If that was even remotely possible, then God help us all, he thought. It would mean the world had almost already reached the point of no return and there was probably no helping it. He looked at his watch and noticed the date. It had only been a few days but he felt as if he'd already spent months on the matter of the prophecy and the Third Secret of Fatima. He was exhausted; he was sleeping fitfully and yet all the while he had to keep up the pretence of being on top of things. Something just isn't adding up, he thought. I'm going to talk to Michael again the first chance I get. Maybe he's found out something more.

Peter wondered exactly what he was going to ask his brother when he snapped out of his introspection, as one by one he heard the others slowly put down their copy of the document. Finally everyone had finished and they sat in a silent group, each immersed in their own thoughts.

Gadaleta was the first to break the silence. 'This is all kind of unbelievable, Professor,' he stated glibly.

Muntz was about to react when LeSarus held up his hand in a conciliatory gesture. 'Professor, I'm sure we all share Mr Gadaleta's thoughts, that this is so fantastic it does seem unbelievable, but not in the way it sounded. None of us doubt the authenticity of your finding. It's just that, well yes, it does seem unbelievable.'

Now Emery piped up. 'Peter, it's all very well to say we believe in the authenticity of the Professor's finding but, let's face it, without the original, no one's going to believe this.'

'Yes I know that,' Muntz agreed. 'That is why it is so important that I retrieve the original.'

'I think we are missing the point here, Mr Emery,' Christina said. 'Can we take the risk not to believe this is authentic?'

'Yes, good point,' Emery conceded. 'I guess we just have to assume it is authentic and figure out how we can get back the original. Tell me, Professor, how accurately does your translation reflect the original meaning?'

'A good question, Mr Emery. I took a long and painstaking time over the translation, often necessarily substituting a word with one I felt fitted the intended meaning more accurately, or perhaps made it read better, or be more understandable. For example, in the original document, the exact translation of a specific word he used would be something like, antagonist to the good messenger, which for simplicity of meaning I interpreted to mean the Antichrist.'

The men continued questioning Muntz on various aspects of the translation.

Gadaleta interrupted, 'Professor, I'm particularly interested in what your translation refers to in references to terrorism. Could you please elaborate your interpretations of that?'

'The prophecy clearly refers to revelations by a deity of female form, delivered to shepherd children, which in my mind relates clearly to Fatima, and specifically the Third Secret, that has been suppressed by the Church. Mentonidus warns that should the world ignore Her demands, then a great holocaust will visit the earth, by way of wars, atrocities and mayhem hitherto unheard of. He states that this will come from the East and refers to a great ball of fire, which will engulf man's greatest architecture, claiming many lives. He goes on to warn that this one event will mark the beginning of an ongoing conflict, which will differ to all before, and the ensuing chaos will eventually disrupt civilisation as we know it.'

'A great ball of fire,' Emery mused. 'And man's greatest architecture. Any clue as to what he may be referring to, Professor?'

Muntz shrugged his shoulders. 'I have been trying to figure that out. It could refer to any number of buildings around the world.'

'Including, I dare say,' Peter ventured, 'the Sydney Opera House.'

'Do you think the great ball of fire could be a nuke?' Emery asked.

'Yes, it's quite probable. He states emphatically that the conflagration will come from the sky, and after all, as you would have read within the reference to Hiroshima, he also spoke of a great ball of fire coming from the sky.'

Emery continued his line of questioning. 'So if this document truly is authentic, and judging by the accuracies to date, it would seem we can expect some serious terrorist atrocity in the future. Any idea when, Professor?'

'With the exception to the events of Fatima, most of the events he writes about are fairly broad in terms of chronology, yet if you analyse minutely the way he dates events one from the other, then it would be my strong guess that we are right there, in terms of time. Without placing an exact date on it, I would suggest anytime between now and the year 2002 at the latest.'

'Christ,' Emery swore, and then remembering the company he was in added, 'sorry.'

'Getting back to this Antichrist,' Gadaleta said, 'do you believe there is such a thing?'

'You'd better believe it,' Christina replied. 'My uncle has carried out immense research on the matter, and the coming of the Antichrist has been foretold by just about every prophet known to man, including Jesus Christ.'

'I'm sorry, Christina,' Gadaleta continued, 'but with respect to your beliefs, I'm afraid I find all this to be rather like something out of a Dennis Wheatley novel.'

Christina smiled indulgently. 'Don't condemn Mr Wheatley out of hand, Mr Gadaleta. He had more of an understanding of these things than you may think. Most of his books, although fictional, are based on a solid grounding of research as well as a keen understanding of the occult.'

'OK, so assuming you're right,' Gadaleta said, 'who is this Antichrist, and what's his purpose in life?'

'Ah, I still detect some cynicism, Mr Gadaleta,' Christina said, 'but that is to be expected. According to my uncle, and putting it in as simplistic terms as possible, the Antichrist is to Satan, what Jesus Christ is to God.'

'You mean, that the Antichrist is the son of Satan?'

'No, not the son, but the messenger or servant.'

'And all this is assuming there is such a thing as the devil, and a Hell, and all those other nasty things that scare children to make them behave.'

'There is no doubt, Mr Gadaleta,' Christina continued, 'that the greatest trick played by Satan on mankind, is to make us believe he doesn't exist. He has convinced us that we are far too sophisticated to believe such nonsense, and, in the meantime, he is able to carry on his work uninterrupted.'

Gadaleta turned to Peter. 'Do you believe all this stuff?'

Peter shrugged. 'There are forces of which we have little understanding,' he replied.

Gadaleta turned his attention back to Christina. 'And what would that work be? This work the devil is carrying out, and the purpose behind it?'

'If you go back to the Revelations in the Book of the Apocalypse, you will find there is no mention of Lucifer being cast into Hell, along with the other fallen angels. Hell, as we think of it, has come about through evolution of folklore, mainly during the Dark Ages. It was difficult for peasants to relate to a pure spirit existing within a certain state, away from God. People created Hell in their own minds, and within their own capacity of understanding. As being burned was considered the worst conceivable torture, they invented Hell as a place of burning to tie in with their own understanding of ultimate suffering. You see, the Apocalypse states clearly that Lucifer and his angels were cast down to Earth, which has become Satan's domain. Evil is not something created. It is a state brought on by free choice. To put it as succinctly as possible, it irks Satan to be surrounded by goodness. It is in his interest to be surrounded by evil, for the sake of evil. That way he undermines God's very creation. Do you understand?'

'Yes, I think so,' Gadaleta answered, 'but sorry, I can't say I'm convinced. But you still haven't answered my question. Does anyone know the identity of this Antichrist?'

Muntz answered, 'Up till now, I would suggest that only Satan's most trusted disciples would be privy to his identity. But now, as you have read in the prophecy document, it is steeped with clues to his identity. I believe he does exist and his time is near. It is also clear that he is a person of enormous influence and power on a global scale, and is surrounded with disciples who are also in positions of awesome power and influence.'

LeSarus asked, 'In your opinion Professor, is there anything that can be done to avert all this, this disaster?'

'Most certainly. The key to all of this would seem to lie within the Third Secret of Fatima, which is supposed to contain explicit instructions of what to do to avert disaster.'

Now Emery threw a question at the Professor. 'If this Fatima secret is so goddamned important, then why has the Catholic Church suppressed it?'

'I would have thought that had become patently obvious, Mr Emery,' Christina answered. 'My uncle is adamant that the Luciferians have infiltrated into a position, or positions, of power within the Vatican.'

'What?' Emery asked. 'Are you saying that Satanists run the Vatican?'

'Not only possible, but probable. Do you recall the untimely death of Pope Leo Alexander I?' Christina continued without waiting for an answer. 'Just before he died he recalled the entire

College of Cardinals. This was most unusual considering he'd only just been elected. The cardinals had only just returned home following the conclave. Can you imagine the inconvenience, not to mention the expense?'

'What are you getting at, Christina?' Gadaleta pressed.

'What I'm getting at is this. According to my uncle, the Pope had only just been elected. It is on public record that shortly after his election he visited Sister Lucia. She was the last survivor of the shepherd children who had seen the apparition at Fatima. Almost immediately following that meeting he recalled the cardinals and announced his intention that he planned to address an extraordinary announcement to the world.' Christina paused, glancing from Emery to Gadaleta. 'He obviously had something very, very important to announce, wouldn't you agree?'

'Hmmm, I see what you're getting at,' Emery said, rubbing his chin.

Christina continued. 'Almost immediately following this announcement he died and his untimely death has never been satisfactorily explained.'

'So do you think the announcement the Pope was about to make had something to do with the Third Secret?' Gadaleta asked.

'My uncle is convinced of it, and his guess is that he was murdered because of it.'

'If he's right,' Emery observed to Gadaleta, 'we may well be on to one of the greatest cover-ups of all time.'

'And we already know,' Peter added, 'that the highest ranking cardinal on earth has gone to extreme measures to get his hands on the prophecy.'

'Yes, but don't forget, we only have the word of Archbishop Voitra for that,' Emery countered. 'It wouldn't stand up in a court of law.'

'Yes,' Gadaleta agreed, 'Scott's right. If we were to act on the evidence we have, and considering the rank and standing of Cardinal Morova, we'd be laughed out of court. Not to mention being hit with a libel suit that would spin your heads.'

'So what do you propose we do gentlemen? Nothing?' Christina asked, frustrated.

'I didn't say that,' Emery shot back, 'but you have to trust Tony and me on this. We don't want to jump the gun and tip our hand.'

'That's right,' Gadaleta agreed. 'The only facts we really have, are that Archbishop Voitra stole a document from Professor Muntz, and caused him grievous bodily harm.' Emery sounded as though he were giving evidence in court. 'And he was an accessory to attempted murder. The rest is unproven testimony on his part and, at this point, I would suggest there is no reason why we should trust him. How do we know for example that he isn't involved with a terrorist group? For all we know, he may have thrown all this bullshit about Morova as a smoke screen to shift attention away from whoever he may be really associated with.'

LeSarus and the others were shocked at this possibility. 'My God,' LeSarus said, 'I would never have thought of that!'

'That's all right, Peter,' Emery soothed. 'Tony and I have had a little more experience at this sort of thing. Mind you, that's not to say we are dismissing what the Archbishop told us. There may well be something rotten within the Vatican. It's just that we have to prove it.'

Peter asked, 'Just to satisfy my curiosity, Scott, how would you go about proving or disproving the Archbishop's allegations?'

'I would think Rome would be as good a place as any to start,' Emery answered.

Chapter 32

⟡⟡⟡

As the Lauda flight began its descent to Da Vinci Airport in Rome, Peter LeSarus watched wistfully from the window. His companion Christina Kelly leaned across, craning her neck for a glimpse of the Eternal City. LeSarus wondered if Christina shared his melancholy. In his youth he had talked often about how exciting it could be to visit the centre of the Roman Catholic Church. At the time, he would never have dreamed of the circumstances that would ultimately bring him here. Peter could still scarcely believe it himself, as he looked upon the ancient city below. Gadaleta and Emery were seated across the aisle in the mid section of the aircraft. The two agents had initially insisted on going alone but Peter had convinced them that he and Christina might prove to be useful in potential dealings with fellow clergy. He had added convincingly that they had come to Europe to find answers and they were not prepared to quit now. Reluctantly Emery had agreed, but stressed that he would call the shots. Emery had CIA contacts in Rome and he intended to call on them to see what connections they may have within the Vatican.

Once they checked into their hotel, Emery suggested that Peter and Christina do some sightseeing and acquaint themselves with Rome's history, while he and Gadaleta visited Emery's Roman counterpart.

Peter and Christina decided to walk to fully appreciate the sights, and they headed off towards the Vatican. Dressed in their clerical garb they blended in with the countless clergy on pilgrimage to the centre of world Catholicism.

The previous evening, when Christina had telephoned her uncle to tell him of their plans, he had suggested they call on an old friend of his at the Vatican who may prove useful. Arriving at the Vatican, they proceeded to the administration entrance, which bustled with all the various personnel coming and going about their business. As people arrived at the gate, they flashed their passes to the Swiss Guard. Peter approached the guard, asking him if they could visit O'Shaughnessy's friend. The guard picked up a phone and after punching in the extension spoke briefly. He asked Peter to wait, informing him that Monsignor Giulio Reitanio would come to the gate shortly. Within minutes a short, rotund, jolly-looking Italian priest emerged from the building. He took one look at Christina and embraced her like a long lost sister.

'Aha,' he beamed, 'so you are the niece of my good friend, Brian O'Shaughnessy.'

Christina returned the smile and introduced Peter, who received an equally warm greeting from the jovial Monsignor. He took Christina and Peter by the arm, steering them off into the street. They talked animatedly as they went, until they reached a delicatessen where he ushered them in, to be greeted demonstrably by the owner.

'Ah, Monsignor Reitanio. What a pleasure,' the owner said.

After the Monsignor and his party were seated they ordered antipasto and coffees. When the plate of cold cuts arrived Christina and Monsignor Reitanio spent the next half hour reminiscing about what O'Shaughnessy had been up to since his untoward departure from Rome.

'I never believed for one minute, the things they said about Brian,' he assured Christina. 'But enough about your uncle, we are being self indulgent in front of your friend.' He spoke good English with a delightful Italian accent. 'So tell me, my dear, what brings you to our fair city?'

'My friend Peter and I are researching the Fatima revelations,' she replied.

The Monsignor's eyes clouded over momentarily. 'I see,' he said, 'and why would you be doing that?'

Christina went on to explain her uncle's misgivings as to why the Third Secret had been repressed by the Popes.

'But surely you accept the Holy Father had his reasons, which are not ours to question?'

'I wish it were as simple as that, Monsignor,' Christina sighed. She exchanged a meaningful look with Peter, who gave an imperceptible shrug, as though to say, it's your call.

The exchange was not lost on the Monsignor. 'What is it?' he asked. 'Is there something you wish to share with me?'

'I don't know, Monsignor. It's not that we don't trust you, because we do. It's just that … well, I don't know that we should be involving you in this.'

'Are you in trouble, my dear?'

'In a manner of speaking, we all are,' Peter replied.

'Ah, you speak in riddles, Father LeSarus. Why don't you just tell me what is troubling you? What is the real purpose of your visit to Rome?'

'Very well, Monsignor,' Peter said at last, 'we will confide in you, because this potentially affects all of us. But you must give us your word you will not repeat anything I tell you. I only ask this for your own safety.'

'You have my word. I am, how you say? Intrigued.'

'A good choice of word because what we are about to tell you is, most intriguing.'

Peter and Christina spent the next hour or so taking turns, explaining the events leading up to them making the decision to come to Europe. Occasionally the Monsignor would interrupt with a question in order to clarify a point, but for the most part he listened with rapt attention.

When they finished relating the events to date, they eagerly watched the Monsignor for a reaction. 'My children,' he asked grimly, 'have you lost your faith in God?'

'Good God, no!' Peter and Christina assured him simultaneously. 'But I have lost faith in those who purport to serve Him,' Peter added.

Reitanio pondered silently, trying to choose words appropriate to what he was thinking. 'I should call the little men in white coats,' he finally said. 'But coming from you, Brian's niece, what can I say? It is all so incredibly …' Again he searched for the correct English word. 'Sinister,' he finally said.

'Sinister it is, Monsignor,' Peter agreed, 'but I should point out that our friends from the American government agency have warned us that the plot may well lie with Archbishop Voitra alone, and that any implication against Cardinal Morova could be pure fabrication.'

'I know very little about the Prelate of Prague, and as far as I know, he has only been to Rome once. I believe he was created a Bishop in absentia, during the Communist regime. The only visit he has made to Rome was recently, when the Cardinal Secretary of State, His Eminence Cardinal Morova, summoned him.

'Do you happen to know what the business or agenda of that meeting was?' Christina asked.

The Monsignor smiled. 'Alas no. I am but a humble cleric. Cardinals do not confide in me. The only reason I even know that he was here was because I made the arrangements for him to be met at the airport and escorted here. But perhaps I can see what I can find out. Meet me back here in about an hour.'

Chapter 33

Emery and Gadaleta were having their own meeting in a café in a different part of Rome, well away from the usual tourist haunts. They sat at the back of the café, away from prying eyes, all but hidden from the casual observer. They sat shoulder-to-shoulder in the narrow booth, barely wide enough to contain them, with the man in the pinstriped suit sitting opposite. He was slim with thinning, fair hair that he kept neatly in place with gel. The pencil-thin moustache completed the appearance of a well-groomed but unobtrusive businessman. Paul Slaughter had been a European operative based in Rome for as long as Emery could remember. The two men had collaborated on many cases together, and over the years had become friends.

Slaughter listened attentively, without interrupting as Emery and Gadaleta filled him in on the purpose of their visit. When they had brought Slaughter up to date with all they knew he did not bother to ask questions or make comment. He respected Emery sufficiently to know there was nothing further to add. If there was, then Emery would have left it out for good reason. He simply said, 'I have people in the Vatican. I'll see what I can find out and get back to you.'

Gadaleta placed a handful of Italian lire on the table, and the three men left as unobtrusively as they had arrived.

Chapter 34

Monsignor Reitanio was the first to come back with information. He had spoken to Cardinal Morova's secretary who had confirmed that the Cardinal had held audience with the Czech Prelate, but when Reitanio pressed the issue, asking for the purpose of the meeting the secretary had clammed up. Reitanio thought this was unusual, as Morova's secretary usually liked to gossip and thought nothing of discussing his master's business.

'He was almost rude,' Reitanio said, as he related the meeting.

'Do you think he resented your enquiring about the Cardinal's business?' Peter asked.

'No, no, we often discuss what our bosses are up to. No, there was more to it this time.'

'What do you mean?' Christina asked.

'He seemed afraid. Yes, that's it, he was afraid. As soon as I mentioned the Archbishop, I saw fear in his eyes. He just cut me off and stormed out.'

'And that was it?' Peter asked.

'He muttered something about keeping out of things I didn't understand.'

It was another day before Slaughter contacted Emery and Gadaleta. He asked the two men to meet him at a different café this time, in a different part of the city. No one could accuse Slaughter of setting himself up by establishing a pattern.

Once they were all seated, and satisfied that no one was within earshot, he began to recount what he'd been able to find out. 'I'm sure it won't come as a surprise when I tell you there are many Vatican insiders who believe Pope Leo Alexander I was murdered.'

'Yes,' Emery confirmed, 'there was considerable conjecture at the time of his death and, as I understand it, there was never an autopsy.'

'No, there wasn't,' Slaughter agreed. 'Seems the Papal doctor diagnosed a massive coronary and the cardinals were satisfied with that, or so the Vatican PR machine would have us believe. The truth is, there were many at the time who were outraged at the speed of the funeral and lack of autopsy.'

'Who would have been instrumental in arranging the funeral and making the decision not to have an autopsy?' Emery asked.

'Why, the Cardinal Camerlengo of course. He's the headman of the College and calls all the shots between Popes. Sort of like a caretaker Pope I guess.'

'That's interesting,' Emery said. 'What else did you find out, Paul?'

'Vatican protocol demands that if a document or book is taken out of the archives it has to be signed out to the person requesting it. My contact happened to discover that the Third Secret of Fatima was signed out at the request of Pope Leo Alexander on the night he died.'

'Is that so?' Emery asked, even more interested now.

'That's not all,' Slaughter went on. 'It was never returned. And guess who the signatory was.'

'I'll bet it was Cardinal Morova.'

'Correct. But wait, there's more. Before he died, His Holiness made a copy of the document.'

'You're kidding us,' Gadaleta said, excitement mounting in his voice. He could scarcely contain himself as he asked, 'And does your man know where that copy is?'

'Seems the Pope had a close buddy he used to visit – a priest by the name of Bruno Bracciano in some unheard-of, remote village somewhere in the Dolomite Mountains. The Pope sent the copy to him, along with a covering letter. And I happen to have a copy of that letter.'

'You are unbelievable,' Emery congratulated his friend.

'Yeah, I know I'm good,' Slaughter laughed, sharing his friend's jocularity, 'we're lucky the Vatican never throws anything out, but what I don't know is whether or not this Father Bruno Bracciano is still alive. He'd have to be somewhere in his seventies and I don't know whether or not he kept the document. He may have died, and the secret may have died with him.'

'Only one way to find out,' Gadaleta said, jumping up from behind the table.

Chapter 35

Cardinal Morova's private secretary had served him for almost a decade, after Morova had plucked him out of the Vatican Bank where he had worked as a clerk. As was befitting his senior position as assistant to a cardinal, he was promoted to Monsignor. The Monsignor disliked Morova, sensing something sinister about the man, which he could not quite put his finger on. He had been privy on numerous occasions to the man's utter ruthlessness, destroying without hesitation or pity the career of anyone foolish enough to attempt to thwart him. He loathed working for him, but was afraid to let his feelings be known and had resigned himself to the fact that he could never leave voluntarily, for he knew too much for the Cardinal to ever let him go.

The meeting with Monsignor Giulio Reitanio had worried him. He was not averse to a little harmless gossip, but was not happy when people asked specific questions about his boss's business. Why would Reitanio want to know about the Czech Archbishop's visit? Although he and Reitanio were friends, this did not give him the right to compromise him by questioning him about the Cardinal's confidential matters.

He feared Morova terribly, and following a sleepless night he made a decision to tell his master about Reitanio's probing. The decision had nothing to do with loyalty, but rather it was based on his deep-rooted fear. How did he know that Reitanio's questions were not a test devised by Morova to trap him? My God, the man was cunning enough to contrive such a scheme to test his assistant's loyalty. If he failed to report the matter, and Morova had indeed instigated it as a trap … he shuddered at the prospect.

'Why did you not come to me immediately after Monsignor Reitanio meddled into Vatican State affairs?' Morova demanded.

Although it was chilly in the cardinal's office, the secretary began to sweat, stammering for a suitable response. 'At the time, Eminence, I did not think it was important.'

'You did not think it was important?' Morova echoed menacingly. 'At what point did you decide it was important, and why?'

The monsignor continued to stammer, searching for an answer, but was cut off as Morova leaped up from behind his desk with speed and agility belying his age. His face was red with rage and the veins in his neck and temple stood out like cords of rope. 'I will not harbour disloyalty!' he shrieked. 'Do you hear me?' He gave no time for a response. 'You are privileged to be personal assistant to the highest-ranking Cardinal in Christendom. I expect you to be my eyes and my ears. Is that clear? You are to report everything to me. Everything. No matter how inconsequential it may seem to you. If it concerns me, I wish to hear of it. Do you understand?'

He's mad, the Monsignor concluded. Stark, raving mad. But he kept these dark thoughts to himself. Like a chastened schoolboy, he nodded his head silently, eyes averted.

'Good,' Morova continued more sedately, recovering from his outburst and touching a hand to the still throbbing vein in his temple. He returned to the chair behind his desk. 'We live in difficult times, Monsignor, and the Church has enemies everywhere, enemies determined to undermine the Church. You only need to look at what is happening around the world. It is everywhere. Satan is doing his work well.'

The Monsignor remained silent, staring at a spot on the floor.

Morova continued. 'You must understand, Monsignor, that only His Holiness and I truly understand the big picture. Now, would you please arrange as a matter of urgency for Monsignor Reitanio to attend us.'

Relieved to have been let off so lightly, the Monsignor hurried from the room. Just as he reached the door, Morova called after him. 'Oh, Monsignor, it is not necessary to divulge the purpose of my summons.'

⚜

As Monsignor Reitanio was ushered into the Cardinal's office, he felt an overwhelming sense of foreboding. He had no doubt the summons was a result of his meeting with the Australians. He cursed himself for questioning the Cardinal's secretary.

The Cardinal was busy at his desk when Reitanio entered and as the door closed, Morova seemed oblivious of his presence. He stood in awkward silence in front of Morova's desk, feeling like a schoolboy reporting to the headmaster for punishment. He continued to stand in silence, considering it prudent not to interrupt the Cardinal's work. The Cardinal would acknowledge him when he was ready, he figured. He continued to wait for an interminable length of time and began to wonder whether Morova was so engrossed in his work that he was unaware of his presence. He decided to make a noise, coughing politely and shuffling his feet, which had the desired effect, causing the Cardinal to look up in surprise.

'Why, if it isn't, Monsignor …' he grappled with the name, as though trying to remember it.

Reitanio decided to assist him. 'Reitanio, Eminence. I am Monsignor Giulio Reitanio.'

'Are you now? And am I supposed to know you?'

Morova's response confused Reitanio. 'Excuse me, Eminence? Your personal secretary summoned me. The Monsignor told me to make haste, that you wished to see me immediately. I dropped everything, coming as quickly as I could.'

'My personal secretary summoned you?' Morova asked, feigning surprise. 'And did he say what it was I wished to discuss?'

'No. I'm sorry, Eminence, he did not.'

Morova seemed puzzled, and then, his face brightening, said, 'Ah yes,' as though his memory had at last been refreshed. 'Tell me Monsignor Reitanio, what is your role here at the Vatican?'

'I am a clerk, Eminence.'

'A clerk?'

'Ah, well, yes. I suppose that describes what I do. I work in …'

'I did not ask where, or for whom you work,' Morova interrupted, all traces of geniality gone. The Monsignor was still standing, becoming increasingly uncomfortable, and switching his weight from one foot to the other. Morova must have noticed his discomfiture. 'Would you like to sit down, Monsignor?' he asked in an affable tone.

Reitanio thanked him with a grateful smile, moving towards one of the chairs facing Morova's desk. As he reached for the back of the chair, Morova stopped him dead in his tracks. 'Well, I'd prefer you stand.'

Reitanio's hand froze in mid air, his face reddened by the humiliation. 'As you wish, Eminence.' His initial foreboding was now replaced with anger at his treatment thus far. 'May I ask, just what it is Your Eminence wishes to discuss with me?'

'Let me hear you recite the affirmation of faith,' Morova growled.

'I beg your pardon?' Reitanio asked, taken by surprise.

'I beg your pardon, Cardinal, or Eminence,' Morova corrected.

'My apologies, Eminence, it's just that, well, you surprised me.'

Morova leaned forward, placing his hands firmly on the desk, he spoke slowly and distinctly, his voice menacing. 'You heard me Monsignor, recite the Catholic affirmation of faith.'

'But why? I'm sorry, I don't understand, Eminence.' He added the last word as an afterthought, completely flustered.

'Because I am ordering you to. You do know the words, don't you?' he added caustically.

Reitanio could see there was no point in arguing further, so he began to recite the affirmation, repeated every day, at every mass by millions of faithful Catholics around the world.

I believe in God the Father Almighty,
Creator of Heaven and earth;
I believe in Jesus Christ,
His only Son, our Lord,
He was conceived by the Holy Spirit
and born of the Virgin Mary.
He suffered under Pontius Pilate,
was crucified, died, and was buried.
He descended to the dead.
On the third day He rose again.
He ascended into Heaven
and is seated at the right hand of the Father.
He will come again to judge the living and the dead.
I believe in the Holy Spirit,
the Holy Catholic Church,
the communion of Saints,
the forgiveness of sins,
the resurrection of the body,
and life everlasting.
Amen.'

Morova allowed him to complete the affirmation uninter-rupted. When he had finished Morova looked up and said, unmistakeable menace in his tone, 'You dare to stand here, in the office of the Secretary of State of the Vatican, within the very heart of Christ's Church and affirm your Catholic faith.'

'Eminence,' Reitanio pleaded, 'I am confused. You are speaking in riddles. I, I don't understand.'

'Then do you understand this?' Morova thundered, standing up from his chair, and walking around his desk towards the hapless Monsignor till their chests nearly touched. 'You and Satan's cohorts have been plotting against me, the Holy Father and Mother Church.'

A feeling of dread enveloped Reitanio, and for the first time he began to harbour doubts about his friend O'Shaughnessy. He knew that O'Shaughnessy was no longer a practising priest, having been de-frocked for his involvement in the Vatican bank scandal. At the time and ever since, Reitanio had steadfastly believed his friend was innocent of the charges. But now, standing before the second highest official in the Catholic Church, he was no longer so sure of himself. After all who was he, a lowly Monsignor cleric, to side against a cardinal? Perhaps there really were things going on which were beyond his scope of understanding. He began to shake under the unerring glare of Morova, and his resolve began to evaporate. Morova was quick to seize on this, and speaking more gently, he finally invited the Monsignor to take a seat.

Reitanio settled his bulk into the chair, head bowed, looking utterly miserable, as Morova continued in a conciliatory tone. 'Greater and wiser men than you have been tricked by Satan, my son. The important thing is that you now recognise your folly and make a clean breast of it. You must understand that now, more than ever before, the Catholic Church is in great danger, and frankly my son, we are losing the battle.'

Deeply affected by this statement and Morova's apparent sincerity, Reitanio begged for the Cardinal's forgiveness, asking what he could do to right the wrongs he may have unwittingly inflicted.

Morova waved a hand. 'I forgive you freely, my son, for obviously you knew not what you were doing when you chose to side with Luciferians. As to what you can do to amend the damage you have caused, simply tell me all you know about those who approached you for information.'

Reitanio was almost pathetic in his gratitude, happily blurting out all he knew. He related everything LeSarus and Christina had told him about Morova, blushing at times and apologising for having doubted the Cardinal. Morova reassured him that he'd been tricked by the devil's disciples, and urged him to continue. Reitanio told him about the Fatima copy, and the plan to travel to the Dolomites in the hope of retrieving it from the late Pope Leo Alexander's friend.

At this point Morova questioned him about details of their departure, their mode of transport, how many were in the party and the route they were taking. Reitanio was able to deliver all this information, as LeSarus had confided freely in O'Shaughnessy's friend.

After Morova was satisfied he had gleaned all the information, he suggested the Monsignor take a few moments to reflect in prayer, offering him the use of his personal chapel. Reitanio agreed gratefully as Morova led him by the elbow to the tiny chapel adjoining his office.

As the Monsignor knelt, head bowed in prayer, he did not hear Morova stealthily approaching from behind. Reitanio felt a sharp jab in his neck as Morova plunged the deadly hypodermic syringe into the exposed jugular vein. He turned, hands frantically clawing at the needle jutting from his neck, but it was too late. Morova had already injected the deadly concoction. As it started to take effect, Reitanio's dying brain had just enough rational time left to understand the truth. Then his mind stopped and he collapsed sideways from the kneeler.

He was dead before he hit the floor.

Morova stepped over the body and returning to his office he picked up the phone, dialling a number known only to him.

A familiar voice came on the line and Morova said, 'It's me. There is a mess in my chapel that needs cleaning up. Please see to it immediately.'

Without waiting for a response he hung up and dialled another number. When his call was answered he gave the same curt greeting as before. This time he spent a longer time on the phone, giving explicit instructions to the person on the other end and describing an exact route to the Dolomite Mountains.

He then made a third call. After issuing instructions, he finished by saying, 'And I want something special for the Archbishop. Something spectacular, do you hear me? Make sure you eliminate the secretary too,' he added, almost as an afterthought.

Chapter 36

After renting a car, Emery and Gadaleta picked up Peter and Christina and to their surprise told them they were leaving. With Gadaleta at the wheel, they set off from Rome heading north to Florence. They didn't stop to take in the sights of the famous Medici city, but drove on without rest, heading north towards the Austrian border and the mighty Dolomite Mountains. They stopped at Bologna to refuel, where they grabbed a bite to eat and stretched their aching muscles. Feeling refreshed, they continued their journey through Padova and began to wind their way up the tortuous mountain road towards their final destination, the tiny village of San Martino di Castroza, nestled in a valley deep within the mountains at an altitude of about 3000 metres. The scenery was spectacular with impossibly rugged cliffs reaching up to touch the sky. As they climbed higher the contrast of dusted snow made the cliffs look even more imposing.

Gadaleta was still at the wheel, concentrating on the winding, slippery road, barely wide enough for two vehicles to pass. In most places there wasn't even a guard rail to separate them from the sickening abyss dropping vertically from the road for 1000 metres. Whenever they approached a hairpin curve in the road Gadaleta would plant the palm of his hand on the horn, having quickly learned the reckless nature of local drivers.

'These Italians only have two speeds,' he complained, 'stationary or flat out.'

Christina laughed from the back seat, adding, 'Any speed in between seems to be a serious indictment against their manhood.' Her laugh was a nervous attempt at jocularity, as twice they had been nearly forced off the road, with one wheel spinning desperately in space, screaming to regain traction. She wished they would arrive and get off this road.

They were all nervous and no one had spoken for some time, when Peter broke the silence, hoping to alleviate the tense atmosphere in the car.

'Can you believe that Pope Leo Alexander I used to climb these mountains?'

Emery turned in his seat, thankful for the distraction. 'You're kidding me. You mean, like really climb, with spikes and ropes and all that serious climbing stuff?'

'Yes,' Peter confirmed, 'he was an accomplished mountaineer and he and his friend, Father Bruno Bracciano, used to spend days climbing on these cliffs.'

'How do you know all this stuff?' Gadaleta asked.

'We picked up a copy of his biography while we were waiting for you.'

Gadaleta was about to respond but was interrupted by a shuddering thud from behind. They were hit with such force that Emery's door exploded open, and he was flung from the car. 'What the hell …?' Gadaleta said, desperately fighting to regain control as the vehicle lurched dangerously close to the edge. 'Christ, why didn't Scott have his belt on?' He brought the car under control and was about to pull over to go to Emery's assistance. He glanced at the rear view mirror and saw a large, black saloon right on his tail. There was no sign of Emery. 'Idiot,' he shouted and then started pouring out a torrent of vile abuse, momentarily forgetting who his passengers were. He was pulling over when they were rammed again, only this time harder. Gadaleta wrestled with the wheel, suddenly becoming silent as he must have realised they were being rammed deliberately. Peter and Christina turned in their seats to take a look at the driver behind them. There were two men in the car, and even in a sedentary position it was obvious the passenger was a man of huge proportions. Both men wore grim looks of determination as the driver increased speed, lining up for another charge.

'Watch it, Tony,' LeSarus warned, 'He's going to hit us again.' They braced themselves for the crash, which nearly sent them off the road again.

'What on earth is going on?' Christina cried out from the back seat, fear in her voice. Peter placed a protective arm around her shoulder and she slid towards him, cringing.

Gadaleta did not answer, concentrating and fighting with the wheel.

They were approaching another hairpin curve, and Gadaleta knew that if they were rammed at the apex of the curve, nothing would stop them going over the cliff. As he was about to negotiate the curve he watched the vehicle behind him in his mirror. It was creeping up to deliver the fatal charge. Without warning, Gadaleta wrenched the wheel over, and at the same time he hit the brakes hard, crashing into the sheer cliff rising up from the roadway, causing the car to come to a gut-wrenching stop. In the back seat Christina screamed, and Peter held her closer. Then, in the same split second, the vehicle behind them raced alongside and Gadaleta threw the gear lever into drive, simultaneously flattening the accelerator. The wheels spun, spitting gravel as the vehicle shot forward, ramming into the rear-side of their antagonists. The black car slewed sideways from the impact. They could see the driver fighting with the wheel, desperate to regain control as his car slid towards the cliff edge, and then, with sickening inevitability, the vehicle launched into space. LeSarus caught a clear look of the terror-filled faces of the stricken men as they plummeted, with the sure knowledge they were about to die.

Christina's scream was extinguished as her head exploded with pain as their own car finished upside down, pressed hard up against the cliff. She lost consciousness.

Chapter 37

Archbishop Voitra glanced at the luminous clock on his bedside table. It read 1:20AM, only three minutes since he last looked. He wondered if Father Hruska was also experiencing a sleepless night. So much had happened. He was glad he'd sent the young priest to visit his family. Voitra needed the solitude to reflect on what he'd done. Hruska had tried to argue, not wishing to leave his master alone, but the Archbishop told him he wanted time alone to meditate on his sins.

He reflected on how he had been duped by Morova and could not believe he'd fallen for his treachery.

His thoughts were interrupted by a noise downstairs, but he decided it was merely the creaking of the ancient building. There it was again, on the stairs. This time there was no denying it. Someone was climbing the stairs to his bedroom and he wondered if Hruska had decided to return. He thought this strange, considering the time and decided he had better investigate. It was not uncommon for homeless people to seek a free bed and a meal, and tonight was cold. Switching on the light, he tentatively opened the door, ready to scold whoever had decided to pay him an unwelcome visit at such an ungodly hour.

He never saw the blow coming.

The baseball bat connected between his upper lip and just below his nose, hurling him backward into the bedroom. He landed on his backside dazed, the taste of blood at the back of his throat. Spitting out a mouthful of broken teeth he tried to focus on the silhouetted figure of his attacker. The shape filled the frame of the doorway and with deliberate purposefulness was making its way toward him. He saw the boot flying towards his head and instinctively lifted his arms to cover his face but he was not fast enough. In a blur of speed the boot connected with his mouth, and he gagged with pain. The force of the kick sent him sprawling onto his back. Instinctively he doubled over into the foetal position to protect himself from further blows. Blood was filling his throat, and he nearly choked on his remaining shattered teeth. Another kick caught him on the side, smashing ribs. He struggled to get to his knees, desperate to crawl away from his unknown assailant but caught another cruel kick to the groin, causing him to retch. He had no time to recover as another kick followed immediately, this time to the side of his head. He saw stars, but no longer felt pain, and was dimly aware of more kicks, landing indiscriminately, one after the other until finally he sank into merciful oblivion.

⋟✦⋞

The assailant stopped to admire his handiwork with a detached, professional sense of pride. His victim's face was an unrecognisable, bloody pulp of raw meat, yet he was still alive, and would regain consciousness, the attacker noted with satisfaction. His instructions were clear. This one was to receive special treatment.

He worked quickly, knowing his job would be far easier while his customer was still unconscious. Despite his strength, he knew from past experience how even slightly built men are capable of calling on superhuman reserves of resistance when subjected to excruciating pain. The pain would come later, after the Archbishop regained consciousness. The assailant almost felt sorry for his victim, wondering what act of transgression he had committed to warrant such special consideration, but quickly shrugged off the sentiment. After all, he was a professional.

A red cloud of agony slowly penetrated Voitra's consciousness, as he tried to comprehend what had happened to him. Wave after wave of nauseating pain engulfed his body. He tried to move but his muscles would not obey. Slowly his tortured brain began to remember the beating. He tried to cry out but only managed a weak moan and then realised there was something in his mouth, choking him. It felt like cotton, which he tried to extricate with his tongue. His nose was so clogged with blood he had difficulty breathing. His entire body was now wracked with pain, and he felt enormous pressure pulling at his limbs and chest, threatening to suffocate him as he laboured for every breath. He tried to open his eyes but they were so puffed his lids would not obey. Through the lids of his eyes, he was aware the light was on, and then, ever so slowly, he managed to force one eye partly open. To his great confusion, he was looking down on his bed, and could not understand his perspective. He tried to turn his head to figure why he could not move his arms, but only managed to turn it ever so slightly. But it was enough. He screamed silently into his gag.

He was crucified to the ceiling of his own bedroom.

Chapter 38

Christina tried moving her head and winced as pain stabbed through her neck. Gingerly she touched at her throbbing head and felt a bandage. She looked down at the crisp sheet tucked up to her chin, wondering whose bed she was in and how she had got there, and then, realising she was naked she blushed, speculating on who had undressed her. Slowly her memory came back and she remembered the accident. Then, with a start, she remembered it had been no accident. Someone had tried to kill them. Fighting back the panic threatening to overtake her, she forced herself to ignore the pain and take stock of her surroundings. The small room she was in did not resemble any hospital room she'd ever seen. The walls were of rough logs with the cracks separating them filled with straw and pitch to keep out the wind. Beside the bed was a chest of drawers with an array of photographs, which she guessed must have been of the family members who lived here. As well as pictures there was also a pitcher of water standing in a basin, with a washcloth and towel folded neatly next to it. A straight-backed, wooden chair completed the sparse furnishing. The only other decorations apart from the family photos were a framed picture of the Sacred Heart of Jesus and a small wooden crucifix. From these simple observations, Christina was able to deduce that she was in a private home, the occupants were Catholics and most likely they did not have running water.

She tried to sit up and was rewarded with another sharp pain in the neck. She gritted her teeth and persevered, till finally she succeeded. The exertion taxed her strength, and the throbbing in her head increased. She sat still for a while, waiting for her breathing to return to normal and hoping the pain would subside. She swung her legs out of the bed and, wrapping the sheet around her, tried to stand, only to crash to the floor as her rubbery legs crumpled under her weight. The noise must have alerted the occupant, for almost immediately the bedroom door opened and a heavy-set, matronly woman entered the room. She took one look at Christina, sprawled half-naked on the floor and rushed to her aid, clucking in concerned Italian. She bent down and hooking an arm under each armpit, she easily helped Christina off the floor and back on to the bed, where Christina flopped back exhausted. The woman continued to fuss, arranging the quilt and fluffing the pillows.

Christina smiled gratefully at the woman. It was difficult to determine her age. She was large-boned and buxom, dressed in black with tufts of greying, dark hair escaping from under a tight black scarf. She returned the smile and then spoke again in rapid Italian, gesticulating with her hands. Christina understood that she was to wait where she was, and that she, or someone else would soon return. The woman hurried from the room, closing the door behind her as if fearing her charge might attempt to get out of bed again. She was only gone a few minutes when the door burst open and there stood Peter LeSarus. She had never been so relieved to see anyone in her life.

'Welcome back to the land of the living,' he greeted, with a warm smile which failed to hide the look of concern in his eyes.

Christina winced with pain as she struggled to sit up again.

Peter rushed to her side. 'Whoa, steady on. Just take it easy. You've had a nasty whack on the head.'

'Where am I?' she demanded. 'How did I get here, how long have I been out of it? I remember the accident. How are the others? Is everyone else all right?'

'Everyone's fine,' Peter assured her, 'but it was no accident. Someone tried to run us off the road. You were the only one hurt.

Emery was lucky. He was thrown out of the car, but apart from a few bruises and grazes, he's all right. As I said, you copped one on the head. I think you were concussed.'

Christina fingered the bandage on her head.

'You've been out of it for two days.'

'Two days,' Christina echoed. 'The other car, what happened to them? I saw it go over the cliff. Were they killed?'

'They tried to kill us, Christina.'

'Were they killed?' she repeated.

'I'm afraid so,' Peter answered.

'Oh my God, Peter, what have we got ourselves involved in?'

Peter shrugged his shoulders. There was nothing more he could say.

'Where are we? What happened after the accident?'

'We're in San Martino di Castroza.'

'Oh, so we made it.'

'Yes finally, but you wouldn't believe how difficult it was. This village is tiny, I mean really tiny. Trying to organise a tow truck, an ambulance and rescue services was a nightmare. You were lucky to have slept through it all.'

'What about Father Bracciano, did you find him? Does he still have a copy of the document?'

'Christina, slow down. There's plenty of time.'

Peter began to relate what happened following the crash.

⚜

After they crashed into the cliff they were stranded, as there was hardly any traffic on the backwoods mountain road. Christina was unconscious and they could not guess at the seriousness of her injuries. Their greatest fear was being caught by the dark, after which the temperature would plummet to below zero. Peter, who was frantically worried about Christina, volunteered to set out on foot and follow the road in the hope of finding help.

After walking for a couple of hours he finally stumbled onto a tiny village where he was met by the curious inhabitants. He tried explaining that he needed help but no one could understand him and his frustrated hand signals were watched with bemusement. Just as he was about to give up in frustration, the small crowd parted, allowing a man dressed in the black smock of a priest to approach Peter.

A priest, thank God, Peter thought, and tried communicating in Latin. To his relief the priest understood and Peter introduced himself, urgently explaining their plight. The priest gave orders to a couple of the men who left, returning in a few minutes in an old, dilapidated truck.

'They will drive back to collect your friends,' the priest assured him. 'Now come, we will go inside, I will call the police and get you a hot drink. Once you are sufficiently rested you must lead me to the unfortunate deceased. We must minister to their souls.'

Peter guessed the man's age at somewhere around sixty, but it was difficult to tell. He looked lean and fit, with the leathery, weatherbeaten features of someone who had spent a great deal of his life outdoors. Handing Peter the coffee, the priest left the room, returning in a couple of minutes dressed in an anorak with a neatly curled mountaineer's rope draped over his shoulder. He handed an anorak to Peter, and told him to put it on, explaining that it gets very cold in the mountains.

By the time the two drove back to the crash scene in the priest's car the truck was already returning with its passengers. As they passed, the priest honked his horn and waved but did not stop. He pulled up when he spotted the vehicle lying on its roof. Jumping out, he methodically unwound the rope, anchoring it to the car's bumper. When he was satisfied that the rope was secure, he asked Peter if he wished to accompany him down the cliff to the other car.

Tentatively, Peter peered over the edge and was overcome with vertigo.

'It is all right,' the priest assured him. 'I will go alone. You wait here for me.'

Peter could not help but admire this elderly man's courage and felt ashamed at his own fear. 'No, no,' he insisted, 'I will go with you. You may need help.'

'You know how to abseil?' the priest asked.

'Um, I'm not sure. What does it mean?'

The priest chuckled. 'You had better wait here,' he advised as he threw the anchored rope out into space.

Peter watched as the priest hooked himself onto the rope, and then walked backwards to the edge of the cliff. Without hesitating he leaned back, disappearing over the edge.

After what seemed an eternity, the taut rope went slack and Peter knew the priest must have reached bottom. He crawled on his belly to the edge to peer over but could see nothing due to the overhanging angle of the cliff. He resigned himself to wait, but after a while began to pace nervously. What if he's hurt, Peter thought uneasily. He could be at the bottom with a broken ankle, or God only knows what injury. Suddenly he decided he couldn't just wait.

Peter fetched the spare abseiling hardware from the car, and began trying to figure out how it worked. Although he'd watched the priest, he wished he had paid closer attention. After a few attempts he managed to secure himself into the harness. Next he clipped on a karabiner to which he attached the figure eight abseiling ring. That was the easy part. The difficult part was getting the rope correctly attached to the ring. Finally, after a few attempts, he felt reasonably sure he had it right. He leaned his weight against the rope and it seemed to work. Slowly, he inched backwards towards the drop like he had seen the priest do it. As his feet reached the edge he experienced a sudden panic attack and lurched forward away from the precipice. What if I haven't done it right? he thought. I must be insane. He tried his weight against the rope again, testing to see if the system would hold. It seemed to do the trick but he still couldn't be sure. His imagination took over and his courage deserted him. About to give up and extricate himself from the harness, he thought again of the priest possibly lying injured at the bottom of the cliff. Don't be such a bloody coward, he hissed at himself. With renewed determination he mouthed a silent prayer and backed to the edge again. This time when his feet felt the edge he hesitated for only a second, not trusting himself to pause. Shutting his eyes, he stepped gingerly down the face.

To his great surprise and delight it worked. He still lacked the courage to look down, concentrating instead on taking one vertical step after another. After a while he began to feel he had the knack of it and feeling bolder, he increased his pace. Without warning, his feet gave way as he reached the overhang and he dropped, hitting his head on the rock face. Instinctively he dropped the rope, raising his hands to protect his face. The instant he let go, the braking mechanism ceased, and he plummeted down the cliff. He screamed as he fell, clutching desperately at the rope, trying to arrest his fall. Just as he thought he was about to die, the rope went taut, bringing him to a shuddering stop. He wasn't sure what had happened, and then, just as he thought he'd regained his composure, he began to descend again, but at a controlled rate. He could not understand how this was happening as his hands were not even on the rope. Finally he felt his feet touch the ground and he sank to a sitting position, breathing heavily.

'That was a close call,' the priest observed, 'I wish you had warned me you were coming down.'

He explained to Peter that he was just about to crawl into the wreck of the car when he heard Peter scream. He managed to leap at the rope, grabbing it and applying tension, arresting his fall.

Peter thanked him, and then apologised for his untimely entrance, explaining he'd been worried he may have been hurt.

'Well, thank you for your concern, but I have done this many, many times. But no need to apologise, you displayed great courage to abseil down a cliff when you have never done it before. But come, we must administer to the immortal souls of these two unfortunate men.'

Peter began to wonder how they were going to get back up the cliff. In answer to his thoughts the priest explained that they would return the way they had come by utilising jumars, or ascenders. He only had one pair of this apparatus with him, so he explained to Peter how it worked and sent him slowly and laboriously back up the rope, a foot at a time. When Peter reached the top he tied the jumars onto the rope, and lowered them down to his companion.

By the time they had returned to the village it was late at night and the police had been and gone. Emery and Gadaleta were waiting in the priest's house when the two returned, with Christina still billeted in the farmer's house. The police had been satisfied it had been a tragic accident and said they would make arrangements to recover the bodies the following day. No one had suggested the possibility of foul play as Emery warned they did not need the police complicating things at this stage. The Italian priest welcomed his guests, begging them to make his home their own. Emery asked Peter if the priest was Father Bruno Bracciano. Peter was amazed that in all the excitement it hadn't occurred to him to ask the priest the same question.

'Alas, no,' the priest answered in Latin. 'I am Father Sebastian. Alas, Father Bracciano has been dead for many years.

I now look after his small flock of parishioners alone.' He went on to ask how they knew of Father Bracciano, and what business they had with him.

Peter explained that they were researching the Fatima phenomenon. 'It would seem that the Third Secret, as documented by Sister Lucia, has gone missing and we understand that Father Bracciano had a copy.'

'How intriguing,' Father Sebastian exclaimed, 'but what makes you think Father Bracciano would have a copy of such an important document?'

Peter explained that the former Pope's private secretary had confided in them, and had given them a copy of a letter sent to Father Bracciano by his late friend, Pope Leo Alexander I.

Father Sebastian asked if he could see the copy of the letter. Emery readily agreed, producing the letter. Father Sebastian read the letter with great interest before returning it. 'My, my,' he observed, 'it would seem my dear friend was handed a great cross to bear by his friend, the Pope.'

At Emery's prompt, Peter continued. 'Father Sebastian, did Father Bracciano ever discuss this with you?'

'No, he did not.'

'How long ago did he die?'

'Very soon after learning of the Pope's death.'

Emery grew increasingly frustrated as Peter translated. 'Ask him,' he said, 'whether he was here when the letter was delivered to Father Bracciano?

'I do recall something of importance being hand-delivered from the Vatican. Father Bracciano had to sign for it. I remember he became agitated after reading it, but he died soon after, without telling me what it was about.'

'I see,' Emery said. 'Does he know what Father Bracciano did with the document? I mean, if he died soon after receiving it, it must have been among his personal effects.'

Peter relayed the question.

'Had I seen anything like what you refer to, I would certainly remember it. May I ask what this is truly all about, Father LeSarus?'

'I fear it could be to your detriment to tell you Father. There are men who will stop at nothing to ensure the document never sees the light of day again.'

'I see,' Father Sebastian mused, 'and these men you speak of, did they have anything to do with your, ah, accident?'

'We do not wish to place your life in danger as well, Father. Suffice to say, we have reason to believe that Pope Leo Alexander I was murdered for actions he was about to take as a result of studying the Third Secret.'

'And you cannot tell me what your role is in all of this?' Father Sebastian persisted.

'Father, believe me, it is safer for you not to know, but we are determined to uncover the truth and to deliver that truth to the world.'

'I see. And how do I know you are not the evil ones wanting to destroy this document?'

'A fair question,' Peter agreed, 'and one that I really can't answer to your satisfaction. Guess you'll just have to decide whether or not you feel you can trust us.'

'An honest answer. But come, it is late, and we are all tired. Why don't we pray on the matter and speak again in the morning?'

Chapter 39

Christina had listened with great interest to Peter's account with hardly an interruption.

'That was last night, Christina,' Peter finished, 'and brings you right up to date with everything that happened since you were injured.'

Christina was acutely aware of her nakedness beneath the sheet, pulling it even closer to her chin, she asked, 'Where is Father Sebastian now?'

'He went out early to assist the police in recovering the bodies.'

'Do you think he knows more than he's letting on?'

'That's what Gadaleta and Emery suggested. They think he's hiding something.'

'From what you've told me,' she said, 'and without having spoken to him myself of course, I would tend to agree. Do you think we should take him into our confidence?'

'I don't think we have anything to lose.'

By the time Father Sebastian returned, Peter and Christina had spoken to Gadaleta and Emery, and all agreed there was nothing to be lost in taking the Italian priest into their confidence. They all knew that without his help they had reached a dead end in locating the missing Third Secret. Perhaps there was nothing more he could add but they had no choice but to exhaust every option open to them and, for now, this seemed to be the last one left. As Christina was still bedridden they invited the priest to her room.

Father Sebastian greeted Christina warmly when he was ushered into the small room, barely large enough to accommodate them all. Peter sat on the edge of Christina's bed, while the others sat on the extra chairs the owner of the house had provided.

'I am so glad you are feeling better,' Father Sebastian conveyed to Christina.

Christina thanked him, while Peter interpreted for the benefit of the laymen. 'Peter told me how you helped us, and I cannot thank you enough for your generosity and hospitality.'

'Any priest would have done the same,' he replied.

'Peter conveyed your reservations about our motives. I understand your suspicions; anyone could come here making all sorts of claims.'

The priest nodded, but said nothing.

Peter said, 'My friends and I discussed the situation while you were away this morning, and we have agreed to be open with you.'

'I think that would be a good thing,' Father Sebastian nodded again, gesturing for Peter to continue.

Without holding anything back, Peter recounted all they knew, including their experiences to date.

'And this prophecy document you speak of, do you have a copy with you?' Father Sebastian asked. 'I would very much like to see it.'

Peter opened the valise he'd brought with him, removing a manila envelope. 'I brought the copy from Professor Muntz in anticipation of showing it to Father Bracciano.'

He opened the envelope, removing the document and handed it to Father Sebastian who took it with trembling hands and began to read. He read the entire document without comment, occasionally emitting a tut-tut sound, and shaking his head as he read something that probably caused him particular concern or amazement. Finally he returned the document to Peter, who replaced it in the envelope. All eyes were on Father Sebastian, awaiting his reaction. He continued to sit silently for some time before finally speaking in a voice choked with emotion.

'This document is truly incredible, and finally I understand many things that were previously a mystery. You say this was written almost four thousand years ago, and that it has been authenticated?'

'Yes,' Peter confirmed.

'Then this is truly amazing, and of course quite unbelievable, although I am now convinced you are genuine, gentlemen. I can understand why some people would not want this revealed.'

'Father Sebastian,' Peter prodded gently, 'is there anything else you can tell us?'

Father Sebastian seemed to be wrestling with a mental turmoil. There were tears in his eyes as he looked around at the people in the room.

'My name is not Father Sebastian,' he whispered.

He had everyone's attention.

'I am Bruno Bracciano.'

They all stared at the priest as though he were a ghost.

Ignoring their reaction, Father Bracciano continued. 'Giuseppe, or Pope Leo Alexander I, was my great friend, and I miss him terribly. I always suspected his death was never explained satisfactorily. When I learned he'd died so soon after sending me that letter I did not know what to think – or believe. It was a long time before I could bring myself to open the sealed envelope he'd entrusted to me. When I finally did, I understood why he had recalled the cardinals so soon after his election. And it was then that I knew without a doubt, that he had been murdered.' He then added, 'I am not a brave man gentlemen. I am ashamed to say that I lacked the courage to pursue it.'

'Please, Father Bracciano,' Emery asked, 'why do you think he recalled the cardinals?' Peter translated.

Father Bracciano frowned, considering the question carefully before replying. 'I do not think it is my place to offer an opinion on that. I would prefer you came to your own conclusion after you have studied the document for your self.'

Peter had mixed emotions at this response. He was disappointed that Father Bracciano would not share his conclusions with them, but at the same time he felt a thrill of excitement, which, judging by the look on Christina's face, she shared. Eagerly Peter asked, 'So it still exists?'

'Oh, yes. It exists all right,' Father Bracciano assured him.

Gadaleta and Emery were watching the priests and the nun closely, sensing something important. 'C'mon Peter,' Scott Emery pleaded, 'let us in on it. What did he say?'

Peter ignored the question. 'And do you have it with you?'

'I hid it where it could never be found.'

'Could you take us to it?' Peter asked.

'I daresay you may be up to such an adventure,' he said. 'As a matter of fact I will need help, I'm not as young as I used to be.'

'Where did you hide it?' Peter asked.

'In a cave not far from here, but it is very difficult to reach.' He smiled sheepishly. 'You see, it is a thousand metres up a sheer cliff.'

Peter paled at the thought of accompanying this remarkable old man on another mountaineering expedition. He translated for the benefit of the others.

Emery said, 'One of us should go. With respect, Peter, Tony and I have more experience at this sort of thing.'

'What sort of thing?' Peter asked. 'Scaling a sheer cliff?' He gestured with his eyes at Emery's protruding belly.

'Well, OK, point taken. I'm not as fit as I used to be, but Tony is, and he's had extensive survival training.'

Peter translated for Father Bracciano.

Bracciano listened to the objection and then replied, shaking his head, 'None of you are experienced climbers, and besides, I must be able to communicate with the man I take. You certainly look fit enough and you have already proven your courage and that you have a calm head for heights. More than one will only get in the way.'

Begrudgingly, Gadaleta and Emery had to acquiesce.

'How difficult is the climb, Father?' Christina asked, hoping her voice did not betray her nervousness.

'I first attempted it with Giuseppe when we were much younger men. He was an excellent climber, but it was without doubt the most difficult climb either of us had ever attempted. To the best of my knowledge no one else has ever repeated the achievement. When Giuseppe and I climbed it we found the cave and we commented on how it would make an excellent hiding place. The cave is protected by a great overhanging roof, making it impossible to abseil to from the top.'

Christina, sounding even more nervous now, asked, 'Father, the late Pope was an accomplished mountaineer, so what makes you think that Peter, with no experience, could possibly make it?'

'I will do all the climbing, and Peter will follow me using the ascenders which he already knows how to use. While I'm climbing, it will be Peter's job to protect me.'

'Protect you? I don't understand,' Christina said, perplexed.

'Let me demonstrate how two climbers would tackle a dangerous climb while protecting themselves.' He took a notebook from his pocket and drew a diagram of two climbers on a cliff. 'Climbers protect each other with a technique called belaying.'

It sounded strange to hear the priest use a technical term in English, interspersed with the Latin, but it was only one more oddity in this whole experience, and Peter decided he would just have to revise his definition of normality.

'Which means the second climber anchors himself to the rock face,' the priest continued. 'He then pays out a rope to the leader who, as he climbs, threads the rope through various devices he has attached to the rock face. Should the leader fall, he would only drop as far as his last fixed point. Do you understand?'

Peter translated and the others nodded as they studied the simple diagram.

'Good. So now you understand why I need someone to accompany me, to protect me in the event of a fall, which at my age is quite likely.'

Peter shuddered. 'What if I can't hold you?'

'Oh, don't worry about that. It has nothing to do with strength, even though you do seem to be a strong young man. We use a device called an arrestor which, as its name implies, is designed to arrest a fall.'

'I see,' Peter said, not at all convinced he would be up to the task.

'Don't worry, Father LeSarus, you have a big heart, and with a little more coaching and a lot of faith, I believe you will be able to follow me. But if you truly want the document, do we have a choice?'

Chapter 40

The two men set out from the village at two in the morning, because, as Father Bracciano explained, they had to be on the face by daybreak in order to complete the climb and get off before nightfall. Father Bracciano had managed to outfit Peter with climbing gear borrowed from a parishioner of similar size. Father Bracciano utilised their time on the walk to advantage, explaining the equipment and the basic techniques of climbing to Peter. The younger man, who was accustomed to the outdoors, found he was beginning to enjoy the older priest's company immensely.

They wore hiking boots on the approach to the cliff-face, which they would later change for the less comfortable, slim, tight fitting, vibram-soled climbing shoes. They each carried a backpack filled with food, water, chocolate for energy and climbing hardware, and each man carried a 50 metre, perlon-sheathed climbing rope draped over his shoulder.

The massif they headed for was clearly visible from the village, dominating the skyline with its ominous dark, buttress shape. They set out on an easy path through a thick pine forest, illuminating their progress with headlamps, leaving their hands free for the scramble over the rough scree slope leading up to the base of the cliff. The air had a cold bite, causing their breath to vaporise and Peter was grateful for the warm climber's anorak. After a while they walked on in silence, each immersed in their own thoughts, conserving their breath and energy for the gruelling climb ahead.

When they emerged from the forest, they stepped on to the start of the scree slope, an unstable pile of rubble that had fallen from the cliff over the millennia. It was made up of a morass of loose stones and rocks ranging in size from ankle breaking pebbles to boulders the size of a cottage. Father Bracciano expertly negotiated their way among the boulders, sure-footedly heading upwards towards the base of the cliff. At times there was no way around some of the giant boulders and they had to climb up and over them.

When they finally arrived at the start of the climb proper, they stopped at the base of a thin crack that bisected the great expanse of cliff. Bracciano took off his pack and began rummaging through the climbing hardware, arranging it in an orderly cluster on a belt around his waist. By the time he'd completed this task he carried a huge array of pitons and karabiners. He uncoiled the climbing rope, fastening one end to his climbing harness with a bowline knot, finished off with two half-hitches. The first streaks of dawn began to illuminate the face, turning it from coal black to blood red. Peter leaned back and peered up at the cliff they were about to negotiate, awed at the immensity and steepness of the great precipice which seemed to lean out, giving him a sense that it would topple down onto them.

'The route we'll take is straight up this crack,' Bracciano explained. 'It's a natural fault line, which will enable me to climb up by jamming my feet and hands into the fissure.'

'It looks incredibly steep,' Peter exclaimed in wonder, unable to believe that anyone could possibly climb the sheer cliff.

'Yes, it is,' Bracciano chuckled, 'it's actually steeper than vertical, which means it is slightly overhanging all the way up. If you were to drop a plumbline from the top, it would finish up quite a long way out from the face, making it impossible to abseil back down once we are committed to the climb.'

This piece of news did nothing for Peter's confidence. 'So how do you climb something steeper than vertical?'

'It does make for difficult climbing, but it's not impossible, provided you know what you're doing, and have the right equipment. When you follow me using the ascenders, you will be suspended clear of the wall. For me, the awkward part is if I fall. It makes it a bit tricky to get back onto the face.'

'Well let's pray that doesn't happen.'

'Don't worry, I'll be placing plenty of protection, as you'll soon see.'

This was all sounding very worrisome to Peter. 'So if you fall what do I do?'

Without answering, Father Bracciano proceeded to anchor Peter to a nearby boulder, attaching him to it with a stout length of webbing.

'There,' he exclaimed, admiring his handiwork, 'it would take a bomb to dislodge you.'

Next he attached another length of webbing to the same outcrop, snapping a karabiner on to the end of the loop he formed. He then snapped the rope through the gate of the karabiner and screwed it shut. He tied the other end of the rope to Peter and showed him how to pay it out as he ascended, and how to utilise the karabiner as a pulley to brake him in the event of a fall. Peter wasn't at all sure he'd mastered all there was to know, and was about to tell Father Bracciano, but before he could open his mouth the older priest, amid a loud clanking of hardware, began to climb.

'Ah, Father Bracciano, before you go further, may I ask a question?'

Father Bracciano paused, turning his head. 'Yes, what is it?'

'How old are you?'

Father Bracciano smiled as he replied. 'I was seventy-two last birthday. Why do you ask?'

Peter shook his head in astonishment at this remarkable man who was starting out on a climb, which would have daunted experienced climbers half his age. 'No reason, just be careful,' he added.

Peter paid out the rope as he had been shown, and watched with admiration as the elderly priest skilfully made his way up the natural fault-line of the cliff face. Somehow it was a thing of beauty to perceive, as the old man seemed to effortlessly glide up the rock. Every 5 metres or so he would stop, choose a piton of the right dimension and hammer it into the crack. He then attached a karabiner, clipping in his lifeline before continuing to the next safety point. Just as Peter thought he would lose sight of the climber, the 50 metres of rope had all but paid out. There was a longer pause this time and then Peter heard Bracciano shout that he was securely attached and Peter could commence his ascent.

Peter detached himself from the belay point he'd been anchored to and began to clumsily fiddle with the jumars, until finally satisfied, he began to ascend. At first his progress was painfully slow and deliberate, as he wrestled with the combination of actions required to slither up the rope. The jumars, or ascenders, were clamped to the rope and by pressing a trigger, the locking mechanism released, enabling him to alternately slide each one in turn upwards. Releasing the trigger, the ascender re-clamped onto the rope, allowing him to place his weight on it. Thus he was able to climb up the rope by way of a series of sliding steps. After about 20 metres he began to get the hang of it, and settled into a steady climbing rhythm. As he made his way up the sheer face he began to appreciate the difficulty of the climb and his admiration for the skill, courage and fitness of the elderly priest increased even more. Reaching each point where Father Bracciano had placed a piton and karabiner he had to unclip the rope and remove the hardware, clipping it on to his own waist-line to be used again on the following pitch.

When he finally reached Father Bracciano, he found him anchored to a piton hammered into the rock face, hauling in the slack rope in time with Peter's accent. As Peter reached him he allowed himself to look down for the first time, causing his head to swim with vertigo. From this perspective the pine forest they had trekked through looked like a miniature forest adorning a model railway. Father Bracciano helped Peter attach himself to the anchor point.

'No time to rest,' he said, 'that was only the first of ten pitches before we reach the cave. And this was probably the easiest,' he added.

'What, you mean it gets harder?'

'Yes. Take a look above you.'

Peter craned his neck to look up at the towering cliff soaring above their heads. They were suspended directly below a massive overhanging ceiling, and Peter could see no possible way of climbing it. 'There is no way a human could climb that,' he stated categorically.

'Not free climbing,' Bracciano agreed, 'the only way to get over that is by mechanical climbing, using etriers.'

'I'll take your word for it,' Peter marvelled, not at all convinced it was possible.

'Once I get over that roof, I'll bring you straight up. It's comparatively easy after that. But I'm afraid you'll have to try to move more quickly. We're behind schedule. I don't want to be caught on the face by the dark.'

'I'll try,' Peter promised, 'I think I'm getting the hang of it now.'

Without further ado, Bracciano unclipped himself from the anchor and began to climb towards the massive overhanging roof jutting 5 metres out from the cliff, obscuring the upper part of the climb. Reaching the base of the roof, he stopped to bang in a piton and attached a karabiner, into which he clipped a length of nylon webbing knotted into a series of loops. He placed a foot into one of the loops and stood up in it, allowing him to reach higher and repeat the process with another etrier, stepping from one to the other. He methodically continued this procedure along the ceiling of rock all the way out to the end of the overhang. Finally he hauled himself up and over the lip, disappearing from Peter's view.

Peter waited patiently, feeling the thumping of his racing heart, as he tried to prepare himself mentally for his turn.

Finally he heard the shout above. 'I'm secure, you can start climbing.'

Peter fitted the ascenders, more quickly now than before, and as he unclipped from his suspended perch, he launched out into space, as the rope took his weight and swung him out away from the cliff. He cried out in terror, wildly grabbing at the rope above him. When he'd reached the full arc of the pendulum he swung back, crashing into the cliff, winding himself. A stream of blood poured into his eyes where his forehead had slammed into the cliff. Finally the swinging stopped leaving him spinning crazily, directly below the massive ceiling of rock. He wiped the blood from his eyes and waited for his heart to stop racing. Gripping the ascenders until his knuckles were white he began his ascent in mid-air.

At last he hauled himself over the lip to find a grinning Father Bracciano comfortably standing on top of the overhang. 'What kept you?' he asked bemused. Noticing the cut on Peter's forehead he apologised. 'Mea culpa, I should have warned you that you would pendulum as soon as you unclipped.'

Peter wiped a hand over the cut and muttered, 'That's all right. It was fun.'

'Congratulations. That was the crux, the hardest part of the climb. It is more or less a straightforward climb from here to the cave.'

He examined the cut declaring it was only superficial, and began to ready himself to continue.

'Please,' Peter pleaded, 'can't we rest for just a short time? I need to steady my nerves.'

Father Bracciano laughed. 'All right,' he agreed, 'five minutes. You've earned it. We'll eat some chocolate.'

Peter gratefully removed a chocolate bar from his pack. 'I know this may sound like a stupid question,' he began, 'but once we get to the cave, how do we get down again?'

'As I said before, it would be impossible to backtrack down a climb like this because of the overhang, and there isn't a rope long enough for us to abseil. And once again, because of the overhang, we couldn't do it in stages, because by the time we reached the end of the rope, we'd be too far out from the face.'

'So how do we get off?' Peter persisted.

'The cave is about halfway up the cliff. Once we retrieve the document, we have no alternative but to continue climbing to the top. You see, this buttress is like a half dome. It's only steep on one side. Once we get to the top we just walk off and around, back to the village.'

Peter was relieved at not having to descend the way they had come, but wasn't sure he relished the thought of climbing all the way to the top of the massif.

The next pitch went without incident, and Peter found he was beginning to enjoy himself. He began to understand what it was that drew people to the giddy heights of mountains. Although he was still scared, he was experiencing a sense of pure physical achievement that he'd rarely felt before. His admiration for the old priest continued to grow, knowing that no matter what, he would never be capable of leading a climb of this magnitude and difficulty.

They continued on for two more pitches before Bracciano called a break. 'This is a safe, comfortable ledge,' he declared. 'We can rest here and have some breakfast.'

The nice ledge could not have been more than 40 centimetres wide. Bracciano anchored them to the wall above, and the two sat with their feet dangling in space. They ate a sparse meal of dried beef, bread and cheese, washing it down with water, which Bracciano urged Peter to drink sparingly.

Having finished the meal, Bracciano set off almost at once and it took all of Peter's willpower to force his now aching limbs to start working again.

They climbed on resolutely, with Peter beginning to think there was no end to the cliff, that it must stretch on forever. He was reminded of the children's story of Jack and the Beanstalk.

As he continued to monotonously climb the rope, Peter began to feel the effects of fatigue. His muscles ached, and any previous sense of exhilaration had been replaced with boredom at the repetitive movements up the rope. At the end of each 50-metre pitch Bracciano would wait for Peter to reach him, and then immediately take off on the next one. Peter lost count of the number of pitches they had completed. Catching up to Bracciano at the end of the current pitch he snapped on to the anchor and was about to plead for a rest when Bracciano declared, 'This is the last one.'

'The last one?' Peter repeated. 'What do you mean, the last pitch?'

'Yes,' Bracciano smiled. 'See that small clump of overhanging rock about 15 metres straight up?'

Peter peered straight up the wall, and there, just where Bracciano was pointing, he saw a prominent bulge of rock. 'Yes, I see it,' he said excitedly. 'What is it?'

'It's a small but tricky overhang, and just above it is the entrance to the cave.'

Compared to the long, 50-metre pitches they had been climbing, this one seemed almost inconsequential.

'I'll get going,' Bracciano announced. 'We can have lunch in the cave, where you'll be able to stretch out flat on your back.'

The luxury of this thought appealed immensely to Peter; his former lethargy disappeared and he felt a growing sense of excitement now that they were so close to the mysterious document. A mystical awe overcame him as he contemplated the document which was now almost within his reach, and which contained the spoken words of Our Lady.

Father Bracciano harboured his own thoughts, as he inched his way up the remaining few metres below the small but technically difficult bulge that was all that separated him from the sacred document he'd secreted away so many years before. He was overcome by a wave of nostalgic guilt as he thought that perhaps he should not have hidden the document, but instead revealed it to the world. But how? Who was there then, that he could have trusted? He still wasn't totally convinced that he could trust the man climbing with him, or his companions. But the document had to be finally revealed to the world, as was intended by the Virgin Mary. It had been kept a secret too long. Either way, the consequences were almost too terrible to comprehend, whether it was revealed or remained hidden. Damned if I do and damned if I don't, he thought bitterly.

He had reached the overhang, snapping himself out of his thoughts, willing himself to concentrate on the difficult moves ahead. The bulge he had to negotiate had no natural fault. Not even the tiniest crack to drive in a piton. The only way to negotiate it was to free climb it. To anyone but the most skilled rock climber it would be perceived to be perfectly smooth in texture. But Bracciano expertly felt for the tiny hint of ripples that he would use as minute finger and toe friction holds. His fingers searched over the smooth rock, till at last he felt what he was looking for. His middle finger disappeared into a hole like that of a ten-pin bowling ball. Displaying incredible finger strength, he flexed, pulling his entire weight up on the one finger. His feet desperately searched for the slightest roughness to give purchase to the sticky, smooth soles of his climbing shoes. He found traction. If his next move did not work he would fall. Desperately he lunged upward with his other hand for the hold that had to be there. It was. Gratefully his fingers curled around the comfortable jug-handle, and his feet followed up the impossibly overhanging bulge. Made it, he thought triumphantly, just as his strength was about to fail. Panting from the incredible effort he hauled himself up the last remaining centimetres toward safety. Just as he congratulated himself on succeeding, an explosion of pain erupted in his chest, shooting out into his left arm. As he fell, he knew with certainty he was experiencing a massive heart attack.

⚜

Peter was watching Father Bracciano with consternation, sensing he was having a difficult time negotiating the tricky overhang. He breathed a sigh of relief when it became apparent he'd made it over. Just as he relaxed he was shocked to see Father Bracciano fall. Instinctively he braced himself for the expected impact of the falling climber. Father Bracciano seemed to be falling in slow motion, legs and arms spreadeagled, tumbling end over end.

Peter prayed the pitons would hold. The slack in the rope tightened as the falling body passed the highest piton. Peter felt the jarring pull as the accelerating weight stretched the rope, arresting the fall, but only for an instant. With a sickening twang, the force of the fall dislodged the piton from the crack, and Father Bracciano continued to plummet. The second piton did not even give pause as it was ripped out of its purchase. Only one piton remained. If it did not hold then the falling priest would fly past Peter and the full force of the fall would concentrate on the belay anchor, which was already straining under Peter's weight. With a loud snap, like the crack of a stock whip, the rope went taut and stretched with all the energy of the accelerated force concentrating on the last remaining piton. Peter stared at it, horrified, already resigned to being jerked off his precarious perch. The piton held. Father Bracciano pulled up to a shuddering stop, dangling almost level with Peter's face. He was spinning wildly at the end of the rope, legs and arms grotesquely spread. Eventually the spinning came to a stop and then slowly, he began to spin in the opposite direction. The silence was eerie, broken only by the haunted whistling of the wind. Peter tried to reach out to stop the spinning, but he was just out of reach. Father Bracciano hung motionless and quiet at the end of the rope, seemingly lifeless and Peter was not sure if he was dead or unconscious. Finally the spinning came to a halt, and Peter found himself staring at Father Bracciano's face. The eyes were closed and his skin was a sickly, bluish hue. The disconcerting silence was suddenly broken by a sickening, grating sound. Peter looked up towards the source of the sound and to his horror it was the piton. It had moved, ever so slightly. He quickly checked his own anchor point, and despaired when he saw that the force of the fall had loosened it too. If the piton gave way, then Father Bracciano would fall past him, and the renewed shock on the already loose anchor would almost surely tear him away as well.

Peter was on the verge of panic, when Father Bracciano gave out a low moan and his eyes fluttered open. He groaned in pain, then shook his head, taking a few moments to become lucid. Slowly his precarious predicament registered, and as his eyes focused on Peter, he smiled weakly. 'Sorry my friend, it would seem I have placed us in somewhat of a fix.' He tried to raise his arms in a futile effort to grab hold of the rope, to relieve the pressure under his ribcage, allowing him to breathe more easily. His skin was still alarmingly blue and a stream of saliva dribbled in a thin rivulet from the corner of his mouth. He let out another groan and gave up his attempt to grab the rope. He was gasping for breath.

'Keep still,' Peter warned, as the piton moved a fraction.

The slight movement of the piton was not lost on Father Bracciano. 'Cut the rope,' he ordered in a weak, yet urgent voice.

'No! I can't do that.'

'Do as I say,' Father Bracciano ordered, more loudly this time and with authority. 'You have no choice. If you don't, we'll both go.'

'There must be another way,' Peter pleaded. 'Try to swing yourself, so I can reach you. That way I'll be able to pull you in, and hook you on to my belay.'

Bracciano coughed from the exertion of speaking. He breathed in short, shallow gasps before he could continue. He chuckled weakly. 'And then what will you do? Unless I'm highly mistaken, I've had a massive heart attack. What are you going to do, strap me to your back and climb us both out?' he asked.

'There's got to be something I can do,' Peter insisted.

'There is. Cut the rope and give yourself a chance. I'm finished anyway.'

'I can't do that,' Peter cried.

'Listen to me,' Bracciano hissed urgently through gritted teeth, obviously in pain, and having trouble breathing. 'I'm dying anyway. You have to continue the climb yourself. You must secure Our Lady's document. Save yourself and take it back.'

'I tell you, I can't. Even if I did, there is no way I could finish the climb myself.'

'Listen to me, Peter, there comes a time in all our lives when we have to rise above what we think we are capable of. This is your time. You have to finish the climb. The overhang is difficult, but not impossible. You're young, you're strong, and you can. You must! The cave is just above the bulge. Go into the cave, it's about 15 metres deep. At the far reaches of it you'll find a cairn of rocks. The document is under the pile of rocks in an airtight container.' He paused, catching his breath before continuing his instructions. 'After the cave, you still have a fair climb to the top, but it's much easier. Once you get to the top, you just walk off. Skirt the top of the ridge, and it will gradually take you back to the valley. You should be able to find the village fairly easily from there. Have you got all that?' he demanded.

Yes, yes,' Peter replied shaking, 'but there must be another way.'

'There's not. Now listen to me. You've watched me climb, Peter. You've seen how I do it. Now you must do it too.' Suddenly they froze as the piton slipped further out of its flimsy purchase. It looked like only one third of its length was still embedded in the fissure. Bracciano's dead weight would pull it out any second. 'In the name of Jesus Christ and all that's holy, cut me loose before we both go!'

'I just can't,' Peter cried, tears of frustration streaming down his face.

Bracciano's voice took on a desperate edge. 'Hurry man. Do it now, before it's too late. If not to save yourself, do it for humankind and the Church. Our Lady's message has to be revealed to the world! Please! I was a coward. I couldn't bring myself to expose the Church. It's now up to you.'

The piton shifted again and Bracciano dropped a few centimetres. The two men stared at each other, not daring to breathe. Peter was desperately weighing up Bracciano's words. Enough people had died already. He made a decision. He must return with the Third Secret, no matter what the consequences. Reaching into the pocket of his anorak he removed his clasp knife. He opened it, testing the razor sharp blade on his thumb. He took one more look at Father Bracciano who nodded his head. 'Do it,' he mouthed.

Peter touched the blade to the rope and began to saw. The sharp knife parted the rope with ease. He looked up just before the final strand parted, his eyes blurred with tears. Father Bracciano was smiling. Peter made a futile attempt to return the smile; and then he was alone.

Chapter 41

Peter remained still for a long time, eyes tightly shut. Finally he shook himself out of his overwhelming lethargy. If he didn't make a move soon his nerves would fail him. He vowed to himself that Father Bracciano's death would not have been in vain and felt overcome by the incredible burden of obligation to recover the document. With trembling fingers he unclipped the karabiner securing him to the cliff, being careful not to look down for fear of freezing up. Standing up on the tiny shelf, he shuddered as he realised that for the first time since commencing the climb there was no rope above him to arrest his fall should he slip. Hugging the rock face, he felt a vacuum in his bowels, and then, to his disgust, realised he had soiled himself.

With renewed determination he groped above his head, found a hold and began to climb. After a few feet he began to gain confidence. He continued climbing, slowly and carefully, each movement purposeful and deliberate until he reached the bulge. His heart sank in despair. This is just impossible, he thought. The rock was as smooth as a polished sculpture. He was standing on a fairly good-sized foothold, his fingers exploring the rock above, searching for any sort of purchase he could grab hold of to haul himself up. But it was no use. Just as he was about to give up, he felt an indentation. His searching fingers had found the finger hold Father Bracciano had used. But it was just not possible for Peter to repeat that feat. He had to find something more substantial to hold on to. He continued to grope desperately, but there was nothing else. He looked around frantically, searching for another way around the bulge, and then he glanced down and froze. He began to shake uncontrollably and he was afraid his legs might buckle, as the reality of his desperate situation sank in. He was trapped on a foothold, unable to go up or back down, and he would remain here till his already depleted strength finally gave out and he plummeted to the rocks far below, or froze to death where he stood.

He shut his eyes and began to pray. Then with enormous resolve he shook off his malaise and with a great sense of determination, he cried out, 'DAMN YOU! I'm not going to just die. If I have to die, then I'll die trying.'

Reaching up, he jammed his finger into the hold as best he could, and then, before his courage deserted him again, he pulled up with all the strength of his being. His feet clawed at the sheer rock, desperate to find purchase. Just as he was about to give up and let go the sticky vibram soles miraculously gripped and he was able to take some weight off his agonised finger. He lunged up as Father Bracciano had and to his amazement and relief, his hand wrapped around a hold as big as a jug handle. Crying from the strain, he used every ounce of his remaining strength and hauled himself up and over the lip of the bulge. He collapsed on a broad ledge, rolling away from the abyss. He lay on his back, his chest heaving, his entire body shaking from the gargantuan effort.

When he finally recovered he looked around, surveying his surroundings. The ledge extended about 20 metres along the cliff and was about 5 metres wide, allowing him to get to his feet safely without the danger of toppling off. He looked around and to his despair saw no evidence of a cave. With a sinking heart he moved towards the cliff towering above him from the ledge. At the foot of the cliff he saw what appeared to be a step. He climbed up on to it and saw that it was freestanding rather than abutting to the cliff – and there behind it, he saw the opening of the cave. The step hid it from prying eyes, even from the vantage point of an aircraft. No wonder Father Bracciano had considered it such a safe hiding place. The cave was invisible until one stood immediately over it, and the mouth was only a couple of metres wide and maybe half a metre high. Peter lowered himself onto his belly, peering into the cave. The interior was pitch black. He took off his backpack and rummaged around for his headlamp. He placed it on his head, switched it on and peered into the cave again. He was amazed at what he saw. The lamp illuminated the interior of a huge cavern. He could hear water dripping, which over countless millennia had formed the fabulous stalactites and stalagmites hanging from the ceiling and jutting up from the floor. Some had joined forming great pillars, which seemed to support the roof 5 metres above. He wriggled through the entrance and then stood up, gazing around in wonder. The surrounding rock consisted of a giant pocket of limestone which aeons ago had become entrapped within the much harder, outer rock. Seeping water had excavated the softer limestone, forming the cavern.

Eagerly, Peter began to make his way towards the back of the cave. Suddenly there was a great flurry of sound, accompanied by screeching and he was shocked as something hit him in the face, sending him sprawling onto the damp floor. Bats. Thousands of them, disturbed by the light, were scurrying for the entrance to escape the intruder. He hugged the floor, his arm covering his head, till the last of the creatures departed. Regaining his feet, he smiled at his initial fright and continued towards the back of the cave. It was deeper than he had expected, but finally, the light illuminated the back wall. He began to search for the cairn of rocks, scanning the entire back wall, but to no avail, discovering nothing more than a roughly scattered clump of rocks that could have once been a cairn. He rummaged through the rocks but found nothing. He was desperately disappointed. All the danger they had been through, and now Father Bracciano was dead, and for what? There was nothing here. But perhaps Father Bracciano's memory over so many years had let him down and he had forgotten where he had hidden the document. Peter took heart at this thought and renewed his search, this time determined to cover every inch of the cave if need be, refusing to leave empty handed.

He would have to systemise his search, he decided. He walked the entire length of the back wall of the cave, dragging his foot in the dust to mark a roughly straight line. When he reached the end he stepped out a metre and repeated the process. He'd seen this system of searching on a television news story when a team of police were searching for a body, and he remembered it was called searching to a grid. Patiently Peter shuffled from one end of the cave to the other. He'd just passed a large stalagmite when something caught his periphery vision. There was something on the floor of the cave just behind a stone column. At first it looked like a bunch of rags. He moved closer to inspect the find. It wasn't a bunch of rags, but what appeared to be a climber's outfit, complete with boots. He knelt down for a closer inspection and with a start, realised he was looking at the remains of a human being. The remains were curled in the foetal position, with the knees pressed up to the chest, which is why he did not immediately recognise it as a body. Whoever it had been, had been dead a long time for all that remained was a skeleton. The skull was obscured by a black balaclava that Peter gingerly removed, not sure what he expected to find. The back of the skull had a gaping hole the size of a fist. Whoever this was, had met a violent death. He turned the skeleton over gently, unzipping the anorak, hoping to find something that would identify the victim. He rummaged through each pocket, but to no avail. There was no wallet or anything else to give him a clue. He undid the shirt, finding

307

another layer of cotton that turned out to be a rollneck skivvy, as worn by skiers and climbers. On a hunch, he prised back the collar, and there, glittering in the torchlight, was a distinctive gold cross on a chain. He removed the chain, carefully placing it in a zippered pocket of his own anorak. He completed his painstaking search of the cave, concluding that the document – had it ever been there – was now gone.

Chapter 42

❧✦❧

The sun had set, and Christina sat in a corner of Father Bracciano's house chewing on a finger nail. Emery sat on a chair opposite, absently flicking through a magazine, while Gadaleta peered through the window.

Christina broke the silence. 'I thought Father Bracciano said they'd be back before dark.'

'The sun's only just gone down,' Emery observed.

'But what if one of them is hurt?' Christina persisted.

Emery smiled. 'You mean, what if Peter is hurt?'

Christina blushed furiously. Had her feelings for Peter become so transparent? When she first met him, she had to admit the man was very attractive physically, but she very quickly dispelled this. Long ago she had accepted a life without the prospective comfort of a mate. After all, she had made her decision when she chose to be a bride of Christ. But now? Her situation had certainly changed after India, and she wasn't even sure if she should still call herself a nun. She felt terribly confused. She had admired Peter, right from their very first meeting, respecting his courage for standing up to the Church, irrespective of the consequences. Yes, he was a man of strong character, she decided, prepared to live by his ideals whatever the outcome. She liked his decisive manner, the way he took charge of a situation at times of crisis, like after the bombing of the hotel. And when he had walked into her room after she'd been hurt, his look of concern had touched her and she had felt safe. She smiled at the memory, recalling her embarrassment at being naked under the sheets. It had been a confusing mixture of self-consciousness, yet at the same time a thrill of something she had not felt for a very long time. But she was being stupid, she decided. There could be no future for her with Peter. After all, he had never given even the slightest hint of being attracted to her, and why would he? He is a priest. What she was experiencing, she decided, was akin to a schoolgirl crush on a strong, attractive man. She vowed to banish such thoughts from her mind.

'I think it's too early to be jumping to conclusions, Christina,' Emery said, snapping her out of her reflections. 'Father Bracciano is very experienced, but he's not as young as he used to be. It's obviously taking them longer than he expected.'

'That's right,' Gadaleta agreed, turning from the window, 'and besides, they left in the dark, so I guess it's no big deal if they come back in the dark.'

'And what if they don't come back?' Christina shot back, her imagination taking over.

'Then there's nothing we can do about it tonight,' Emery replied pragmatically. 'I share your concerns, but all we can do is trust that Peter is in good hands, and that probably his lack of experience slowed Father Bracciano down.'

'But what if Peter, I mean, one of them, or both of them for that matter, are lying out there somewhere hurt? They may be in desperate need of help. Pretty soon, the temperature is going to drop below zero.'

'There's still nothing we can do about it in the dark,' Emery repeated. 'Now cheer up and stop thinking the worst. Chances are, they'll walk in the door any minute.'

'Scott's right, Christina,' Gadaleta said. 'If they don't make it tonight, they'll bivouac outside. Bracciano knows these mountains like the back of his hand. He'd know where to hole up if they got caught by the dark. If they're not back tonight, I suggest we recruit that guy, who lent the gear to Peter, to guide us to the buttress first thing in the morning. Meanwhile, I suggest we all get some rest. It could be a big day tomorrow.'

⚜

As the red dawn began to streak the sky Christina was already dressed and eager for positive action. She examined her reflection in the mirror, touching the dark circles under her eyes. The nightmare had been so vivid. Peter's lifeless body, lying broken on the rocks below the cliff. She had woken screaming, her limbs twisted in the sweat-soaked eiderdown. With resignation she stepped out into the cold, striding resolutely to the priest's house where she found the men also dressed and ready to go. She looked questioningly at Emery, who shook his head.

'Sorry, Christina, they didn't come back.'

'Obviously spent the night out,' Gadaleta said, feigning cheerfulness.

Christina's heart sank, the memory of her nightmare still too vivid. 'What now?' she asked, the tremor in her voice betraying her pent-up emotion.

'The villager has agreed to guide us to the bottom of the massif. I'm hoping we'll meet them coming back.'

'But didn't Father Bracciano say they would walk off the top? That it was impossible to climb back down the cliff?' Christina asked, puzzled.

'Ah, yes, that's true, but Tony and I figured it might be a good idea to see if we can get a clue to what happened by going to the base of the cliff first.'

Christina fought the panic in her voice. 'You mean, to see if you can find their bodies at the bottom of the cliff?'

Emery hesitated, exchanging looks with Gadaleta. 'No, no, Christina. Not at all,' he assured her without conviction.

Gadaleta said, 'It's just that, well, you know, one of them may be hurt, and we figured that if that is the case, the best place to start is at the bottom.'

Christina closed her eyes and prayed. Oh please God, let him be all right.

Emery looked at his watch. 'We'd better get going Tony. Christina, we'll be back just as soon as we can. And don't worry. I have a gut feeling that they're OK.'

Christina stared at him. 'But I'm coming with you.'

'I don't know if that would be a good idea,' Emery said, 'considering the knock on your head.'

'Don't try to stop me,' she cried, eyes blazing.

Gadaleta said, 'Look, Christina, be sensible about this, you'd only slow us down.'

'Don't you dare try to stop me,' she repeated.

Emery looked at Gadaleta, who shrugged.

By the time the sun was up in the sky, they were well and truly on their way through the pine forest, with the Italian guide setting a blistering pace. He had explained that, to save time, a second search party had left simultaneously for the top of the buttress, taking the gentle slope from behind. If the men were trapped on the cliff they had no idea what to do, as the Italian had made it clear that he was neither capable nor willing to attempt the climb and it was an impossibility to abseil down the cliff from the top. This information did little for Christina's already frayed nerves.

They continued on in silence, not letting up the pace nor stopping for a rest till they reached the scree slope, where they rested for fifteen minutes, after which the Italian took up the lead again, negotiating the tricky, boulder-strewn scree slope.

Being fitter and more accustomed to this type of exertion, the Italian was soon well in front of the others. Gadaleta and Emery were labouring along, at least a hundred metres behind, and despite their earlier reservations, Christina was faring better than both of them. They heard the Italian cry out excitedly. Christina took off towards the voice, and both men picked up their pace, hurrying to catch up as the Italian continued to call out. There was no mistaking the urgency in his voice.

Christina rounded a large boulder, and what she saw made her gasp and stop dead in her tracks. The Italian was on his knees examining a crumpled body. There was a great deal of blood staining the surrounding rocks. The face was unrecognisable and the neck was askew with the head grotesquely facing in the wrong direction. Christina screamed and fainted.

When she came to, Gadaleta was helping her into a sitting position, trying to get a few drops of water between her lips.

The sight of the mangled body flashed back to her and she thrashed against Gadaleta, desperate to regain her feet. 'It's Peter, isn't it?'

'Whoa, hold on, Christina. Calm down. It's not Peter.'

She continued to struggle, hysteria taking over.

This time Gadaleta shouted. 'It is not Peter. Do you understand? It's Father Bracciano.'

His raised voice finally got through. 'Not Peter?' she asked, as though not trusting what she'd heard. 'Let me go. Let me get up. I want to see for myself.'

'It's not pretty,' Gadaleta warned.

'Please, I must see for myself.'

Gadaleta helped her up. She took one look and simultaneously felt relief and horror. She averted her eyes from the grisly scene and threw up.

'Shit man,' Emery said to Gadaleta. 'Come and have a look at this.'

He held up the short length of rope, still attached to Bracciano's waist. The Italian and Gadaleta stared at it. The

Italian took it from Emery for a closer inspection, and then made a cutting gesture with the flat of his hand.

'That's right,' Emery said, 'this rope didn't break. It was cut.'

They made a cursory search of the immediate surrounding area, but there was no other body to be found. They stared up at the forbidding cliff looming over their heads.

'Shit,' Gadaleta exclaimed, 'I don't know what happened up there, but it may well be that Peter is still up there, trapped.' He gestured to the Italian, mimicking climbing up the cliff. The Italian shook his head vigorously. There was no way he was going to contemplate that climb.

Christina had recovered her composure. She had seen the Italian's gesture of refusal. 'If Peter is up there, we must get to him.' She grabbed the Italian by the lapels of his jacket, shaking him vigorously. 'You must climb,' she said, repeating Gadaleta's mimicking gestures.

'It's no use, Christina,' Gadaleta said. 'The man won't climb. The best thing we can do is return to the village to see if the other party may have had better luck.'

⚓

Word quickly spread through the small village as the three men and Christina returned, carrying Father Bracciano's body on a makeshift stretcher. Men, women and children converged from their cabins, silently weeping, paying their last respects to their beloved pastor. The Italian climber excitedly explained where and how they found the body. The cut rope raised much speculation as to the circumstances of the fall, with some gesticulating angrily at the strangers in their midst. It was agreed that the police should be called without delay. Meanwhile, the search party that had set out to the top of the massif by way of the back route along the plateau had still not returned.

Chapter 43

⟶ ✦ ⟵

Peter LeSarus spent a restless night within the protected confines of the cave. At first light he ate the meagre remains of his food, re-filled his water bottle from the dripping roof of the cave and set out with trepidation to complete the climb to the top of the dome. Without a backward glance he began the ascent. To his great relief, he found that Father Bracciano had been right, the wall above the cave did not present anywhere near the difficult climbing they'd experienced before. Peter made his way up another fissure in the rock above the cave, and the angle was not nearly as steep. As he climbed higher the crack began to expand till it became so wide that Peter found he was able to comfortably fit his whole body into it, which made him feel much more secure, as he was not as exposed to the dizzy drop. Relentlessly he kept climbing, only resting when he felt too tired to continue. The cliff above seemed to go on forever and soon the ledge where the cave was had all but disappeared from his view. When the sun passed its zenith in the sky, Peter realised he'd been climbing steadily for eight hours, and he began to worry that he might not finish the climb before nightfall. He shuddered at the prospect of spending a night exposed on the cliff, doubting he could survive the sub-zero temperature. Angrily, he forced these negative thoughts from his mind. He had to stop for a rest and to drink some water. He looked up to see if there was any sign of an end to the climb and his heart leaped with joy, as there above him, less than 50 metres up, he spotted trees at the top of the escarpment. He could hardly believe it. He was near the top. He set out again, with a rising sense of elation. He would make it. Then after about

40 metres of relatively easy going the chimney-like fissure he was climbing in came to an abrupt end. He could not believe it. He'd come so far, only to find his way blocked with only a mere 10 metres or so to go. He felt sick as he surveyed the almost perfectly smooth, overhanging rock impeding his way. Then he noticed something curious. There was a line of bolts sticking out of the sheer rock at regular intervals of approximately one metre apart. Father Bracciano and his friend, Giuseppe, must have placed them there on their original ascent. Stretching up, he managed to touch the first bolt. It was rusty but felt sound. On closer inspection, he figured a hole had been drilled into the rock and the bolt had been hammered in to nearly its entire length with just the head exposed. His heart sank with despair. Father Bracciano must have been carrying some sort of climbing aid to clip on to the bolts. He remembered the etriers used to climb the overhang by clipping onto the pitons. All of the climbing hardware had gone with Father Bracciano. He speculated as to the possibility of gripping the bolt with his fingers and hauling himself up, one at a time, but quickly dismissed this notion as impossible. As the reality of his situation sank in he wondered whether he would die from exposure or by falling onto the jagged scree slope one kilometre below. He began to weep, not from fear of dying but from sheer frustration. All of this will have been in vain, he thought, Father Bracciano's death, everything, and the mystery of the body in the cave would never be resolved.

Resigning himself to his fate, he wedged his body tightly into the chimney-like fissure and began to pray. After a while, he found his mind wandering, contemplating his life. He wondered at what would have been had he chosen a different path to that of serving Christ. He couldn't help wondering if he had wasted his life. He found himself fantasising about what could have been had he pursued a normal career, along with a loving wife and children. He was daydreaming, and in his dream he pictured himself coming home from work to a modest cottage in the suburbs. The front door opened and his loving family greeted him. There was his wife with two young children, and an excited dog completed the picture. The dog was jumping up at him, determined to lick his face. His wife was smiling and the children, although faceless, were beautiful and they were all greeting him adoringly. He leaned down to kiss his wife affectionately and in his mind, he saw her face. It was Christina.

He woke with a start. He must have dozed off. He wasn't sure what had awakened him. At first he thought he'd heard voices, but quickly dismissed the thought. He'd been dreaming. Then he heard it again. It was unmistakeably a voice calling in Italian. He froze, listening intently. Yes, there it was again. It was definitely someone calling out. Peter screamed at the top of his lungs. 'HELP! HELP! I'm here!' He was looking up at the top of the cliff when suddenly a face appeared, staring down at him in wonder. Peter wasn't sure who was the most surprised. The face was joined by another and then another. Men were talking excitedly. Within minutes a rope snaked down, and with shaking hands, Peter grabbed it, attaching it to his waist.

Chapter 44

When the police arrived at the village they were anxious to question the foreigners about the circumstances surrounding the death of Father Bracciano and the missing foreigner. The police sergeant in charge commented in broken English that the village seemed to be attracting an unusual amount of excitement since the strangers' arrival. He questioned Christina, Emery and Gadaleta at length about the reason the two men had undertaken such a dangerous climb, particularly considering Father Bracciano's advanced age.

'Stupido,' the police sergeant observed. 'Matto,' he added, making a twirling gesture with a finger around his ear.

Although reluctant to take the police into their confidence, Emery decided it would be prudent to give them at least a part of the story. Emery and Gadaleta presented their credentials, which greatly impressed the small town policeman who had never dealt with foreign security agents. Emery explained that the two men had climbed the cliff to retrieve a sensitive Papal document which had been entrusted to Father Bracciano many years ago.

The policeman's questioning was interrupted by a loud commotion outside. They all rushed to a window and saw pandemonium. The other search party had arrived, and they were surrounded by what appeared to be an angry mob of villagers, jostling and jeering. Christina did not wait for the others. She rushed out the door, calling Peter's name. The crowd parted as she rushed toward them, and when she spotted Peter surrounded by his rescuers, she stopped dead in her tracks. All of a sudden, she felt very unsure of herself, and instead of rushing into his arms, which is what she wanted to do, she just stood there, grinning and feeling foolish.

Peter saw her, and was about to say something when Christina was joined by Emery, Gadaleta and the policeman who cleared a path and ushered them all back into the cottage, closing the door behind them. Although he was deathly tired, Peter assured them he was up to giving the police a statement. With emotion in his voice, he recounted how Father Bracciano had suffered a heart attack, fallen, and then insisted that Peter cut the rope to save himself. The police sergeant listened attentively, taking notes, occasionally interrupting to clarify a point.

When Peter completed his statement, the sergeant shut his notebook and said, 'There is much, how you say,' he searched for the correct word, 'precedent,' – pronouncing it 'precedenta' – 'for such a thing. When men go climbing, and one fall and the other he can't help him, then he must cut the rope to save himself. No?'

As the news filtered to the crowd outside Christina heard their anger diminish, replaced by howls of grief. Everyone in the room nodded their heads in agreement with this sentiment, relieved that the police sergeant was an understanding man. However, he went on to warn that the outcome would be subject to an autopsy. If the findings confirmed a heart attack, then Peter would be free to go.

Now Emery asked the one question they had all been dying to ask, 'What about the document, Peter, did you find it?'

They watched Peter expectantly. 'No,' he said shaking his head, 'and it's a good thing the police are here.' He went on to describe his search of the cave, which failed to locate the document. 'I did see a pile of rocks, which could have been the cairn Father Bracciano described, but if the document had ever been there, it's not there now.'

'What do you think happened, Peter?' Emery pressed.

'Well, I do know that someone else climbed up to the cave after Father Bracciano secreted the document, and whoever it was, took it.'

'How can you be sure?' Gadaleta asked. 'Father Bracciano himself said that no one else, to his knowledge, had ever made that climb.'

'Well, at least one other person did,' Peter responded, 'and he's still up there.'

They all stared at him, 'I don't understand Peter, what do you mean?' Emery asked.

'There's a body in the cave, or at least what's left of it.'

The policeman was all attention. 'What you mean, a body?' he demanded.

'There is a skeleton in the cave, and unless I'm greatly mistaken, he was murdered.'

The policeman retrieved his notebook flipping it open, as Peter continued. 'The skeleton is dressed in climbing gear and the skull has a hole the size of a fist.'

He unzipped a pocket and retrieved the cross and chain. 'I found this around the neck of the deceased,' he explained, handing it to the police sergeant.

The sergeant examined the cross closely before commenting. 'This is very interesting. Many, many years ago a climber from here fell into a crevasse. But his body was never recovered. He and his friend were from this village.'

'This friend of the lost climber,' Gadaleta asked, 'you say he also came from this village?'

'Yes, yes, from this very village.'

'And does he still live here.'

'No, no. He's gone. He left after his friend was killed. But the widow of the man that was killed, she still lives here. I think I had better show her this cross.'

320

The widow of the lost climber tearfully confirmed that the cross had belonged to her missing husband. She was adamant, as it had been a present from her on their wedding day. What had been a closed file on a death by misadventure suddenly re-opened into a murder investigation.

'I'm sorry,' the policeman apologised to Peter, 'but now it would seem you are a witness to what looks like a murder. You must not leave the country. I have to ask you to give me your passport.'

Reluctantly, Peter surrendered his passport and they all decided that as there was nothing more they could learn at the village, they would head back to Rome. They gave the police the address of the hotel they had stayed at previously.

Within days of arriving in Rome, Peter was relieved that an autopsy supported his claim that Father Bracciano had suffered a heart attack. The police also told him they had traced the second climber from the village and that he was already in police custody, having been charged with murder. The police had retrieved the skeleton from the cave by winching a policeman onto the ledge by helicopter and a DNA test confirmed he was the climber purported to have fallen into a crevasse. Peter questioned the accommodating police sergeant about the missing document and was told the man denied knowledge of it. He claimed his friend had been hit by a falling rock and, fearing the consequences, he'd made up the story about the crevasse.

When Peter related this news to the others, Emery was convinced the man was lying, and told Gadaleta to use whatever clout he had with the authorities to question him. Meanwhile Emery announced he had other pressing agency business in Rome and would catch up with them later.

Chapter 45

Cardinal Morova was in a morose mood when he greeted his visitor, and seemed distracted when he waved an arm, gesturing him to take a seat.

'I've got to tell you, Cardinal,' his visitor began, 'I don't much like coming here. What if someone recognises me?'

Morova brushed aside the visitor's concerns as if they were of no consequence, seating himself behind his desk.

'I am disappointed you have failed to rid us of those meddlesome Australians. You have had ample opportunity, and it would seem they simply refuse to let go. Now you tell me that a copy of the Third Secret has survived after all these years. That is very troubling,' Morova stated, barely able to control his rage. 'After destroying the original, I understood there were no other copies in existence. Yes, this is very troubling. Do you know where this copy is?'

'As I told you on the phone,' the visitor replied, 'it turns out that Pope Leo Alexander I sent a copy to his friend, Father Bracciano, who was too terrified to do anything about it, so he just hid it.' The visitor then reiterated everything that had happened since the Australians arrived at Father Bracciano's village. He completed his account of the facts by saying, 'The Italian climber is now under arrest for murder. He denied knowledge of the document. Says his friend's death was an accident.'

The knuckles on Morova's writhing hands were white with tension. 'And what do you think?' he demanded.

'I think he is lying. It's all too much of a coincidence.'

'Yes, yes, I see,' Morova said. 'But, has it ever crossed your mind that this Peter LeSarus may have found the document?'

'What do you mean?'

'LeSarus climbs to the cave with Father Bracciano. Father Bracciano comes to an unfortunate end. LeSarus gets to the cave and finds the document as well as a body. Would it not make sense for him to tell everyone the document was not there? And that whoever had accompanied the deceased climber must obviously have taken it? Would it not be a perfect ploy to blame some innocent climber of stealing the document, when in fact LeSarus has it all along?'

'No, no, I don't consider that a possibility,' the visitor replied. 'He's not that smart. And besides, what would be his motive?'

'On the contrary. I suggest this LeSarus is much smarter than you think. As for a motive? I would have thought that was obvious – to put us off the scent. They know someone is trying to kill them. They are not sure, although from what you have told me, they suspect I am behind it, but they have no proof. And they certainly do not know how I am tracking their every move.'

'Yes, you may be right. I suppose it could make sense for LeSarus to pretend he does not have the document.'

Morova's voice took on a menacing tone. 'If that document exists it has got to be destroyed. Do you understand? It must be destroyed and I do not care how many more people go with it.'

'I understand perfectly, Eminence, but, I would suggest it prudent not to kill the Australians right now, at least until we're sure they don't have it.'

'Yes, yes, all right,' Morova agreed impatiently, waving his hand dismissively, 'find out whether they have it. Then I want them out of the way, finally. No more mistakes. So what is being done about the Italian climber? You say he is in police custody.'

'Yes, that's right. He's been charged with murder. Gadaleta is pulling strings to get in to interview him.'

'And you are confident that he will get the truth from him?'

'Gadaleta is very good at what he does. He'll find a way to get the truth.'

'Very well then, but I must be kept informed.' Morova stood up, ushering his visitor to the door, where he held out his hand. Respectfully, Scott Emery leaned over to kiss the Cardinal's ring.

Chapter 46

Scott Emery, or Zoltan Myer as his Jewish family called him, hated Christians. He hated Jews as well. Having been brought up in what was referred to as Hell's Kitchen in the Bronx in New York, he was the only child of hardworking, Orthodox Jewish parents who had made an art form of suffering, considering it a virtue. At an early age he had come to the realisation that being Jewish in a Christian world made him the target of derision and racial hatred.

'The Goyim, they hate us, 'cos we are smarter than them,' his father would say, tapping a forefinger to his temple. He would go on to explain, 'Cos we're smarter, we make all the money, and they don't like that.'

Young Scott used to wonder about this. If the Jews made all the money, then how come his family and their neighbours continued to live in wretched poverty? He concluded that there were Jews and then there were Jews. Some were smart, but then there were the schmucks as his father called anyone who was a loser, despite being a loser himself. The schmucks worked for the smart Jews who ripped them off as mercilessly, and if not more, than they did the Goyim.

As he grew older, Scott began to hate Jews even more than he hated Christians. After all, weren't they of the same race and supposed to help each other? In his mind, the wealthy Jews were even worse than the wealthy Goyim, because after all, you didn't expect favours from the Goyim. The wealthy Jews tended to exploit the poor Jews more mercilessly than they did the Goyim because the Jews were an easier target. He hated his parents and all they stood for. They were losers and it was their own fault that they meekly accepted their pathetic fate in life. Oh yes, they complained all right, but only among themselves. They never had the nerve to speak out to their bosses or landlords. They would never make demands or do anything to raise themselves above their miserable lot in life. They were put on this earth to suffer and they did this exceptionally well.

Scott Emery was determined to raise himself above his parents' abject wretchedness. The first thing he did after leaving home was to change his name. By playing with the letters in Myer, he added an e and changed it to Emery. There was nothing he could do with Zoltan, but being an avid fan of Randolph Scott, the tough-guy, Western movie star, he took his name.

The one thing Scott Emery understood was the power of education. He put himself through college, where he excelled, and later passed the stringent entrance exams to join the CIA. He saw this as an opportunity to get back at the corrupt Christians and the Jews he hated so much, by taking them down through official channels.

He served in Vietnam where the army decorated him for thwarting a massive Vietcong ambush. Although he carried out his duties in an exemplary manner, he was nevertheless of the firm opinion that America had no business being there, but he kept these sentiments to himself, knowing such sentiments would do little to further his own cause.

Later on in his career he was placed in charge of a covert investigation in Afghanistan to infiltrate the camps of potential terrorists. His swarthy complexion and knowledge of Middle Eastern languages qualified him eminently for his role. It was during his term in Afghanistan that he had inadvertently been introduced to Satanism. Although at the time he did not realise what it was, it was an ideal he embraced immediately and with enthusiasm. The people he met had a doctrine he had harboured unwittingly all his life and he became a willing disciple almost immediately. He was introduced to a group meeting, at which he hung on to every word. He was amazed at the worldwide extent of influence of the organisation, which was committed to righting all the historic wrongs of the world. He learned that the Jews were as guilty as the Christians, and America in particular had much to answer for. Greed and territorialism were the common denominators for the woes of the world's downtrodden. The Catholic Church, he learned, was steeped in hypocrisy and unparallelled avarice. He discovered there were forces at work to right all these wrongs, and he became a willing participant in the organisation.

His position with the CIA presented him with the opportunity to feed information to his new allies, assisting in the ongoing struggle for righteousness. As his position became increasingly important to the organisation, and he gained more and more trust, he was introduced to powerful men in influential positions in government, the media, the judiciary and even the clergy.

He was later posted to Rome, where he met and befriended Monsignor Morova, head of the Vatican Bank, and his Irish-Australian assistant, Father Brian O'Shaughnessy.

When the bank all but collapsed, and O'Shaughnessy became the scapegoat, Emery played a duplicitous game. Morova thought he had the support of the American agent, while at the same time, Emery would have O'Shaughnessy believe he was sympathetic to his case, doing what he could to assert the man's innocence. Emery believed in never burning his bridges – one never knew when an ally could prove useful.

When O'Shaughnessy contacted him, Emery was surprised, as he had not heard from him since O'Shaughnessy had been expelled from Italy. Nevertheless, Emery agreed to help out

O'Shaughnessy's niece, when he'd heard she was in trouble. When he discovered what it was that she and her friend the priest were looking for, his interest was piqued. And when he learned of what was potentially at stake, he decided it was time to renew his contact with Cardinal Morova, sensing the Secretary of State may be prepared to pay handsomely for the tip-off. He was not wrong. But he could not have predicted the reaction his call would generate, nor the intrigue it would unleash. Morova had briefed him on the importance of the Third Secret, as well as the potential ramifications, should the document ever be released to public scrutiny. Emery began to realise there was more at stake than dollars. Ever since then, Emery had kept Morova closely informed on all their movements, with Morova orchestrating behind the scenes. Morova had organised the assassins to head the 'investigators' off on the mountain road, intending to run them off the cliff. Emery had been prepared for the attack, ejecting himself from the vehicle at the first impact. Emery had also tipped Morova about Archbishop Voitra turning against him, resulting in the Archbishop's gruesome death.

Emery would have preferred to interview the Italian prisoner personally, but he had to concede that Gadaleta was well connected in Rome and he did not wish to press the point for fear of raising suspicions. He would have to be patient and rely on Gadaleta to find out what he could.

Chapter 47

Gadaleta had little trouble getting in to see the Italian prisoner. After all, he was owed some heavyweight favours from the local police, and a request to question a murder suspect about a missing Church document was no big deal. At the police station he was introduced to an affable young policeman who would act as translator. He was shown to the man's cell where he found an elderly, but fit-looking, Italian. He deduced from the fear in the man's eyes that this one would cooperate fairly quickly.

The interpreter introduced Gadaleta, explaining to the prisoner who he was and advised the man to cooperate. The man looked at Gadaleta beseechingly, and spoke in rapid Italian, locking his hands together in a gesture of prayer.

When he'd finished, the interpreter said, 'He is pleading for you to help him, he swears he is innocent of the crime. He claims it was an accident, that his friend was hit on the head by a falling rock, which killed him instantly.' The interpreter explained all this in a dispassionate monotone, as though reading evidence in a court.

'Ask him,' Gadaleta said, 'that if he is innocent, why did he lie about his friend being lost in a crevasse?'

The policeman conveyed the question in the same emotionless monotone, and then waited for the response.

'He says he was scared. He could not bring the body down and so he left it there and concocted the story about the crevasse.'

'What was he scared of?'

After the question was relayed in Italian, the man paused, seemingly searching for an answer.

'What was he scared of?' Gadaleta repeated, more loudly. 'Tell him to answer me.'

The interpreter repeated the question in the same disinterested monotone, without matching Gadaleta's raised voice.

The man eyed Gadaleta nervously, the tone of the raised voice not lost on him. He cast his eyes down and began to speak haltingly. Soon he seemed to warm to his story and continued on for some time without interruption.

'What did he say?' Gadaleta demanded impatiently, when the man finally finished.

'He said that he and his friend were in the church one evening and they overheard the priest praying.'

'Go on,' Gadaleta pressed.

'They heard him asking for guidance about what to do about a precious legacy left to him by the Papa. They thought it was a treasure and so when the priest set out from the village alone the next day, they followed him. They were amazed when they saw him start on a climb that everyone knew was so difficult and dangerous. Next day they decided to attempt the climb themselves, to see if the priest might have hidden something along the route.'

'And? Did they find something?'

'He says they came across a cave, where they found an old document wrapped in oilskin and covered with rocks.'

'What did he do with it?'

'He says they began to read the document, and it scared them. Then he claims a rock fell from above, killing his friend. He says he read this as an omen from God, that they should not have been tampering with the document.'

'But what did he do with it?' Gadaleta demanded. 'Does he know where it is? This is very important.'

The policeman asked some more questions, and then with a look of triumph said, 'Yes, he knows where it is.'

Gadaleta could scarcely contain his excitement.

⚊◆⚊

When Gadaleta returned to the hotel the others, including Scott Emery, were waiting expectantly for his news.

'Did you get to speak to the prisoner?' Emery asked for all of them.

'I sure did,' Gadaleta replied with a grin.

'And?' Emery pressed. 'What about the document? Does he have it?'

Gadaleta was enjoying himself. 'No, he doesn't have it,' he answered, still grinning.

'You look like the proverbial cat who caught the canary,' LeSarus observed. 'C'mon, Tony. You're obviously dying to tell us something, why don't you just get it out and be done with it?'

'Knowing Tony as I do,' Scott Emery said, 'I believe he'll tell us in his own good time. Isn't that right, buddy?'

Gadaleta laughed good-naturedly at his friend's observation. 'All right,' he conceded, 'I know where it is.'

The others pressed around him, everyone suddenly talking at once.

'Whoa,' he said holding up his hands in a gesture to quieten them. 'Hold on, give me a chance. I'll tell you what I learned. Firstly, I believe the old fella is innocent. I don't believe he killed his partner. What I do believe is, that they found out about Father Bracciano wanting to hide something on that climb. They thought it was something valuable, probably Church treasure, and so they made the climb hoping to steal it. As it turned out, they made it to the cave, searched it, and to their disappointment all they found was the document. They opened it and read it. What they read apparently scared the hell out of them, and they weren't sure what to do with it. Their first reaction was to just leave it where it was. They returned it to its hiding place in the

331

cave, and recovered it with rocks. Then, as they stepped out of the cave to climb out, he claims a boulder came crashing down on to his friend's head, killing him instantly. This left our little Italian in a huge state of confusion and shock. He believed it was divine retribution for attempting to steal what he now thought of as a sacred document. There was nothing he could do about his dead friend so he dragged him back into the cave. He then figured that as his friend had died as a result of them trying to retrieve whatever Father Bracciano had hidden, he owed it to him not to leave empty handed. So he decided to take the document with him, despite his dread of what it contained.

'When he returned to the village, he couldn't bear to face Father Bracciano, knowing he'd stolen the document. So he fabricated the story about his friend falling into a crevasse. He led a rescue party to the place where he said the accident happened. Naturally they found nothing and, following an inquest, the verdict was death by misadventure. Soon after that he left the village, running from his guilt, taking the document with him.'

'So where is it now?' Emery asked impatiently.

'I thought you agreed, I would tell you in my own time,' Gadaleta answered mischievously.'

'All right, all right, just get on with it.'

'He decided to head for Rome where he has a sister, whose husband is a builder. He figured she'd put him up, and the brother-in-law would give him a job as a labourer. This little arrangement worked well for a time till his brother-in-law fell on hard times and had to let him go. He couldn't find other work and the family were getting a little sick of their uninvited guest who spent his days loafing around the house and generally making it look untidy. This caused a fight between his sister and her husband, who wanted him out. Suddenly, our friend had a brainwave. He remembered the document, and wondered if it may have some value. He showed it to his brother-in-law explaining he'd stolen it from a priest but omitted details. The brother-in-law, being a simple builder, had no idea about these things, but sharing his greed, suggested he show it to a friend who was worldly and wise, and would probably know if it were worth anything. Turns out that this friend is a powerful, local Don.'

Christina looked up surprised. 'You mean "Don" as in "Godfather in the Mafia" type Don?'

'That's exactly what I mean.'

'Oh! I thought that nowadays that sort of thing only existed in novels and movies.'

Gadaleta and Emery laughed, as Emery explained. 'The Mafia still exists, Christina, but not the way it did in the old days. Most of it is all legit, big business now. This Don, although he is pretty old now, still heads up one of the most powerful families in Rome.'

'So what did this Don say about the document?' Christina asked.

'He told our friend that he would have it checked out by his people to find out if it had value.' Gadaleta answered.

'Tony,' Peter cut in, 'you're telling us that the Third Secret of Fatima is now in the hands of the local mafia?'

'It would seem so.' Gadaleta replied.

'Oh that's just great,' LeSarus said. 'So how do we get it back?'

'I guess we get in touch with this Don, and ask him if we can have it,' Gadaleta said.

'And how do you propose we do that?' LeSarus asked caustically. 'Do we look up Mafia in the local phone book and give him a call?'

'No, not we,' Gadaleta said seriously, 'he wouldn't talk to Scott or me. My suggestion is that the approach comes from you and Christina.'

Peter and Christina exchanged looks.

'You approach him as a concerned priest and nun, searching for an important Church relic.'

Christina looked worried. 'Do we know how or where to make contact with this man?' she asked.

'According to our friend, he has lunch at the same restaurant every day where he holds court, so to speak. He told me where the restaurant is. I guess that's as good a place as any to start.'

With considerable trepidation, Peter and Christina agreed to attempt to meet the Don at the restaurant the following day. Meanwhile, Emery took his leave of the group explaining he still had unfinished business to attend to and he would look forward to hearing how they fared.

Chapter 48

Back at their hotel, Peter felt awkward. Standing behind Christina as the clerk handed her the key he detected a faint, but unmistakeable scent of perfume. He'd also noticed that she'd recently taken to wearing a slight hint of lipstick. Ever since he returned from his epic on the mountain he sensed something had subtly changed between them. The carefree, friendly spontaneity of their relationship had somehow disappeared, replaced by drawn-out, uncomfortable silences. He could not define it; it was far too esoteric in its nature for him to grasp. She had become somewhat aloof, and he had to admit, he had caught himself acting towards her in similar fashion. It was not because he wanted to – on the contrary. He could not remember having felt so aware of a woman, and yet it was this very perception that appeared to be driving him from her. He wondered if she sensed this, and that perhaps this was the cause for her own withdrawal.

'Well, I guess I'll go to my room now,' Christina said, interrupting his thoughts.

'Um, sure,' Peter replied self-consciously. 'I guess I will too. After all, we do have a big day ahead of us tomorrow.' He tried to make light of the awkward moment. 'After all, it's not every day you get to meet with the Mafia.'

Christina's laugh lacked conviction and she made a trite attempt to return the humour. 'Not unless you happen to be going to a Mario Puzo movie.'

Peter did not return the laugh. 'OK, I guess I'll see you in the morning.' He felt foolish – like a schoolboy after his first date.

Christina turned to go, and then stopped abruptly, as though she had forgotten something.

'Oh, by the way,' she said, 'I think I should call Uncle Brian, to bring him up to speed.'

Peter had been so pre-occupied with his mixed emotions, that he had all but forgotten O'Shaughnessy. Christina's statement jerked him back to reality. He remembered what Piggott had told him, and found himself wondering yet again whether Christina knew. He dismissed the thought immediately, convincing himself anew, that there was no way she would be involved. But despite his conviction, he wanted to be there when she spoke to her uncle. 'Good idea,' he agreed. Normally he would not have thought twice about suggesting she make the call in his presence, but now, he stammered when he said, 'Ah, do you want to make the call alone, or would you like me to be there with you?'

Christina did not hesitate. 'Why, of course you should be with me. Uncle Brian will probably want to talk to you.'

Relieved at her response, Peter checked his watch. 'It's nearly six in the evening,' he did a quick mental calculation, 'which means it's four in the morning in Sydney.'

'A little too early, even for Uncle Brian. Let's give him a couple of hours.'

'How about I come to your room at eight, then?'

'Perfect,' Christina agreed.

⚜

At almost precisely 6:00AM Piggott picked up the phone. He greeted Christina without emotion, nor did he ask how she was. Christina knew he was much too proper for that. He asked her to hold, and in a moment she heard the familiar voice of Uncle Brian's 'Hello.'

Christina greeted him enthusiastically. 'Oh, Uncle Brian, you won't believe the adventures we've had since Peter last spoke to you.'

'Christina, it's great to hear from you. I do hope you are both all right. I must tell you, I've been somewhat concerned. Did Scott Emery look after you?'

Neither O'Shaughnessy nor Christina noticed the almost inaudible click on the line as an extension was picked up in another room of O'Shaughnessy's house.

Christina spent the next twenty minutes relating all that had happened since they were rescued by Emery in Prague.

'Scott Emery has once again proven he's a loyal friend,' O'Shaughnessy observed. 'I must get him something very special.'

Christina concluded her report, 'That's all I can tell you for the moment, Uncle Brian.'

'From what you've told me, you're both very lucky to be alive, Christina. I'll have a word with Peter, if he's there.'

Christina handed the phone to Peter, but kept her ear close to the earpiece.

After exchanging greetings, O'Shaughnessy came straight to the point, expressing his concerns. 'Peter, I'm sorry to have placed you and Christina in such jeopardy. I had no idea it would come to this. I really think you should abandon everything and just get on the next plane home. I must say that I'm not at all happy about you and Christina meeting with this Mafia fellow.'

'We're too close now to just drop it,' Peter protested, 'and besides, Tony Gadaleta will be keeping an eye on the restaurant.'

'Very well, Peter, but it's against my better judgement. Please take care of Christina. As I said before, she is all I have.'

※※※

O'Shaughnessy hung up and asked Piggott to reserve a flight for one to Rome.

Piggott carried out his instructions with one addition. He booked two tickets on separate flights.

Chapter 49

Peter and Christina stood outside the restaurant with a powerful sense of the unreal, but knowing that Gadaleta was parked discreetly across the street with a clear view of the restaurant gave then some small comfort.

'I can't believe we're doing this,' Christina remarked.

They were in a part of the eternal city that was frequented by local businessmen, artisans and tradesmen, well away from the traditional tourist haunts. Gadaleta had run some checks, and was told that this was where Don Amiglio held court, routinely enjoying a luncheon of antipasto, veal or spaghetti, washed down with the ubiquitous Chianti and water. The word from Gadaleta's source was that the Don was no longer concerned about enjoying a lifestyle of habits and patterns as the days were long gone when a person of his profession never travelled the same route two days running, or ate at the same restaurant for fear of being gunned down. Those had been tough days, but he had been young then, as well as ruthless, and it was the life he had chosen.

Today, no one referred to them as 'the mob', they were now respectable businessmen, and to the casual observer, the Don was just another old man, relishing retirement. But the reality was, Gadaleta was assured, that Don Amiglio still reigned over his empire with a tight fist, except nowadays it was more like running a company, and the Café Rosa was his boardroom. Locals still came seeking favours or asking his help to settle disputes, be they business or domestic, and for one so old, his mind was still sharp and he had lost none of the wisdom, which was legend, and that had been instrumental to his long, successful reign. Gadaleta's source had warned him that bodyguards and lieutenants always closely surrounded the Don. He advised that those seeking an audience did so on a strictly informal basis, which meant simply arriving and asking to see him. 'You're either in, or you're not,' the man had said. 'And if you're not, then there's nothing you can do about it. It's final.'

'It does seem unreal, doesn't it?' Peter replied to Christina's observation as he surveyed the restaurant. 'Who would believe that we, a couple of ordinary Australians, would be seeking audience with a Mafia boss in Rome?'

'Yes,' Christina agreed, 'if it wasn't so scary, it would almost be verging on the comical.'

It was as typical an Italian restaurant as Peter could imagine, with tables placed on the footpath covered with the traditional red chequered tablecloths. The place was alive with Italians sipping from ridiculously tiny coffee cups and engaged in loud, animated conversations. At first observation, Peter thought all the tables were taken, when Christina grabbed his arm, steering him urgently to an empty one she had spotted.

Peter held the chair for Christina as he looked into the interior of the restaurant, trying to catch the eye of one of the frantically busy waiters, flying in all directions, in what appeared to be ordered chaos.

A waiter, noticing they had seated themselves, rushed over, indignation written all over his face. He began to protest, but stopped short when he noticed they were clergy. His demeanour changed abruptly as he greeted them warmly.

'Do you speak English?' Peter asked.

'Si, si,' the waiter replied grinning, eager to show off his language skills. 'I speak English very good. Welcome, Holy Father and Holy Sister.'

Peter ordered coffee, and when the waiter returned with their order, Peter asked, 'I understand that Don Amiglio can be found here.'

The waiter's cordial expression froze as he asked suspiciously, 'And what would a Holy Father want with Don Amiglio?'

'Is he here?' Peter pressed.

'Maybe yes, maybe no, Father. He is a busy man.'

'If he is here, would you please tell him we wish to speak to him?'

'And if he were here, what would I tell him that you wish to speak to him about?' the waiter asked, without committing himself.

'Would you please tell him that a priest and a nun have travelled all the way from Australia to find an important Church document, and we believe he may be able to help us?'

The waiter was about to ask another question, thought better of it, and shrugging his shoulders, disappeared into the restaurant.

From where he was sitting, Peter was able to follow the waiter's progress. He watched as the man approached a table at the back of the restaurant where he leaned over and whispered into the ear of a man who had his back to the entrance. The man listened intently, then turned to look in their direction. He turned back to the waiter and nodded. Peter expected the waiter to return, but instead he disappeared into the kitchen. The man the waiter whispered to stood up and walked around the table and leaned over an elderly man. The elderly man also turned to look in their direction and gave Peter a slight wave. The first man left the table and headed in their direction.

Christina had been watching Peter's expression intently, too afraid to turn around in her seat. 'What's happening?' she demanded.

'We're either about to be invited to meet the Don, or we're about to be evicted,' Peter whispered, just as a man of gigantic proportions reached their table. He wasn't that tall, or at least he didn't seem that tall, perhaps because the unbelievable breadth of his massive shoulders belied his height. Besides the sheer enormity of the man, his singular, most distinctive feature was an angry scar running in a jagged line, like lightning, from his forehead, down over his eye and finishing on the side of his chin. Peter and Christina exchanged nervous glances, and now, faced with the disconcerting reality of a Mafia mobster, Peter experienced trepidation at what now seemed a foolhardy mission.

The man leaned over. 'The waiter tells me you wanna speak to the Don,' he announced, more as a statement than a question.

'Well yes,' Peter began to explain, trying to sound as natural and affable as possible.

The man cut him off. 'You come with me,' he gestured to Peter. Pointing to Christina he said, 'You wait here.'

Peter looked questioningly at Christina, and was about to protest, when she smiled and said, 'I'll be all right,' she assured him. 'You go. I'll wait here for you.'

The giant pulled back Peter's chair, then ushered him through the restaurant to the table at the back, where a man seated next to the elderly man stood up, gesturing for Peter to take his seat. As he sat down, Peter nodded to the men around the table who were silently appraising him, not quite sure how to proceed. The old man spoke softly to the giant, gesturing towards Peter. The big man said, 'This is Don Amiglio, he wants to know what you want.'

Peter inclined his head respectfully towards the Don, and said, 'Please tell Don Amiglio that my friend and I would like to thank him very much for taking the time to talk to me. We wish to speak to him on a matter of grave importance to the Catholic Church.'

The man translated for the Don, who nodded his head, acknowledging Peter's respect, then gestured for the man to continue.

'The Don says okay, but what is this grave matter of the Church you wish to discuss?'

'We have come a long way searching for a very important Church document, and we have reason to believe that the Don may know where this document is.'

'What makes you think the Don knows anything about this document?'

Peter related his story about the climb with father Bracciano, and how he found the body of the climber, which led the police to the man now in custody, who claimed he gave the document to the Don.

The Don did not wait for the translation, but spoke to the big man, who listened attentively, before translating back to Peter.

'The Don, he wants to know, how come all of a sudden there is all this interest in this document, and why is it so important?'

'I beg your pardon?' Peter asked, his senses suddenly alert. 'Has someone else expressed interest in this document?'

'Yeah. Only yesterday. Some American. He came here to see the Don about a document. He said to watch out for a man and a lady who are pretending to be priest and nun. He told the Don that these two, they want to steal the document.'

The Don pulled at the big man's sleeve. The man leant over, placing his ear near the Don's mouth.

'The Don wanta know if you are the ones who are pretending to be a priest and a nun.'

'I assure you, sir, that I am a priest, and that my companion is a nun,' Peter protested. He reached into the inside pocket of his jacket, but was stopped as the giant clamped a vice-like grip on his wrist. 'I was only retrieving my passport,' Peter explained, wincing with pain.

'We see about that,' the giant said. Without relinquishing his grip on Peter, he reached into his pocket, extracting Peter's wallet.

He flicked it open, producing the passport, which he handed to Don Amiglio.

The Don flipped through the pages and then scrutinised Peter's image. 'Ha,' he grunted, and then to Peter's surprise, addressed him in passable, but heavily accented English. 'This means nothing. I have six passports, all in different names.' Peter was dismayed to see his passport disappear into the Don's inside coat pocket. He was about to protest when the Don continued. 'Tell me Father, if that is who you really are, why are you so interested in this document which you say someone give me for the safe keep?'

'Don Amiglio,' Peter said, 'firstly, let me assure you that we are who we say we are, despite what someone else may have told you.'

'We soon see about that,' the Don replied, 'but now you tell me what is so important about all this. How come, all of a sudden, everyone wanta know where this document is? Is it worth money?' he asked shrewdly with a hint of a smile.

Peter decided to take an affirmative stand. 'Do you have it, Don Amiglio?'

'Maybe, maybe not. Depends on if it is worth something.'

'No, I wouldn't think so. It has no commercial value. But having said that, there may well be people, enemies of the Church, who may go to great lengths to secure the document. And I suppose in all honesty, these people may be prepared to pay money to get their hands on it.'

The Don thought about this for a while, and then said, 'You seem to give honest answer. So tell me, you would pay me money for it?'

Peter was taken aback by this question, and took time to consider his answer. 'I suppose I would, if I could. But I guess I would rather appeal to your sense of decency to return it to the Church.'

'Hmmm,' the Don replied, weighing up the answer. 'Okay. Is fair answer. Now you tell me why this document she is so important.'

'Very well, Don Amiglio. We have reason to believe it is a copy of the Third Secret of Fatima.'

'And this is important?' the Don asked.

'Important enough for us to believe a Pope was murdered because of it.'

The Don crossed himself, a gesture that surprised Peter. 'You say the Papa was murdered?'

'We don't have proof, but we have reason to believe it is true.'

The Don sat in silence digesting this, before he spoke again. 'Why would someone murder the holy Papa? That is, how you say, a sacrilege.'

'Indeed it is,' Peter agreed, 'and should give you some idea of how important this is, and the lengths that some people will go to, to get their hands on the document.'

'I have read this document and it made no sense to me. Please tell me, what does it mean?'

'Before I do that, Don Amiglio, I should tell you about another document, recently discovered by an archaeologist. It is a prophecy, warning of grave consequences if the Third Secret of Fatima is not acted upon. And I hasten to add, that the Blessed Virgin Mary stipulated that Her revelation was be released to the world no later than 1960.'

The Don crossed himself again at the mention of the Blessed Virgin, and Peter wondered if the man, a Mafia boss, could truly be religious or if he was merely superstitious. Peter went on to explain in more detail about the Prophecy and how it was linked to the Third Secret of Fatima. The Don listened attentively without interruption.

When Peter finished, the Don sat for a long time deep in thought. Finally he said, 'I tell you what I'm gonna do, Father. I'm gonna hold on to your passport,' he gestured towards where Christina was patiently waiting, 'and my man here, he gonna get your friend's passport. 'If you are who you say, then we talk some more.' His tone took on a menacing quality, 'But, if like the American says, and you are not who you say …' he made a cutting gesture across his throat, 'then you won't need the passports again anyway. You capiche?'

⊁⊹⊱

Christina was not happy about surrendering her passport, but realised she had no choice. The giant's parting words were that he would be in touch one way or another. They hurried away from the restaurant, avoiding Gadaleta's car, in case they were being watched. Peter quickly filled Christina in on the gist of the conversation with Don Amiglio.

'This American worries me,' Peter said. 'Who, apart from us, would know that we were intending to see the Don?'

Up to this point, Christina had listened without interrupting. 'The only ones who know what we are about are Scott Emery and Tony Gadaleta.'

'And your uncle,' Peter reminded her.

'And my uncle,' Christina agreed, 'but he's in Sydney, and he's not an American. Emery and Gadaleta are.'

'What are you saying, Christina? That Scott or Tony are trying to sell us out?'

'Who else knew?' Christina persisted.

'No, I can't believe that,' Peter said. 'Why would they sell us out?'

'I don't know the answer to that,' Christina replied, 'but don't you think it's just too much of a coincidence?'

Peter thought for a moment. 'That driver,' he said, 'the one who tried to kill us on the mountain road, how did he know where we would be?'

'But Scott and Tony were in the car with us,' Christina argued. 'They could just as easily have been killed if the driver had succeeded.'

'That's true,' Peter mused, 'but there's something you don't know. Scott was thrown out of the car at the first impact.'

Christina raised an eyebrow. 'Look, it could all just be a coincidence.' Just as she said this, they rounded a corner and Gadaleta pulled up to the kerb. She hurried on, her voice lowered. 'But under the circumstances, I suggest we keep tight lipped from now on, and that includes Tony Gadaleta.'

'I think that's sound reasoning,' Peter agreed as he opened the car. 'Let's just wait and see what the Don comes back with.'

Chapter 50

Scott Emery was deep in thought in the back of a cab, as it sped east, leaving the outskirts of Rome behind. He snapped out of his reflection, as he realised the cab driver was talking to him.

'I beg your pardon?' Emery said, 'I mean, did you say something?'

'Si Signore, I was saying we are now driving along the famous Appian Way.'

'What?' Emery asked, irritated at the interruption.

'The Appian Way. You know, where the Spartacus was a-crucified.'

'I beg your pardon?' Emery asked again, not sure what the man was talking about, and becoming even more annoyed at the intrusion on his thoughts.

'Spartacus, you know, like the famous actor, Kirk Douglas. Spartacus, he was very famous man. Here they crucify him.'

'Is that right?' Emery replied, adding sarcastically, 'well why don't you tell someone who cares?'

'Scusi?' the Italian driver asked, the meaning of the cheap quip lost on him.

'I said, oh it doesn't matter. Look, do I look like a tourist to you?' He didn't wait for a reply. 'Tell you what; I'll do you a deal. Let's you and I agree on a clear line of demarcation. You do the driving, and I'll do the thinking, fair enough?'

'Scusi?'

'Let me put it as plainly as I can. Drive, and shut the fuck up!'

'You mean, you not want me to talk?'

'You're a fast one all right. The deal is, shut-up for the rest of the trip and I'll give you a tip.'

The driver took the hint and continued on in silence, heading towards the outer lying acreages favoured by the wealthy.

Emery was excited. The Don had summoned him to his home to discuss handing over the document. He had decided not to mention his breakthrough to Cardinal Morova, preferring to surprise him after he had successfully secured it. He smiled at the thought of Morova's reaction when he would melodramatically present it on his desk.

When Emery received the call on his cell phone, a man with a heavy Italian accent informed him that the Don would be pleased if Signore Emery would join him for dinner at his residence. Emery suspected the man on the phone was the ape he'd met at the restaurant with the Don, and he shuddered involuntarily. Emery could look after himself, he had no doubt about that, and there were many who, if they were still alive, could have testified to the folly of underestimating him. Despite his confidence in himself, the ape, as he referred to him, was not a man he would like to go up against. Instinctively he touched his hand to his side to feel the reassuring bulk of his .45 Smith & Wesson revolver. He didn't care how big the man was, a .45 calibre bullet is a great equaliser. Still, he thought, it was highly unlikely it would ever come to that. He felt certain the Don had invited him to dinner to do a deal. Like all mobsters, greed was his motivation. The Don would be thinking he was sitting on a valuable piece of merchandise, and he'd invited Scott over to talk turkey. Emery didn't care how much he had to pay. He knew Morova would happily compensate him, plus a handsome bonus. Yes, Morova would be prepared to pay anything to get his hands on it and destroy it. Emery understood only too well the consequences for

Morova if the document ever went public. Christ, it would mean the end of Morova, his cronies and a lot of other things too.

The crunching sound of gravel jolted him out of his reverie. The cab had slowed to a crawl as they made their way along a driveway flanked by tall spruce trees. Emery turned in his seat, noticing that the road was well out of sight. At the end of the drive the cab stopped in front of a large, iron gate which carried a sign warning intruders that it was electrified and that the property was protected by patrolling guard dogs. As if to confirm this message, four large Doberman Pinschers appeared as if from nowhere, pacing excitedly on the other side of the gate, eyeing the intruders noiselessly. Emery was impressed. These were highly trained guard dogs that understood their job was not to keep intruders out, but to make sure they didn't get away, in the unlikely event that someone managed to get inside. As the cab stopped, a bright searchlight came on, and Emery noticed a camera on top of the gate.

A metallic voice boomed from a speaker adjacent to the camera. 'Welcome, Mr Emery. Would you please step out of the cab and send the driver away.'

Emery did as he was told, paying off the driver, who knew better than to ask questions. Emery was left standing alone as the cab disappeared around a bend. Sensing the silent scrutiny of the camera, he was wondering what would happen next, when the gate slid silently open. His first reaction was alarm, as the barrier between him and the dogs was removed. Instinctively his hand felt for the reassurance of the gun nestled under his armpit, and immediately he cursed his folly, realising the movement may not have been lost on whoever was observing him from the other side of the lens.

The metallic voice boomed again. 'Would you kindly step through the gate Mr Emery, and wait. Please do not move when you are inside.'

Once again, Emery followed the instructions, keeping a watchful eye on the dogs, which were also watching him intently, lips drawn back menacingly, teeth bared in a silent snarl. The gate slid closed behind him and almost immediately he heard the sound of an approaching car, and then he saw it from the periphery of his vision, not daring to take his eyes off the dogs for even a second.

When the car stopped a familiar figure stepped out and Emery recognised the ape. The ape put a whistle to his mouth and blew into it, and although no sound came out, the dogs immediately dispersed, disappearing as quickly as they had appeared. The ape said nothing, gesturing for Emery to get into the back of the car, and then climbed in beside him. The car took off following the drive, which meandered uphill between the neat rows of trees. They continued for at least a kilometre before they came in sight of a house perched on top of a hill, surrounded by manicured gardens. To say the house was elaborate would have been an understatement

The car pulled up in front of the house and the ape climbed out, gesturing for Emery to follow him up the front steps, where he opened the door and they entered a large, marble foyer, adorned with ancient statues and expensive art works. Emery did not have time to admire the works as he was speedily whisked through a long corridor till they reached a set of double doors that the big man flung open, ushering Emery through.

Emery stepped into a room the size of a ballroom, dominated by a massive table, which he estimated would have comfortably seated fifty. As he turned, surveying the room, Emery saw he was not alone, for sitting at the head of the table was the Don himself, resplendent in a black silk smoking jacket with a bright red scarf around his neck, elegantly tucked into the jacket.

'Welcome to my humble home, Mr Emery,' the Don greeted, 'I'm very happy you could come.'

'The pleasure's all mine,' Emery responded.

'Please, come, sit by me,' the Don invited, gesturing to a chair by his side. 'We will have a nice dinner, okay? And then we will talk some business about this document you want so bad.'

As Emery seated himself next to the Don, he noticed the ape took up a strategic position directly behind his chair, causing Emery to feel distinctly uncomfortable. A servant entered the room pushing a serving cart, with a large, silver soup tureen. After serving the Don and his guest, he retreated as silently as he entered. The Don made small talk, mainly about the history of the surrounding district, to which Emery only half listened, wishing the Don would get down to business. When they had finished the second course of veal and garden salad, the Don poured an expensive cognac, and then offered Emery a cigar, which he declined. The Don shrugged and proceeded with the ritual of lighting his own cigar. When he was finally satisfied it was burning properly he took a long puff, contentedly blowing a cloud of blue smoke.

'Ah,' he exclaimed, 'a good cigar with fine cognac is one of the few pleasures left to me, Mr Emery.'

Emery smiled, taking a sip of his own brandy.

'Now, Mr Emery, down to business,' the Don finally exclaimed.

Emery fidgeted in his chair, leaning expectantly towards the Don. About time, he thought. He was finally going to get his hands on the Third Secret of Fatima. He wondered how much the Don would make him pay, but it didn't matter. Any price would be worth it, just to see the look on Morova's face when he finally presented it to him.

'Tell me, Mr Emery,' the Don continued, 'this document, it is very important to the Church, no?'

'The document is a forgery, meant to embarrass the Church,' Emery explained, 'and to cause confusion among the faithful. I have been assigned to track it down to ensure it doesn't fall into the wrong hands.'

'Ah, I see. Mr Emery, I am a simple businessman. This forgery you speak of. How much money is it worth to the Church?'

'Don Amiglio, I was hoping to gain your cooperation. I had hoped you would give up the document of your own volition, to save the Church acute embarrassment.'

The Don laughed, as if he'd just heard a funny joke. 'Ha, ha. You make a good joke. That is very funny. You were hoping I would just give you the document, outa the generosity of my heart. Let me tell you something Mr Emery. As I said, I am just a simple businessman.' He made a sweeping gesture with his arm. 'You look at my house and you think I'm very rich, hey. Well, let me tell you. The Church, she is rich. She is the big business. Compared to the Church, I am a very small, and poor businessman. Capiche?'

Emery nodded.

'So, let's cut the bullshit, Mr Emery. How much will you pay for this embarrassment to the Church?'

'I guess we would be prepared to pay whatever it takes to secure the document, within reason,' he added cautiously.

'Aha, within reason.' The Don clapped his hands in glee. 'So we must agree what is reasonable.'

'Yeah, I guess so.' Emery was beginning to feel uncomfortable.

'Would you think that maybe ten thousand US dollars is reasonable?'

Emery pretended to give this amount some thought. 'I believe I could sway that,' he responded, excited at how cheaply he may be able to get hold of the document, knowing that Morova would gladly pay ten times that amount.

'Aha, so if ten thousand is reasonable, how about twenty?'

Emery knew he'd fallen into the trap. This bastard is very shrewd, he thought. He'd have to be more careful. 'That's starting to sound like a whole heap of money we're talking about now, Don Amiglio,' he said cautiously, 'but yeah, maybe I could get approval for that.'

The Don thought about this for a while, then suddenly and unexpectedly, his demeanour changed. 'You know what I think, Mr Emery?' without waiting for an answer he continued, 'I think you are one big bull-shitter, Mr Emery, that's what I think.'

Emery, taken by surprise, stammered. 'Now wait a minute. I'm not sure I understand what you mean.'

'I tell you what I mean,' the Don growled, 'You think I come down witha the last rain, as you Americans say. Well let me tell you, I seen a lotta rain over the years, and no one, but no one, try to cheat Don Amiglio.'

'I assure you, Don Amiglio, I am not trying to cheat you. As I explained, I am a lawyer, retained by the Vatican to secure this potentially embarrassing document. Naturally, part of my job is to secure it with a minimum of expense to the Church, that's all. I'm just doing my job. I'm negotiating. I'm sure you can understand that.'

'Your job, ha.' The Don scoffed. 'You come to me with a story of being the lawyer. Well, you know what I think? I think that you are not the lawyer. I think you the fucking cop, that's what I think.'

Suddenly Emery was very nervous as he felt a sheen of sweat break out on his forehead. He tried to stay calm but could not resist the urge to feel for the reassuring, hard bulge under his armpit. That was his fatal mistake. Emery could not believe that such a big man could move so quickly. Before his hand even touched the fabric of his jacket, the ape had grabbed it, pulling it behind his back so hard that Emery screamed in pain as he heard his shoulder pop out of its joint. With a simultaneous blur of speed the ape's other hand was inside Emery's jacket, removing the gun from its holster.

'So watta we got here, eh?' the Don marvelled, 'a lawyer Johnny that packs the heat. What's a respectable lawyer man like you, working for the Church, needing to carry the piece, huh?'

Emery knew he was in desperate trouble. Instinctively he drew both knees to his chest, kicking out hard against the table. He flew backwards crashing into the giant, hoping to catch him off balance and knock him to the floor, giving himself a fleeting second's head start to get the hell out. Instead, he felt as though he'd crashed into what might as well have been a brick wall. The last thing Emery was aware of was the garrotte wire slipping expertly around his throat. The ape pulled on the wooden handles with such force that the wire almost decapitated Emery, killing him instantly as it cut through his windpipe.

Chapter 51

Peter LeSarus woke from a deep sleep. He glanced at the luminous clock on the bedside table. It read 3:00AM. He wondered what had woken him so suddenly. As if in answer, there was an urgent knock on the door of his hotel room. He climbed out of bed, groping for the light switch, wondering who on earth could be knocking on his door at this hour. His first thought was, Christina, but he quickly dismissed this. There was no way she would come to his room at this hour. If she needed to speak to him urgently she would have called his room extension. Then, remembering the bombed hotel in Prague, he picked up the phone to call security. As he began to dial the number, he heard an urgent, muffled voice.

'Father LeSarus, please open the door. I must talk to you.'

Replacing the handset, he slipped on his robe and padded barefooted to the door, pressing his ear against it. 'Who's there?' he demanded.

The voice repeated the urgent plea. 'Please open the door, Father LeSarus. I must talk to you.'

This time Peter recognised the voice, and in amazement, opened the door.

Piggott pushed past Peter, even before the door was fully opened.

'What on earth …?' Peter gaped.

'Please excuse the late hour, Father,' Piggott apologised breathlessly, 'I had to warn you. Your life is in peril.'

Peter was now fully awake, staring wide-eyed at his unexpected visitor. 'Piggott,' he exclaimed, 'where did you come from? I mean, what are you doing in Rome? And what do you mean peril?'

'There's not much time,' Piggott warned. 'Do you mind if I sit down?'

'No, of course not. Sorry, I seem to have forgotten my manners. It's just that, well, I must say you did take me by surprise.'

'Yes, I'm sorry about that, sir, but there is no time for niceties.'

'Piggott, please sit down. Can I get you anything?'

Piggott shook his head, 'No thank you, sir.'

'Then tell me what this is all about.'

'Very well, sir. Have you mentioned to anyone else anything I said to you that evening after the dinner?'

'No, I gave you my word. I haven't even mentioned it to Christina.'

'Thank God for that,' Piggott said, sounding enormously relieved. 'At least he doesn't know you suspect anything.'

'Piggott, what on earth are you getting at?' Peter asked.

'Father LeSarus, O'Shaughnessy is on his way to Rome, as we speak. I figure I have about eight hours head start on him.'

'O'Shaughnessy is coming here? But, how? I mean, what about the emphysema? I thought he couldn't fly.'

Piggott laughed without humour. 'He no more has emphysema than you or me.'

'What? But then, why would he invent such a thing?'

'Because he wanted you to go to Europe to find the Third Secret of Fatima, as well as the prophecy.'

'Why couldn't he have gone himself?'

'Because he knew that if Cardinal Morova ever got wind that he was back in Europe, he would have him killed.'

Peter shook his head. 'Go on.'

'Brian O'Shaughnessy has always claimed that he was framed by Cardinal Morova over the Vatican Bank scandal and as a result was imprisoned for it. His hatred for Cardinal Morova has festered all these years, and revenge has become an overwhelming obsession.'

'But you told me that O'Shaughnessy is not all he makes out to be, and when I asked you what you meant by that, you said he was guilty of embezzling the money from the Vatican Bank.'

'That's right,' Piggott agreed. 'You see, his father's bank was in deep trouble and O'Shaughnessy bailed him out with the money he syphoned off.'

'In that case, if what you say is true, that he did steal the money, then he got what he deserved.'

'Yes, but Morova got off scot-free and he was responsible for far greater losses than O'Shaughnessy. Morova handed O'Shaughnessy over to the authorities like a sacrificial lamb, and he's never forgiven him for it.'

'So what makes O'Shaughnessy think that Cardinal Morova would have him killed?'

'Because O'Shaughnessy knows for a fact that Morova killed the last Pope, but he's never been able to prove it.'

'And he thinks that the Third Secret can be linked to the murder of the Pope?' Peter guessed.

'Precisely,' Piggott agreed, 'because he believes that the Pope was about to announce to the College of Cardinals that he intended to enact the demands of Our Lady, and that was something Morova had to stop at all costs.'

'But why?'

'Morova lives only for power. O'Shaughnessy believes that something about the Third Secret threatens that power and if the Pope were to act on the demands of Our Lady, Morova would lose his power. The last thing Morova wants is a Pope he can't control.'

'This is insane, Piggott, are you telling me that all this madness over a document is so that one old man can retain his power base?'

'Sir,' said Piggott. 'You of all people would know that men have done a lot more for a lot less than the control of one of the world's richest and most powerful institutions.'

Peter thought about this for a moment. 'Yes, I suppose you do have a point, Piggott, but you said my life is in danger. I already know that. There have been two attempts on my life and on Christina's. But why did you have to come here to Rome to tell me and what has it got to do with O'Shaughnessy coming to Rome?'

'O'Shaughnessy is coming to Rome to kill you,' Piggott answered matter of factly.

Peter stared at Piggott, not believing what he'd just heard. 'What? Why would O'Shaughnessy want to kill me?'

'Because you have outlived your usefulness. You have all but led him to the location of the copy of the Third Secret.'

'Why would that necessitate him killing me? I don't understand,' Peter said, confused.

'When Brian O'Shaughnessy was in prison he had a lot of time on his hands to think. His hatred for Morova is equalled only to his hatred of the Church, and it was then that he hatched his plan. By finally bringing the Fatima secret to world attention, he would kill two birds with one stone. Prove Morova is a murderer, and bring the Church undone.'

'I can understand the reasoning behind that,' Peter said, 'but I still don't see why he would want to kill me.'

Piggott took his time before answering, weighing his words carefully. 'Christina contacted him when you were on the mountain and told him things he did not want to hear.'

'Like what?' Peter demanded.

'You must understand that Brian O'Shaughnessy is more than just fond of his niece. As he himself has said to you, she is all he has. He harbours an unhealthy possessiveness towards her. You were useful to him while you were protecting her during your enquiries, but now you are in the way.'

'What are you saying?' Peter demanded, wondering where this was going.

'Christina admitted to her uncle that she has fallen in love with you.'

Peter stared at Piggott, his heart suddenly pounding.

Chapter 52

By the time Christina met Peter for breakfast, Piggott had long gone. He promised Peter he would stay close, but advised him not to let on what he knew, and to act as though he knew nothing. Piggott was certain that as long as the document was still at large, Peter was safe. The news about Christina's feelings towards him had come as a complete surprise, and now his emotions were in turmoil.

As they chatted over breakfast, the bellhop approached Peter with a note. It was a summons from Don Amiglio to attend his residence for dinner. Peter wondered where O'Shaughnessy was, and why he hadn't contacted them. He was feeling decidedly edgy and the lack of sleep that night had not helped his frayed nerves.

That evening Peter and Christina were heading in a taxi along the same fateful route taken by Emery the previous night. On route, they speculated as to what the outcome of the meeting might be, but Peter warned Christina not to get her hopes up. 'Don't be fooled by his grandfatherly image. I think it's fair to speculate that if he agrees to a deal, there will have to be something in it for him.'

'I wonder why he's summoned both of us this time?' Christina mused.

'I'd suggest,' Peter ventured, 'it's probably because if he doesn't like what he hears he'll want to get rid of us without leaving someone behind, who is going to ask questions.' He sensed Christina stiffen and immediately regretted what he said, so he added. 'I'm sure I'm being melodramatic. More likely I would say he wants to strike a deal, and wants both of us there to agree on the spot.'

'I hope you're right,' Christina said, 'but maybe we should have confided in Gadaleta.'

'I thought we agreed on that,' Peter reminded her.

'I know we agreed,' Christina said, 'but I still feel a bit nervous going into a Mafia house, with no one knowing where we are or what we are doing. If the Don decided to harm us, no one would even know we went there.'

With these sentiments in mind they were ushered nervously into Don Amiglio's elaborate dining room. Christina was reminded of the children's tale about the fly being invited into the spider's parlour for dinner.

The Don was already seated at the head of the table in animated conversation with someone sitting next to him, but whose identity they could not make out as he was partly concealed in shadow, with his back to the door. The Don stood up from the table, greeting his newly arrived guests.

'Good evening, Father and Sister,' he welcomed amiably, 'I am so glad you could join us. I also asked an old friend to be here.' He gestured at the figure seated at the table. 'He is an expert in such matters and I thought it would be good for him to share his knowledge with us. Let me introduce you.'

The figure at the table turned towards the newcomers and as he turned, the light illuminated his features and the scarlet skullcap perched on his head.

'Reverend Father and Sister from Australia, may I introduce you to my old and good friend, His Eminence, Cardinal Morova.'

Peter and Christina were completely stunned, struggling not to reveal their discomfiture. Morova seemed just as taken aback, staring at them and then back at his host. He had obviously not been forewarned as to who his fellow dinner guests were to be.

Morova was the first to regain his composure, his lips parting in a grimacing smile. 'Don Amiglio, it is always a pleasure to meet with fellow clergy,' he said in perfect English, 'especially ones who have travelled such a long way. Please introduce me.'

Don Amiglio was clearly enjoying himself, grinning as he introduced Peter and Christina to the Cardinal. With reluctance, Peter stepped forward to kiss the Cardinal's ring, and Christina followed suit.

After they had all been seated, with Peter and Christina facing the Cardinal and Don Amiglio seated at the head of the table, the Don began, 'My dear friend, Lucca, you are perhaps wondering why I asked you here to meet my new friends, the Holy Father and Sister from the Australia?'

'Indeed I am, Paulo,' Morova replied, displaying unfeigned interest. The familiarity of address was not lost on Peter.

'Might I suggest then,' said the Don, 'that we do the business much better with full stomachs. We eat, then we talk.'

No sooner had this been said than a door opened and a man in a dinner suit, complete with white gloves, entered the room, pushing a trolley. He lifted the lid from the silver food server, revealing a veritable mountain of steaming spaghetti in bolognaise sauce which he proceeded to heap on to their plates. They washed the delicious pasta down with red wine, which the Don poured personally.

'This is a good wine,' he commented genially, 'the grapes, they come from my own vineyard. The wine, it is very rich, no?' he asked.

No sooner had they finished, than they were served a second course, this time veal parmagiana. For a man who appeared as small and frail as the Don he had an enormous appetite. The same could not be said for his guests, each of them picking at their dinners, impatient to get on with the business at hand.

After the second course had been cleared the Don stood up from the table, inviting his guests to join him in his study. The butler re-appeared, producing cognac glasses and offering the men cigars. The Don and Morova accepted, but Peter and Christina graciously declined. Everyone settled comfortably into the large, leather lounges, and when the two men were satisfactorily puffing their Cubans, the Don began.

'So, now we no longer have to worry about being hungry, we can talk the business.'

Peter and Christina leaned forward expectantly.

'Firstly,' the Don said, 'I would like to thank my good friend here, Lucca, the big shot from the Vatican, for joining us tonight, eh.' He raised his glass to Morova who inclined his head, acknowledging his friend's thanks with a mirthless smile. 'First I gotta explain to you, Father and Sister, that Lucca and I, we go back a long time. Isn't that right, Lucca?' He didn't wait for acknowledgement. 'You see, we know each other since we be the bambini. His father and my father were great friends in the old days. They helped each other a lot, and now I ask my friend here tonight to help me to make some decision about this document, that you, and I think, plenty others, are so interested in.' He chuckled.

The Don leaned over and retrieved a manila folder from beside his lounge, placing it in front of him on the coffee table. He then went on to explain for the benefit of Morova how the document had come into his possession and how Peter and Christina had tracked it down.

'You know me, Lucca. I am just a simple man. I used to do some business, till I got too old. Now I just sit in the coffee shop. Anyway, I read this document, and I gotta tell you, it scared me. The Father here,' he gestured to Peter, 'he tell me all sorta things, and I think it best you have a look and you tell me what to do.' He opened the folder and passed the contents to Morova, who took out his glasses and began to read.

He'd only read a few lines before he put the document down and refolded his glasses, returning them to his pocket.

'I am familiar with this document, Paulo,' he announced matter of factly, 'and I know who these two are.'

Don Amiglio looked up surprised. 'What? You say you know these people?'

The Cardinal scowled, clearly displaying his contempt. 'Oh, yes. I know them, not personally, but I know of them. And I know all about this document. It is a fake. Contrived by enemies of the Church to discredit Her. As for these, these persons,' he pronounced it as though the word were an obscenity, staring ominously at each in turn, 'yes, they were clergy. That is, before they were excommunicated for heresy.'

Don Amiglio looked up, surprised.

'Is that true?' the Don asked. 'You are no longer the priest and the nun?'

Peter responded for both of them. 'Don Amiglio, let me begin to answer that by firstly emphasising that until now neither of us has been excommunicated, and even if we had, I am sure his Eminence the Cardinal will verify that once a man is ordained a priest it is for life. No power on earth can undo that, not even a Pope. Yes, the Church can impose restrictions on a priest, like banning him from administering the sacraments, or a priest can apply to be released from his vows, but no one can undo the sacrament of Holy Orders. So, to answer your question, I am still very much a priest, and Sister Christina is still very much a nun.'

'Is this the truth, Lucca?' he asked, looking confused.

Morova smiled patronisingly at the Don. 'Technically what he says is true, but nevertheless they have been ostracised from the Church. The Church no longer recognises them.'

'Don Amiglio, please hear me out,' Peter pleaded.

The Don nodded for him to continue.

'It may be true that we have been renounced by the Church, but there are mitigating circumstances.'

'I don't know this word, how you say it, miti …?'

'I beg your pardon, Don Amiglio,' Peter apologised, 'what I meant was that there were reasons justifying our actions. The actions we took which brought us into disrepute with the Church. We acted according to our own consciences, doing that which we believed in, and still do believe in.'

'Ah, I understand. Please, continue,' he waved his hand.

'There are no mitigating circumstances acceptable to the Church for heresy and the breaking of vows,' Morova interrupted angrily.

'And what of the murder of a Pope?' Peter demanded.

Morova gave the Don a look, suggesting Peter was mad.

'What murder of what Pope?' the Don asked.

'Don Amiglio,' Peter pleaded, 'please. You agreed to hear me out. The Cardinal here claims that the document you have is a forgery designed to embarrass and harm the Church. Well, let me tell you, the previous Pope entrusted that document to his best friend because he feared for his life. He feared for his life because he had made the decision to act on the document, as was ordained by the Blessed Virgin to Sister Lucia.'

'Bah,' Morova spat the word contemptuously. 'Sister Lucia was and is a fraud. The Church now recognises that. We have evidence that she and the other two shepherd brats were in alliance with Satan. That is why the Church suppressed the document. It is a fake.'

'What do you have to say to this, Father LeSarus?' the Don asked.

Peter reached into his jacket pocket retrieving a letter that he handed to the Don. 'This is a letter from Pope Leo Alexander I to his closest friend, Father Bruno Bracciano. If you will read it you will see he asked his friend to keep the copy of the Third Secret of Fatima in safekeeping. The letter goes on to say he was about to make a radical announcement, and it was because of this he feared for his life.'

The Don looked at the letter, turning it over. 'It has the Papal insignia,' he motioned to Morova, visibly impressed.

'Any printer can forge the Papal insignia,' Morova hissed.

The Don ignored him and began to read.

<hr>

My Dearest Friend Bruno,

We live in troubled times, as never before. Since taking up the cross as Christ's representative I have become privy to a situation so alarming and so serious that I cannot begin to explain the potential ramifications to Mother Church and to mankind. All I can say is, God help us, and have mercy on our souls. I have had the most alarming revelation, and I beg you to pray for me, so that God grants me the wisdom to deal with it correctly as failure could result in Armageddon.

I know that sounds dramatic, but believe me my trusted friend, when I tell you that the forces of evil are more active and more advanced than you and I would hitherto ever imagined possible.

How I long for the simplicity of my previous life, and like Christ in the Garden of Gethsemane I would give anything for this cross to be taken away from me. But that is not to be. The Holy Spirit chose me to be Pope; as such I have no say but to do what I must to resolve what is without doubt the most critical challenge in history. How I long for the simplicity of striding out with you my friend, to the clean air of the mighty Dolomites, to glean your wisdom. But alas, I cannot even entrust in you the true nature of this crisis. Believe me when I tell you that it is for your own safety that I keep you in ignorance, in order to protect you from the evil that surrounds us. I know not who to trust as the evil permeates even the walls of our most sacred Vatican.

I beseech you to hold a most important document in trust for me and for the world at large. You are the only person whom I can trust. Suffice to say that it is divinely inspired and holds the truth and future of mankind within its contents. It is a copy of the original, and for your own protection and sanity, I implore you to resist opening it, but rather keep it within your most sacred care.

I have called for an extraordinary conclave of the Sacred College of Cardinals, at which I will make a momentous announcement, which will change the Church, as we know it, forever. There will be those who will stringently oppose what I must do, and consequently I do believe my life is already in danger. In the event of my untimely death, I have no doubt that those who oppose me will destroy this sacred document. Therefore it is imperative a copy is kept in a safe place. Only in the event of my death do I ask you to open and read the contents and take what action you deem fit.

Should it come to that, I seek your forgiveness in advance for the trauma it will bring to your life.

Your dear friend,
Giuseppe

After the Don finished reading, he sat in silence. Slowly and deliberately he removed his reading glasses, placing them on the table in front of him, on top of the letter.

Suddenly Morova reached out, grabbing for the letter. The Don made no attempt to stop him. Morova began to read, moving his head from side to side, as his eyes scanned the lines, mouthing the words. When he finished, he screwed the letter up in a ball, throwing it to the floor in disgust.

'This is preposterous. Can't you see that this is all part of the plot?'

The Don said nothing as he leaned down to retrieve the document. He then spent some time fastidiously smoothing it out. He replaced his glasses and began to re-read the letter. When he finished he addressed LeSarus. 'You truly believe that the holy Papa was going to do what it says in that document?'

Peter did not reply immediately, but sat still for a while staring at the ceiling, as though he might find the answer up there. Finally he said with slow deliberation, 'Yes, I believe he was, Don Amiglio. I believe the Pope recalled the cardinals to announce his intention to meet the demands of the Third Secret and that is why he was murdered.'

Morova could no longer contain himself. He leaped up from his chair spitting with anger. 'Don Amiglio, this is absurd! In the name of the Holy Roman Catholic Church, I demand you hand over that document and the letter immediately. This man has just proven who he is working for. The Devil! Do you hear me? The Devil himself.' He grabbed the crucifix around his neck, theatrically thrusting it in Peter's direction.

Don Amiglio was shocked by the outburst, which was so out of character. The door burst open, and the giant bodyguard came running in.

'Don Amiglio,' he called, alarm written all over his face, 'are you all right?'

The Don waved a hand, assuring him that he was in no immediate danger, but then gestured for him to remain in the room.

The Don addressed Peter again, serious indecision showing in his eyes. 'I not know what to believe. You are a priest. My friend is a cardinal and he says this is, how he say ..., propostrio?'

'Is it preposterous?' Peter challenged. 'The demands come from the Mother of God, as do the warnings of what will happen if these demands are not met. Read it again, Don Amiglio. It is all there in the letter.'

The Don thought about this for a while. 'No,' he announced, making a decision, 'I don't need to read it again. My friend the holy Cardinal, he already told me this writing is the bullshit. And I think a cardinal knows more about these things than a priest. Especially an excommunicated priest,' he added for good measure.

Peter challenged. 'Then what would you say, Don Amiglio, if I were to tell you there is another document? A document that supports the validity of the Third Secret of Fatima.'

'What, another document?' the Don demanded. 'How many documents are there?'

'It is the ancient prophecy I told you about at the restaurant. It has been scientifically authenticated at nearly four thousand years old,' Peter explained.

'Another Satanic forgery no doubt,' Morova mocked. 'Paulo, I must insist you give me the document so that it can be finally destroyed for what it is – the devil's work. Let me warn you as a friend and as a cardinal, that anyone harbouring or assisting these evil people will be damned to eternal hellfire along with them and he who they serve.'

The Don appeared shaken by this, crossing himself to ward off such a calamitous possibility.

Peter reached into his jacket again, this time producing a copy of the translation of the prophecy and handed it to the Don. 'Before you make a final decision, Don Amiglio, please read this. It is the part of the prophecy that makes direct reference to the Third Secret and The Blessed Virgin's warnings.'

The Don replaced his glasses and, unfolding the paper, he began to read. Morova started to interrupt again, but the Don held up a hand silencing him.

※※※

The Don was visibly distressed as he removed his glasses. He rubbed the bridge of his nose with two fingers, placing the copy of the prophecy on the coffee table. His eyes darted backwards and forward from LeSarus to Morova, as if in great confusion. Finally, he seemed to have come to a decision.

'Father LeSarus, I think I have read enough of this stuff. I don't know what it is all about, and I don't think I wanta know too much more. I have known the Cardinal for a long time and he is a cardinal after all. You are only a priest who I don't know, and you come from the Australia, which I'm not even sure where it is. I find out you are to be excommunicated. You tell me there are reasons for this. Well, I don't care about no reasons. The fact is, that you never told me this before. You kept it from me.'

Peter was about to interrupt, but Don Amiglio silenced him with a gesture as he continued. 'So I think I must believe my friend the Cardinal, here. I give him the document like he asks. To you and your friend here,' he gestured at Christina, 'I gladly give you back your passports. I don't ever want to see or hear from you again. I think you are scary and big trouble for me. Now, you go way from my house. Don't ever come back, or next time there will be trouble.' He glanced ominously over his shoulder towards the ape. 'You capiche?' He made a sign to his bodyguard to escort them from the house.

The giant stepped forward to carry out his boss's orders, when Peter suddenly had an idea. It was desperate, but he had to give it a shot. It was their last chance. He held up a restraining hand, causing the giant to pause.

'Don Amiglio, wait, just one second.'

'No, I no wait any more seconds. You leave my house now.'

Peter saw Morova triumphantly retrieving the document and the Pope's letter from the coffee table.

'Don Amiglio, I beg you. This is far too important. May I speak for just one moment? Please.'

Christina was watching Peter intently, wondering what he was up to. Something in Peter's tone made the Don hesitate. He paused, holding up a hand to his bodyguard, who stepped back, but kept a wary eye on Peter. 'OK. What is it you wanta say?'

'Don Amiglio, we have reason to believe that it was the Cardinal here who murdered Pope Leo Alexander I.'

Morova began to interrupt with another outburst of outrage, but the Don held up a hand silencing him. 'And you can prove this?'

Peter hurried on for fear of being interrupted again. 'No, I can't prove it.' He held up a hand. 'But I put it to you that this is so critically important, it should be put to the Pope himself.'

Morova would not be silenced any longer. Bursting out with an expletive he said, 'You're insane. Who do you think you are? The Pope would never see you and even if he would, he couldn't, he is a sick man.'

'Cardinal Morova,' Peter continued, 'you are Secretary of State. If you were to tell the Holy Father that it is a matter of critical importance, he would see us.'

'I tell you it is not possible. It is madness.' With that, Morova made an angry farewell gesture to the Don and made to leave the room, with the documents safely stashed inside his voluminous robes.

The Don gave an almost imperceptible signal to his bodyguard, who immediately blocked the Cardinal's exit.

'Lucca, please wait, uno momento.'

Morova glared at the bodyguard, then at the Don. 'What for? Are you, my old friend, going to take the word of these, these renegades? Take their word over mine, a cardinal, the Secretary of the State of the Vatican?'

The Don hesitated, once again unsure of what to do. Desperate, Peter decided to take one, final gamble.

'Don Amiglio,' he pleaded, 'you have read the Third Secret of Fatima, as well as part of the prophecy. You now know what will happen if these documents are authentic and are ignored. Can you afford to take the risk, and not make certain that it is truly a directive from Our Lady Herself?' He was playing on what he had observed of the Don's deeply ingrained superstition. He watched the Don closely, and saw his resolve wavering. He took a deep breath and then threw his last frantic punch line. 'Don Amiglio, you still hold our passports. Keep them.' Christina shot Peter a look as if asking if he were completely insane. 'Yes, keep them,' Peter continued. 'Then, if the Pope agrees that the document is a fake, then we are at your mercy.' Christina rolled her eyes as Peter continued. 'I am prepared to bet our lives on this.' Christina shot him another look, more urgent than the first, which he ignored. 'Don Amiglio, we are prepared to stake our lives. What is the Cardinal prepared to stake?'

Don Amiglio stared at him, then turned to his old friend who was eyeing Peter belligerently. 'Lucca, the Father here has put a challenge to you. He has shown much honour and proven he gotta big balls. Scusi, Sister,' he apologised to Christina for his language before continuing. 'He is prepared to stake the life of him and his friend on this. What you have to say to this, Lucca?'

Morova was flustered, not at all sure how to handle this turn of events. Without being able to think of anything else to say, he said, 'This is ridiculous.'

'Lucca,' the Don continued, 'I cannot refuse him this. It is like the old days, when honour was everything. You must give me back the document. Make the appointment with the Holy Father. If you do not do this, then I will give the document to Father LeSarus. If the Holy Father he say they lie, then I take care of them myself. Capiche?' he asked ominously, watching Peter closely.

.

Chapter 53

'Have you gone mad?' Christina challenged when they were safely in a taxi heading back to Rome.

'Sorry,' he apologised. 'I know it was a long shot, but I didn't know what else to say. Morova already had the document. I had to come up with a drastic ploy.'

'Drastic? That's some understatement.'

'Look,' Peter reassured her, 'I have no intention of placing your life in danger. As soon as we get back to Rome, you're going to the Australian embassy. Tell them your passport has been stolen, and that you believe your life is in danger. They'll grant you asylum.'

'And what about you?' she demanded.

'I'll just have to hope the Pope backs my story.'

Peter was tempted to tell Christina about his late night visit from Piggott, but instinct told him to keep it to himself – for now at least.

'Backs your story,' Christina spluttered, 'you know the word is that the Pope has no idea of who he is, let alone be able to back your story, or anyone else's for that matter.'

Peter had no answer to this, so he merely shrugged his shoulders.

By the time they entered the hotel foyer it was past midnight and they were surprised to receive a note from the captain asking them to contact Room 309, irrespective of how late they were. Peter picked up the house phone and feigned great surprise when O'Shaughnessy came on the line.

'Brian? How on earth? What are you doing here?' He turned to Christina. 'It's Brian, your uncle. He's here in the hotel.' Christina's surprise matched Peter's, as he replaced the receiver. 'I don't know how, or why, but your uncle is waiting for us in Room 309.'

O'Shaughnessy embraced them warmly when they entered his room and laughed good naturedly when Christina asked at least a dozen questions without drawing breath. He held up both hands, 'Hold it! Give me a chance. Why don't I get us all a drink and I'll tell you everything.'

Once they were all settled with a drink in their hand, O'Shaughnessy began. 'I thought I'd surprise you,' he chuckled. After you told me you were so close, I couldn't resist. I made a decision to get straight on a plane and join you. Besides, I figured you might still need some help.'

'But Uncle Brian, your emphysema, how did you manage to get them to let you fly?'

O'Shaughnessy grinned like a little boy who had been caught out. 'I got a doctor to give me an extra strong dose of cortisone, which seemed to do the trick. And as for them letting me fly, well, I just failed to disclose my condition, didn't I,' he said with a twinkle.

You're a good liar, Peter thought as Christina admonished her uncle thoroughly. 'Oh, Uncle Brian, I really thought you had more sense.'

'You know better than that,' he said fondly, still grinning. 'Now then, where have you two been at this late hour? Why don't you bring me up to date?'

Christina did most of the talking, while Peter had to restrain himself from blurting out what he'd learned from Piggott. He decided to take a wait-and-see attitude and let O'Shaughnessy show his hand. Meanwhile Peter determined to remain vigilant.

'It seems you may have painted yourself into somewhat of a corner, Peter,' O'Shaughnessy remarked when Christina had finished.

'Well, we'll see about that,' Peter responded. 'I can only hope that when I get to see the Pope with Morova and the Don, he'll be lucid.'

'Hmmm,' O'Shaughnessy mused, 'I hate leaving anything to chance, particularly if your life is at stake.'

'I agree with your sentiments,' Peter answered, 'but sometimes we don't have a choice.'

'We always have choice, my dear boy.' O'Shaughnessy paused for a moment and, yawning, said, 'You'll have to excuse me, it's been a long flight and I simply must get to bed. I'll see you both in the morning.' He stood up, shook Peter's hand and gave Christina a kiss and a hug, and left them, rejecting any suggestion from Christina of further help or fussing.

As O'Shaughnessy left Peter wondered where the old man was really going and what he was up to. For one crazy second, he actually considered going to bed with a knife under his pillow. He shook his head in amazement.

Chapter 54

When Sister Mary Magdalena received the call in the early hours of the morning she was overcome by a sense of humility. The caller explained that the Pope's longstanding personal nurse had suddenly taken ill and would she be able to stand in to look after the ailing Pontiff. The nursing nun readily agreed, promising to be ready to be picked up within the hour, at the hospice where she lived and worked.

The priest who spoke perfect Italian, but with a strange accent, deposited her at the Vatican where he had a hurried, whispered conversation with the Swiss Guard on duty, before ushering her in to the Pope's private quarters where he briefed her on his condition. She was told he was still asleep and was handed a chart, detailing the physician's orders for medication. She checked her watch, noting it was nearly six o'clock, the time designated to administer the first of his drugs. The priest then suggested she check the medication schedule. When she queried this, he simply explained that the Pope's regular physician was indisposed, and that it seemed a good idea – just to be on the safe side. And then he was gone.

Sister Mary thought that all of this was highly unusual.

She read the order and frowned.

My God, this must be a mistake, she thought. She read the order again. It was quite emphatic. An injection of Rohypnol before the Pope was even awake. Silently, she entered his bedchamber where the Pope seemed to be sleeping peacefully. She quietly left the room to re-read the instructions yet again, fearing she may have misunderstood. No, there it was. The instruction was clear, 250 mg of Rohypnol to be injected just prior to awakening. Confused, she flipped the page to read the previous day's instructions, and sure enough the instructions were the same. She continued to flip pages, noting that the tranquilliser had been administered each morning at the same time every day for the last week.

This is definitely not right, she thought. Why would the doctor order a powerful tranquilliser like Rohypnol to be administered before the Pope awoke? It made no sense. The poor man would barely be able to wake up, and when he did he would remain in a state of stupor. She noted there was an order to re-administer the drug every four hours throughout the day, and then again, finally, just before he was due to retire.

Sister Mary Magdalena made a momentous decision.

⚜

The Pope's eyes flickered open, and for the first time in as long he could remember, he felt alert and alive. Tentatively, he made his way to the bay window, where he pulled back the heavy curtains and looked out at a still deserted St Peter's Square, with the sun's imminent arrival heralded by a streak of red across the sky. He opened the double window and drank in the sweet smell of Rome, revelling in the unfamiliar sensation of elation and excitement of a new day.

Sensing the door opening, he turned to see an unfamiliar, elderly nun, dressed in the white habit of the nursing sisters.

⚜

'Holy Father, you are awake,' Sister Mary Magdalena exclaimed, genuflecting.

The Pope crossed the room, extending his hands, bidding the nun to stand. 'Yes,' he said, 'and I have never felt better. You are not my regular nurse, Sister,' he observed.

'No, Holy Father. Your regular nurse is ill and I was asked to stand in.'

She decided not to discuss the drug orders, but determined to speak to the doctor on the first available opportunity. Something was going on and she did not like it. She offered to help the Pontiff dress, which help he cheerily dismissed, announcing he felt quite capable to do it himself.

~·~

Once the Pope finished dressing the nurse helped him to his private chapel where he celebrated mass, taking longer than usual, revelling in the exhilaration of communicating to God through prayer with a clear head. He prayed for enlightenment and for a continuation of the wonderful feeling of health that had overtaken him.

He began to believe what he'd vaguely suspected for a long time. He had clouded memories of injections. He racked his brain, wondering who was responsible for this and why, and how long it had been going on. Vague suspicions were forming in the Pontiff's mind, but for the moment he would simply wait and see what developed.

His mind went back to the time he was elected Pope, following the sudden death of his predecessor. He remembered having a long meeting with his Secretary of State, Cardinal Morova. He recalled questioning him at length as to the purpose of the extraordinary recall of the College of Cardinals, ordered so shortly after his predecessor's own election, but had failed to receive a satisfactory answer. The Cardinal had pleaded ignorance. But the Pope did not call for a gathering of cardinals without discussion with his Secretary of State.

When the Pope emerged from his private chapel he took breakfast, eating more heartily than he had in years. His private secretary interrupted his breakfast to announce that Cardinal Morova had requested an urgent audience, along with three other people. He did not know who the other people were, and the Cardinal preferred not to state the nature of business to be discussed. Instinct warned the Pope to continue with a façade of appearing to be not quite lucid. He absently nodded his agreement, gesturing with a weak hand wave of resolve.

Chapter 55

Peter woke to the incessant ringing of the phone. O'Shaughnessy had kept them up till 1:00AM. Peter had hardly slept and could barely open an eye to check the time on the illuminated clock by his bed. It read 6:05AM. When this is all over, I'm going to sleep for a week, he thought wearily, happy to have survived the night, and as he groped for the phone he noted the chair still wedged tightly underneath the doorknob where he had left it when he went to bed. The voice on the phone caused him to sit bolt upright, fully alert. It was the now familiar voice of the Don's bodyguard.

Without so much as a greeting, the voice said, 'You and the Sister are to meet Don Amiglio and Cardinal Morova at the Vatican at four o'clock this afternoon. The Cardinal has arranged for an audience with the Holy Papa.' He went on to give details of precisely where at the Vatican they were to meet. 'The Swiss Guard will be expecting you. Don't be late.' The line went dead.

Peter jumped out of bed and picked up the phone again. He dialled Christina's extension. She must really be out to it, he thought after he had let it ring for what seemed an interminable length of time. He decided he should call O'Shaughnessy. The phone was picked up on the second ring, and O'Shaughnessy came on the line, sounding wide awake and refreshed. Doesn't the man ever sleep? Peter marvelled.

'Brian, it's Peter. The meeting with the Pope has been set up for four this afternoon.'

'Splendid,' O'Shaughnessy remarked jovially.

'I wish I could share your enthusiasm,' Peter responded.

'There, there, my boy. Let's be optimistic about this.'

'It's difficult to be optimistic when everything I hear tells me the Pope doesn't know what time of day it is.'

O'Shaughnessy chuckled into the phone. 'I have a good feeling about this. I'm almost certain you'll find the Pope will be most receptive.'

Peter wondered. 'Do you know something that I don't?'

'Remember what I said. Leave nothing to chance.' Before Peter could press further, O'Shaughnessy changed the subject. 'Have you informed Christina?'

'No. I tried to, but she's not answering her phone.'

'Poor dear. No doubt she's exhausted. Let her sleep, we have plenty of time. Why don't I meet you for breakfast in, say, half an hour?'

Over breakfast, O'Shaughnessy proved to be entirely non-committal over his optimistic feelings about the Pope. He brushed it off as a gut feeling, refusing to be drawn further on the matter. Peter wondered whether this was the truth, but his instinct told him O'Shaughnessy was holding out.

'So, I suppose we should discuss our game plan for the meeting,' O'Shaughnessy suggested.

'It's very simple,' Peter said, 'if, and I emphasise the word, if the Pope is capable of a discussion, then I present him with the facts, and the translation of the prophecy, while Don Amiglio presents him with a copy of the Third Secret, and I hope like hell he buys it, whatever it is.' Peter grimaced. 'On the other hand, if he rejects it, or, as is the more likely scenario, he isn't capable of understanding, well …' his voice trailed off.

'Not much of a plan,' O'Shaughnessy reflected with the hint of a twinkle in his eye.

'Do you have a better suggestion?'

'Well, yes. Now that you mention it, I do.'

'I'm listening,' Peter prompted, growing a little terse with what he took to be a display of pomposity. He was very mindful of Piggott's warning, and was wondering what O'Shaughnessy had in mind.

'For starters, I'm coming with you.'

'You're what?'

'Hear me out, Peter. I'm the last person Morova will be expecting to see, and surprise is the best offensive. It will totally unsettle him. But more importantly, I'm privy to a mountain of information that you simply do not have. It will be critical to back everything we put to the Pope with first-hand evidence, not anecdotal.'

Peter could not disagree with this. He thought about the ramifications of O'Shaughnessy's plan, and decided he would prefer to have him where he could see him, if and when the Don relinquished the document. 'Very well, I agree with your plan. But meanwhile, I want to get Christina into the safekeeping of the Australian Embassy.'

'Yes, yes, that's wise, and we should do that this morning, just in case we come up against unexpected snags.'

⚜

Peter knocked on Christina's door and waited. There was no sound from within, so he repeated the knock, only louder and more incessantly. 'Christina, it's Peter. It's time to get up,' he called through the door. There was still no response. He checked his watch and glanced at O'Shaughnessy, a troubled frown creasing his forehead. 'That's strange. We did have a late night, but …'

'Here, let me,' O'Shaughnessy said, stepping up to the door and pounding it with his fist. 'Christina,' he yelled, 'it's me, Uncle Brian.'

The door adjacent to Christina's opened and an elderly woman poked her head out. She gave them a dirty look of disapproval and was about to retreat, when Peter called out. 'Scusi, uno momento, prego. Do you speak English?'

'Of course I do, young man,' she responded stiffly in perfectly correct English. 'I am English, you know,' she sniffed. 'What is all the commotion about?' she demanded, full of righteous disapproval. 'It's not enough that the young, uh, lady and her, her guest woke me up at five in the morning, but now the two of you are banging on her door with absolutely the same disregard for others.'

'Excuse me?' Peter interrupted. 'You mentioned a guest?'

'Yes,' she replied haughtily, 'they had the most frightful row. Woke me up. But it's no use knocking. They left.'

'They what?' Peter demanded, a knot forming in the pit of his stomach.

'You heard me, young man. They left. They had a huge row, and then they left. And I might add, the man had the appearance of a gentleman, but he certainly did not act like one. He was dragging the lady. He was very rough. A lover's quarrel, no doubt.'

Peter took a deep breath before he asked his next question. 'You saw this man?'

'What do you think I've been saying? Of course I did. I was about to step out of my room to knock on the door, when they came out.'

'Can you describe him?' O'Shaughnessy asked.

'Certainly. There's nothing wrong with my eyes, you know, nor my memory.'

She gave a detailed description of Christina's abductor, causing Peter and O'Shaughnessy to stare at her, open mouthed.

Just as Peter recovered from the initial shock and was about to respond, Gadaleta came striding up the hall towards them.

'Hey, Peter, where've you been? I've been trying to contact you since yesterday.'

Peter introduced Gadaleta to O'Shaughnessy.

Gadaleta shook O'Shaughnessy's hand warmly. 'So you're Scott's buddy from Australia. I've heard all about you. But speaking of Scott, I seem to have lost him. Can't raise him anywhere.'

'Seems he's not the only one missing,' Peter said dryly.

He filled Gadaleta in on what they had learned from the old lady, who had retreated back into her room, muttering and shaking her head.

Gadaleta asked, 'And you say you both recognise the description?'

O'Shaughnessy and Peter looked at each other and O'Shaughnessy answered for them. 'There's no doubt about it. The description fits my man Piggott to a tee.'

'Who's Piggott?' Gadaleta asked.

'He's my manservant, but to the best of my knowledge, he is, or should be, back in Sydney.'

'Afraid not,' Peter said, 'he's here in Rome.'

'What?' O'Shaughnessy turned to Peter, surprised. 'You mean to say, you've known all along that Piggott is here, in Rome?'

Peter immediately regretted letting on.

Gadaleta was looking quizzically from one to the other.

'I think you had better let me in on what you know, Peter,' O'Shaughnessy said, 'for Christina's sake.'

Chapter 56

꘏꘎꘏

Christina woke with a start. She felt as though she'd only just put her head down. Switching on the bedside lamp she glanced at the clock which read 4:47AM, and then reached for her gown, irritated at the persistent rapping at her door, which is what woke her. Peter must have forgotten to tell her something, but what could be so urgent that it couldn't wait till a respectable time? She opened the door, still half asleep, fully expecting Peter and was about to admonish him when her jaw dropped.

'Piggott?' was all she could manage.

'My sincere apologies for the early hour, Miss Kelly, but unfortunately this could not wait for a more appropriate time.'

'But, Piggott, where, how, I mean, what are you doing here?'

Piggott glanced furtively up and down the hallway, and in a hushed voice asked, 'I'm so sorry for the inconvenience, but do you mind if I come in?'

Christina stepped aside, allowing Piggott to enter the room and closed the door behind him. She was wide awake now. 'I'm sorry, Piggott, you caught me by surprise. What on earth are you doing in Rome? Does Uncle Brian know you are here?'

'Ah, no, he doesn't, but he soon will.'

'Piggott, what is this all about?'

'Your uncle is on his way to Rome,' Piggott glanced at his watch, 'as a matter of fact, he should be here by now.'

'Well, I can tell you he is,' Christina replied. Peter and I just had a meeting with him in his room. Now, would you please tell me what's going on?'

'May I sit down?' Piggott asked, gesturing to the sofa.

'Yes, of course,' Christina said, sitting on the edge of the bed.

'I'm afraid I have bad news about your uncle,' Piggott began.

'Bad news, what do you mean?' Christina demanded, fear in her eyes. 'Is he all right?' She glanced at the clock. 'He was fine when I left him a few hours ago.'

'Yes, yes,' Piggott reassured her, 'there's absolutely nothing wrong with his health.'

'The emphysema. He should never have flown …'

'As I said, Ms Kelly, there is nothing wrong with his health.'

'I'm sorry, I don't understand. You said, bad news, what is it?'

'There's no easy way to tell you this, Ms Kelly …'

'Go on,' Christina pressed, by now feeling quite alarmed, 'just tell me.'

'Very well, as you wish. You see, your uncle does not suffer, nor ever has suffered from anything more serious than influenza.'

'But then, why would he …? Oh, this is ridiculous. What are you saying, Piggott?'

'I'm afraid your uncle has been using you, Ms Kelly, and Father LeSarus.'

'Using me? What do you mean?' Christina's demeanour suddenly changed.

'Your uncle feigned emphysema, so that you and Father LeSarus would hunt down the Third Secret of Fatima. He is so consumed with hatred for the Church in general, and Cardinal Morova in particular, that he will stop at nothing to destroy both.'

'How? Why, what do you mean, destroy?'

'As soon as your uncle learned that you and Father LeSarus had all but retrieved the Third Secret document, he booked a plane to Rome. I learned of his intentions, so I caught an earlier plane to arrive before him in order to stop him.' Piggott paused, waiting for a response, and when none was forthcoming, he added, 'And to stop him killing Father LeSarus.'

Christina stared, lost for words. 'You, you're insane. Why would he want to kill Father LeSarus?'

'If anyone is insane, Ms Kelly, it is your uncle. I'm afraid his sojourn in the Italian prison rendered him such. You see, he is obsessively possessive of you.'

'I don't understand.'

'You're not aware that Father LeSarus is in love with you?'

Christina stared, incredulous. Could it really be true? 'Father LeSarus is in love with me? Why, I mean, what makes you think such a thing?'

'Because he called your uncle and told him. He announced his intention to ask for your hand.'

Christina's head was swimming. She could feel the pulse racing in her veins. 'I don't believe you,' she finally managed to say.

'I assure you, ma'am, that it is true.'

'I simply don't believe it. I don't believe that Peter would discuss such a thing with my uncle before speaking to me. And even if he did, well, my uncle is certainly neither possessive nor insane. In fact, I believe, that for whatever reason, which I cannot fathom, you are making all of this up.'

Piggott's hitherto polite disposition evaporated as his eyes hardened. Suddenly, Christina was afraid. She stared into the man's eyes, and what she saw was madness. 'Get dressed,' he ordered abruptly.

'I beg your pardon?' Christina said defiantly, putting on a brave face. 'I'll do no such thing. And now, if you don't mind, I'll thank you to leave.'

'And I'll thank you to get dressed,' Piggott responded, standing and taking a threatening step towards her.

Christina reached for the phone. Piggott moved quickly, wrenching the handset from her hand, and then ripping the cord from the wall he smashed the phone against the wall. Christina stared at him in amazement, then, recovering from her shock, she made a dash for the door. Once again, Piggott proved too fast. Blocking her path, he struck her with his open hand, sending her sprawling.

Christina looked up from the floor in amazement, barely able to believe that Piggott had struck her. She placed her hand to her cheek, where an angry red welt was already clearly visible. 'Why are you doing this?' she pleaded, confused.

'He has to be stopped. Do you hear me?'

'Who has to be stopped?'

'Enough questions.' Piggott was looming over her. 'Now get dressed, you're coming with me.'

'I'm not going anywhere,' Christina yelled, frantically trying to crawl away.

Piggott reached down, grabbing Christina's gown and tore it from her, leaving her cowering in her pyjamas. 'Now get dressed, or I'll do it for you.' To emphasise his threat, he went to the wardrobe, ripping clothes out and throwing them at her. 'Now put something on.'

Christina curled into a ball. 'I'm not getting undressed in front of you, you bastard.'

'If you think I'm interested in what you've got under that, then you flatter yourself,' Piggott sneered. 'You women are all alike. You think that men are only interested in one thing. Ha! Once you've taken a close look at it, you really wonder what all the fuss is about.'

Christina slowly stood up, and turning her back to him she undressed, then quickly slipped on her street clothes. 'Where are you taking me?' she demanded, stalling for time, her mind racing furiously. She had to get away from him and warn Peter and her uncle.

'Don't worry about that,' Piggott answered, grabbing her arm and moving towards the door.

'Just a minute,' Christina demanded.

'What is it?'

'Shoes. I have to put some shoes on.'

'Be quick about it.'

She peered into the wardrobe as if searching for shoes, but grabbed the umbrella, spinning around and smashing it with all her strength in Piggott's face. She was gratified when Piggott screamed in pain and she saw blood spurt from the wound she'd inflicted. But her jubilation was short lived as Piggott tore the umbrella from her grasp and punched her with a closed fist.

⚜

An elderly woman poked her head out of the door next to Christina's room and gave a disapproving frown to which Piggott responded with an apologetic smile as he dragged Christina down the hall. 'Lovers' quarrel,' he muttered.

Chapter 57

Peter was about to respond to O'Shaughnessy's question when the older man's cell phone began to ring. As he retrieved the phone from his pocket O'Shaughnessy remarked. 'No one who has my number knows where I am.'

'Piggott knows you're here,' Peter said as O'Shaughnessy took the call.

Peter and Gadaleta were watching O'Shaughnessy's expression closely and they saw the colour drain from his face. He tried to respond to the caller, but was cut off in mid-sentence. He continued to listen carefully, nodding his head. Finally he spoke. 'Don't be a fool, Piggott. Let Christina go immediately, do you hear me, Piggott? Piggott! …

He replaced the phone in his pocket and said, 'He hung up.'

'Piggott's got Christina,' Peter said.

'Yes, I'm afraid so,' O'Shaughnessy responded despondently. 'He threatened to kill her.'

Peter felt sick. 'Good God. Kill her? Why would he want to kill her?'

'I think you'd better tell me all you know, Peter,' O'Shaughnessy said.

'Did he say where he's holding her?' Gadaleta asked.

'No, of course not.'

'Come on, then,' Gadaleta said, 'We can't talk here. Let's head downstairs to the coffee shop, and yes, Peter, you'd better tell us all you know.

Peter told O'Shaughnessy and Gadaleta about his late night visitor, holding nothing back.

When Peter had finished, O'Shaughnessy was incredulous. 'And you believed him?' he marvelled.

Peter looked sheepish as he answered. 'He was very convincing, and besides, he'd already put doubt in my mind when he followed me to the car after your dinner party.'

'So, if you doubted me way back then, why on earth did you agree to the trip?'

'I was intrigued, and I wanted to find out for myself. And besides …' his voice trailed off, and he turned his eyes away from O'Shaughnessy.

'Besides what?' O'Shaughnessy demanded.

'It doesn't matter,' Peter said.

'Good God, man, you're blushing. What is it? Come on, out with it.'

Peter smiled awkwardly. 'Christina,' he said softly, then added, 'the thought of going abroad with her appealed to me.'

'Well, I'll be,' O'Shaughnessy exclaimed, slapping Peter good naturedly on the thigh, 'you're in love with my niece.'

The colour in Peter's face turned an even deeper red as Gadaleta guffawed and said, 'That's certainly no secret.'

'Okay, that'll do, you two. Please, Christina's in danger,' Peter said, recovering his composure. He then filled Gadaleta in on the meeting with the Don and the meeting that had been set up with the Pope for that afternoon.

Gadaleta whistled. 'Why on earth didn't you confide in Scott and me? I mean, you two may never have got out of there alive.'

Peter explained why he and Christina had decided to no longer trust the two Americans.

Gadaleta rubbed his chin thoughtfully. 'From what you've told me, I can't say I blame you. He sat silently pensive for a while. 'I wonder,' he finally said.

'What?' O'Shaughnessy prompted.

'I was just wondering why I haven't been able to contact Scott.'

'You think that …' O'Shaughnessy began.

'Let's just say, I'm curious, but it's a little early to be jumping to conclusions.'

'Brian, you still haven't told us what Piggott said,' Peter reminded him.

'It would seem that Piggott has gone off the rails,' O'Shaughnessy announced, bitterness in his voice. 'To put it succinctly, he told me he has Christina hidden away someplace where we will never find her.'

Peter felt desperate as he asked, 'Why on earth has he taken her? What's he got against Christina?'

'Nothing,' O'Shaughnessy answered. 'He has nothing against Christina. It's me, I'm afraid.'

'What do you mean?' Peter asked.

'He's using Christina as a lever against me.'

'But why?' Peter insisted. 'To what purpose?'

'Now try to stay calm, Peter. We'll find her, that's a promise. Piggott demanded that when we meet with Morova this afternoon, I'm to tell the Don that the Third Secret is a hoax. If I don't …' He didn't finish the sentence.

'If you don't, he'll kill her,' Peter finished for him.

'Peter, don't be an alarmist. I told you. We'll get her back.'

'He'll kill her,' Peter said, his voice breaking with emotion. 'That's what you said. My God, we've got to find her.'

Peter jumped out of the booth and was making for the door, when Gadaleta held up a restraining hand. 'Hold on, Peter. Where do you think you're going? Where will you begin to search?' Gadaleta was also on his feet now, placing a comforting arm around Peter's shoulder, steering him back to the booth. 'Come on, sit down. We have to think this through.'

Peter calmed down and returned to his seat.

'Don't worry, Peter,' O'Shaughnessy reassured him. 'We'll find her.'

'How?' Peter demanded. 'We have no idea where he took her.'

'Look, if we don't find her by four o'clock, then I will drop the Third Secret, and to hell with the consequences,' O'Shaughnessy assured him.

Peter sat silently, mulling over this. He looked O'Shaughnessy squarely in the eye and said, 'No you won't. This is bigger than you, me, Christina, all of us. We can't just let it go. For God's sake, man, we can't sacrifice humanity for the life of one person, even if it is Christina.' Angrily, he brushed away a tear, and with a new and fierce determination he said, 'We'll just have to find her, that's all there is to it.' He checked his watch. 'And we've got less than eight hours to do it.' O'Shaughnessy squeezed Peter's elbow reassuringly.

Gadaleta had said nothing during this exchange, and now he looked up, a smile on his face. 'There may just be a way, you know.' He pulled out his cell phone and made a call. When he'd finished, he announced. 'This may take a few hours.'

'So what do we do in the meantime?' Peter asked, agitated.

'We wait,' Gadaleta said. 'Meanwhile, I have some shopping I need to attend to.'

Chapter 58

The car rolled to a stop and when the engine was cut the only sound that could be heard was the chirping of crickets and the occasional hoot of an owl. The car door opened and slammed and the crunch of footsteps on gravel approached the rear of the car. Christina held her breath, fighting to hold down the nausea threatening to overcome her. Her stomach was queasy from the motion of the car, as well as the fumes from the exhaust, and she had begun to panic at the thought of throwing up. With her mouth securely gagged, she would have drowned in her own vomit. She estimated they had been travelling steadily for approximately forty minutes, but without being able to refer to her watch she couldn't be sure, as her close confinement would probably have distorted time. At first she had done her best to try to keep track of turns and the time elapsed from one to the other, but she had finally given up on this as an impossibility. For all she knew, they could be anywhere. Without warning the trunk opened and the glaring beam of a high-powered torch blinded her. She felt rather than saw something cutting through the electrician's tape, freeing her ankles as she was roughly hoisted into a sitting position. Her legs were manhandled over the edge of the trunk and she was ordered to stand. As she transferred her weight she noticed that her legs had lost all feeling due to her confinement. They would have buckled and she would have fallen, had she not been propped by a steadying hand. Slowly, feeling tingled back into her legs as the blood began to circulate.

'Come on then,' the unmistakable voice of Piggott ordered, 'I haven't got all night.'

Her hands were still securely fastened behind her back, and as Piggott had made no move to remove the gag, Christina made urgent, muffled sounds, beseeching him to remove it so she could breathe properly.

'All in good time,' he said, prodding her in the back, forcing her to move forward. She stumbled in the dark, tripping on a tree root, causing her to crash face first into the brush, unable to break her fall with her hands. Piggott dragged her to her feet, and with a steadying hand under her arm, she lurched forward, as Piggott shone the torch onto the ground in front of her, illuminating a rough track, flanked by low scrub and an occasional, stunted tree. To add to her discomfort, it began to drizzle and before long her clothes were soaked, clinging to her skin.

Shivering from the cold, she staggered on with Piggott forcing the pace, until finally they arrived at what seemed to be the entrance of a cave. By now, the grey of an overcast dawn began to illuminate their surroundings and Piggott switched off the torch. The entrance to the cave was blocked by a solid, rusted iron-gate, held shut by a thick, padlocked chain and a prominent sign displaying a skull and crossbones, no doubt warning of the dangers of entering.

Christina watched as Piggott set to the padlock with a large set of bolt cutters he'd carried from the car, making easy work of the rusted metal. The hinges protested with a loud creak as he pushed the gate, and she wondered how long it had been since anyone had entered the cave, if that was what it was. He pushed Christina ahead of him through the open gate, closing it behind them, re-locking the chain with a new padlock he produced from his pocket.

As they entered the cave, Piggott switched on the torch, revealing a tunnel hewn from the soft rock. Christina was really frightened now, wondering what manner of place this was as she became convinced that Piggott meant to kill her. Desperately she began to look for opportunities to escape, but as they continued they were surrounded by nothing but the smooth walls of the tunnel. Even if she could break away, the exit was now securely locked and the only other option was straight ahead into darkness. At least if she could speak, she might at least learn what his motive was, and maybe she could reason with him. She stopped suddenly, causing Piggott to crash into her and she began again to make the loud muffled noises. Piggott angrily pushed her forward, but she held her ground, making out as though she were gasping for breath. Piggott pushed her again, but this time she sat down, shaking her head in a defiant gesture of refusal.

Piggott sighed. 'Very well,' he acquiesced, 'no one can hear you now anyway.' He stooped and ripped the tape from her mouth. Gratefully, Christina sucked in a lungful of air, and Piggott waited patiently, giving her time to recover. 'Happy now?' he said, dragging her to her feet again.

'Wait,' she pleaded, 'just give me a moment to catch my breath.'

'All right then, but don't take for ever.'

Christina took a few deep breaths. Trying to keep the trembling out of her voice she asked, 'Where are we? What is this place?'

'Never mind,' he answered brusquely, 'suffice to say, no one will ever find you here.'

'Why, Piggott? Why have you brought me here? What have I ever done to you, except show you kindness?'

'Kindness?' he sneered. 'What would you and your family know about kindness?'

'I'm sorry, I don't understand. Have I done something to offend you?'

'Shut up, and get moving,' he ordered.

Christina was beginning to despair, when suddenly a pile of rocks and rubble blocked her path – evidence of an old, partial cave-in. That explained the warning sign at the entrance. Piggott prodded her on, and when she looked at him questioningly, he said, 'Go on. Keep moving. There's just enough room to get past the cave-in.'

By flattening her back against the wall, she managed to squeeze past the obstruction, and when she cleared it she found she had reached a dead end. Then she saw that the floor opened up, with a set of steep steps carved out of the rock, with a steel railing attached to the wall.

'Go on,' Piggott urged, 'down the stairs.'

This could be the chance she was waiting for. The steps glistened with moisture and she turned to Piggott. 'You'll have to undo my hands. There's no way I could get down those slippery steps without holding on to the rail.'

Piggott thought about this for a moment, and finally he said, 'All right, but don't try anything.' He cut the tape and Christina gratefully rubbed the circulation back into her hands.

Gingerly she began to descend the steps, hoping that Piggott would be right behind her. 'I can't see where I'm going,' she complained. 'You'll have to come down with the torch.'

Piggott fell for it and began to follow her down the steps. She waited till he was almost on top of her and then made her move. She spun around, grabbing Piggott by the arm and bending low, she used her body as a lever, and with the aid of gravity, managed to throw Piggott over her shoulder in a clumsy, but effective judo throw. He was taken completely by surprise, but his weight was too much for Christina, and losing her balance, she crashed down the steps, entangled with Piggott. Piggott crashed heavily on to the earthen floor with Christina landing on top of him, which broke her fall. To her relief, he did not move and she figured he was either unconscious or dead. Thankfully, the torch was not damaged, and Christina grabbed for it. To her amazement she found herself in a large chamber with niches carved into walls adorned with paintings and statuesque reliefs depicting saints and various religious themes. At the end of the chamber, she saw the start of another tunnel disappearing into blackness. The niches in the walls were in tiers of four from the floor to the ceiling and each one was tenanted by a macabre occupant; skeletons, elaborately dressed in the outfit of a bishop, complete with mitre, the pointed bishop's hat. Finally it all became clear. She was in one of the many early Christian catacombs that were prolific in and around Rome, where the early Christians buried their dead and carried out their secret religious services to escape the persecution of Romans. She remembered reading that there were more than sixty catacombs in Rome, with hundreds of miles of tunnels and galleries and tens of thousands of tombs. While thousands of pilgrims visited the catacombs daily, this one had obviously been closed due to the cave-in. Piggott had certainly chosen well in his choice of a hiding place.

Tentatively she got to her feet and shone the light into Piggott's face. He remained perfectly still. She knelt beside his inert form, rolling him over to get at the pocket where she'd seen him deposit the key to the padlock. Her hand groped in the pocket, but it was empty. Damn it, she thought, I could have sworn he put it in this pocket. She rolled him over again, and this time when she tried the other pocket she was successful and with great relief she extracted the key. She clasped it tightly in her fist and without a second look, bolted up the steps.

She reached the top and was about to squeeze past the cave-in when she stopped. What am I doing? she thought. I can't just leave him there. I didn't even check to see if he was breathing. He may still be alive, and seriously hurt. With a resigned sigh, and considerable reluctance she turned, retracing her steps. She cautiously approached Piggott's inert form, and reaching down she placed a finger to his neck, feeling for a pulse. She had no time to register a pulse, nor did she need to, as Piggott suddenly came to life, grabbing her hand in a vice-like grip.

'Nice try, girlie,' he said, simultaneously using his free hand to backhand her across the face. She fell to the floor stunned, just long enough for Piggott to re-apply tape, once again securing her hands behind her back. 'That should hold you, bitch.'

Christina began to sob, more from frustration than anguish. Why had she gone back? She could have been stepping out of the entrance by now, free of this lunatic.

While before Piggott had presented a cool, detached façade, Christina now found herself looking into the eyes of a crazed man. 'You wanted to know why I'm doing this?' he began. 'All right, I'll tell you. I suppose that if you are going to die, you should at least have the right to know why.'

Christina's heart sank as Piggott confirmed what she had already suspected. He was going to kill her.

'But whether you live or die,' he continued, 'will depend on your uncle.'

Hope soared again. Perhaps she did have a chance after all. She waited expectantly for him to continue, not daring to interrupt.

'You know that I devoted all of my working life to your uncle's father.'

Christina nodded, not trusting her voice.

'Did you know that towards the end, he couldn't even wipe his own arse?' He didn't wait for an answer. 'I had to do it for him. I had to do everything for the disgusting old bastard. He pissed his pants and I had to clean him up. Every night, he'd wet the bed, and I had to change the sheets. But did I complain? No, I just did it. And what thanks did I get?' Piggott was no longer looking at her. His eyes had taken on a glazed quality, and he seemed to be talking more to himself. 'Meanwhile, where was O'Shaughnessy, his son? Enjoying a holiday in an Italian prison for embezzling Church money. But you know what? The money was never recovered. He sent it all to his father, who was as guilty as he was.' Piggott paused, reflecting, seemingly lost in his thoughts.

Christina now spoke up. 'But, Piggott, you know as well as I do that Uncle Brian was innocent. He was framed by that Cardinal Morova.'

Piggott snapped out of his reverie with a maniacal laugh. 'Framed? Huh!' he snapped. 'He wasn't framed. He was guilty as hell. And by the time they let him out, that filthy bastard of his father got what he deserved and finally died. And what did I get for cleaning up his filth all those years? I'll tell you what I got. Nothing! That's what I got.' Then as an afterthought he added, 'Oh yes, I was given the opportunity to continue on as little more than an indentured slave. Pandering to every whim and fancy of your spoiled and condescending uncle.'

Christina now clearly understood that Piggott was motivated by an all-consuming hatred, but she was still confused. She asked, 'But what do you hope to achieve by kidnapping me, and,' she faltered, 'and killing me?'

'What do I hope to achieve?' Piggott replied. 'I'll tell you what I hope to achieve. Money! That's what I hope to achieve. Money, as payment for my years of service and humiliation.'

'You intend to hold me for ransom?'

'In a manner of speaking, yes. But for more money than your uncle could possibly afford, despite his considerable wealth.'

'I don't understand.'

'Cardinal Morova.'

'Cardinal Morova?' Christina repeated, puzzled. 'What has he to do with this?'

'Everything. You see, when I learned what it was that you and your friend LeSarus were searching for, I knew that Cardinal

Morova would be very interested. So I called him, and you know what? He is prepared to be very generous, very generous indeed to make sure the Third Secret is finally destroyed, once and for all. Now I understand that a meeting has been set up with the Pope for tomorrow at four. If the Pope sees the document, you die. It's as simple as that. If on the other hand, your uncle surrenders it to Morova, well, you see, your fate is in your uncle's hands. It was Cardinal Morova who directed me to this excellent hiding place. No one's been in here for years. It's been shut indefinitely. Too dangerous.'

Christina was staring at Piggott with disbelief in her eyes. 'Do you have any idea what the Third Secret is?' she asked, incredulous, and without waiting for an answer she continued. 'It is the key to salvation of the world, a key given to humanity by the Mother of God. To destroy it would be akin to destroying the world.'

'Bah!' Piggott scoffed. 'Superstitious mumbo jumbo! Now get up,' he ordered, 'we've wasted enough time.'

Piggott forced Christina into the next tunnel, which was larger than the entrance tunnel and honeycombed with burial niches, similar to those in the chamber. They passed through a number of other chambers, but still Piggott continued on relentlessly through the twisting and turning labyrinth, occasionally prodding his prisoner to move faster.

They arrived at another chamber that was larger and more elaborately decorated than all of the previous ones, but what was most discernible about this one was the sarcophagus dominating the centre of the room, with a pair of marble angels, swords drawn, standing guard on either side.

'You can rest now,' Piggott declared. 'This is the end of the line.'

'What are you going to do?' Christina demanded, fear in her voice.

'You should be happy here,' he announced. 'You'll be in good company. I understand that the sarcophagus contains the remains of one of your saints. You can bunk in with him.' He laughed at his own witticism.

Christina noticed that the heavy, stone lid of the sarcophagus had been partially moved, leaving an opening just big enough for a person to climb into. Piggott gestured to the opening. 'Get in,' he ordered.

Christina looked at him, terrified. 'If you think I'm getting into that, then you're mistaken,' she said, desperately fighting to contain the panic threatening to overcome her. She had no more time to debate the issue, as Piggott struck her on the side of the head with the torch.

⚜

As consciousness began to creep back, Christina was disoriented. She opened her eyes, but could not understand why she could not see and then became aware that her hands were secured behind her back. Something sharp was digging into her, and shifting her weight, she probed with her fingers to ascertain what it was. Then suddenly, memory flooded back as she realised she was lying on top of bones. Panicking, she sat up and to her horror, her head crashed into the cold, hard lid of the sarcophagus. She screamed.

⚜

Piggott smiled at the sound of the muffled scream as he dialled the number of O'Shaughnessy's cell phone.

He then made another call. 'I have her,' he said without preliminaries, then added, 'and O'Shaughnessy knows. He'll give you no trouble this afternoon.'

The voice on the other end said, 'You have done well. Go to this address. A man there will give you the money.'

Piggott's hand trembled as he scribbled down the address, already planning on how he would spend the money.

Morova hung up and dialled a number. 'When a man called Piggott arrives, I want you to kill him. Do you understand?'

He replaced the phone. He was taking no chances.

Chapter 59

Driving along the A59 Harrogate to Skipton road, through the North Yorkshire Moors in England, tourists could be forgiven for thinking they had suddenly come across a set from a science fiction movie. They would be surprised to see a massive complex of domes, vertical radio masts, and satellite dishes as well as over 5 acres of buildings. All in all, should they take the trouble, they would count twenty-six domes and dishes, standing like silent sentinels aimed skyward, gathering a constant barrage of information from orbiting satellites. Should the curious tourists enquire at nearby Harrogate, they would be told they had passed the Menwith Hill facility, a Defence Department communication station.

In truth, Menwith Hill is the largest, top-secret spy station in the world, housing more than fourteen thousand American NSA personnel backed up by four hundred UK Ministry of Defence staffers. Although it is a joint venture between intelligence agencies from USA, Australia, New Zealand, UK and Canada, the driving force behind it is the US National Security Agency or NSA. The facility is the hub for an automated global, satellite interception system, codenamed ECHELON, the existence of which continues to be staunchly denied. In scope, it is the greatest surveillance system ever devised, capturing virtually every electronic communication sent anywhere in the world, be it phone, email, fax or any other system of electronic communication. Surveillance satellites act like gigantic vacuum cleaners, scooping up the electronic communication, which is then beamed to the ever-vigilant satellite dishes at Menwith Hill.

ECHELON never sleeps, working tirelessly, twenty-four hours a day, seven days a week, processing millions of messages every hour, with beyond state-of-the-art computers searching and filtering targeted keywords, phrases, phone and fax numbers as well as specified voiceprints. Messages that generate a keyword hit are tagged for future analysis. These keywords are managed by Dictionary Managers who add, delete or change specific keyword criteria, depending on the changing needs and requirements of the relevant agencies. The extraordinary capability of ECHELON to capture all communication traffic in the world is spectacular technology in itself, but what is even more extraordinary is ECHELON's capability to filter, decrypt, scrutinise and sort this huge array of messages and data into specified categories for analysis by the various, secret government agencies. As the continuing stream of billions of electronic signals flood into the system, they are fed into a massively elaborate system of computers called SILKWORTH, which go to work on voice recognition and pre-programmed Dictionary key words and phrases.

Rodger Whiteman, a Dictionary Manager, was about to finish an uneventful shift, when he received a call from his shift supervisor.

'Rodger, we have a code Alpha on our hands.' This was the code for top priority, potentially life-threatening circumstances, which usually meant that somewhere in the world, a field agent was in trouble.

Whiteman was instantly alert, the golf game he'd been looking forward to forgotten. 'Shoot,' he said, squaring his shoulders over his keypad, ready to input data.

The supervisor commenced relaying the information he'd received from the caller at CIA headquarters in Washington. He did not know the state of the emergency, or whom it affected, and he knew better than to ask, as did Whiteman. Their only job was to capture the call. 'Key words are Piggott,' he spelled it using the international phonetic spell system, 'O'Shaughnessy. Key phrase is Third Secret of Fatima.'

Whiteman repeated each word and phrase, spelling each as he entered them on his keyboard.

Satisfied that Whiteman had not made even the slightest mistake, the supervisor continued. 'Call was made approximately forty-seven minutes ago from a location in or around Rome, Italy.'

⚬━✦━⚬

Gadaleta's cell phone rang, and he picked it up on the first ring. His face was a mask of concentration as he pulled a note pad and pen from his inside pocket and began to jot down coordinates. When he'd finished, he repeated the numbers back to the caller, and then said, 'Thanks Sam, I owe you one.'

Peter and O'Shaughnessy were watching him expectantly as he replaced the phone in his pocket, still studying the piece of paper he'd torn from his note pad.

'Well? Peter asked impatiently.

Gadaleta looked up with a triumphant grin. 'We've got the bastard!'

'Are you sure?' Peter asked, not believing it could be quite so simple.

'I'm sure,' Gadaleta assured him. 'It took ECHELON three hours to filter out the call.'

Peter and O'Shaughnessy looked at each other, shaking their heads in disbelief. Like most civilians they had no idea such technology existed.

'So where is she?' Peter demanded.

'I can't be sure,' Gadaleta answered matter of factly.

Peter spluttered in frustration. 'But, but you just said you were sure.'

'The only thing I'm certain of,' Gadaleta corrected him, 'is where Piggott made the call from. I have GPS coordinates that

407

are accurate to a metre. Whether Christina is there, or whether Piggott is, I don't know. But it's a start.'

O'Shaughnessy checked the time. 'We have five hours.'

Peter asked, 'How do we find where these coordinates are?'

Gadaleta grinned, pulling an object from his pocket that looked like a child's electronic game. 'This is what I went shopping for.'

'What is it,' Peter asked.

'A portable sat-nav. This will guide us to exactly where Piggott was standing when he placed the call on his cell.'

'What are we waiting for?' O'Shaughnessy said.

As they raced out of the hotel, Peter paused at the reception desk, grabbing a tourist map of Rome and its environs.

Chapter 60

'Are you sure this is the right place?' Peter asked, looking around despondently.

Gadaleta frowned as he checked the coordinates against the sat-nav. 'I'm positive.'

'Is it possible that ECHELON gave you the wrong coordinates?' O'Shaughnessy asked, sharing Peter's frustration.

'Anything's possible, I guess,' Gadaleta replied, 'but highly unlikely.'

'Why would Piggott call from here?' Peter wondered. 'We're in the middle of nowhere.'

Gadaleta shrugged. The sat-nav had led them to the outskirts of Rome on to the Via Appia, where they proceeded along the ancient, cobbled road.

'Stop the car,' Gadaleta ordered Peter, who was driving. 'We're very close. According to this, the call was made about 300 metres over there,' Gadaleta had said pointing in a direction ninety degrees to the road.

The three men were stumped. The surrounding countryside was barren, except for some brush and stunted trees, and the only buildings were a few scattered ruins.

'Damn it,' Gadaleta swore, looking around, 'this place is so desolate there's not even a place to hide a body.'

Peter winced, causing Gadaleta to mutter an apology for his insensitivity.

'I just don't understand it,' O'Shaughnessy said. 'I'm trying to think like Piggott, but for the life of me I can't understand why he would stop the car, then trudge all the way over here to make a call. We must be in the wrong spot,' he concluded dejectedly.

They stood around for a while longer, hoping against hope for inspiration that might solve the mystery. Finally, they had no choice but to accept defeat, and with heavy hearts they made their way back to the car.

This time, Gadaleta got behind the wheel, with Peter opting for the back seat. He was in no mood for conversation.

Just as Gadaleta started the engine, Peter had a hunch and pulled out the tourist map he'd taken from the hotel. 'Hold it, Tony,' he said.

'What is it, Peter?' Gadaleta asked, turning in his seat.

Peter didn't answer, as he studied the map for a while and then excitedly yelled, 'I've got it!'

'What is it?' O'Shaughnessy demanded.

'We're in the right place after all,' Peter declared, his excitement mounting.

'But there's nothing here!' Gadaleta said, his hands raised in a gesture of helplessness.

'The call was made underground,' Peter announced, barely able to contain his excitement.

'I beg your pardon?' O'Shaughnessy asked, puzzled.

Peter leaned over the front seat, shoving the map under O'Shaughnessy's nose. 'This is roughly where we are,' he said, pointing to a spot on the map with his finger.

'Okay,' O'Shaughnessy said, failing to see the relevance.

'Don't you see it?' Peter said, his excitement mounting.

'See what?'

Peter jabbed his finger at the map. 'That,' he said triumphantly. 'It's a mark denoting a tourist attraction. It can't be more than a couple of hundred metres from where we are.'

O'Shaughnessy looked even more puzzled. 'So we're a couple of hundred metres from some tourist attraction. So what? Tony said the coordinates were accurate to within a metre.'

'And so they are,' Peter agreed. 'We are parked right on top of the spot.' He flipped the map over to the legend, running his finger down to the icon he'd pointed to. 'It's the entrance to a catacomb.'

Gadaleta turned the key, switching off the engine as Peter was already climbing out of the car. 'Peter, you're a genius. Of course, it all adds up. He's hidden Christina in a catacomb. The area is riddled with them. Some of those tunnels go for miles.'

Peter was running.

Chapter 61

Gadaleta and O'Shaughnessy could not keep up with Peter as he ran though the scrub to where the entrance to the catacomb should be. He saw the cave in the distance and increased his speed, desperately praying he would find Christina inside, alive. When he spotted the iron gate, he screamed over his shoulder. 'Hurry up, over here. I've found it.'

When the others arrived, puffing from their exertion, they found Peter desperately shaking the gate with both hands, sheer frustration etched on his features.

'Damn it,' he exclaimed, 'it's got a great big chain on it.' He kicked the gate, almost sobbing by now.

Gadaleta stepped over to examine the chain and padlock. 'It looks like you were right, Peter. This is a brand new lock. And look at this,' he said, stooping over to pick up something that had caught his eye. 'Well I'll be,' he exclaimed, holding up the old, rusted lock. 'This has been cut with bolt cutters.'

This observation prompted Peter to launch his body at the gate in a renewed frenzy of desperation.

'Whoa there. Hold it Peter,' Gadaleta said. 'You'll do yourself an injury if you keep that up.'

'So how are we going to break in?' Peter implored. 'We don't have bolt cutters.'

'No, we don't,' Gadaleta agreed calmly, 'but we have this,' he said reaching inside his coat and producing a .38 Smith & Wesson revolver. 'Step back,' he ordered. He waited till the two men were at a safe distance before firing a shot at the padlock, shattering it.

Peter brushed past, hurling himself at the gate that now burst open. 'Christina,' he screamed into the blackness. 'It's me, Peter. Can you hear me?'

Gadaleta caught up with Peter, placing a restraining hand on his shoulder. 'Keep it down, Peter,' he ordered. 'We don't know whether or not Piggott is still in there. If he is, then you've certainly warned him that we're here.'

Peter put his hands on his face and groaned quietly.

'Look, I'm just as anxious to find Christina as you are, but there's no point taking unnecessary chances. This place has been shut down for years for a reason. I suggest we proceed with extreme caution.' He turned to O'Shaughnessy. 'You'd better wait out here for us.'

O'Shaughnessy was about to protest, but Gadaleta cut him off. 'If Christina's in there, and we all barge in after her, and something happens to us, then that's it for her.'

O'Shaughnessy could not dispute this logic and agreed to wait. 'I don't suppose somebody thought of bringing a torch?' he asked as Peter and Gadaleta entered the tunnel.

Peter looked expectantly at Gadaleta, who held up his key ring, displaying a miniature penlight. 'It's not much,' he said, 'but it's better than nothing. I just hope the battery holds out.'

When they reached the cave-in, Peter's heart sank yet again, before they discovered that it was possible to squeeze past. They continued on through the tunnel and were about 30 metres from the steps when they were suddenly plunged into darkness. 'Damn,' Gadaleta said, shaking the penlight. 'Battery's dead.' They continued on blindly with Gadaleta in the lead, their hands groping the wall for guidance, when suddenly the floor disappeared and Gadaleta, with a surprised yelp, dropped into the hole. Peter heard him crash hard at the bottom of the steps, and anxiously called out. 'Tony, are you okay?'

Gadaleta groaned in pain, and with feigned jocularity said, 'Mind the first step, Peter, it's a bastard.'

Peter inched forward until his feet found the hole, and groping carefully with his hands, he found the railing, and gingerly made his way down the slippery steps till he reached the chamber, nearly stepping on Gadaleta. 'Are you okay?' he repeated anxiously.

'Damn it,' Gadaleta replied, pain in his voice, 'I think I've broken my ankle.'

Peter helped him into a sitting position, propping him up with his back to a wall.

'Leave me here, Peter. You go on, but be careful.'

Peter didn't argue. He moved off, this time on his hands and knees, feeling his way for any more unpleasant surprises that may be lying in store. He came to a solid rock wall, and followed it until he found the entrance to the next tunnel. He continued on relentlessly at a painfully slow pace, negotiating two more chambers, each time succeeding to find the next leg of the labyrinth. He'd never experienced such absolute, black darkness, and as claustrophobia began to play on his imagination he fought back the rising panic. His mind began to play tricks as he saw flashes of phantom light making him even more jumpy. He began to have serious doubts about finding Christina alive in this inky blackness devoid of all light. What if she were hurt, or even unconscious? For all he knew, he may have already crawled right past her without even knowing it. He decided to take his chances and to hell with Piggott. He called her name at the top of his lungs and then listened, but there was no response.

He crawled on for another 20 metres or so, before calling her name again. Still nothing. He repeated this every few minutes. He felt what he thought was another wall in front of him and followed it, expecting to find yet another tunnel. He reached a corner and followed the wall at a right angle. In a very short distance, he found another corner, and realised that what was in front of him was not a wall at all but a freestanding object. Then he felt another shape, and running his hand along it, it became evident that it was a statue. He felt exhausted, physically and mentally, and leaning up against the stone object he decided to rest a while. He called out again, and again there was no reply. He waited a couple of minutes, and just before crawling on he called again. Nothing. He began to move on, and froze. He listened intently. He could have sworn he'd heard something. His mind must be playing tricks. But no, there it was again. He was certain of it.

'CHRISTINAAAAA,' he screamed at the top of his lungs.

Then he heard it, and this time there was no mistaking it. It was a muffled cry. He spun around on his hands and knees, doing a full three-sixty-degree turn, desperate to figure from where the sound had emanated. He called out again, and then listened so hard he could hear his own heart. The sound was repeated, and this time there was no mistaking where it came from. It was inside the freestanding stone box. He stood up, running his hands over every inch of the object.

'The bastard,' he said out loud as realisation set in. Piggott had buried her alive inside a sarcophagus. Peter's searching fingers found the lip of the lid and with all the strength he could muster he strained to lift it. It didn't budge a millimetre. He screamed in frustrated anger, beating his fists against the stone sarcophagus till he felt the warm trickle of blood.

He was beaten. There wasn't a thing he could think of doing. He considered crawling his way back to get Gadaleta to help him, but immediately dismissed the idea. The man had a compound fracture and there was no way he would make it. He heard another muffled sound from inside the tomb that prompted him to try again. He strained at the lid so hard he thought he might pop a vein, and then sank to the floor in despair. Because he could see nothing, there was no way of telling how securely fitting the lid was, and he began to fear that Christina might run out of air. He wondered how Piggott had managed to manoeuvre the enormously heavy lid into place and began to suspect that he must have had an accomplice to help him.

Peter decided to inspect the sarcophagus once again, more minutely than before. Carefully, and with great concentration, he fingered the stone, moving around the sarcophagus as he went. He tripped. He stooped to feel for whatever it was that had tripped him up, and then, to his immense and unbelievable joy, his fingers curled around the solid, cold steel of a crowbar.

He whooped out loud, jumping up and down, holding the bar over his head as if he were an Indian doing a war dance, brandishing a spear. Piggott had a crowbar! That's how he moved the stone, and when he'd finished, he'd been too lazy to carry it back out with him.

⚜

Christina had lost all concept of time. Her initial horror at being entombed alive with a skeleton had slowly been replaced with an increasing state of lethargy as the limited air in the confined space began to foul with her own carbon dioxide. Eventually she fell asleep and as the poisonous gas built up within the sarcophagus, she slipped into a deeper sleep, which would soon become a coma from which she would never awaken. She dreamed, and in her dream she heard Peter calling her name. Even in her sleep, her lips turned up in a smile at the sound of his voice. Slowly and inexorably, as if willing itself to live, her oxygen-starved brain fought for consciousness and her eyes flickered open. She gagged at the foul air, and then, as if from a great distance, she heard her name being called. She was acutely aware of her surroundings and marvelled at the reality of her dream. Then she heard her name called again, only this time it seemed closer. Could it be that she wasn't dreaming? Was there really someone out there calling her?

She listened, and then there it was again, and she knew she was not dreaming. She tried to call out, but her mouth was dry, and all she could manage was a weak moan. Then she heard her name again. She ran her tongue around her mouth, desperate for saliva. She tried again, and this time she managed to call out, albeit still weakly, but certainly louder than the moan. Her effort was rewarded by an instant response as she heard her name again, only this time there was urgency in the call, and now she felt certain it was Peter. Then she heard an anguished cry of what sounded like incredible frustration, followed by a dull thumping sound on the sarcophagus. She held her breath, wondering what was going on. She tried to call out again, but her voice refused to cooperate.

She listened for a long time, but all was quiet, and she was beginning to despair, thinking the worst, when suddenly she heard the most beautiful sound in her life – the grating sound of stone moving on stone.

Then she felt a rush of sweet air.

⌐◆¬

Peter forced the tip of the crowbar between the lid and the sarcophagus and put all his weight to it, and to his intense relief the stone moved. He re-positioned the tip, this time getting a better purchase, and levered again, this time moving the lid far enough to allow him to insert the bar into the now-open crack. He gave an enormous heave and the lid slid and fell to the ground. He all but dove into the tomb in his haste to ascertain that Christina was inside and still breathing. He groped blindly with his fingers and felt the warm, smooth skin of her face. He wept with joy as he helped her sit up, and then gently lifted her out. Christina was making mewing sounds, her arms still firmly secured behind her back. He set her carefully on the ground and then bit the restraining tape, freeing her hands. Christina wrapped her arms fiercely around Peter's neck as he hugged and kissed her in a fever of love and relief.

417

Chapter 62

At exactly 3:47PM Peter deposited Gadaleta at a hospital about five kilometres from the Vatican. Satisfied he was in good hands, Peter hurriedly made his leave and raced back to the car where Christina and O'Shaughnessy were anxiously waiting, with the engine still running. Looking dirty and dishevelled and sporting numerous lacerations and abrasions, Christina insisted she was up to joining Peter and O'Shaughnessy for their rendezvous with the Pope.

'We'll never make it in time,' O'Shaughnessy called from the back seat as Peter braked to a stop, his progress totally impeded by the chaotic Roman peak hour traffic.

Peter responded by leaning yet again on the horn, but his protest was lost, merging with the frustrated honking of hundreds of likeminded, frustrated Roman motorists. Peter made a decision. 'Brian, get behind the wheel,' he ordered, jumping out of the car.

'Peter, what are you doing?' Christina demanded as O'Shaughnessy climbed out of the back seat and moved around to take his position in the driver's seat.

'Brian is right, we'll never make it in this traffic, and if we're not there by four, we forfeit. You and Brian stay with the car and I'll run on ahead. I'll try to stall them, tell them you're stuck in traffic.'

'Then I'm coming with you, Peter,' Christina said.

'No, you'll only slow me down.' Without waiting for a response, Peter took off, disappearing into the thick traffic of Via Cresenzio. At Piazza del Risorgimento he swung left, dodging curious tourists, oblivious to the abuse of a couple he very nearly knocked down as he sprinted into Via Di Porta Angelica.

His lungs were burning, and the muscles in his pumping legs screamed for respite, but he was on the home straight with only six blocks to go before he entered the Piazza San Pietro. He glanced at his watch, causing him to collide with another pedestrian. He didn't pause to apologise. It was three minutes to four. He wasn't going to make it. He increased his pace. At five minutes past four he entered St Peter's Square and without letting up raced across towards the entrance to the Vatican. When he finally came to a stop, he doubled over, sucking air into his tortured lungs, causing the Swiss Guard on duty to give him a suspicious look.

Breathlessly, Peter gasped, 'I'm here to see Cardinal Morova.'

The guard looked at him distastefully, noting the filthy, mud-caked clothing, before replying, 'Cardinal Morova has just left. Might I assume you are the, er, gentleman he was waiting for?'

'Yes, yes. My name is, Peter LeSarus, Father LeSarus.'

The guard looked at his watch and stated the obvious. 'You are late.'

'Yes, I'm sorry about that, the traffic. Look, please tell the cardinal I've arrived.'

'I'm sorry, the cardinal has retired.'

Peter was about to protest when he spotted Don Amiglio disappearing into the recesses of the Vatican. 'Don Amiglio,' he called frantically, causing people to turn and stare.

Don Amiglio paused and then turned. He saw Peter at the entrance and hesitated. Peter called again. 'Don Amiglio, it's me, Father LeSarus. He watched as Don Amiglio called to someone out of Peter's line of vision. Then the unmistakable figure of Cardinal Morova appeared, and the two men walked back towards Peter.

'Ah, the Reverend Father LeSarus,' Don Amiglio greeted. 'My friend the Cardinal here, said you were not coming.'

'Wouldn't have missed this meeting for anything,' Peter said, not without a hint of sarcasm. 'We were held up in traffic.'

'We?' Morova queried.

'Yes,' Peter replied, 'Christina, and ...'

Morova did not let him finish, as he asked, eyebrows raised, 'The nun, Sister Christina? You say she is with you, where is she?' he asked looking around anxiously.

'She's with the car, still stuck in traffic.'

Morova's anxiety turned to scepticism. 'I see. Then she should be along at any moment?'

'Yes, hopefully.'

'Come then, we cannot keep His Holiness waiting.' He addressed the Swiss Guard. 'When, or should I say if, a nun by the name of Sister Christina arrives, please escort her to join us in the Pope's audience chamber.'

The Guard nodded respectfully.

'You are hardly dressed appropriately for an audience with the Pope,' Morova observed caustically, gesturing to Peter's soiled clothing.

Peter shrugged. 'Yes, well, ah, I had a small accident on the way here. Car troubles.'

Morova eyed him with unconcealed hostility. 'Very well then, let's get this farce over and done with.' He opened the door to the audience chamber, stepping aside, 'Don Amiglio,' he gestured politely for the Don to precede him through the door.

The Pontiff sat slumped forward on his official red chair. The men approached, each taking his turn to genuflect and kiss the Ring of the Fisherman. The Pope barely acknowledged their presence, managing only to lift his hand a few centimetres. Morova took charge, beckoning for the men to be seated in the chairs set up before the Pope.

'Holiness,' he began, ' I will speak in English for the benefit of one of the men here, who does not speak Italian. I apologise for the necessity of disturbing you when you are so obviously unwell, but a matter of grave importance has come up. It is a matter which, unless arrested immediately and finally, could cause serious embarrassment and grief to the Church.' He paused, waiting for an acknowledgment or permission to continue, neither of which came. The Pope did not move, head slumped on his chest. It looked as though he was asleep.

Morova glanced smugly at LeSarus, and then at Don Amiglio, with a clear look of, I told you so. He continued on regardless. 'I have been made aware of a document which I know to be a forgery. This document must be destroyed before it gets into the wrong hands. My friend here,' he gestured at the Don, 'Paulo Amiglio, came into possession of the document by an accident of good fortune, and wisely, he brought it to my attention. This other man would harm the Church by making the document public. He has tried to convince my good friend that the document is genuine. Consequently, he has insisted on Your Holiness being the arbitrator as to what is to be done with it.'

The Pope gave no sign of having heard a word of what Morova had said.

Morova turned to the Don. 'You see, I told you it was a waste of time disturbing His Holiness with this matter. He is too unwell to comprehend what I am talking about. Perhaps now you will finally hand over the document and accept that this man and his companion are the villains I told you they were.'

The Don looked dismayed, not at all certain what to do. Peter watched him closely, waiting to see if he would hand over the document when there was a knock on the door.

Morova looked annoyed as he called out impatiently, 'Who is it?'

The door opened to reveal the Swiss Guard. 'Your Eminence, I apologise for the intrusion, but you gave specific instructions to escort Sister Christina to the chamber. Well, she is here.'

Morova looked as though he'd just seen a ghost. 'Here?' he asked, incredulous. 'You say she's here?'

'Why look so surprised, Cardinal Morova?' Peter asked with a hint of malicious satisfaction. 'After all, we were expecting her.'

Morova shot Peter a vitriolic look, and then turned to the guard. 'Well, what are you waiting for, show her in.'

The guard paused, looking uncomfortable. 'Your Eminence, there is a gentleman as well. He insisted on accompanying Sister Christina.'

'Gentleman, what gentleman?' Morova demanded.

Before the guard had a chance to reply, O'Shaughnessy swept past him into the room, closely followed by Christina. 'Well, well, well, how good to see you, Lucca, after all these years.'

Morova stared, speechless, his mouth open, eyes flashing undisguised hatred.

O'Shaughnessy bowed to the Pope and Christina genu-flected, by which time Morova recovered from his initial shock. 'How dare you come in here unannounced?' He turned to the hapless guard who looked positively uncomfortable, sensing he'd done the wrong thing by allowing O'Shaughnessy to convince him to escort them both to the audience. 'Remove this man from the Papal audience immediately,' Morova ordered. 'And see to it that he is held in custody till we are finished.'

The guard took O'Shaughnessy by the elbow and was about to manhandle him from the room when suddenly he froze in his tracks.

'I will read the document,' the Pope announced in a firm voice.

Everyone in the room, with the exception of O'Shaughnessy, spun around startled. The Pope was sitting up straight and alert, his hand extended in a palm-up gesture. Morova could not conceal his surprise as Don Lucca obsequiously handed over the document, genuflecting as he did so. Morova was about to object but thought better of it. O'Shaughnessy was grinning.

The guard, still unsure of what to do, looked questioningly at Cardinal Morova who dismissed him with a curt wave, whispering, 'I'll deal with you later.'

Pope Leo Alexander II gestured for everyone to be seated and putting on his reading glasses he began to read.

The silence in the room became oppressive as they waited, intently watching the Pope's face for a tell tale sign of emotion. They were disappointed, for he read the entire document with a stony, expressionless countenance, giving nothing away. When he finally finished, he looked up briefly, as if to reassure himself that no one had left, and then began to read again, from the beginning.

At last he placed the document on his lap, and looking distinctly troubled, he sat in silence, seemingly reflecting on what he had just read. Those in the room continued to wait patiently and Morova opened his mouth to speak but thought better of it. After what seemed an interminable length of time, the Pope addressed Cardinal Morova.

'I take it, Eminence, that what I have just read is supposed to be the revelation of the Third Secret of Fatima?'

'That is what these people would have us believe, Your Holiness. But it is a lie. A fake.'

'How can you be so sure?'

'Because what it says is preposterous,' he replied pompously.

'Yes, yes,' the Pope mused thoughtfully, 'but then again ...'

'Holiness?' Morova queried.

'Preposterous perhaps, but then again, if it were truly the Third Secret of Fatima, it would warrant a Pope to convene a gathering of the College of Cardinals, would it not?'

'Holiness,' Morova protested, 'it is just too bizarre to contemplate.'

'Holiness, please hear me out,' O'Shaughnessy interrupted, and then stopped, surprising even himself at having the temerity to speak before being addressed by the Holy Father.

'And what do you know of this, my son?' the Pope asked.

'Holiness, excuse my impudence for speaking out.' The Pope waved aside the apology, beckoning him to continue. 'It is my belief, Holiness, that when your predecessor read this document, he called for a Conclave of Cardinals to announce his intention to fulfil the demands made by Our Lady, whatever they might be.'

The Pope nodded sombrely. He picked up the document again and re-read a few lines. Satisfied, he removed his glasses and said, 'Our Lady's demands seem very clear and unambiguous.'

O'Shaughnessy said nothing and the Pope continued. 'I take it you have not read this document, my son.'

'No, Your Holiness,' said O'Shaughnessy.

'Nor you, my daughter?'

'No, Holiness,' Christina said.

'Nor you, my son?' he said to Peter.

'No, your Holiness.'

'And you, Don Amiglio?'

'I have, your Holiness, although I confess it is beyond my simple understanding.'

'You,' the Pontiff said to Morova, 'have, of course, read it.'

'Yes, Holiness, although ...'

The Pope held up a hand. 'Enough.' Then turning back to O'Shaughnessy he asked, 'But how can you be sure that this is a true copy of the Fatima document, my son, if you have not read it?'

O'Shaughnessy went on to explain how they had discovered the letter from Pope Leo Alexander I to Father Bracciano, and had set out to find him. He went on to recount how Peter and

Father Bracciano had climbed the mastiff to retrieve the document, resulting in the old priest's death, and how this led to Don Amiglio receiving the documents, and here they all were.

The Pope listened to all this attentively, and then asked, 'Is this true, Don Amiglio?'

'It is true, Your Holiness, that a man did hand this document to me, and he did tell me that he found it in a cave high up on a mountain, as this man has just said.'

'But Holiness,' Morova protested, 'the document is a lie.'

The Pope again silenced him with a gesture of his hand. 'I do believe there is a way to authenticate this document,' the Pope said. 'The original Third Secret of Fatima should still be safely locked away in the Vatican archives, should it not?' he asked Morova.

Morova stammered. 'Why, I don't know, Holiness.'

'Do you have reason to suspect it may not?'

'Ah, well, no, I mean, it could have been removed by your predecessor, Holiness, without my knowledge.'

'But you are the keeper of the keys, are you not?'

'Well yes, Holiness, but …'

The Pope cut him off. 'So that would mean, Eminence, that even if I would wish to retrieve an archive, I could not do so without your knowledge, is that not correct?'

'Um, not necessarily, Holiness. There are two keepers of the keys.'

'Yes, you are quite right, Eminence. But nevertheless, even the keeper of the keys must sign the registry book if anything is removed from archives, is that not so?'

Morova looked visibly sick, as the clever trap closed shut on him. Not trusting his voice, he simply nodded agreement.

'Very well then,' the Pope declared triumphantly, 'let us call for the Captain of the Swiss Guards, and you may personally accompany him to retrieve the original document.'

The others waited with the Pope while Morova and the Captain proceeded to the Vatican archives. By the time they returned the Pope had thoroughly acquainted himself with his visitors and was in a grievous state of concern at what he'd been told regarding their suspicions about his Secretary of State. They related all they had learned since setting out on their search for the truth. When the name of Archbishop Voitra was mentioned the Pope came to attention, for he had received news of the man's violent death.

⚔

Throughout the conversation, Don Amiglio sat silently, taking it all in, fearing that his friend the Cardinal may have duped him. It is one thing to kill for business, he thought, but to kill a Pope or an archbishop, that was something else again.

⚔

When Morova and the guard re-entered the room the Captain stood respectfully by the door, while Morova tentatively approached his Pontiff.

'Well?' the Pope demanded. 'Did you bring me the document as I asked?' Morova stood as though rooted to the spot, his eyes downcast, unable to look up. The Pope addressed the guard. 'Captain, did you accompany His Eminence to the archive room?'

'Yes, Holiness, as you ordered.'

'And?' the Pope pressed.

The guard was looking decidedly nervous, as he caught Morova glaring at him. 'Ah, it would seem, Holiness, that the document is missing.'

'I don't understand, Captain. Please explain. If it is not there, then it must have been signed out. Was it?' the Pope demanded.

'Ah, yes, Holiness, it was signed out.'

'So pray tell us the name of the signatory, Captain.'

426

The guard hesitated, nervously pulling at his tight collar, avoiding eye contact with Morova.

'Come now, Captain. You have nothing to fear here,' the Pope reassured him. 'Tell us the name of the person whose signature you saw.'

'Holiness, the signature was that of His Eminence, Cardinal Morova.'

'You are sure of that?'

'Yes, Holiness, there is no doubt.'

'And was the signature dated?'

'Yes Holiness, it was signed out the day prior to the passing away of His Holiness, Pope Leo Alexander I.'

'I see,' the Pope said, his eyes never leaving Morova. 'And tell us Captain, did the book state the purpose for the removal of the document by the Cardinal?'

'Yes Holiness. It was signed out at the request of Pope Leo Alexander I, but was never returned.'

'Thank you, Captain. You may go. But we may need you again soon. Please be so kind as to wait outside our door.'

As the Swiss Guard retreated, the Pope continued to glare icily at Morova who was still standing, staring at his feet and looking decidedly miserable. 'No doubt you had forgotten removing the document for my predecessor, the day prior to his untimely death, Cardinal Morova.'

Morova looked up with the grateful expression of a drowning man who had just been thrown a lifeline. 'Yes, Holiness. That is it. It happened so long ago, I had forgotten.'

'So, Cardinal, now that your memory is refreshed, pray tell us the purpose of my predecessor requesting the Fatima document.'

'It is not my place to question my Pontiff, Holiness.'

'Quite right,' His Holiness agreed. 'As you served my predecessor so closely, you would recognise his handwriting, I take it.'

'It has been so long, Holiness.'

'Yes, indeed. But would you indulge us anyway, and look at this letter that has come into our possession and give us your best opinion as to whether it is authentic?' He handed Morova the letter from Pope Leo Alexander I to his friend in the Dolomites.

Morova glanced at the letter, and then looked up at the Pope. 'I cannot say, Holiness. Not with any degree of certainty,' he added.

'Please take your time Cardinal Morova. Take a longer look.'

Morova studied the letter again, seemingly taking his time, then looked up and feigning sincere disappointment, shrugged his shoulders. 'As I said, Holiness, it has been so many years and I read so many papers.' He bowed his head.

'Then please indulge us a little further. Let us assume the letter is authentic. Can you imagine why His Holiness was in fear for his life?'

'I really cannot, Holiness,' Morova answered lamely.

'Cardinal Morova, this document, which I am told is a genuine copy secreted away by my predecessor, which you refer to as a preposterous forgery, calls for … how should I put it? Extraordinary measures.' Morova remained silent, fidgeting nervously, waiting to hear what was to come. The Pope continued. 'I can well understand, if this truly is a faithful copy of the original, why the Pope would fear for his life, and why he would call an extraordinary Conclave of the Cardinals. Furthermore, I refuse to believe that a Pope, any Pope, would instigate such measures without first conferring with his Secretary of State. So tell me, Cardinal Morova, what was the purpose of the conclave he was about to call?'

Morova looked like a terrified fly trapped in a web with the spider slowly approaching. His mind was in turmoil, racing frantically to find a way to extricate himself. More lies would only serve to implicate him more deeply, so he decided on one desperate ploy. He shrugged his shoulders, this time in resignation.

'Holiness, you have been ill. I did it for the Church, to protect Her.' He had everyone's attention.

'You did what to protect the Church?' the Pope asked.

Morova ignored the question. 'You see, Holiness, the document you hold truly is an authentic copy of the so-called Third Secret of Fatima.'

LeSarus and O'Shaughnessy exchanged looks of triumph at this admission and Christina squeezed Peter's arm. They had not expected it would be this easy, that Morova would confess so soon. Don Amiglio sat stony faced, staring at the man who had lied to him. But none of them could have guessed what was to come next.

Chapter 63

Cardinal Lucca Morova stood before the Pontiff defiant, eyes blazing with the self-righteousness of a crazed zealot. All prior signs of fear and anxiety had disappeared, replaced with defiant arrogance as he demanded, 'Why do you think the Secret was repressed?' Without waiting for an answer he continued. 'Because they knew. Your predecessors all knew that which you do not.'

The Pope was visibly taken aback by Morova's sudden change in demeanour, shifting uncomfortably in his chair before asking, 'What is this thing you speak about, of which I do not know?'

Morova paused for effect before replying. 'What your predecessors knew was that the children of Fatima were Luciferians.' He paused again, allowing the bombshell to sink in. Everyone was staring, as if at a madman, as he continued. 'Yes, Holiness, they, including that witch, Sister Lucia, were disciples of Satan and that document was perhaps his greatest lie to mankind. Oh yes, he had everyone fooled for a long time. It was a brilliant plan, the miracles and all. But the truth is, the Virgin Mary never appeared at Fatima. All the miracles purported to Her name were nothing but cheap tricks of the devil.'

The Pope had turned pale, attempting to make sense of what Morova was telling him. In a tremulous voice he asked, 'And what of Pope Leo Alexander I?'

'Can't you see, Holiness? I had no choice. I had to protect Christ's Church.'

'What, what do you mean, you had no choice?' the Pope pressed.

'Leo Alexander I was a victim of deception,' Morova was ranting now, 'by that evil nun. She had convinced him, and then there was no stopping him. Can't you see? I had no choice. He had to be stopped.'

'Then it is true? You murdered him?' the Pope asked in disbelief.

'Murder is not the word I would have chosen, Holiness. I would prefer, dispose.'

'Oh, my God.' The Pope buried his face in his hands, head shaking in despair as he struggled to come to terms with what he had just heard.

Morova continued, as though trying to get a point across to a slow-learning child. 'Holiness, try to understand, he was under the influence of Sister Lucia, the most powerful Satanist the world has ever known. Leo Alexander sold his soul to the devil. He called a Conclave of Cardinals to do the unthinkable! It would have resulted in Satan's final triumph!'

'No!' shouted O'Shaughnessy, jumping to his feet, causing the Pope to flinch at the sudden outburst. 'You are the evil one. You are the Antichrist.'

'I?' Morova asked calmly. 'I think not. Why don't you tell them who you really are, Mr O'Shaughnessy?' Morova challenged. 'You see, we have known about you for a long, long time, since before you defrauded the Vatican Bank.'

Christina turned to look at Peter, then at O'Shaughnessy, while Peter sat impassively, looking straight ahead while O'Shaughnessy seemed nonplussed.

'I beg your pardon?' O'Shaughnessy asked.

'Yes, we know about you, all right,' Morova continued, 'you were defrocked as a priest for embezzlement and then went on to preach sedition and heresy. But you did not stop there. Why don't you tell them about Sodalitas Petitore Reapse? That unholy coven you founded. Oh yes, the Vatican knows all about your Satanist group. Yes, Mr O'Shaughnessy, we have been watching you closely for many years.'

O'Shaughnessy laughed. 'But this is ridiculous. Sodalitas what?'

'Is it?' Morova demanded. 'You would be acquainted with one by the name of Scott Emery, would you not?'

Christina and Peter as well as the Don pricked up their ears at the mention of the familiar name. 'I don't see what he has to do with your preposterous accusations,' O'Shaughnessy protested. 'But yes, I do know him, as you well know.'

'Then you would also know,' Morova continued, 'that Mr Emery is an operative with the United States government? The CIA to be precise.'

'Yes, yes, we know all that,' O'Shaughnessy said impatiently with a dismissive hand gesture.

Morova continued as though he had not been interrupted. 'He is the leading European authority on subversive terrorism. For years now he has been liaising with the Vatican, sharing information relating to you and Sodalitas Petitor Reapse.' Don Amiglio paled visibly at this news. Morova continued. 'Sodalitas Petitor Reapse. How ironic that your secret society of Satanists should adopt a name meaning seekers of truth when in reality you are propagating the greatest of lies.'

'Uncle Brian?' Christina asked, incredulous. 'What's this all about? What's he talking about?'

'Your uncle duped you, Sister Kelly, as he did you, Father LeSarus, as he has hundreds, if not thousands of others who believed his evil lies.'

Christina was eyeing O'Shaughnessy with doubt-filled eyes, as Peter continued to sit expressionless. 'Uncle Brian?' Christina asked again.

'Don't believe a word he's saying, Christina,' O'Shaughnessy replied. 'What did you expect? He's desperate, and a self-confessed murderer. How can you doubt me and even begin to believe his lies?'

The Pope who had been listening intently interjected. 'Enough,' he ordered sternly. Everyone had been so caught up in the banter between O'Shaughnessy and Morova they had all but forgotten they were in the presence of the Pope. 'Cardinal Morova,' the Pope continued, 'we would like to re-visit the circumstances surrounding our predecessor's demise.'

'As you wish, Holiness,' Morova agreed. 'The document of the so-called Third Secret of Fatima had been archived long ago as seditious material against the Church, as had many other such documents over the centuries. It came as a surprise, therefore, when Pope Leo Alexander I ordered me to retrieve it for him. When I asked the purpose of his request he was dismissive, telling me it was of no concern to me. Naturally I obeyed and delivered the document. He asked to be left alone. It was some time later that he re-summoned me. He told me he had studied the document and was amazed that, contrary to Our Lady's specific instructions, the document had not been made public. He was of the belief there was a conspiracy to thwart the divine wishes of the Mother of God. He told me it was his firm opinion that the forces of darkness had plotted to keep this sacred document a secret for all these years. He then told me it was his intention to implement Our Lady's demands.

'I listened respectfully to His Holiness, and when he had finished I attempted to dissuade him from his decision. "Holiness," I pleaded, "please try to understand that great scholars have studied this document and after much deliberation concluded it is not the revelation of the Blessed Virgin Mary, but rather the distorted lies of Satan."

'Having said this, his demeanour changed before my eyes. He took on a strange look, as though he had taken on a new persona.

It was frightening. Even his voice changed, sounding more like the growl of a beast than the voice of a human being.'

'And what did he say?' the Pope urged.

'He said, "Morova, you are a fool, as are all your sanctimonious kind. Don't you see? God is dead. Satan rules, and his is the kingdom to come."'

The Pope leaned forward. 'What?' he asked, 'Leo Alexander I said that?'

'That is exactly what he said, Holiness. I swear to God and to all that is holy. I stared at him, believing he'd gone mad, at which point he let out a maniacal laugh that chilled my blood. "Join us, Morova," he cried, "He will give you power over men such as you never dreamed possible."

'It was then, Holiness, that I knew with certainty he was mad. I argued with him, telling him he was crazy and that I would expose him. He laughed at this, saying, "You will expose me, Morova? That is a joke. I am the Pontiff. I am the undisputed leader of the most powerful political machine known to man. And all that power belongs to him, the Prince of Darkness, whose rule is already at hand. You cannot begin to understand the powers we are dealing with."

'At that moment, Holiness, I knew what I must do. It was as though I had a revelation. I had to kill him, before it was too late. Don't you see? I was chosen as the saviour of the Church, of Christianity, of mankind. And so, kill him I did.'

When Morova completed his account everyone in the room sat in stunned silence, till finally the Pope spoke up. 'And tell me, Cardinal Morova, what of me?'

'What do you mean Holiness?'

'Do you perceive me as also being a threat to the Church of Christ?'

'Why, of course not, Holiness, why do you ask?'

'Is it not true I have been drugged all these years? A virtual prisoner, my mind trapped in a fog of narcotics.'

For the briefest of moments Morova looked uncomfortable, but quickly regained his composure. 'You are right, Holiness. I did have you drugged. You see, I had a vision. A vision from God. I saw myself as the protector of the Church. I could not risk allowing another Pope to undo all the good I had done.'

'I see,' the Pope answered thoughtfully. 'Cardinal Morova, as a priest I cannot condone killing under any circumstances and I will not begin do so now. However, neither is it for me to judge you. Civil authorities will judge your actions. Whether or not the circumstances that drove you to killing a Pope can be condoned is a matter between you and God. As for what will be done about this document that has been brought to my attention, that is a matter on which I will deliberate.'

He turned to the Don. 'Don Amiglio, we thank you for keeping this document in trust, and we thank you for bringing it to us. Will you be satisfied to leave the decision as to what is to be done with me, your Pontiff?'

'Most assuredly, Holy Father,' the Don agreed.

'Very well then, you are excused. This is now a Church matter.' The Pope pressed a small button concealed from sight beneath the armrest of his chair. Immediately the door opened, and the Swiss Guard entered the room, snapping to attention. 'Captain, we are finished with Don Amiglio. Will you be so kind as to escort him out?'

The Don did not look unhappy to leave the room.

When the door closed behind them the Pope gestured to Morova to be seated and addressed the others. 'We are prepared to be benevolent,' he began. We understand that for reasons best known to yourselves, you each chose a path contrary to that of the Church. We are prepared to offer you Papal dispensation from

435

your vows if that is what you seek. On the other hand, we are also prepared to offer absolution for your sins should you show contrition, in which case we would grant a Papal proclamation reinstating all your clerical powers.' He paused, 'Pray tell, each of you, which is it to be?'

For a while no one spoke up, as they digested the Pope's offer. Finally, O'Shaughnessy spoke up.

'Holy Father, I think I can speak for all of us by thanking you for your benevolence and generosity of spirit.' The Pope gave a slight nod to acknowledge O'Shaughnessy's gratitude. 'However, Holy Father, with the utmost respect, I do believe you have missed the point.' The Pope raised an eyebrow, but O'Shaughnessy continued on. 'Irrespective of what you have been told by His Eminence, Cardinal Morova, we all three have acted in good conscience. The path we took was as a result of seeing many wrongs and it has only been our intention to try to right those wrongs.'

'That may be, my son,' the Pope replied, 'but all too often, as frail humans, we make mistakes, as well intentioned as we may be.'

'But, Holy Father,' O'Shaughnessy protested, 'there is far more at stake here than you are aware of. Cardinal Morova has admitted to having you drugged all these years, keeping you in ignorance. He has attempted to convince you that I am a Satanist.' The Pope made a sign of the cross at the mention of Satan. 'I assure you that nothing could be further from the truth,' O'Shaughnessy continued. 'Furthermore, he has attempted to convince you that Sister Lucia, along with the other shepherd children, were Satanists. This is obviously falsehood of the highest order.'

'Continue, my son.' He had the Pope's attention.

'This blessed document, which Cardinal Morova refers to as Satan's work, the Third Secret of Fatima, is a divinely inspired message from the Blessed Virgin Mary. It simply cannot be ignored, Holiness, I beseech you.'

'Proof, my son. What proof have you that this is a message from the Mother of God?'

'I have proof, Holiness.'

'Oh?' the Pope leaned forward expectantly.

'Proof? How can you have proof?' Morova challenged. The Pope silenced him with an impatient gesture.

'There is another document, Holiness,' O'Shaughnessy said, 'a document of which I believe the Cardinal has some intimate knowledge.'

The Pope leaned forward, his curiosity piqued. 'And what is this document, my son? Do you have it with you?'

'Yes I do, Holiness, although it is only a copy of the translation of the original papyrus.'

'A copy of a translation,' Morova sneered. 'Do you expect His Holiness to accept your absurdities on the strength of a copy of a translation of some imaginary papyrus?'

'The papyrus is not imaginary, as you well know. It was stolen at your behest, Eminence, and delivered to you.'

'Lies, all lies,' Morova protested. 'Holiness, can't you see that this evil man will do anything to discredit me?'

Once again the Pope held up a silencing hand. 'This copy, you say you have it with you?'

'I do, Holiness,' O'Shaughnessy answered, retrieving the copied translation from the inside pocket of his coat. 'What I have here, Holy Father, is a true copy of a translation of a prophecy written down and hidden, almost two thousand years before the birth of Our Lord, by King Mentonidus. The original papyrus from which this was faithfully translated was subjected to the most stringent scientific tests authenticating the date of its writing.'

'We will see it,' the Pope commanded, holding out his hand. He took the copy from O'Shaughnessy and began to read. When he had finished reading he placed the translation on his lap, removing his glasses. 'Father O'Shaughnessy, this is very difficult to believe. It is just not possible. No one could have prophesied the future with such clarity and accuracy.' He shook his head in amazement and disbelief. 'When did you say it was written?'

'The prophecy has been scientifically dated to three thousand seven hundred years ago, Holiness.'

'Impossible,' the Pope said. 'Such details could not have been known so long ago.'

'I swear to you on all that is sacred, Holy Father, that the prophecy is genuine.'

'And isn't it convenient that you cannot produce the original?' Morova sneered. 'Surely this is the proof Your Holiness was seeking that this man is a fraud.'

'If it is proof you are seeking, Holy Father,' O'Shaughnessy continued, 'I can prove that Cardinal Morova has – or had – possession of the original papyrus.' Morova cocked his head to one side as the Pope gestured for O'Shaughnessy to continue. 'One of your very own archbishops can testify that the papyrus was stolen and delivered to Cardinal Morova. Might I suggest you arrange a telephone connection to Archbishop Voitra, Prelate of Prague?' O'Shaughnessy announced triumphantly, delivering the ace in his deck.

'What?' Morova gasped theatrically. 'You did say Archbishop Voitra?'

'That's what I said,' O'Shaughnessy shot back.

'Holiness, you may have been informed, Archbishop Voitra was only recently the victim of a most brutal murder.' Morova allowed this to sink in before adding, 'Another one of your coin-

438

cidences, O'Shaughnessy? Perhaps you should tell us why you chose this particular archbishop as your witness.'

'Enough,' the Pope snapped. 'We have had enough surprises for one day. I have made my decision. Father O'Shaughnessy, there seem to be many mysteries surrounding yourself and your colleagues. Nevertheless my original offer stands. As for you, Cardinal Morova, it is our considered opinion that you have acted for the continuing good of the Church, as misguided and over-zealous as some of those actions may have been.'

Morova bowed his head in recognition of the wise decision, his mouth turning up in the slightest of smiles.

'However,' the Pope continued, his countenance stern, 'we cannot overlook the fact that you took it upon yourself to ostensibly disempower your Pontiff.' The smile vanished from Morova's face as the Pope continued. 'Nor can we overlook the fact that you have murdered. Consequently, it is our decree that you be stripped of your rank of cardinal. Furthermore, at the conclusion of these proceedings, it is our civil duty to hand you over to the authorities.' He lifted a hand to curtail the anticipated objection from Morova. 'As for this, this document. We are of the opinion that our predecessors were wise to have suppressed it. We recognise it to be what it is, a masquerade. To even consider acting on that missive would bring about a new dark age in the history of the Church and the faithful. We have a fiduciary duty of care to the Catholics of the world to uphold the sacred teachings of Jesus and of His disciples, as well as to maintain the status quo of Mother Church. The document is far too dangerous to archive. We are of the opinion that it really is the workings of Satan, and as such it is our command that the copy of the document shall be destroyed, ridding us of this evil once and for all.'

In spite of everything, Morova managed to look smug and triumphant.

'Holy Father,' O'Shaughnessy jumped to his feet, 'you cannot do this.'

'Silence!' the Pope shouted. O'Shaughnessy sank back into his chair, crestfallen.

Peter LeSarus got to his feet. 'Holy Father, may I speak?'

'We have not heard much from you, Father LeSarus, so you may speak, but briefly. Bear in mind we have made our decision on this matter.'

'Thank you for your indulgence, Holy Father.' Peter reflected a while, gathering his thoughts. 'Whenever I was in doubt as to what course of action I should take in life I would ask myself the question: what would Jesus have done in a similar situation?' The Pope nodded his approval. 'By asking myself this question, I made the decision to break the sanctity of the confessional seal.'

Peter disregarded the Pope's look of disapproval. 'I did not make that decision lightly, Holy Father. I was painfully aware that I would be the first priest in the history of the Church to have done so. I also knew that by that action I would forever place a potential taint of mistrust on the sacred seal.'

'Your violation is not only a grievous sin, my son,' the Pope observed, 'but also a sacrilege. But as we have already stated, it is within our benevolent Papal power to forgive you your transgression, thus reinstating you to the grace of God.'

'Thank you, Holiness. Your benevolence is boundless,' Peter agreed. 'However, it is not forgiveness I seek.'

Brow creased in puzzlement, the Pope asked, 'Then what is it you seek?'

'The truth, Holiness.'

The Pope did not reply, gesturing for Peter to continue.

'Christ empowered His priests as judges to whom sins should be revealed in order that they pronounce forgiveness or retention.

I cannot believe it was His intention that paedophiles seek protection and asylum behind that seal.'

An angry cloud descended over the Pope's features. 'Be careful, my son. It is not for you to interpret that which Christ our Saviour intended.'

'No, it is not, Holiness,' Peter readily agreed. 'But nevertheless, from my experiences it has become clear to me that many of the interpretations of Christ's intentions are erroneous.'

'You have been warned, Father LeSarus.'

'Holy Father, please indulge me a little further.'

Again, the Pope gestured for him to continue, but less patiently this time. He did not look happy with where this seemed to be heading.

'Cardinal Morova has insisted that the revelation of Fatima is a Satanic inspiration. In the first and second revelations of Fatima we were warned that to ignore Our Lady's demands would carry grave consequences. History has already recorded the consequences of the Church's refusal to sanctify Russia as decreed in the first revelation. If one were to truly believe that the third revelation is a divine message to mankind, then one would be foolish to ignore it. If it is the words of Our Lady, then you, as Pope, now have the opportunity to heed Her warnings before it is too late. You have the opportunity to reverse all the evil that has enveloped the world and to set a new course of enlightenment. You have the opportunity to put an end to poverty and to divisiveness, to war and suffering. The alternative is to ignore Her clear and specific directives and suffer the consequences unto the world.'

'We have already covered this ground, Father LeSarus,' the Pope interrupted testily, 'and we have made our decision.'

'Yes, Holiness,' Peter agreed, 'but that decision was made without you being aware of all the facts.'

'Oh,' the Pope said looking puzzled, 'and what facts might those be?'

'Holiness, your dilemma here is who to believe.' The Pope nodded at this. 'On the one hand, Cardinal Morova accused Brian O'Shaughnessy of belonging to a society of Satanists, determined to destroy the Church. He, on the other hand, claims to have had divine inspiration, causing him to take on the role as protector of the Church. Brian O'Shaughnessy has accused Cardinal Morova as being the Satanist. Cardinal Morova has made accusation that Sister Lucia was the greatest Satanist of all, claiming the apparitions at Fatima were a plot hatched by Lucifer himself to dupe the world.' Peter paused. 'The reality is, Holiness, that neither of them are right.'

Peter could clearly see he had the Pope's attention, and for that matter, everyone else's. 'Cardinal Morova was correct in that Brian O'Shaughnessy is not what he purports to be.' O'Shaughnessy shot Peter a quizzical look, while Christina, appearing to be thoroughly confused, looked from one to the other. Peter continued. 'He is not however a Satanist, and neither is Cardinal Morova. All along Cardinal Morova has acted from a genuine concern to protect the Church.' Morova looked up, surprised at this unexpected support, but surprise turned to confusion as Peter continued. 'As misguided as that concern may be, Cardinal Morova, by his own admission, was driven to murder by his schizophrenic compulsions to protect the Church against real and imagined adversaries. I have it on authority, Holiness, that Cardinal Morova has been diagnosed as being hopelessly insane.'

Morova's eyes flashed as he jumped to his feet to refute the accusation. The Pope held up a restraining hand. 'You will remain seated, Cardinal Morova,' he ordered, 'and you will not interrupt again.' Reluctantly Morova resumed his seat as the Pope asked

Peter, 'You say you have this on authority, Father LeSarus. I assume you can provide us with proof.'

'Yes, of course, Holy Father. When we were warned that Cardinal Morova was plotting against our lives I decided to do some checking of my own. Unbeknown to my companions, I took Father Bracciano into my confidence. It was from his rectory that I telephoned my brother in England, asking him to utilise his connections to undertake discreet enquiries about Cardinal Morova. When Cardinal Morova was hospitalised some time ago, after he was found in his room with horrific injuries, the official explanation was that they were self-inflicted as a result of a violent attack of epilepsy. My brother's connection managed to interview the medical staff in attendance. When Cardinal Morova was admitted, he was in a semi-conscious state and was reportedly ranting about having been seduced by Satan, who he claimed, was a woman of unnatural beauty. In his delirium he re-lived the experience further, claiming that it was she who had inflicted his injuries. The attending physician was sufficiently alarmed as to recognise the need to call in a consulting psychia-trist. Following numerous drug-induced hypnotic sessions, it came out that in Cardinal Morova's tortured mind, he was convinced that the devil was attempting to use him to discredit the Church. He also claimed to have had a divine visitation during which he was told how to thwart the devil to protect the Church from her evil plans.'

Morova could no longer contain himself, leaping again to his feet, he shouted, 'It is all true,' he screeched. 'It was not a figment of my mind. You just don't understand.'

The Pope watched Morova with compassion, not interrupting this time, allowing the man to continue his ravings. 'You just don't understand,' Morova sobbed, 'none of you understand the evil of Satan. You have not looked into her eyes. How could you understand?' Shoulders heaving, and racked with uncontrolled sobs, Morova resumed his seat.

Peter waited for Morova to calm down before continuing. 'Because of the Cardinal's high office, the psychiatrist was hesitant about revealing his diagnosis, choosing instead to report an explanation of epilepsy.' Peter reached into his pocket, producing a document that he handed to the Pope. 'This is a copy of the psychiatrist's notes, Holiness, which were obtained by my brother's connection, and subsequently faxed to me.'

Christina and O'Shaughnessy were almost gaping at Peter now, incredulous that he had found all this out and kept it to himself. The Pope read the report, shaking his head. And then he asked Peter, 'And what of Father O'Shaughnessy here? You said he is not all he purports to be. Please elaborate further, my son.'

'Ah yes, Brian O'Shaughnessy,' Peter reflected, turning to Christina's uncle. O'Shaughnessy shifted in his seat, returning Peter's gaze. 'No, Brian O'Shaughnessy is not a Satanist, Holiness, as claimed by Cardinal Morova, but he might as well be.'

O'Shaughnessy sat passive faced without revealing the slightest hint of emotion. Christina was staring at Peter, her mouth open. Peter leaned over, and giving her hand a squeeze, he whispered, 'I'm sorry, Christina.' He turned his attention back to the Pope. 'Brian O'Shaughnessy is a clever man, and an opportunist of the worst kind.' Peter gestured towards Christina. 'His niece here was taken in by him, as would I have been, had I not been tipped off early in the piece.' He now addressed Christina again. 'I'm sorry, but I decided not to confide in you till I knew the whole truth.' Christina continued to stare from Peter to O'Shaughnessy. Her uncle remained silent, his arms crossed defiantly over his chest.

'O'Shaughnessy gave me the first clue to his treachery when I was invited to his home for dinner, where he first alluded to a conspiracy within the Church. In order to lend credibility to his accusations he told me about the *Titanic* conspiracy which he substantiated at the time with some compelling documentation. By the time I left that evening I was feeling confused and more disillusioned than ever before. O'Shaughnessy's butler, Piggott showed me to the door. I recall being surprised at the time that Piggott walked me all the way to the street and waited till I was in the car, at which time he told me that O'Shaughnessy had in fact embezzled Vatican funds, but that he was also the head of an immensely powerful, international cartel, whose aim, inspired by the *Titanic* conspiracy, was to embezzle the Vatican's wealth to an extent that would have made his original crime seem like a misdemeanour.'

'What?' the Pope and Christina gasped in unison.

'Really, Peter,' O'Shaughnessy responded, 'this is too ridiculous for words. It's even wilder than Morova's accusations. We already know about Piggott's treachery. For goodness sake, he nearly killed Christina.'

'That was a separate issue, and one you hadn't counted on,' Peter responded. 'Piggott was driven by greed and disillusionment, as well as a hatred towards you and your family. When he learned of your plan, that served only to reinforce his hatred, and he became obsessed with righting what he considered a terrible wrong to him. Judging by Cardinal Morova's surprise that Christina was going to show up it's obvious that Piggott tipped off Cardinal Morova, who no doubt promised to pay him a great deal of money to thwart you.'

Peter continued his address to the Pope. 'O'Shaughnessy hatched his incredible scheme after deciding that no matter what the contents of the Third Secret it would have to be something so radical that it inspired more than one Pontiff to suppress it. O'Shaughnessy was at a disadvantage in that he never learned what the Third Secret actually was. How could he? So few people

445

ever did. But it didn't matter; he was prepared to gamble on the logic of his supposition. O'Shaughnessy often bragged that he leaves nothing to chance, but like many obsessed men he has his blind spots. And like Cardinal Morova, his own paranoia and dishonesty forced him to limit the number of people he could trust, and to take some things for granted. My brother Michael says that this is a common weakness and failing of conspirators.

'Regardless, O'Shaughnessy sold his plan to a handful of the world's wealthiest and most powerful individuals. The plan was to publicise the Third Secret of Fatima, give it undeniable credibility through the support of the prophecy of King Mentonidus, and through public pressure force the Pope to succumb to Our Lady's wishes.

'You see, although O'Shaughnessy appeared to be an exile from the Church he never lost contact with the network that he established while working within the Vatican bank. In spite of his protestations of innocence, O'Shaughnessy was guilty of embezzlement. His initial motive was to save his family's bank from ruin. Certainly, he was caught. Maybe he even wanted to be caught; it may have been all part of a greater long-term plan to control the Church later. Who would suspect that a man, who had been so thoroughly disgraced, would continue to hold such power? What were a few years of jail compared to the insurance it would bring? It was all a ruse. And it worked, and O'Shaughnessy's hatred of Cardinal Morova, while real, was also only a ruse to distract attention to what was really going on.

'My brother and I also surmised that in embezzling the Vatican Bank O'Shaughnessy left a trail of people who were so hopelessly compromised they were forced to comply with his later schemes or risk ruining their own lives. No doubt there were others who were complicit from the very beginning. The Church has been around a long time, Holiness, and perhaps even at the time that O'Shaughnessy joined the bank there were people already there who were either planted by, or corrupted by, the individuals who O'Shaughnessy would later approach. Such men, unlike O'Shaughnessy and Cardinal Morova, leave little to chance. This is not to say that O'Shaughnessy was not thorough though. He also has his dupes, like Monsignor Reitanio, who were quite willing to help his "innocent friend."

'If you conduct an internal investigation, Holiness, you may find that O'Shaughnessy's cabal continues to function not only in the bank but in other parts of the Vatican at the highest levels. His network has intimate ties with the consortium of wealthy individuals that he formed a quarter of a century ago. Ironically, it's those very inside contacts that probably assisted O'Shaughnessy to ensure that your sedation was stopped.'

At this the Pope let out a sigh of what sounded almost like despair. 'Go on, Father LeSarus,' he said.

'The original plan of the consortium that O'Shaughnessy brought together was that after the Third Secret was revealed, the Church would be destabilised. The consortium, working with the inside network at the Vatican Bank would then place itself in a position of trust, in theory to administer the Church's incredible wealth, but in reality the consortium would utilise that wealth for its own ends to gain even greater world economic domination. It would be the Vatican Bank scandal all over again, but this time there would be no "scapegoat" since that wasn't part of the plan this time.

'We don't know what the cabal's original plan was, but they came very close to success in 1978 when your predecessor seemed to be about to disclose the Third Secret of Fatima to the world. However, the original plan was thwarted when Cardinal Morova murdered the Pope and destroyed the original Fatima document for misguided reasons of his own. Scott Emery is a member of O'Shaughnessy's consortium. His role in all this is still unclear to me and there seem to be things about him that even O'Shaughnessy didn't know about. He successfully ingratiated himself with Morova in order to ascertain whether or not the original document still existed. After informing O'Shaughnessy that Morova had destroyed the original, they needed another irrefutable document supporting the validity of Fatima, since it was evident that Sister Lucia could be of no further help in this regard. It had been difficult enough getting her to record the revelation the first time. Perhaps she too succumbed to the influence of Morova. She might even have interpreted your predecessor's death as a sign that the Secret was now not to be revealed. I don't know, you could ask her.

'O'Shaughnessy had to come up with something. It was then that he came up with his great hoax.' Peter paused to gauge O'Shaughnessy's reaction so far, but there was no reading the man's emotions as he continued to sit impassively, staring straight ahead. Christina's eyes were also on her uncle, but O'Shaughnessy avoided eye contact.

'What was this great hoax?' the Pope pressed, now well and truly caught up in Peter's narrative.

'The Prophecy of King Mentonidus, Holiness,' Peter answered. 'O'Shaughnessy knew that he needed absolutely irrefutable evidence of the authenticity of the Third Secret, since the Church had already complicated matters enough. The only thing that would do, would be an ancient document supporting the Fatima claim, but such a document didn't exist. He would have to create one. But such a document would inevitably be subjected to the carbon 14 test and any other test that could conceivably be developed. While it is possible to fool the dating tests, such tampering was not infallible. O'Shaughnessy needed something absolutely infallible. Such techniques to fool the tests did not exist, but the consortium had funds, and they could develop them. It took years, in fact almost twenty years, but they were patient men. The potential reward was worth the wait, and there were always side benefits from producing techniques to fool dating tests.

'So they were finally able to create a document, but their problem was how to introduce it to the world. The answer came quite fortuitously. When Christina returned from India with stories of the Nag Hammadi finds and the investigations of Professor Muntz, O'Shaughnessy was delighted. Muntz, a frustrated, desperate and yet highly-respected academic was about to make his greatest and most controversial discovery.'

O'Shaughnessy finally broke his silence, 'You knew all along?' he marvelled.

'No, not all of it. But once Piggott told me of your scheme, with considerable help from my brother's intelligence contacts, I managed to put the rest of the pieces of the jigsaw together. The one other person I confided in was Tony Gadaleta. He was the only one, apart from my brother, who I felt I could trust. As a result of what I told him he spoke to some senior associates in the CIA. They did some investigating of their own and through a simple process of elimination it wasn't too difficult for them to track down the scientist with sufficient technical knowledge and expertise to forge the papyrus and fool anyone conducting a carbon 14 test, a prism cryptography test, or any other test you might name. The scientist, like many of his type, was a naïve man, and a little pressure was all that was required for him to reveal who had funded him.'

'But what made you suspect that the papyrus was a forgery in the first place?' O'Shaughnessy wondered. 'Piggot didn't know anything about the papyrus.'

'I was suspicious from the moment Piggott told me that you were not all that you seemed. I didn't know who was lying, or who was telling the truth, if anyone. But I decided to play along. I was curious.

'I couldn't be sure of anything, but when we were finally able to talk to Doctor Muntz and we got to read the full translation of the prophecy I remembered thinking that something didn't add up. I didn't realize at the time how literally true that was.

'The clue was the dates mentioned in the document. Their accuracy was supposedly the papyrus' greatest strength, but also its greatest weakness. The papyrus mentions, very specifically, that the Fatima Secrets would be revealed in two thousand, less eighty-three years, after the coming of Jesus Christ – supposedly 1917. But scholars, and even the Church, with few dissenters, recognise that Christ was born in 4BC, and that our calendar is the result of an error that arose in the Dark Ages. The papyrus should have read in two thousand less seventy-nine years. That is to say, 1996 minus 79 equals 1917. The Fatima visitations occurred one thousand nine hundred and twenty-one years after Our Lord Jesus Christ's coming, not one thousand nine hundred and seventeen years, as our calendar would have it. If the prophecy, and the papyrus, had been real, the prediction would have been true to what had actually occurred, not to a dating error of medieval scribes. Not even Hans Muntz, the translator of the papyrus, picked that up. He was very disappointed when I told him. It wasn't much to go on, but it was enough to get me asking the right questions.

'You put too much faith in technology, Brian, and not enough in history. It was a fatal mistake, one of many.' O'Shaughnessy was now stooped forward in his chair, his face buried in his hands.

Peter continued. 'Perhaps you felt you had waited too long to act, but you got sloppy. You hadn't counted on Professor Muntz confiding in his old friend, Archbishop Voitra, or on what the Archbishop would do. Naturally the Archbishop would tell his superior. Maybe if you had investigated Professor Muntz a little further you might have chosen another man.

'Another mistake was Piggott, who you completely took for granted. Perhaps if you hadn't you would have bought his loyalty, instead of his enmity.

'Your whole plan depended on getting the Church to reveal the Third Secret. You didn't have the Secret, so you had to have a prophecy. Then you didn't even have that. It must have been hard for you, Brian, when I told you that the prophecy had been stolen. At that point you had neither the prophecy nor the Third Secret. If Monsignor Reitanio hadn't discovered that Pope Leo Alexander I had written to Father Bruno Bracciano, and that there was still a chance that you could provide His Holiness with incontrovertible proof of the Third Secret, what would you have done? Maybe you had some other plan up your sleeve. It's obvious that you thought Archbishop Voitra would come to the rescue. But the Archbishop's dead, conveniently for Morova, or so he thought. You underestimated Morova's viciousness. Perhaps His Holiness and the police will have to investigate that death too. Perhaps you had another plan. The police will have many questions, I'm sure.

'Your final mistake,' Peter said, 'was me. No doubt you thought you had the perfect dupe, a disillusioned priest, cheated of his ideals, desperate for a purpose, desperate to find his faith again in a Church that had betrayed him. You probably even knew of my brother and his connections and counted on me to use them. What you hadn't counted on was how much my brother's contacts already knew. They already had most of the information; they just didn't know how it all fitted together. You even dangled Christina as bait, and I took it. You just underesti-

451

mated how much I was willing to do and find out in order to prove to myself that she had nothing to do with this.

'All of it might even have worked, if Piggott hadn't tipped me off on that very first evening.'

Peter felt no sense of triumph; in fact, it all felt a little hollow.

He turned his attention back to the Pope. 'So there you have it, Holiness, the truth. Hopefully, God will grant you the wisdom to decide what action to take. You must decide whether or not you believe the Fatima revelation is authentic. Suffice to add that your predecessor died as a result of his own belief.'

Peter looked at Christina with unmistakeable fondness. His only regret was that she had to witness the denouncement of her uncle. Tentatively, he smiled at her, not at all sure of what her reaction to all this would be, and what she would think of him, being the one who had exposed her uncle's treachery. To his immense relief, she returned his smile, and reaching up, she took his hand in hers and gave it a squeeze.

The Pope paused for a moment and pushed the button under the armrest of his chair. The Swiss Guard promptly returned. 'Captain,' the Pope said. 'Please escort Cardinal Morova and Mr O'Shaughnessy to separate holding cells. We consider them to be a security risk and we will need to inform the civil authorities.'

Morova and O'Shaughnessy, the great enemies, were now both silent, utterly defeated as they were led from the room with nothing more to say. Watching them leave, Peter noticed a tear roll down Christina's cheek as she watched her uncle depart, without so much as a backward glance at her.

He turned his attention back to the Pope. 'There is just one more thing, Holiness.'

The Pope seemed lost, wrestling with a decision. 'And what would that be?' he asked.

'Your Holiness asked whether I would seek reinstatement as a priest.'

'I did, my son, and I would gladly do it, if that is your wish.'

'No, Holiness, it is not.'

The Pope's face dropped at this response as a look of profound sadness overcame him. 'I am truly sorry to hear that, my son. Perhaps at a later date, when you have had time to pray.'

'No, I don't think so, Holiness,' Peter replied gently, and he looked into Christina's eyes. She was still holding his hand. 'Because, you see, Holiness, I have decided to embark on a new vocation.'

'I see,' His Holiness replied sadly. 'And might I ask what that vocation will be?'

Peter squeezed Christina's hand. 'Holy matrimony, Holiness.'

The Pope beamed. 'Then you have our blessing.' The Pope closed his eyes and took a deep breath, as if coming to a decision.

'Perhaps I can offer you a small wedding gift,' he said. And with that, Pope Leo Alexander II, Bishop of Rome and successor to Saint Peter, handed Peter the envelope.

With trembling fingers Peter took the document and looked at the translation of Sister Lucia's account of the Third Secret of Fatima. He could barely focus his eyes.

So many people have died for this, he thought.

He began to read.

He read it again.

And he read it again. Not quite believing it.

Now, he thought, I finally understand.

With tears running down his cheeks he looked at the Pope. 'Holiness,' he asked, his voice a croaked whisper, 'with your permission?'

The Pope nodded.

Peter looked at Christina. Through eyes filled with tears she never looked more beautiful to him than at that moment, dirty and unkempt from her trial in the tomb.

With trembling hands Christina took the document and read. After a small eternity she handed the folder back to the Pope. 'Thank you,' she said. 'It all makes sense now.'

The Pope smiled and with a twinkle in his eye said. 'As for our decision on the Third Secret of Fatima? Well then, you have cast an entirely different light on the matter, and as such, we have decided, that like our predecessor, Pope Leo Alexander I, we too shall convene a Conclave of Cardinals.'

Coda

Although *Satan's Church* is a work of fiction, many of the events depicted are based on documented historical facts.

The circumstances surrounding the fictional characters, Julius Wheeler and the paedophile teacher John McGregor, are based on actual events witnessed by the author while at school, and have since been documented in the public domain following the Australian Royal Commission on paedophilia.

The Catholic Church has been plagued by scandals pertaining to paedophilia, but it seems to continue in its cavalier attitude towards these disgraces.

For example, Cardinal Bernard Law was forced to resign in disgrace as Archbishop of Boston, following proven allegations that he turned a blind eye to child abuse, transferring the offending priests to other parishes. In spite of this, the Vatican chose him to conduct mourning services for the late Pope John Paul II, in one of the Vatican's great basilicas in Rome. His important role at the Pope's funeral caused an outcry of rage from Boston Catholics, where he is considered the embodiment of church complicity in paedophilia.

This ongoing problem of protecting paedophilic clergy has by no means been limited to the Catholic Church, as was witnessed when Australia's Governor General, Dr Peter Hollingworth was forced to resign in 2003 following public outrage of his mishandling of child abuse allegations when he was Anglican Archbishop of Brisbane.

The events relating to the near collapse of the Vatican Bank are also based on fact. When Albino Luciani was elected Pope John

Paul I in 1979, he ordered an investigation into the corrupt Vatican Bank. This turned up a gigantic financial scandal, ending with the Vatican paying out $244 million to outraged creditors of Banco Ambrosiono, which eventually folded with losses estimated at $3.5 billion. There are those of the belief that Pope John Paul I was given the poison cup as a result of his interference.

The recounting of the apparitions of the Blessed Virgin Mary to the shepherd children at Fatima is, again, factual as reported and accepted by the Vatican. The miracle of the sun did happen as depicted, and was witnessed by more than 70,000 people.

The suppression of the Third Secret of Fatima by various Popes is also a fact. Notably these Popes were, John XXIII (1958–1963) and Paul VI (1963–1978). Pope John Paul I (1978–1978) only reigned for thirty-four days before suddenly dying under controversial and mysterious circumstances, and as such his reign was too short to suggest that he too actively suppressed the Third Secret. Pope John Paul II began his reign in 1978 but the world was made to wait a further twenty-two years into his reign before Cardinal Joseph Ratzinger finally 'revealed' the Third Secret to the world on 26 June, 2000. However the controversy did not stop there, and for many there are still numerous questions which need answering. There are those who adhere to the belief that the secret was not revealed in full, as well as those who claim it may even have been fabricated.

Pope John Paul II 'studied' the message while recovering from the assassination attempt against him in 1981. He was later purported to have made verbal reference to tidal waves (tsunamis?) and burning cities (9/11?) based on his reading of the Third Secret, and yet the final, published, official version makes no mention at all of any coming cataclysms.

Pope John Paul II was quoted as saying, that there was and is now an 'apocalyptic' battle being waged between good an evil.

There are those who claim a cabal within the Vatican replaced the original document with a forgery, which was passed on to Pope John Paul II. Many question whether or not Cardinal Ratzinger (elected Pope Benedict XVI in April 2005) duped or lied to the public. There have even been claims that the Sister Lucia who told interviewers that the released Third Secret was genuine, was in fact an impostor, and that the real Sister Lucia had either died or had been sequestered.

It was officially reported that Sister Lucia Marto, the last survivor of the Fatima children, died at the Convent of Carmelites in Coimbra, Portugal on 13 February, 2005, aged ninety-seven.

Pope John Paul II died soon after on 2 April, 2005, aged eighty-four.

There are many sites on the Internet with as many arguments for and against the material that the Vatican finally released in 2000. However, after reading what the Vatican officially released, the question remains:

Why all the fuss?

Considering the contents of the official version, why would one Pope after another have suppressed the document for forty years after it was supposed to have been made public in 1960?

It just does not make sense.

The following is the official translated English text of the Three Secrets of Fatima.

Draw your own conclusions.

⚜

First Secret

'Our Lady showed us a great sea of fire, which seemed to be under the earth. Plunged in this fire were demons and souls in human form, like transparent burning embers, all blackened or burnished bronze, floating about in the conflagration, now raised into the air by the flames that issued from within themselves together with great clouds of smoke, now falling back on every side like sparks in a huge fire, without weight or equilibrium, and amid shrieks and groans of pain and despair, which horrified us and made us tremble with fear. The demons could be distinguished by their terrifying and repulsive likeness to frightful and unknown animals, all black and transparent. This vision lasted but an instant. How can we ever be grateful enough to our kind heavenly Mother, who had already prepared us by promising, in the first Apparition, to take us to heaven? Otherwise, I think we would have died of fear and terror.'

❦

Second Secret

'You have seen hell where the souls of poor sinners go. To save them, God wishes to establish in the world devotion to my Immaculate Heart. If what I say to you is done, many souls will be saved and there will be peace. The war is going to end: but if people do not cease offending God, a worse one will break out during the Pontificate of Pius XI. When you see a night illumined by an unknown light, know that this is the great sign given you by God that he is about to punish the world for its crimes, by means of war, famine, and persecutions of the Church and of the Holy Father. To prevent this, I shall come to ask for the consecration of Russia to my Immaculate Heart, and the Communion of reparation on the First Saturdays. If my requests are heeded, Russia will be converted, and there will be peace; if not, she will spread her errors throughout the world, causing wars and persecutions of the Church. The good will be martyred; the Holy Father will have much to suffer; various nations will be annihilated. In the end, my Immaculate Heart will triumph. The Holy Father will consecrate Russia to me, and she shall be converted, and a period of peace will be granted to the world.'

Text of The Third Secret of Fatima

From Congregation for the Doctrine of the Faith in Vatican

COMPLETE TRANSLATION OF ORIGINAL TEXT:

VATICAN CITY, JUN 26, 2000 (VIS) – Given below is the complete translation of the original Portuguese text of the third part of the secret of Fatima, revealed to the three shepherd children at Cova da Iria-Fatima on July 13, 1917, and committed to paper by Sr. Lucia on January 3, 1944:

'I write in obedience to you, my God, who command me to do so through his Excellency the Bishop of Leiria and through your Most Holy Mother and mine.

'After the two parts which I have already explained, at the left of Our Lady and a little above, we saw an Angel with a flaming sword in his left hand; flashing, it gave out flames that looked as though they would set the world on fire; but they died out in contact with the splendour that Our Lady radiated towards him from her right hand: Pointing to the earth with his right hand, the Angel cried out in a loud voice: 'Penance, Penance, Penance!' And we saw in an immense light that is God: 'something similar to how people appear in a mirror when they pass in front of it' a Bishop dressed in White 'we had the impression that it was the Holy Father'. Other Bishops, Priests, men and women Religious going up a steep mountain, at the top of which there was a big Cross of rough-hewn trunks as of a cork-tree with the bark; before reaching there the Holy Father passed through a big city half in ruins and half trembling with halting step, afflicted with pain and sorrow, he prayed for the souls of the corpses he met on his way; having reached the top of the mountain, on his knees at the foot of the big Cross he was killed by a group of soldiers who fired bullets and arrows at him, and in the same way there died one after another the other Bishops, Priests, men and women

Religious, and various lay people of different ranks and positions. Beneath the two arms of the Cross there were two Angels each with a crystal aspersorium in his hand, in which they gathered up the blood of the Martyrs and with it sprinkled the souls that were making their way to God.'

As you can see, the official version shows a number of disturbing images but unlike the second secret there are noticeably absences of any references by Our Lady of what these images mean, or how to avert the presumed gloomy future that they predict. It is possible that the above is an accurate, albeit incomplete text. If that is the case, it would suggest that Sister Lucia wasn't actually lying, but telling a half-truth, and on such quibbles whole dogmas are defended.

It may be that it is not the apocalyptic vision that caused so many Popes to disobey the 'Mother of God' – the Church is, after all, familiar with and well accustomed to apocalyptic visions. Reading the text as it stands, it's difficult to understand why the Church suppressed the secret for so long.

However, could it be rather that the Virgin Mary had felt that only through a particular course of action could the Church find its true path again, from the path of error into which it had strayed? A path that includes defending the indefensible – such as protecting paedophiles and making deals with arms makers, drug traffickers and murderers, not to mention harbouring and assisting Nazi war criminals; a path that has surely led to the Church losing any credibility it may have ever had as a purported protector of the weak, the downtrodden and the poor; a path upon which if it continues, could quite probably lead to the Holy Roman Catholic Church becoming, in effect, Satan's Church.

I have, in this work, assumed that the Virgin Mary had something very radical in mind, a true test of the values and mission that the Church espoused, a test so radical that Church hierarchy has completely failed or refused to rise to Her challenge, a test so profound that more than one Pope actually presumed to disobey and, or disregard the Mother of God. A test failed so completely that the fundamental credibility of the Church is called into question again and again as it struggles under the enormous weight of its own hypocrisy. A secret so staggering in its implications that ministers and princes of the Church would be prepared to lie, cheat and even murder to keep it concealed.

You be the judge.

Here now is the text of the Third Secret of Fatima, as revealed to Pope Leo Alexander II, Peter and Christina:

This will be the third and final revelation I will make to you, and into your hands, Lucia, I entrust my message to the world. Unlike your cousins who I will take to heaven soon, you will be left behind to bear witness to my word and to the wishes of my Son. But fear not, for despite what may happen, you, as well as all those who are righteous to themselves and to the teachings of my Son, will also join me in heaven.

My Son is angry at what His Church has become, and were it not for my intercession, He would have smote it before this day, as did God, His Father smite the evils that were once known as Sodom and Gomorrah. He did give his life on the cross, so that He would save mankind from the enslavement of Lucifer, and upon His favourite Apostle, Simon Peter, He laid the foundation stone of the legacy of His Church. That very Church that He founded has gone the way of Babylon the Harlot, measuring its success by the acquisition of spiritually worthless baubles and trinkets to the exclusion of the needs of His children who die starving and sick, ignored by those hypocrites who pertain to speak in His name and who revel in the pomp and ceremony of their own perceived importance.

461

I now say this to you, Lucia. I have interceded with my Son, who would deny me nothing, asking Him to hold back the fiery angel of destruction. Humanity can yet avoid the wrath of God upon themselves, but to do so, certain things must be done. The first I have already spoken of, being the consecration of Russia. I have warned of a far greater war. This will come to pass, should my first demand not be met. The war would be delivered unto the nations by a disciple of the Antichrist whose depth of evil has never before been witnessed.

This message is to be delivered to the Holy Father in my name and the name of my Son.

The Church, which was founded by my Son, Christ the Lord and which calls itself the Holy Roman Catholic Church, must relinquish and divest itself of all its worldly riches, and only by sacrificing its material wealth, will it regain the spiritual wealth ordained by its founder. The fruit of this earthly wealth must be distributed under the stewardship and wisdom of the Holy Father, and as inspired to him through the intervention of the Holy Spirit, among the needy of the world, in such a way that the impoverished nations will be able to rise in majestic dignity and thus tend to the needs of their sick and starving children as ordained by God. By doing thus, the Church will set such example to the nations that they will truly believe and understand and take unto themselves the Church of Christ, thus heralding a new age of true universal catholic unity, peace and holiness, thus paving the way for the return of Christ, my Son, who will forever vanquish His enemies and establish His Kingdom on Earth.

The Holy Father must deliver this message to all people of the world by no later than the year of 1960. Failure to achieve this demand by the new millennium will result in the recognition by the people of the False Prophet, who, in imitation of John the Baptist will point to the Antichrist, proclaiming him as the saviour of the world. The Antichrist will have come into power through lies and deceit by means of communicating to all of the masses simultaneously and at the same time, and by working great miracles he will claim to be God and he will be worshipped. And then as foretold in Revelation, 'And the angel cried mightily with a strong voice, saying, Babylon the great is fallen, is fallen, and is become the habitation of devils, and the hold of every foul spirit, and a cage of every unclean and hateful bird. For all nations have drunk of the wine of the wrath of her fornication, and the kings of the earth have committed fornication with her, and the merchants of the earth are waxed rich through the abundance.'

All of this will come to pass if my word is not heeded.

If you would like to contact the author, please visit his website: *www.camlavac.com.au*